ON THE
HIEROPHANT
ROAD

JAMES
CHAMBERS

RAW DOG
SCREAMING
PRESS

On the Hierophant Road © 2021
by James Chambers

Published by Raw Dog Screaming Press
Bowie, MD

First Edition

Cover Image: Bradley Sharp
Book Design: Jennifer Barnes

Printed in the United States of America

ISBN: 978-1-947879-37-9

Library of Congress Control Number: 2021941734

RawDogScreaming.com

Previously Published

"A Cat's Cry in Pluto's Kitchen" first appeared in *Clockwork Chaos*. Neal Levin and Danielle Ackley-McPhail, eds. Howell, NJ: Dark Quest Books, 2013.

"The Flying Rock" first appeared in *Bad-Ass Faeries 4: It's Elemental*. Danielle Ackley-McPhail, Lee Hillmann, L. Jagi Lamplighter, and Jeff Lyman, eds. Howell, NJ: Dark Quest Books, 2014.

"Grilg Friendly" first appeared in *Barbarians at the Jumpgate*. Bruce Gehweiller, ed. New York: Padwolf Publishing, 2010.

"He Who Burns" first appeared in *Dragon's Lure*. Danielle Ackley-McPhail, Jennifer Ross, and Jeffrey Lyman, eds. Howell, NJ: Dark Quest Books, 2010.

"I Am the Last" first appeared in *Fantastic Futures 13*. Robert E. Waters and James R. Stratton, ed. Farmingdale, NY: Padwolf Publishing, 2012.

"The Kind Old Fellow" first appeared in *Sick: An Anthology of Illness*. John Edward Lawson, ed. Baltimore, MD: Raw Dog Screaming Press, 2003.

"Meet the Tuskersons" first appeared in *Walrus Tales*. Kevin L. Donihe, ed. Eraserhead Press, Portland, OR, 2012.

"Mother of Peace" first appeared in *By Other Means (Defending the Future, Volume 3)* Mike McPhail, ed. Howell, NJ: Dark Quest Books, 2011.

"The Price of Faces" first appeared in *Qualia Nous*. Michael Bailey, ed. Written Backwards, Calif., 2014.

"The Star Gazers" first appeared in *If We Had Known (Beyond the Cradle)*. Mike McPhail, ed. Stratford, NJ: eSpec Books, 2017.

"Super-Villain Showcase #53: 'Enter the Deep Loa'" first appeared in *With Great Power*. John L. French and Greg Schauer, eds. Howell, NJ: Dark Quest Books, 2014.

"Upon Wave, Wind, and Tide" first appeared in *Mermaids 13*. John L. French, ed. Farmingdale, NY: Padwolf Publishing, 2012.

Acknowledgements

I am indebted to the editors and publishers who first guided and published many of the stories collected in this book. Thanks especially to Danielle Ackley-Mcphail, Michael Bailey, Kevin Donihe, John L. French, Mike McPhail, Greg Schauer, and Robert Waters. Likewise, much gratitude to the readers who supported the various anthologies in which they appeared. My thanks once again to my colleagues-in-letters in the Top Secret Beta-Reading Group as well as my Sand Sharks crew. Their support, feedback, and enthusiasm remain, always, invaluable. To my family, who unselfishly allow me the time and space it takes to write, your support means everything to me, and I'm grateful for your constant patience. Many thanks to John Edward Lawson and Jennifer Barnes for their outstanding work as publishers and their long-standing support of my writing and of many other writers and the literary community in general.

For William

Contents

The Price of Faces

I. At the Body Forge

For weeks after the accident, in dreams or in a swirling, anesthetic darkness, Coar saw the impossible: Coar saw one's birth face. Its stare bored into Coar as if scanning through one's *elem* to the raw life matrix code beneath with a gaze far too solidly mounted in flesh. The murky face haunted Coar. One could never know one's true birth face, which belonged not to a self but only to a body, stripped away in the first six months of life, removed to the body forges for nurturing and management on the International Life Interface. Birth faces held only identity's potential while separation from one's birth face equaled freedom of identity. Yet, the sight of the face disturbed Coar so much because one felt certain it belonged. People said if you looked at your birth face, it would be like looking into a prison cell you'd escaped. Coar understood why.

Despite its disordered, unfinished appearance, the face loomed so near, so tangible that Coar expected it to open its mouth, shout, scream, or cry, and then swallow one down into an inescapable cage of bone and flesh. Instead it only watched Coar as if awaiting the answer to an unspoken question, remaining until the moment Coar woke from a midnight dream or rose from an anesthetic fog in the body forge laboratory, when it dimmed away, leaving Coar equally trapped in blood and muscle as if it had devoured one.

This morning as the anesthesia wore off, Coar floated toward consciousness resolved to hold onto the face. Struggling out of chemical sluggishness, Coar jerked awake into the typical, yeasty, body forge odors of new flesh mingled with the lingering bite of antiseptic cleansers and antibiotic mists. Coar gagged on them as he inhaled deeply and groped across one's mind for the face in the dying darkness, arms grasping in tandem with mental efforts, fingers clutching only empty air. But the face vanished.

"Steady, Coar," Doctor Mills said, easing Coar's arms down. "Let your body adjust."

Edon stood behind Mills, watching from a tall, female body with brunette hair dressed in a fashionably cut suit and skirt, reminding Coar of yet another day of work missed to be here. At least Coar assumed Edon was still in there since Edon had arrived at the forge in that body this morning. Severed from the International Life Interface by one's injury, Coar perceived only the expressionless faces surgically sculpted to display the *elems*, the life matrix projections that identified a body's inhabitant. Their continued absence from Edon's and Mills' faces told Coar the latest treatment hadn't worked.

No surprise. Coar had known it was a long shot.

Mills' plan to reboot Coar's life matrix via light-induced theta wave recycling and relink it to the 'Face sounded good in theory, but Coar, who'd spent years designing light particle data protocols, knew broken photon matrixes were obstinate. The array of data-laden light in Coar's life matrix—what old-timers still sometimes cheekily called a *soul*—should've bound Coar to the 'Face, but broken, they left one trapped in a single body.

Disappointment rose in Coar like stale oil lifted to a road surface by rain.

"We tried," Coar said. "Maybe the next thing will work."

Mills grunted while studying Coar's electronic chart hanging from the end of the bed.

Edon turned away and answered a buzzing netphone. Anyone could have been in the brunette body, a stand-in hired while Edon skipped to the office, a visiting body forge scientist studying Coar's situation, or even a public relations flack covering up Coar's condition because anything that cast doubt on the safety of the 'Face—as Coar's accident did—verged on heresy. One suspected Edon sometimes body-skipped elsewhere at times when Coar might not notice. Coar couldn't blame one. Skipping across the 'Face came as naturally as breathing.

Coar watched Edon speak into the phone, sun-shadowed near a window, and wondered.

Another Specta network crisis. Ratings plunging every quarter now. More fires to extinguish.

"Don't bitch talk me, Arra. All you do is gripe and guess. Give me some damn results," Edon said and then stroked the brunette body's long black hair before rubbing its forehead then dropping its hand against its thigh.

Coar knew well the frustrated gesture. And *bitch talk*, Edon's pet name for complaining.

So, Edon after all.

Coar's ability to recognize Edon by speech mannerisms and body language despite whatever body Edon wore had thrived since the accident. The stress of Coar's injury and the ratings crisis only heightened Edon's innate traits. Specta demanded more and more time as greater numbers of people stopped watching their programs, and Edon seemed to prefer those problems, which one could grasp, confront, quantify, and perhaps solve. Problems that didn't send termite tunnels hollowing through the foundations of one's existence like the uncertainty of seeking a cure for Coar's damaged life matrix did. Coar only wanted Edon by one's side. Isolation from the 'Face scared one enough without the added pain of the gulf widening between them now that Coar could no longer go where Edon—and almost everyone else on earth—could.

A nurse with a face Coar recognized peeled electrodes from Coar's body. Young, male, a shadow of stubble, and an inch-long, easy-to-overlook scar along the left side of one's nose. The nurse had body-stuck for Coar's last several treatments, along with Doctor Mill's and others. Consistency helped Coar identify one's caregivers. The scar, though, suggested a body choice made for reasons beyond practicality. People discarded scarred bodies. No one had to live with ugliness, and Coar couldn't imagine why anyone would want to. The body forges cleaned and perfected all bodies during regular maintenance. Scars meant embarrassment and pain, tangled lines of tight skin that tugged at one's joints. Scars interlaced Coar's body now, head to toe, remnants of urgent, clumsy repairs made by body forge automatons better built for managing nutrition-to-waste ratios than repairing wounded flesh.

Coar so wanted to be perfect again. The nurse's scar fascinated one.

Noticing Coar's interest, the nurse said, low-voiced, "I'm sorry for what's happened to you." With a glance at Edon still absorbed on the phone, the nurse slid a card from a scrub pocket and pressed it into Coar's hand. An odd change affected the nurse's face; eyes widened, eyebrows rose, and lips parted, breaking its flat, passive stare. It passed too quickly for Coar to be sure what he'd seen. "Life isn't how you think. You can't skip from every problem. Take this in case…. Well, I guess in case nothing can be done, you might need a different kind of help than they offer at a body forge."

"What…?" Coar said.

"My name," the nurse said, "is *David*."

An ancient name. A gendered name.

Coar wondered why David had taken it.

The red and black sign printed on the card delineated the outline of an androgynous, human figure with a stylized drawing of the world centered in its torso. Coar knew it from old news posts and history pages. A forbidden sign with an apostate meaning, illegal for more than a century. On the back of the card, the words: *The World Within Us.* Below that, a name: *Widds.* And a phone number.

Coar shivered.

The nurse—*David*—shifted to shutting down machines and monitors as Mills handed Coar a tablet. Coar hid the card under a leg, unsure why, as he regarded the screen. It showed a scan of Coar's head, broken life matrix represented by a knot of green brightness at the base of Coar's skull.

"Compare this… to *this*." Mills touched the screen, summoning an identical image.

Coar glanced at Edon, wishing one would get off the phone and be with one. Then Coar read the date stamps on the scans—one taken the day of the accident, the other this morning.

Mills dragged them atop one another; superimposed, they made a perfect match.

"They're the same," Coar said.

"That's the problem, isn't it? All we've tried, and yet no change," Mills said. "Your life matrix remains as mangled and dysfunctional as the day of the accident. Fixing bodies is a fool's game. If you'd skipped to the 'Face before the truck smashed your car, as Edon did, you'd still be connected. I wish we could simply scrap this body you're wearing rather than go through all this trouble trying to repair it. Can't do that while you're in it, though, can we?"

"The crash occurred so fast," Coar said. "I hit my head before I knew it was happening."

Mills raised a hand. "No one blames you, Coar. We're simply frustrated we can't heal you. There are one or two more things we'll try, but I'm afraid they're even more of a stretch than today's treatment. If they don't work…"

"What…?" Coar asked. "If they don't work… what?"

Mills studied Coar's face with blank intent, like a staring statue, assessing, Coar guessed, one's damaged *elem*. Coar wondered what it looked like.

"If we don't get you out of that body then we can only wait and hope you heal naturally with time. Otherwise I'm afraid you'll be wedded to this body permanently," Mills said. "I'm sorry, but the damage is extensive. You're too deeply embedded in this nervous system. We could pry you out the way we do infants, but your awareness is too high, and your life matrix isn't as resilient as an infant's. Fifty-fifty it would kill you, ninety-ten you'd come out with severe psychological damage. This body would certainly die, which means if we got you out but not reconnected to the 'Face, you'd be a ghost."

Coar tried to imagine that. "A ghost? Seriously?"

Mills shrugged, a gesture incongruous with his static face and unsettling. "How the hell should I know? It's a figure of speech. Best I can come up with considering no one's ever seen a case like yours before. I'm worried, Coar, because you've been stuck in there longer than is healthy. You have to prepare for side effects."

"What side effects?"

"Depression and anxiety for starters. You can no longer leave your body, Coar. No using and abusing then dumping it to recover while you skip to a fresh one. Right now, we're steadying you with round-the-clock care. Feeding you. Managing your metabolism. Bathing you. Making sure you sleep enough. When you leave here, you'll have to take care of yourself. You get tired, sick, or hurt, you'll have to rest and heal. You get dirty, you'll have to wash. Your body will influence your mental state. You may find it difficult to think when you're hungry or fatigued—or angry or upset. Your blood sugar may drop; your blood pressure may rise. The longer you stay in there, the more you'll identify as male. Do you recall your birth gender?"

"Male," Coar said.

"That might ease things a bit," Mills said. "What was Edon's?"

Coar shook his head. "Never came up."

"No matter. The point is, Coar, you can't skip to another body, so you must learn to manage the sensations you'll experience in this one. It's going to shake you up. You might feel despondent, paranoid, confused. You have to recognize those symptoms and come back for help."

"Understood," Coar said.

"Good. Go back to your room and rest. Tomorrow we'll schedule another session. We'll do everything we can think of before we throw in the towel."

"What about the face I see? My birth face?" Coar asked.

"It isn't your birth face. How could you even know what that looks like?" Mills said. "It's likely a visual artifact produced by your mind to reconcile seeing the same face in the mirror for so long and not seeing your *elem*."

"It doesn't look much like me. It's out of focus."

"Your brain isn't used to the idea of having one face. Before your accident, when was the last time you spent a month—or even a week—in one body?"

"Never," Coar said.

"Exactly. Don't worry. It'll resolve itself." Mills sat in a chair by the door. "I have to get back to the forge now, Coar. We're stripping in 16 new bodies this afternoon. One's work is never done."

Mills settled in the chair and grew still except for the gentle rise and fall of one's chest. Anyone connected to the 'Face would've seen Mill's *elem* blink out as one skipped to a body elsewhere in the forge. To Coar it appeared Mills simply sat down and fell asleep, eyes open.

Coar shifted. The card scraped under one's thigh.

Equipment shutdown completed, the nurse—*David*, Coar remembered—left after a last blank-faced glance at Coar.

Across the room, call concluded, Edon slid the phone into a pocket. Edon had come to all Coar's treatments. How long would one wait for a cure, though, before—*Coar despised the thought*—before leaving one, before moving on? The idea chilled Coar. One never wanted to be alone—especially not alone and cut off from the 'Face. If in fact Coar's life matrix could heal itself, it might happen tomorrow, or ten years from now, or fifty. How could Edon be expected to wait that long? Impatient, passionate Edon, who lived fast and swept Coar along in one's wake.

Coar wiped one's eyes, staving off tears, then slid from bed and dressed, palming the business card into a pocket.

"I'm sorry," Coar said.

Edon smiled then hugged Coar tight.

"It's alright," Edon said. "Everything will be alright."

"I can't face this without you," Coar said. "I need you."

"I know," Edon said.

"But it's so unfair to you."

"It is what it is, love. You'll get through it."

Coar wanted to believe, but Edon's face betrayed no reassurance, and tension in the brunette body—Edon's tension—signaled how much one held back.

You'll *get through it*—not *we*, Edon had said.

What if she leaves me?

Coar shuddered.

She?

I am he, *now. Is Edon…* she?

No. I am he, and Edon is Edon.

Edon is one.

And I am alone.

He squeezed Edon's hand and let one take *him* home.

II. Young Love and Other Day Trips

The final treatments failed, and Coar left the body forge.

One night at home, he startled awake from a dream of his birth face.

The vague face floated beneath the surface of a pool so still its waters mirrored Coar staring into it. He tried to map his reflection onto his shimmery birth face, the similarities enticing, the differences maddening—awakening Coar with a pounding headache.

He rolled over, pressed against Edon's warmth beside him. Although Edon could skip to a rested body to avoid slumber, one went to bed with Coar to help him sleep. Coar exhaled, relieved for the company, then touched Edon's thigh—and knew instantly Edon wasn't there. One—*she*, he found himself thinking—felt wrong. Too still. Too deeply asleep. Too… empty. Once again, Edon had waited until Coar fell asleep then skipped to another body. How many times now? Coar had lost count, but it seemed Edon left almost every night. Maybe one had skipped to the office to deal with the latest ratings fallout. Maybe to see friends. Maybe anywhere, to be with anyone else. Or to be anyone else. Places Coar could no longer go.

He stuffed pillows behind his back and clicked the television remote.

A news show flickered across the screen on the opposite wall. In Morocco, a building collapse; one hundred and fifty bodies lost, all life matrixes escaped via the 'Face to new bodies, no deaths. In Chile, an earthquake; more than six hundred bodies dead, again all life matrixes safely skipped to the 'Face. In Greece, riots over body shortages, pricking up the old debate of cloning versus natural reproduction; three bodies destroyed, no life matrixes lost. The 'Face saved them all; it gathered them, sorted them, and sent them to new bodies. The 'Face now closed to Coar, whose mortality teased him from the images of broken bodies. He wondered how dying felt, afraid he might find out sooner than most. Everyone died, he reminded himself; skipping to the 'Face only delayed it.

Coar found little consolation in that.

"I'm so fucked," he said.

He switched channels to the Specta network. One of Edon's programs appeared.

Two for Flinching, a daredevil game show, where contestants challenged each other to defy their instincts by standing closest to a lava flow, lasting the longest skydiving sans parachute, or taking the most bullets from an old-fashioned six shooter, skipping to a new body before the old one perished. Coar thought it obvious why such shows were failing. When anyone could do the same things for kicks, why would anyone want to watch others do them? He had once told Edon as much, and one agreed. The shows, however, involved teams from different nations, and checked social tensions by uniting people around the common convention of the games. *We're barely keeping things running as it is*, Edon had said. *We can't lose the audience now. Once the last common thread gets pulled, everything unravels.* That rang true. Cities in disrepair. Roads and bridges crumbling. Building collapses, vehicle collisions, and airplane crashes in the news daily. The human work of a millennium decaying. The 'Face and the body forges all anyone cared to maintain anymore, they treated everything else like old furniture.

Coar looked at the sleeping body beside him.

Male, blond, fit. One of Edon's favorites.

Coar had often worn a voluptuous blonde to match it.

Throwing off the covers, Coar slid from bed to yank open his and Edon's closets.

Inside stood rows of glass-doored life chambers, where dormant bodies waited, plugged into nutrition and waste disposal apparatus. Coar's side held three females, three males, a mix of races and body types. Edon's contained five males, four females, revealing a preference for tall, fit physiques and almond-hued flesh. Coar couldn't complain. His eclecticism didn't extend as far as aboriginal, overweight, handicapped, or other extreme bodies; but those were special order and expensive, anyway. It was cheaper to rent them as desired. Any type, anytime, anywhere—for everyone except Coar. He eyed the empty chamber in his closet for the body he wore. *My only body now.* Two empty places waited on Edon's side. One for the male in the bed. The other for a body Edon had bought since the accident and never worn around Coar: a black-haired man.

A body to share with someone new.

It's really over, Coar realized. *Twenty-five years, and it's done and gone.*

How many times has Edon skipped out in that body?

How many times has one—she—left me behind?

No, not she. One.

Edon is one.

One who betrayed me.

Coar slammed shut the doors, then kicked over the chair of the desk in the corner. The blond's eyes snapped open. The body lifted its head and stared at him blankly.

Coar glared back. Rage seethed in him. He wanted to make the body stop staring, to end its mindless breathing, and leave it for Edon to discover, to show he knew what one—what *she*—was doing. He had never before felt such intense emotions. Anger crackled through him, blurred his vision, throbbed in his head. It ran hot and begged release, a conflagration too long denied igniting. Coar grabbed a vase from the desk and hurled it, smashing it against the wall behind the bed. Still the blond body stared at him, glassy-eyed, unknowing.

"Let me out of here!" Coar raked his fingernails across his chest, drawing lines of blood.

He rushed downstairs to the kitchen, to the liquor cabinet, and poured a glass of whiskey. He downed it, poured another, then a third. Heat seeped through his body, soothing him, slowing his mind, dulling his furor. He eyed his reflection in the stainless-steel surface of the refrigerator. His birth face and real face blended into a face Coar couldn't quite grasp. A senseless mess of features. *Is this who I am? A collision of faces? A jumble of identity fragments?* He longed to return to work, to code photons for life matrix sub-strata systems, to wrap his mind around something that still made sense.

He wanted Edon.

He grabbed his phone and dialed Edon's number.

Edon's phone rang in the living room.

Coar traced the ring, stared at the blank blue screen that would've displayed his avatar if he were still connected to the 'Face. He took another drink.

One—Edon—*she*—was leaving him.

Had *left* him.

Alone.

Coar's stomach ached. He tried to remember the last time he'd eaten. In the past he had dined only for pleasure, leaving fed bodies in the life chambers for metabolic systems to balance calories and eliminate waste. Mills had said he would develop a sense of eating for sustenance, but so far that natural rhythm eluded him. After half an hour's discomfort, Coar remembered the sensation in his lower body meant he needed to void his bladder. He stumbled to the little used bathroom and relieved himself.

Afterward, the bottle nearly empty, Coar set out to find Edon.

He knew all Edon's favorite restaurants and shops, lounges and bars. He drove to one after another, disappointed at each, stopping long enough for drinks in the bars, keeping numbed, hazy, holding back the desperation threatening to overwhelm him, wondering if this catastrophe of emotions was what Doctor Mills had warned about. Coar exhausted all the likely locations before he remembered one more.

He drove to the hotel where he'd first met Edon.

His car skidded to a stop by the entrance, jumping the curb and smashing a garbage bin, spilling trash onto the sidewalk. The door attendant came running as Coar staggered from the driver's seat.

"Asshole! What the hell?" said the attendant, clothed in a muscular body. "You drunk? It's illegal to drive with your drinking body, moron."

Coar shoved the attendant aside and weaved into the lobby.

Alerted by the crash and the shouting, every *one* inside faced Coar, trying to make sense of the disheveled one without sense enough to skip out of a drunken body and sober up. Their *elems* invisible to him, Coar sought any sign of Edon. He scrounged up his memories of Edon's newest body. Black-haired, dark-skinned. Male. Tall, of course. As blank faced as all the others. Every second that passed fed his doubt he'd find Edon—and then, by the elevator, a black-haired man ran a hand through one's hair, rubbed one's forehead, touched one's thigh.

Edon.

Coar bolted across the lobby. People cleared from his path.

He brushed past a young man and woman and grabbed the body.

"Edon!"

"What do you want?" said the one Coar held, face emotionless. Coar imagined Edon's *elem* lighting up like fireworks.

"I need you. Come *with* me," he said.

"Let go of me!"

The black-haired body struggled. Coar tightened his grip.

"Come home. Please!" he said. "I can't lose you. Come home, at least for tonight."

"No! I don't even know you! Get your hand off me! What's wrong with your *elem*? Why is it scrambled?"

Coar hesitated. Maybe it wasn't Edon inside this body.

It must be her. This is the body from her closet.

Not her. One. Edon is one, not a body.

You are he, *but Edon is one.*

Still one.

"Don't leave me alone!" Coar said.

The black-haired body cowered as Coar swung and then hammered its face with his fist. The first blow cracked the jaw with a snapping noise. A second punch struck its chest, slamming it against the elevator console. It jolted, sagged limp, and Coar suspected Edon had skipped to the 'Face. But a chain reaction that had been festering in him since the crash and through all the failed attempts to heal him gripped Coar. He couldn't stop himself. He struck the body again, then kicked it, stomped it, punched it, beat it bruised and bloody, the wet smacks of flesh and bone impacts filling the stunned silence of the lobby. Violent energy gushed from Coar, and he channeled it at the shell of the one who'd betrayed him.

Coar beat on the body until he slipped on the bloody tile floor.

Someone said, "*Coar.* Stop it."

Coar looked to the young couple. The man, maybe nineteen, athletic, brown hair, and tall. The female, willowy, thin, red-haired, graceful curves beneath a summer dress.

"It's scrap for the forges. That what you wanted?" the man said.

Coar stared, confused.

"What the hell's wrong with you?" the man said.

Coar's heart galloped. His head spun from too much drink and too great stress, and he tipped into a vertiginous swirl, a man balanced above an abyss. Swaying, he steadied himself against the wall.

"Edon…?" he said.

"You thought I was in that body," Edon said.

Coar nodded. "It's from your closet."

"Shit, Coar. That body cost me a lot of money."

"Who… was in it?"

"Someone I loaned it to for the night. None of your damn business."

"Edon, don't do this. Don't. Leave me. Alone."

Edon sighed. The female body hung off Edon's arm, rested its head on one's shoulder.

"No bitch talk, Coar. I can't stand bitch talk," Edon said. "You're broken. We don't live in the same world, don't speak the same language anymore. I need to be with who I want, and I need to be who I want. You think I want to be with a man for the rest of my life? I don't always want to be a woman or the same age as you or even in the same damn city. If you can't be the people I need you to be, and I can't be the person you need, how can we stay together?"

Coar said, "I don't know."

"We can't."

"I can't live without you," Coar reached for Edon, who backed away.

"No, Coar," Edon said. "Get out of here. Run back to the body forge, to Doctor Mills. When the police come for you, tell them your injury drove you over the edge. I'll back you up. But you can never leave there, Coar. They can care for you in the body forge. I don't ever want to see you again."

Coar searched Edon's passive, plastic face for anything that resembled Edon. It looked naked without an *elem*, so out of sync with its angry, bitter voice. He didn't know who Edon really was. He had never known. An *elem* was only data made visible. A gesture wasn't enough to know one, not truly, not in a way that mattered. Even when he still saw *elems*, Coar had only ever known who people wanted to be when they were with him, had only ever showed them the same—and who was to say how much of any of it was real?

"Go!" Edon screamed.

Coar did. He rushed out into the night's dark grasp as police sirens approached the hotel.

Crying, shivering, he chased block after block, racing, purposeless, into the heart of the city, until cramps in his legs and torso forced him to stop. He sank to his knees by the curb and threw up what liquor remained in his stomach. He couldn't go home, didn't want to return to the body forge. One other choice remained. He fished the card the nurse, *David*, had given him out of his wallet and dialed Widds.

III. Prosopagnosia

"Slow." The woman, Widds, gripped Coar's wrist gently and stopped him from slurping more water. "You'll make yourself sick if you go too fast."

Coar lowered the cup from his lips. Water spilled down his chin, onto his shirt, already stained with crumbs and splotches of food. He took several deep breaths then sipped again. His hands, bound together with rope, gripped the cup awkwardly.

Widds nodded. "Better. Be patient."

Coar bit off a measured piece of bread from his plate and chewed.

"Good, good," Widds said.

The food settled Coar's stomach, helped clear his head. Confusion and fear replaced his rage. He sat in a house outside the city amidst the ruins of an old village, a place no one from the city ever traveled. Widds and David had come in a car when he called and taken him here. Coar heard others moving around the house. Floors creaking. Doors closing. Faucets running. Toilets flushing. But Widds and David kept Coar in the kitchen, feeding him.

After satiating his hunger, Coar asked, "Why did you help me?"

Widds smiled. "You're like us now. Off the 'Face."

"I don't want to be 'him.'" Coar shook his head. "I want to be 'one.'"

"You've been granted a gift. You can live a true life here. If you choose to stay, that is. You're not a prisoner."

Coar raised his bound hands, tied at the wrists to limit the movement of his arms while allowing him the use of his hands.

"You're violent. It's part of the transition. We'll untie you when it passes," Widds said. "The transition, the adjustment—that's the roughest part. Do you want to stay?"

"I don't know what I want," Coar said.

"It's overwhelming," Widds said. "Start with one question you most want answered."

Coar's brain labored under the dregs of alcohol in his blood. His head ached, and light pained his eyes. He had never felt this way before. Widds called it a "hangover."

"Take your time," she said. "We risked sneaking David into the forge with a false *elem* when we heard rumors your caregivers were body-sticking for your benefit. No one noticed him. Maybe while you were there, you wondered about something you saw or something your doctors said?"

"The day I gave you Widds' card," David said, "you woke rough from the anesthesia."

"I saw my birth face while I was under," Coar said. "I see it in my dreams."

He told them how Mills had explained the face.

"Everyone goes through something like that when they disconnect," Widds said. "A reckoning. It *is* a birth face of sorts. Not the one you were born with, but one you can be *reborn* with. Look in that mirror by the sink. Tell me what you see."

Coar scuffed his chair back from the table, stood, and looked in the grimy mirror.

A disjointed mess peered back at him. It possessed elements of the face he'd seen in the blackness of unconsciousness as well as some from the face that belonged to his body, but other characteristics crept in too. Bits of every face he'd ever had. Interference. He rubbed his eyes and tried to describe it to Widds but sounded foolish and gave up.

"What your doctor said is true," Widds said. "But what those who work in the forges see as a disorder, we know is humanity. Your identity is taking root. Once you accept it, you'll see your face clearly. We can help you do that. Or you can return to the city and live in a forge until you die."

"The police will arrest me," Coar said.

"Not here. As long as we stay outside the city, they don't care what we do," Widds said. "Why would they bother anyway? You scared some people and broke a body that belonged to your partner. They have bigger problems. Skipping to the 'Face every time something goes south makes people reckless and indifferent. Things get ruined. Society is breaking down out there."

Coar scanned Widds' face, then David's, both so alien and expressive.

Full of things he'd never seen in other faces.

Presence. Immediacy. Truth.

They terrified him. He wanted to be with Edon, back on the 'Face, skipping bodies; back at work, organizing photon bundles. He didn't belong among outlaws, among the insane who believed physical truth defined one's existence.

The World Within Us.

One body, a singular identity.

A philosophy outlawed a century ago.

Heresy. Madness.

Coar wanted no part of that life. His rage returned in a seismic urge.

Shoving his tied hands together under the edge of the table, he flipped it and pressed it against Widds, knocking her to the floor. Then he slammed David aside and pushed through the door into the next room.

Coar's muscles burned. His head swam with the exertion.

His hands ached, still sore from beating the body in the hotel.

The pain frightened him. It stayed with him. He couldn't skip away from it. He never realized how long pain lasted, how deeply hunger boiled or thirst burned, how tired an abused, sleepless body became. He froze when he saw the people in the next room. Their faces lit up and brimming with emotion. He smelled them, too, their odor so different than the sterile bodies of the forges. Coar raced along a hallway, fumbled with the front doorknob, and then fled outside. People on the porch watched him with curiosity. He stumbled down the steps, fell on the weedy lawn, rose, stumbled to the street. Their gazes chased him. He shunned their faces. Their animate faces. Like his now. Faces of expression. Faces shorn of manipulation and masks. Life embodied in soft wrinkles and moist eyes and cracked lips that would never belong to anyone else. Faces sculpted by experience.

Coar's legs turned to rubber. He collapsed in the street.

He rolled over, spied the distant city lights, a cold luminosity that beckoned Coar at the same time it repulsed him. A massive *elem*, an illusion. Edon dwelled there. Somewhere. As some *one, any* one.

Coar struggled upright. He stepped toward the city.

Stopped.

Widds approached. "We'll drive you back," she said.

"I…." Coar's voice cracked. "I'll be alone."

"Weren't you always alone there?" Widds said.

"…Yes."

"Stay with us."

"I can't bear to look at your faces," Coar said. "And *my* face… it must be grotesque."

"You have a good face. You only need time to understand it. And ours."

"How long?"

"A year, maybe two."

Widds gestured, and David came with a strip of red cloth. "When your mind knows it's right, you'll see your own face clearly. We'll help you. Then you can choose a new name if you want. Not all of us do. To bear the weight of existence in your flesh, to face yourself in the mirror every day, is the price of a real life, Coar. It's a price people on the 'Face never pay, an experience they never obtain."

Widds pulled the cloth over Coar's eyes, taking away the faces and light, and then tied it tight around the back of his head. Coar walked back among the people. Voices came from within the house. He smelled their bodies and felt the air temperature drop as a breeze brushed his skin. Widds guided him, her fingers at his elbow. The others touched him, too, stroked him, squeezed him, patted him on the back. Rope scraped and rustled around his wrists as someone removed his restraints. The sensations belonged to him. Not to a body or a memory. In the darkness of the blindfold, his birth face appeared, steady, yet cloudy, nascent, still awaiting an answer Coar could only now begin to provide.

The Flying Rock

"Everyone should have a chance to fly before they forget how," Daniel said.

The flying rock sat on the far edge of the clearing, and the little meadow looked as if nothing had changed in all the many years since Daniel had last been there. A thick ring of oaks, birches, and honeysuckle bushes still encircled most of it, casting hazy shadows onto the grass, lacing the air with a soft sweetness. Abby and Mike left Daniel and the shaded path for the bright field, where the sunlight formed halos around the edges of their hair. Mike, clutching a toy dinosaur wearing a jetpack, trailed a few uncertain steps behind his big sister. They stopped and stared at the enormous wedge of rock.

"Is that it, Daddy?" Abby said. "How does it work?"

Daniel joined his children and shrugged free of his backpack. He dropped it to the grass and shivered as air hit the patch of sweat it had left soaked into his shirt.

"You climb on and fly," Daniel said. "Nothing to it."

Abby squinted. "For real?"

"Yeah, for real?" Mike asked.

"I wouldn't let you try if I didn't believe you could do it," Daniel said. "Didn't you listen to what Grandma told you?"

"That was only a story, like in storybooks with faeries and wizards," Abby said. "Cause if it's real, why can't you still fly? If I could fly, I'd fly everywhere and never come down. Except for dinner."

"I grew up and forgot how to do it," Daniel said.

"Why'd you forget?" Abby asked.

"I didn't have a choice."

"I'd draw pictures how to do it. Or write it down. So I couldn't ever forget," Abby said.

"You would anyway," Daniel told her. "Everyone does, no matter what. Everyone grows too old to remember how. Most people don't even miss it, because they never realized they knew how to do it in the first place. I brought you here to make sure you know."

"What about Mommy?" Abby said. "Did she fly?"

Daniel thought of Ginny back at the cabin, as preoccupied with accounts and balances as she ever was, even on vacation, as she tried to plan for their future and

23

all the things they needed but couldn't afford. She still rolled her eyes whenever he mentioned the flying rock, except now anger and resentment were layered on top of her exasperation. Daniel was grateful she had even agreed to the trip to his family's cabin, but he knew she had come only for Abby and Mike, who adored their grandmother.

He shook his head and told Abby, "No, your mother never flew. Then it was too late for her. Now she doesn't believe anyone could ever fly. Most people believe they can't fly. Almost everyone, really. That's because most people never flew while they could."

"Maybe you could show Mom how. Then she can come with us," Abby said.

"Mommy's got a lot of work to do, sweetie. Besides, once you've forgotten how to fly, there's no going back," Daniel said. "It's a now-or-never kind of thing. But if you fly while you can, you'll always remember it. Then the memory comes back to you in your dreams, and it's there for you when you grow up."

Mike ran to his father, hugged him, and said, "Daddy, I'm hungry."

"We'll eat lunch soon," Daniel said. "I want you to practice first. Come on, I'll show you how to use the flying rock."

Daniel led his children to the base of the stone, a huge chunk of striped granite that seemed to have fallen from the sky. Its presence in the clearing, as far as Daniel knew, had never been explained. It jutted from the earth on an angle, like a ramp, fifteen feet long, twelve feet high at its tip, and sloped gently enough for a child to climb to the top. Daniel circled to the front of the stone, Abby and Mike following close behind him. On the rock's far side, the clearing continued on a gentle slope for about six feet before the ground declined and plunged in a steep slope toward a stream below, a sharp, thirty-foot drop that made an obvious dent in the tree cover. A winding trail of stones wedged into the face of the slope formed crude stairs to a trail below. The steps descended into a misty gloom. They had been there since before Daniel first came to the flying rock; probably, they had been there for centuries.

"Stay close to the rock," Daniel said. He held Mike's hand and put himself between Abby and the slope. "You can get down that hill if you have to, but it's tricky. Take my word for it. I once tumbled halfway down there and rolled into the stream."

"Did you get hurt, Daddy?" Abby asked.

"A bump on my head, knees scraped, a few cuts and scratches down my back. I was lucky. I could've broken my neck."

"You got boo-boos, Daddy?" Mike said.

"Yeah, but they're all better now, kiddo." Daniel crouched and pointed northwest over the rippling, green quilt of trees that spread outward from the hillside. A powerful gust of wind pushed against his face and swept his hair back. Mike tightened his grip on his father's hand. Abby squinted and pushed her long hair back from where the wind dragged it across her eyes. The children's T-shirts flattened against them and fluttered. "Look. Over that way is Grandma's cabin. See the plume of smoke? Grandma's got the brick oven going. We'll have fresh bread with dinner tonight. If you get dizzy or turned around up here, use that smoke to find your direction. All right, who's first?"

Abby jumped up. "I'll go!"

"Okay, come around to the base of the stone," Daniel said. "Here's what you do. Climb up to the peak but keep your eyes on the stone the whole time. Don't look over the edge. At the top, lie down on your tummy, with your legs straight behind you, stretch your arms out to your sides, and close your eyes. Wait for a good strong gust, like that last one. When it comes, lift your head up, snap your eyes open, and you'll be flying. Think you can swing it?"

Abby was already climbing the stone. "Watch me, Daddy."

She clambered easily up the incline. It amazed Daniel how fearless she was, how much she trusted him. He cherished the excitement in her voice and the way she moved, her slender body so strong and capable that it made him proud. He wished Ginny could have come with them if only to see how happy the children were, but even if she had wanted to—even if she would have made time for what she considered pointless nonsense—he could not have brought her. Daniel's old friends would not come, and the flying would not work with Ginny here. Abby lowered herself to the stone and spread out her arms. Daniel studied the treetops down the slope, watching leaves and branches shake and sway.

"Get ready, Abby, there's a good one coming," he said.

The gust rushed up the slope, rustling leaves, and swirled Abby's hair. She lifted her head. Her excited scream, half shock, half thrill, told Daniel the exact moment she opened her eyes and saw the sky before her.

"I'm flying, Daddy!" she called. "I'm doing it!"

Mike's eyes were glued to his sister; he was enrapt with a mix of curiosity and fear.

Daniel had seen what Abby saw many times when he was a child. The height and angle of the rock combined with the descent of the slope created the illusion for anyone lying in Abby's position that there was no ground anywhere nearby. It was like being a hundred feet in the air, and when the wind kicked up and rushed past your face, it really did feel like flying, especially to a child. *Almost as good as the real thing,* Daniel thought, as the gust faded to a breeze then ended.

Abby spun around and sat up on the rock, her face beaming.

"Did I do it right, Daddy?" she said.

"Perfect, honey," Daniel said.

Mike tucked his dinosaur under one arm and tugged on his father's hand. "My turn. I want to try."

"Up you go," Daniel said.

He boosted Mike onto the stone, and Abby guided him to the peak. Mike squinted and kept his head down, focused on the rock underfoot. He slipped once, skidded, then caught himself and kept going. Daniel jolted, fearing Mike might fall, but even if he did there was only soft grass anywhere he might land. Abby helped her little brother into position, and then slid halfway down the rock to wait. For as far as Daniel could see the trees remained still. Then in the distance beyond his family's cabin, a wave of air moved the branches and rolled toward the clearing, rising and falling with the treetops. It crossed the woods with a fleeting inevitability that saddened Daniel, the beauty of the wind so brief before it was gone and forgotten.

"Get ready. Here it comes," Daniel said.

Air streamed over the slope and enveloped Mike.

"Yippee!" the boy shouted when he opened his eyes.

He stretched his arms as far as he could and stiffened his body, pretending to be an airplane. He laughed until the wind died and then he rolled over, smiling at his father.

"Do it again," he said. "Can I do it again?"

"Sure," Daniel said. "Wait for more wind and take turns while I get lunch ready. Be careful not to fall off, though, okay?"

Abby slid next to Mike and got into position. Daniel retrieved his backpack and opened it. He took out a blanket, which he unfolded and spread on the grass, pinning its corners and edges beneath stones gathered from the meadow. Then he pulled out wrapped sandwiches, apples, and juice boxes, followed by a Thermos of coffee. He took a drink before setting the Thermos beside a small basket, latched closed by a wooden peg pushed through a leather loop.

"Alright, guys, lunch time," he called.

Abby won the race to the base of the stone, but she waited at the bottom for Mike to catch up. They ran together to the picnic blanket. They flopped down and dug into peanut butter-and-jelly sandwiches and sipped from their juice boxes.

"Flying makes me hungry, Dad," Mike said.

"Being awake makes you hungry, kiddo," Daniel said.

"Can we go flying everyday while we're visiting Grandma?" Abby asked.

"We'll see," Daniel said. "Really, it only works like this on windy days."

Mike smeared a blob of jelly from his cheek onto the back of his hand. "Today sure is a good windy day."

Abby pointed at the little basket beside Daniel. "What's in there?"

"Dessert?" Mike asked.

"Nope. That's a treat for some friends of mine from when I was your age. The ones Grandma told you about. They're going to meet us here." Daniel stood with the basket. "I should get things ready for them. You guys eat. I'll be right back."

He walked to the edge of the clearing, knelt down, and opened the basket. He removed a tiny cup and saucer from inside and set them on the grass. Then he poured milk into the cup from a small Thermos. Next he opened a jar of honey, spooned some into the milk, and stirred it. Finally, he took three iced cookies from a plastic bag and arranged them on the saucer. When he was done, he placed the Thermos, honey jar, and spoon back in the basket and walked to another spot along the edge of the clearing. There he prepared a second cup and saucer, this time with petit fours. He continued around the ring, setting five more places, each one tucked into the shady green along the strip of light and shadow at the clearing's edge. As he finished fixing the last cup and saucer, he realized Abby and Mike were staring at him, sandwiches and juice boxes held in mid-air.

"What are you doing?" Abby asked.

"Can we have some cookies too?" Mike said.

"Maybe." Daniel closed the basket and returned to the blanket. He sat down, drank more coffee, and bit into his sandwich. "Those are for my friends."

"Are your friends cats?" Abby asked.

"No." Daniel laughed. "Why do you think they'd be cats? I'm allergic to cats."

"Everyone knows cats like to drink milk from a cup," Abby said. "If they're not cats then who are they? Do they live out here? Why do you want to see them? Are they going to fly too?"

Daniel laughed. "You'll find out soon enough. We have to wait a little while. Now finish your lunches, and maybe I've got an extra cookie or two stashed away for you. Grandma made them special for us and my friends."

"They're faerie cookies," Abby said.

"How do you know that?" Daniel asked.

"Grandma told me. She said she makes them 'just so,' and they're hard to make."

"She's the expert," Daniel said.

The children finished most of their lunches, each taking a second juice box, and Daniel gave them a couple of cookies each, which they happily devoured. He ate some himself and savored their strong, sugary taste and the vague bitterness it masked—the taste of ozone after a storm—the special ingredient his mother preserved that made them faerie cookies. It was one of the flavors that defined Daniel's childhood, a sensory memory that transported him back to when he was Abby's age. Back to better times. *The world has become so dark since then, so filled with wars, and anger, and hatred, and perversion,* Daniel thought. He feared the future he was raising Abby and Mike to face; he worried they would find darker times ahead than he ever could have imagined. He would not always be there to protect them. How things were between him and Ginny, he was not even sure where he would be in a year. The tension between them would break soon. Daniel felt it coming. Then there would be no hiding it from the kids. Worse, the dark sadness that had crept into his soul seemed heavier and harder to shake every year. He wished there was a place like this meadow, safe and removed from the bad things, where they could go and live their entire lives. He finished the last cookie and then cleaned up what was left of lunch before he stretched out on the blanket, resting his head on his backpack.

"Can we go flying again?" Abby asked.

"We need to rest," Daniel said. "Don't you feel sleepy?"

"No. I want to fly again," Abby said, but then she yawned.

Her eyes closed. Beside her Mike was curled up dozing on the blanket, his dinosaur back in hand. Warmth spread through Daniel as the magic of the cookies relaxed him. He waited until Abby nodded off then let himself drift into a light sleep filled with airy dreams, none of which he remembered when he awoke. It seemed only moments later that Abby shook his arm.

"Dad," she said in a loud whisper. "Dad! They ate the cookies and milk."

Daniel sat up. The nearest cup and saucer were empty. He checked the others. Hardly a crumb or a drop of milk was left in them.

"Wake your brother," he told Abby. "They're here."

"Your friends?" Abby said. She knelt beside her brother and rocked him. "Wake up, Mikey. Wakey-wakey."

Mike sat up, rubbing his eyes, and then he snapped awake. "Look! Butterflies!"

"I see them!" Abby said.

Half a dozen, large, brightly-colored butterflies darted around the honeysuckle bushes, splashes of sparkling pink and orange, stripes of furry indigo, flitting from branch to branch, circling, flashing in the air. Mike jumped up and ran to catch one, but Daniel snatched him back.

"Not so fast," Daniel said. "Both of you stay on the blanket until I say otherwise. Promise?"

Abby and Mike agreed, but Daniel knew how hard it was for them to sit still and wait. As he approached the line of honeysuckle, the butterflies flocked around him then scattered as he brushed against them. When Daniel reached the bushes, all but one landed among the flowers. The last one alighted on the grass in front of Daniel and fanned its wings. A fast, soft breeze streamed across the clearing and through the woods, flattening the grass and shaking branches. The butterfly on the grass shimmered. With a burst of pale light, it grew and changed into a woman with oversized, transparent butterfly wings. She stood five feet tall, garbed in a diaphanous blue-and-white dress, which fluttered and snapped as if moved by the wind even when the air was still. Likewise her silken white hair flowed as if caught up in a perpetual funnel of air. A woven silver belt encircled her waist, and an iridescent tiara rested on her brow. Her delicate bare feet dangled several inches above the ground. Translucent, she radiated a gelid, sapphire light. The other butterflies flickered and turned into similar women, each smaller and shorter than the first, none of them as beautiful, yet all of them caressed by the same endless, phantom breeze. They stood among the honeysuckle bushes.

"Danny, you've grown so much," the woman said. Her voice whispered like the wind, a sound that seemed to rise from thin air rather than her lips. "I wondered if you'd ever come back to us."

"I'm sorry it's been so long. I missed you," Daniel said. "I brought my children."

The blue woman floated past Daniel for a better look. "They're absolutely stunning. Like you were when you were a child. Like all children are. Do you remember, Danny, how you used to come visit? How we used to fly?"

"I remember," Daniel said.

"You remembered our most favorite treats, too. Such a sweet boy. You always were so sweet. How's your mother?"

"She's well," Daniel said. "She wanted to come today, but the trail's too much for her."

"Send her my best. I'm so happy to see you." The woman turned to the butterfly-ladies behind her. "Aren't you all happy to see Danny?"

The ladies laughed and nodded, rustling honeysuckle flowers. Their perfume spread in a cloud, the aroma sweeter than before. It reminded Daniel how everything seemed so much more intense in the presence of his old friends. He waved for Abby and Mike to come to him. They hesitated, their eyes wide.

"It's okay," Daniel said. "Come meet my friends."

Abby stepped onto the grass. Mike clutched his sister's hand and followed her. They stopped halfway to Daniel.

"Come closer. It's okay. Really," Daniel said. "Abby and Mike, meet Ariel, the Faerie Queen of the Winds."

With Mike sticking beside her, Abby inched closer. "No way," she said. "For real?"

Ariel glided to Abby and knelt before her. "Absolutely, unequivocally for real."

"Do you live in the woods?" Abby asked.

"I live in the air and the winds, in the sky and the clouds, little one. I live beneath the wings of birds and in the mouths of all living, breathing things," Ariel said. "I live in the enchanted places, in the spaces between time; I live in splendor and glory."

Abby scrunched her face. "Where's glory?"

With a sweeping gesture, Ariel told her, "All around you, if you know where to look."

Mike pushed in front of his sister. "How'd you fit inside that butterfly?"

Ariel laughed and the butterfly-ladies giggled. She crouched and extended a closed hand to Mike. "She and I are old friends, and we know a trick or two." She opened her hand to reveal a butterfly sitting in her palm, fanning its wings. For a moment, it seemed to look at Abby and Mike, and then it leapt into the air and danced away.

"I knew your daddy when he was no bigger than you, Abby," Ariel said, and then she stroked Mike's nose with the tip of her finger. "Even when he was as small as you. I know your grandmother, as well. She and I go back to when she was a child, and I knew her father and his mother, and others older than that. I've known your family a long, long time."

"Do you know my mom?" Abby said.

Ariel's smile faltered. "No, dear one, she never flew."

"That's what I brought Abby and Mike here for," Daniel said.

"Yes, the time is right." Ariel stretched and straightened. "Are you sure it's what you want for them? You remember what it was like?"

"Yes," Daniel said. "I want them to know before their chance is gone."

A flurry of excited whispers rose from the butterfly-ladies.

"You chose a good day. Such a beautiful, luscious wind blows today," Ariel said. "First, let me look into your eyes, Danny."

Ariel took Daniel's chin in her fingers and tilted his head. She stared into his eyes. The touch of her blue gaze made Daniel feel like he was lying on cool grass, watching clouds traverse the sky. It seemed a long time that Ariel held him still, but only a few seconds passed before she let go of him and floated away.

She shuddered. A faint, blue tear ran down her right cheek.

"Daniel," she said. "I'm sorry. You're so lost. So much in your life isn't as you would have it. You've tried so hard, failed so often. There's little love there for you now, and even less understanding, and you're so alone outside your children. And—I'm so sorry—but worse is yet to come. It isn't how I would've had things for you, and yet you've not forgotten what wonders exist in this world. Your light, though buried, is still bright. You honor us. You make us proud. But… you've forgotten more than you realize."

"No," Daniel said, "I remember it clearly."

"Clearly perhaps but not completely," Ariel said. "It's understandable. Memories of time passed in this field do not settle in your mind as memories do in the mortal world."

"I remember flying. I see it in my dreams."

"Only in your dreams?"

"I don't understand," Daniel said.

"You've grown, Danny. You're not like your children. You've gone out into the wide world, forsaken your innocence. You've travelled, and experienced success and failure, richness and loss. You are not the boy you were when you flew. You're no longer free and full of passion. I believe you remember, even as I believe you've flown—in different ways—after you left this place. Flown and fallen many, many times, with no one there to catch you. But I think you've forgotten the price of it."

"The price?" Daniel said.

Ariel frowned. "You *have* forgotten. Not that it matters. You paid it, as did your mother and your grandfather and your great-grandmother and many others through the years. That was our bargain, and no harm ever came to any of you."

"No. I remember," Daniel said. "I…"

"Yes, the knowledge still lives inside you, but you've grown so that you can't recognize what you know anymore. It's like forgetting how to fly. Did you know that? The knowledge of flying still exists in your mind. It never leaves. It's inside all people, but one can never find it again once it's lost," Ariel told him. "All that matters today, though, is that you're sure about letting your little ones fly. Are you sure? If you are, then it shall be done."

Daniel studied the wide-eyed awe in his children's faces, the naked curiosity and excitement only children could experience. For them, the world was still new, its rules fluid, and if it so happened that faeries were real and children could fly, then so it was. They felt little need to question beyond what their senses and their father told them. Daniel envied them that, as he envied them the experience they would have today. Remembering flying was not the same as flying. Experiencing the world as limitless and unbound was not the same as telling himself it was while all its shadows and the inexorable passage of time closed in around him. There were days, especially when he was away from Abby and Mike for too long, days when things were brutal between him and Ginny, days when all his failures weighed on him—on those days his memories of the flying rock and flying were the only things that guided him through the darkness.

"I'm sure," he said. "I want them to fly."

"Then so they shall," Ariel said. "Children! Abby! Mike! Come with me."

Ariel whirled past Daniel and shooed the children toward the flying rock. The butterfly-ladies trailed after her, each one lingering with Daniel for a heartbeat to brush his cheek with a warm, breezy kiss, a touch Daniel found both familiar and unreal. Then they surrounded the flying rock while Ariel led Abby and Mike to its peak and sat them at the edge.

She knelt between them. "Are you ready to fly?"

"Can we really?" Abby said.

"Yes, most assuredly, if you let yourself."

"Okay," Mike said. "I'm ready. Dad showed us how." Still holding his dinosaur toy, he tucked his legs under him to get into position.

Ariel stopped him. "Not like that."

"That's how Dad said," Abby told her.

"That was practice," Ariel said. "This is for real."

"How?" Abby asked.

Ariel took the children by their hands and stood. "Stand with me. Wait for a strong, young wind. When you feel it all around you, think of being light, of being air, of shrugging free from gravity the way you shed a jacket and let it fall to the floor, and then...*you fly*. Get ready. A good wind is coming."

A gust shook the trees and then flowed around Ariel, Abby, and Mike. It pulled Daniel's breath away. It ruffled the butterfly-ladies' dresses and wings and started them giggling again. Dust raked Daniel's face. He blinked tight, and when he opened his eyes again, Abby and Mike were in the air, a foot above the flying rock. They rose with Ariel between them, guiding them, and then the Queen of the Winds released their hands. The children's faces glowed with joy and astonishment as they lifted higher into the air, hesitant as their bodies adjusted to the sensation. Abby stretched her arms out, turned, and began to glide. A fresh wind came, pushing her along, drawing her higher, and she laughed. Mike floated to her side. They hung in the air together, while Ariel hovered below them. Then they darted out over the trees and raced each other before they turned and made a loop. One-by-one, the butterfly-ladies leapt into the air and joined them, watching over them.

Earthbound, Daniel listened to his children's laughter and squeals of excitement. He crept to the peak of the flying rock, dangled his feet over the edge, and watched. Ariel settled beside him.

"They're happy," she said. "They took to it much more quickly than you did."

"I know," Daniel said. "I fell a few times before I got it right."

"We were there to catch you, to make sure you never got anything worse than a bump or a scrape," Abby said. "Then, in a breath, you didn't need us."

"You weren't always there," Daniel said.

The words surprised him. He spoke them not knowing entirely what he meant.

Ariel's expression turned serious.

Daniel thought of his fall down the drop to the stream; he had faltered in the air, landed hard, and only Ariel and her ladies had protected him from serious harm. They had never let him fall too far before he could fly well on his own, and yet they had not shielded him from every danger. He recalled another time, the blue sky whirling around him as he darted and dove and arced over the trees, ranging as far as his family's cabin before circling back only to find that he was flying head-on into a raging darkness—and Ariel and her ladies were only tiny, bright figures standing still in the meadow, gathered upon the flying rock.

Daniel jolted to his feet, poised on the rock's edge. Out over the woods, Abby and Mike looked like birds. He called their names, but they were too far away to hear him.

"Now you remember," Ariel said.

"Can you bring them back?" Daniel asked.

Ariel said nothing. Sadness dampened her smile.

"Please," Daniel said.

"You know I can, but if they are to truly fly, they must do so on their own. As you said, we can't always be there. You know this to be true even if you've kept it hidden from yourself, elsewise you wouldn't have brought them to me."

Daniel studied the sky, clear and blue, except for a gray haze gathering on the horizon. It grew and darkened.

"No," he said.

The winds kicked up. Trees bent and swayed.

The butterfly-ladies fled the sky and returned to the clearing.

Daniel called Abby and Mike again, and this time, they seemed to hear him. They glided toward the clearing. But the darkness on the horizon came on too fast, painting the sky the color of ash and wet clay, spreading gloom through the woods. It was not the darkness that worried Daniel so much as the things that lived inside it. He heard their voices, singing sour melodies and grumbling like far-off thunder; they stirred terrible echoes in his memory. Abby and Mike noticed it now, too. They darted to each other's side. Abby grabbed her brother's hand, and they rushed straight for the clearing, cutting the sky like hawks. Alone, Abby might have made it, but she kept hold of Mike and never glanced back as the darkness overtook them and swallowed them from sight. Wild voices filled the air. The children screamed.

Daniel glanced at Ariel, but the Queen of the Winds would not meet his eyes.

She asked, "Is it only in your dreams that your memories of this live?"

Daniel did not answer. He understood now—or rather he found his way back to an understanding he had possessed long ago and misplaced: On the other side of every light existed darkness. As much as his memories of flying shaped his dreams, they also bred his nightmares.

One of the things in the tempest broke free. Two more followed it. They flew like giant ravens, speeding over the clearing, wicked laughter ringing in their wake, and as they circled, they shrieked with voices that ripped the air like lightning. They wore ragged black dresses, laced with silver threads that sparked and crackled. Bone earrings dangled in their wet, black hair. The Queen of Storms and her retinue. Negatives of Ariel and her sisters, infused with the rage of hurricanes and cyclones, poisoned with the despair of leveled buildings and uprooted trees.

"To fly without risk of falling means nothing," Ariel said. "We watched over you while you learned, but once you were capable, you too faced the storms. No mortal can live in glory alone. That is only for the fae. Abby and Mike must show the Queen of Storms that they accept that, and they will be fine. That is the price."

"If they fail?" Daniel said. "If she refuses them?"

Ariel sighed. "Then another price will be paid."

"What price?" Daniel asked.

"That I can't say unless it is to be exacted, but you may guess."

"Has anyone ever paid it?"

Ariel did not answer. Her expression hardened, and the cast of her eyes frightened Daniel. Her features sharpened, turned almost sinister.

"Ariel?" Daniel said.

"I offer you this, Daniel, as I offered it to your mother and her father and his mother and all those in your line who came before you, all who made the choice you did: If you wish to protect them, I shall give you the power to do so." From the folds of her dress, Ariel produced a round, blue fruit about the size of a plum, with a green stem and leaves. "Eat this and you'll be able to fly long enough to go and bring them back. If you do, though, they will remember nothing of this day, neither flying nor the darkness, and in their minds where the exhilaration of what they are experiencing should live for a lifetime, there will be a dull, aching emptiness that they shall never fill. Then when you return to this clearing, my ladies and I shall be gone. No one in your family shall ever greet us again."

Daniel eyed the fruit in Ariel's hand.

Flashes of lightning illuminated the dark clouds, highlighting silhouettes of those flying within them. Daniel thought he glimpsed Mike and Abby, but he was not sure.

"Glory lies on the other side of fear," Ariel said. "Without awareness of the darkness, would your memories of flying be so rich? Without knowledge of your fears, would you have taken the many risks that have shaped your life? Would you ever have risked truly being father to your children?"

Darkness filled the entire sky. Drops of rain pelted Daniel's face. High above, something screeched. Black and indigo shapes plummeted toward the flying rock. Six of them. They formed into a ring, circling over Daniel and Ariel, singing and squealing with voices like ice scraping across glass. Ariel's ladies cowered in the shadows of the stone.

Daniel refused to look away.

Inside the storm someone screamed.

Over the woods, Abby plunged from the roiling cloud cover and spiraled toward the trees. Mike followed, racing to catch her, his arms outstretched, too slow to close the distance. Abby, facing the sky, reached up for him. Daniel thought of how she had waited for her brother at the bottom of the flying rock, of how they always watched out for each other, even when he was not watching.

He looked for the fruit, but it was gone. Ariel's hands were at her side.

I wouldn't let you try if I didn't believe you could do it.

If Abby thought of anything he had said that day, he prayed it was those words.

She neared the treetops. Daniel could not look away.

Abby vanished into the leaves and branches.

Mike pulled out of his dive and skimmed the treetops, circling, searching.

Daniel held his breath.

"I...," Ariel said, her voice like a dying breeze. "I'm sorry..."

Thunder boomed from the storm clouds. A trio of dark shapes broke from the grayness and flashed toward Mike like needles. Mike cut sideways toward the thin plume of smoke rising from his grandmother's cabin. The storm faeries closed the distance fast.

Ariel gripped Daniel's shoulder. She too was trembling.

"Daniel," she whispered.

The trees below Mike rustled and shook. Leaving a trail of leaves in her wake, Abby rocketed from the woods. She connected with her brother, lifting him, drawing him higher, away from the chasing storm faeries. Together, they disappeared back into the darkness. Lightning flashed brighter, and the clouds churned. The six, circling storm faeries arrowed away from the flying rock to rejoin their flock. The shouts and cries from the blackness increased. Lightning flashes came one after another. Growls of thunder sounded, rumbling from the heavens, shaking the ground even as stinging rain blinded Daniel and tore at his skin, and then—the storm broke. A hole opened in the clouds. Sunlight streamed through it, spreading light outward from the bleak sky, pushing away the gray and black. The thunder faded and the downpour dissolved into a cool mist. In moments the storm disappeared, the storm faeries with it, and Abby and Mike flew back to the clearing.

The Queen of Storms trailed them.

Her ragged black gown swirled around her. The color of an overcast dawn lived in her skin, and black knobs that flashed with white light formed her eyes. Her hair trailed behind her like a pouring rain. She paced the children until they reached the rock. Then with a piercing howl—a cold shriek that drilled through Daniel's bones—she blasted away, leaving a frigid gale behind her.

Daniel wrapped his arms around Abby and Mike and held them tight.

"I'm so sorry," he said. "But I believed. I believed you could do it. And you did."

"It's okay, Daddy," Abby said. "We knew you were watching. We stuck together like you always say we should."

"Yeah," Mike said. Then he jumped into an action pose, thrusting his jetpack dinosaur at Daniel. "Jet Dino was on our side, too!"

"Can we go flying again?" Abby said. "The storm's gone now."

"Yeah, we wanna do it again," Mike said.

Speechless, Daniel nodded. He felt as if he had hardly let go of Abby and Mike before they were back in the air, soaring and laughing once more. The butterfly-ladies leapt from the meadow and joined them. Ariel stood at Daniel's side.

"They're very brave," she whispered.

The sight of his children flying held Daniel too captivated to reply.

Later, Abby and Mike came down to say farewell to Ariel and her butterfly-ladies. They promised the Queen of the Winds they would come back one day. Then the faeries faded into the woods. Daniel and the children lay down to rest and again fell asleep on the picnic blanket. When they woke, it was late in the day, and the sun sat low on the clean horizon. Daniel let Abby lead them home, wondering if he would ever see the flying rock again. Over dinner, the children told their mother about Ariel, the Queen of Storms, the faerie cookies, the butterflies, and how they had flown. Ginny smiled and listened, but when the children were not looking, she rolled her eyes and glared at Daniel. Yet even the sadness her contempt stirred within him was not enough to diminish the joy he felt at the memory of watching his children not only fly but soar. If there were to be dark days ahead, at least they would have that to hold them up until whatever storms came broke and faded away.

Upon Waves, Wind, and Tide

"You begged me to show you," Ebb said.

"I know," Naia said. "But should we really be watching something so personal?"

The two crouched on a low hill above the beach. At the water's edge, frothy surf glowed in the waning moonlight as it coiled itself around the feet of the old man they had trailed from the woods. The wind kicked up, and the man wiped spray from his brow. When Ebb was a boy, they might have had their pick of who to follow on any night, but these days there were far fewer people in the city. He and Naia had staked out the paths to the beach for four days before anyone came, and they had not been surprised to see Caron Tucker appear. Nor would it surprise anyone in the city to find the old widower gone tomorrow. Many had thought it only a matter of time. Bent by age and a lifetime of hard days, Mr. Tucker looked like most who gave themselves back to the water—spent, broken, and lost.

"Oh, don't get squeamish on me," Ebb said.

"I'm not squeamish," Naia said. "It's only—I've never seen anyone give themselves back to the water. Aren't we intruding? He might not want us watching."

"You're bringing this up now?" Ebb said. "He doesn't know we're here. The water will take him, or it won't just the same. But if you want to leave, we'll leave."

"I want to see them." Naia frowned. "I want to see the mermaids."

"Then we stay. But you'll probably see nothing."

"I know." Naia placed her hand over Ebb's, entwining her fingers with his, and shifted closer until their bodies brushed together. "But maybe I will. And *you'll* see. You always do, and if I stay close to you…"

"Maybe." Ebb shrugged. He did not want to raise his hopes that Naia—or anyone else—might ever see the things he saw. "If the mermaids take him. If the others don't come."

"What do the others look like?"

Naia had asked him that before; Ebb gave her the same answer as always: silence. Although it pleased him to describe the beauty and grace of the mermaids, he would give her no idea what the others were like.

A loud *plunk* came from the darkness beyond the breakers. Ebb and Naia scanned the black surface of the sea. Mr. Tucker paced faster along the shifting waterline, his plodding feet scattering languid sprays of water, his eyes cast toward the dense expanse of night that hung over the shore. Out of sight, something heavy splashed, like a big fish jumping. Mr. Tucker froze in place. Naia squeezed Ebb's hand. Together they watched the shifting wave crests brighten and vanish in the moonlight.

"Are they coming?"

"I don't know," Ebb said.

They listened awhile but heard no more unusual sounds. Mr. Tucker resumed pacing. Naia sighed and let go of Ebb's hand. She took an object from one of her pockets and handed it to him.

"I made this for you," she said. "To say thank you. I was saving it for later, but I want to see how it looks on you now."

Ebb uncoiled a loop of braided sea grass, which Naia had fashioned into a strand for him to wear around his neck. A small, perfect nautilus shell dangled from it, fastened by a silver link. The working of the braid was fine and tight, and the silver link was shaped with a twist that made it resemble a pair of conjoined dewdrops. Minus the shell, it matched a bracelet around Naia's wrist, which had a silver dewdrop clasp, and Ebb thought it was the most beautiful piece she had ever made. He slipped the strand over his head and let the shell fall against his chest.

"Where did you get the nautilus?" Ebb said. "You know how hard it is to find one that's not broken?"

"Tell me about it," Naia said. "I've had that one since I was little."

"What? Oh, no, I can't accept it."

Ebb began to slip the necklace off, but Naia stopped him.

"I want you to have it," she said.

She pulled him to her and kissed him.

It was not their first kiss, but it was their most intense yet, and it caught Ebb unprepared. Until that moment, he would not have guessed he could feel any closer to Naia than he already did. She was his best friend since childhood; of all the friends he had ever known only Naia had never been frightened of him. He let the necklace drop to his skin and stroked Naia's hair. In that instant, it seemed to Ebb that all of existence was defined in the heat radiating from Naia's body, in the sweet smell of her skin and hair, in the softness of her lips, and the faint salt flavor of the air forever spiced by the sea. Then the crash of something loud hitting the water broke the spell. Ebb and Naia pulled apart and scanned the sea. Two more loud splashes came. Mr. Tucker knelt in the surf and cried out the summoning words.

"Here I am!" he called. "In the water life began, in the water life survives—I give myself back to the water! I give myself back! Let my life be renewed!"

Naia gasped at the anguish in Mr. Tucker's thick, uneven voice, and Ebb admired her for her compassion. Even though it was discouraged to watch people give themselves back to the water, Ebb had often done so in secret, and he found the words too familiar to move him.

In answer to Mr. Tucker's plea, a series of wild splashes came from the far side of the breakers.

"They're here," Ebb said.

"Where?" Naia said.

"Out there." Ebb pointed. "Swimming in."

"It's getting so dark. Is a storm rolling in?"

Naia squinted at the churning surf dotted with flickers of shadow that refused to resolve into anything recognizable. There was no doubt, though, that Mr. Tucker saw something in the sea. That was clear enough from how he backed away from the water, his hands thrust out in front of him, his face drawn and colorless with terror.

"It's like darkness is leaking into my eyes," Naia said. "I can't even see the moon now."

"It's not them, anyway." Ebb was disappointed. "It's… the others."

"Where? I don't see them."

Naia crawled right up against Ebb and trained her eyes in the same direction as his.

"I can't even see Mr. Tucker, now. It's like… like I've gone blind." Naia rubbed her eyes and looked all around her. "No, wait. I can see you, Ebb, and the hill, and the trail behind us. It's only… only the beach that's… blacked out?"

"That's how it goes," Ebb said. "They won't let you see."

"They let you," Naia whispered. "Why *not* me?"

The sounds of violent thrashing came from the water—followed by screams. Whatever had come for Mr. Tucker was driving him out of his mind with fear. Ebb was relieved that only Mr. Tucker had come tonight. The days when people gave themselves back to the water by the dozens, when the chorus of their voices rose in screams of terror and cries of joy, still echoed in his childhood memories. Mr. Tucker's long last cry faded away; soon after, the splashing died out.

Ebb relaxed.

"The darkness is gone now. The moonlight's coming back," Naia said. "Has Mr. Tucker gone back to the water?"

"Yes," Ebb said.

"Oh, I see him now," Naia said.

Caron Tucker's remains stood at the edge of the surf, his body comprised now only of sand that would be worn down and carried away by the waves, the wind, and the tide.

"I'm sorry you didn't see them," Ebb said. "Maybe… it's better you didn't. When I saw it was Mr. Tucker, I thought the others might come."

"Why?" Naia asked.

"Because Mr. Tucker was a monster," Ebb said. "Sometimes the others come for the monsters."

"Oh," Naia said.

The sound of Naia's disappointment scraped at Ebb's isolation, sweeping away the intimacy he had felt earlier. He stood and brushed himself free of sand. Being alone was nothing new; when it came to this, he had always been alone—and might always be. In all other ways he was lucky to have Naia. He smiled, extended his hand, and helped her to her feet.

"Do you want to go see his sand?" he asked.

Naia shook her head. "Everyone has seen what gets left behind. Let the tide take it."

"Then we should go before the sun comes up," Ebb said.

"Do we report Mr. Tucker?" Naia asked.

"Are you serious? We're not even supposed to be out here. You want people to know you're sneaking around in the middle of the night—*with me*? They'll think you've gone off the deep end too. Anyway, there's nothing to be done for Mr. Tucker. No one will miss him tonight. Let him be found in the morning."

Ebb led the way to the woods that had once been part of a park at the heart of the city. Naia held his hand, uncomfortable in the dark.

It still amazed Ebb that she believed in him enough to have come this far, to the beach in the dead of night in search of sharing a truth it seemed only Ebb would ever see. Nothing he tried seemed capable of helping Naia—or anyone else—to see the things he saw. He wished he knew how to make it happen if only to reassure himself that what he saw was real. His life would be so much easier if someone else confirmed it, especially if it were Naia, but he would not wish on her all that he had suffered. Besides, he was almost certain now his gift of sight could never be shared.

A branch cracked in the woods. Ebb stopped and gestured Naia to stay quiet.

The brush ahead of them rustled.

Footsteps crunched fallen leaves and sand.

"Could it be someone else returning to the water?" Naia whispered.

"Maybe. I don't know," Ebb said.

From the sound of it, several people were approaching. Ebb could not say how many because the footsteps came from multiple directions. He did not want to be discovered in the dark with no way to protect Naia. He pulled her around, thinking to run back to the beach, to head for the water, but then a hard, heavy weight struck the side of his neck. The pain shocked him, and the stone knocked him off balance. He lost hold of Naia's hand and fell. Naia screamed against a riot of crashing as people stormed through the brush, and then the first of many fists pummeled into Ebb's back. More followed, striking his sides, his head, driving him against the ground. A flurry of fists and feet sliced the shadows. Each one jabbed or kicked Ebb, and ignited flares of pain throughout his body. The beating was fast and brutal. Ebb tasted blood in the back of his mouth. His ears rang after several punches to his head. Naia's voice sounded muted and faraway, screaming for his attackers to *stop, to go away and leave him alone*—but they ignored her.

Ebb knew why.

A shrill, commanding voice urged them on.

The voice of Mayor Pearl.

Naia's mother.

One of the attackers kicked Ebb in the chest, his foot cracking apart the nautilus shell.

Naia screamed again. Ebb glimpsed her trying to pull his attackers away, only to be yanked clear by her mother. Naia's cries rose and fell like the noise of waves crashing, receding, crashing....

Ebb grasped their rhythm and used it to blot out the pain.

Like diving underwater.

Cut off from sound and light.

Away from anyone else.

Enclosed.

Safe.

If only the sea was closer...

He could escape there.

No one could ever catch him in the water...

...but the water is so far away...

A fist connected with the back of his head, driving his face to the ground. Dirt and sand filled his mouth. He spit it out and waited for his punishment to be over. It lasted until he thought he could no longer bear it—and when it ended, he lay on the ground, gasping for air. He assessed his condition and sensed that, despite the jumble of throbbing pains throughout his body, nothing seemed broken, although he felt as if all the wind had been knocked out of him. It was a brutal playground beating, and Ebb was familiar enough with those.

"Take him to the beach," Mayor Pearl said.

"No!" Naia said. "Why are you doing this? He didn't hurt anyone!"

Ebb rolled onto his side to see Naia, her mother, and the boys who had beaten him, three of Naia's four brothers: Trak, Donal, and Marts. Ebb was too weak, his thoughts too fractured to even attempt to filter his vision. As he looked at them, he saw how they appeared in the invisible world, and what he saw terrified him. They were all monsters—except Naia, whose beauty was so radiant she seemed translucent and brimming with moonlight. Ebb used her light to distract him from his fear. The sight of her was more than enough for that; and he had learned as a boy how to keep his terror from controlling him—a necessary skill for a child surrounded by monsters.

Ebb pushed himself up onto his hands and knees. Marts put his foot on Ebb's back and drove him back down.

"He's tainted, Naia," Mayor Pearl said. "He's rotten. He's foul. His mind is broken. His madness is a poison that will spread if I don't purge it now. It was one thing to dismiss the things Ebb says he sees when he was a child, but now—he's almost a grown man! The councilors and the people have been asking me to do something about him for years. Ebb frightens people, Naia. He upsets things. He makes people doubt they should return to the sea when their time comes and that puts all our survival at risk. For what? Delusions? Fairy tales of mermaids and monsters and an invisible world that only he can see? What he says he sees isn't real, but the danger it creates *is*. Did you think I didn't know you were out here running around with him? It makes me ashamed you can't see it for yourself, that you're out here in the night doing—oh, god!—I don't even know *what* you're doing."

"That's not how it is. What if—" Naia said.

"Stop it, Naia!" Mayor Pearl shouted.

"—what if it's true?" Naia said. "What if we simply can't see the world how Ebb does? His gift is real. He's a good person. Don't hurt him like this. We should make people see—"

"Naia, enough." Mayor Pearl's voice softened. "I know you don't want this for Ebb. You were friends before his madness. I knew him then too, and he was a fine boy. Never knowing his mother, losing his father so young—he's had a hard life. We all wanted to protect him. We loved him. But... we can't anymore. Not when he clings to heresy. Not when he's misleading *you* and warping your thoughts. He'll ruin everything. It pains me that it's come to this. When you're older and you've gained some experience, you'll see—there's nothing else I can do!"

"But... what if he's right?" Naia said.

"Even if he is, I can't let him be." Mayor Pearl looked to her sons. "I said, '*Take him to the beach*.'"

Hands gripped Ebb. The movement stirred his pains, and he groaned. His feet dragged in the sand as Mayor Pearl's sons carried him along the path. Ebb avoided looking at their faces for too long; each was monstrous and vile, riddled with fear, hate, doubt, and cowardice, warped so far there was almost nothing human left. They looked like...

...but he didn't like to think about that.

The worst was Mayor Pearl; her face was like that of a broken porcelain doll with dead, expressionless eyes set amidst a multitude of fine, angry cracks. She was bitter, unchangeable, and swollen with fear. The world was not how she or the others who lived in the city thought it was. It was not the world they had known before the Flood Times. Yet they refused to see how much its very nature had been altered. Only Ebb saw the truth, with his gift that had come from the sea. It had come to him in darkness forty feet down on a stormy day when his father's fishing skiff capsized and plunged them overboard. He should have drowned that day like his father did, like Naia's, like so many other fathers—but he was too strong a swimmer, even as a child. He washed up on shore, spared, left orphaned, alone, and frightened. He knew the fear Mayor Pearl and the others felt because it was the same fear he had felt when he first realized his gift: fear of living in a world very different from what they understood or wished it to be.

That was not enough, though, for Ebb to forgive or pity them.

They were monsters even if their fear had made them so.

When they reached the beach, the boys dropped Ebb on the sand and then went to see Mr. Tucker's remains. Mayor Pearl joined them by the sand figure.

She lowered her head and spoke the traditional words: "May the waters bless our brother who has gone back to the sea. May his life be renewed and return to us."

Fat chance of that, Ebb thought. He had ideas about what happened to those who gave themselves back to the water, and it was not returning to the city. There were fewer babies born in the city every year, fewer people to tend it. Fewer people, period.

Nothing lasts forever.

The breaking dawn lightened the sea and the sky by the second.

Mayor Pearl walked to the water's edge, searching for something.

A few minutes passed before a motor sound grated against the gentle noise of the surf. A small powerboat appeared from the west, cutting past the needles and bones of the few ruined buildings left standing tall enough to rise above the surface. Piloting it was the Mayor's oldest son, Redley. When the boat drew closer to shore and Ebb saw the anchor in the back, he knew what they intended for him. Naia realized it too, and she screamed.

Mayor Pearl grabbed her daughter's arm and yanked her up short. "Stop that! Don't you understand? The more he goes on about monsters, mermaids, and the others, the more frightened people become? Life's hard enough without worrying that something in the sea will—*will come for them*—that if they give themselves back to the water something horrible might take them and they'll never be renewed. There's only the sea out there, and the sea is the source of all life. The sea returns to us the lives we give it. I can't let him take that away from us. We need the sea to survive, Naia, *all of us*. Even if it means Ebb won't."

"You're cruel!" Naia bolted from her mother. She ran to Ebb, knelt in the sand beside him, and raised the jagged remnants of the nautilus shell on her fingers. "Let's give ourselves back to the water. Right now. Together. Let them take us, and we'll never be apart."

Ebb shook his head. He gasped to speak. "I'm the strongest swimmer… in the entire city. I'll last a long time. I'll… find a way to free myself."

"No," Naia said. "No. Say the words with me. Stay with me."

"They need you, Naia," Ebb said. "They need someone…who'll remember the truth."

"No, Ebb, no," Naia said.

"I'll always be with you." Ebb slipped the necklace off and hung it around Naia's neck. "You'll never forget me."

Trak and Donal dragged Naia off and forced her to sit near her mother.

The powerboat cut through the shallows until it grated against the beach. Redley jumped out and dragged the boat onshore. The four brothers lifted Ebb and threw him onto the small craft. Then Mart clamped a shackle around one of Ebb's ankles; it was linked to a long chain fastened to the anchor. When they were done, Redley and Marts shoved the boat into the water until it floated. Then they jumped in and gunned the motor. The craft sped straight out from the shore, skipping over low waves, and leaving a wake painted pink by the rising sun.

The boat traveled farther and farther from shore, but Ebb felt no fear of the water.

He knew the sea here as if it was his home. He knew its currents and its secrets and what hid in the sand and seaweed below its surface. He knew the maze of fallen buildings and flooded streets, the forgotten wrecks of ships, cars, and buses overgrown with anemones and coral and teeming with schools of green and silver fish. No one could swim as far or hold his breath as long or pull as big a catch in his net as Ebb.

I'm the best swimmer who's ever lived in the city.

But it was not enough to buy him any more tolerance.

If he had kept the things he saw to himself, if he had ended his friendship with Naia before they fell in love…

…maybe then Mayor Pearl would have let him be.

There was more in her condemnation of him than fear that he would endanger the city's survival. That was plain in the fact that she was making Naia watch his execution.

The boat stopped more than half a mile out, where the deep water began.

Redley cut the motor and let them drift.

Ebb stared at Naia's brothers, only a few years older than he was. When he looked at them without his sight, they looked young, handsome, and innocent. *Lies and masks.* If he had never seen behind them, they might have been friends. They might have swum, and sailed, and fished together. Instead, both had bullied and beaten up on Ebb all through school. For as long as he had known them, they had been monsters.

Redley and Marts said nothing as they lifted the anchor and tossed it over the side of the boat. It crashed the water with a wide splash and plunged out of sight.

Ebb scrambled to his feet. The chain trailed away beneath the surface, a silver shimmer drilling down into the dark. As the last of it rattled over the side, Ebb inhaled as deeply as he could, and then dove overboard before he could be yanked into the water. The coolness of the sea embraced him. It was murky and quiet beneath the surface. He readied himself to be pulled into the depths, but the chain went slack, and he found himself swimming toward the dim light of dawn above him. His face reached air. He gasped and struggled to rise, but the chain drew tight. The anchor was locked far below him. Treading water, he kept himself a few inches above the surface. Enough to breathe, enough to see the shore—where the accumulation of deadwood and debris that marked the high-tide line told him his reprieve would not last for long. Naia knelt in the surf, one hand stretched out to him, the other pressed to her mouth. Her mother stood beside her, and even at such a distance, Ebb perceived her ugliness.

Redley started the outboard and steered the boat to shore. When it arrived, the two boys dragged it onto the beach. Then they sat with the others in the sand by Mr. Tucker's effigy and waited.

An hour passed.

The rising sun warmed Ebb's face, and he felt the deepening twinges of muscle fatigue as he treaded water against the weight of the chain.

No one on shore had moved. Ebb knew Naia would not leave while he was in sight, but he wished her mother would take her away. He hated Mayor Pearl more for what she was doing to Naia than to him. He wanted to sink and be done with it to end Naia's suffering, but he found that as long as Mayor Pearl was there, he could not give up. Her presence invoked his defiance, and he took strength from that. He had lived most of his life in defiance; he would not surrender now. They had made him an outcast, beaten him, spurned him, and it had only ever hardened his resolve to give them the truth.

Only Naia had never feared him.

Never hated him.

Had… *believed in him.*

"Naia," Ebb said.

Water splashed over his lips.

The tide rose.

He dove under and struggled to free himself from the chain, but it was impossible. His air ran out, and he returned to the surface.

More time passed, and the waters crept over his face, washed into his mouth.

It was early afternoon when he looked upon Naia for the last time.

When Ebb went under, it was like the day he fell overboard and blacked out near the bottom. That day he had woken safe and sound on the shore…

Maybe…

For a time, there was the quiet gloom of the sea.

Then all became darkness.

Naia let the waters rush over her.

She had not moved or cried. The tide had brought the waves to her chest, but despair paralyzed her. The nautilus shell bobbed in front of her, tethered by dried sea grass that was coming unbraided as the water soaked it. After a while—after Ebb did not resurface—the grass strand broke. The shell drifted away on the current. Naia watched it go.

Mayor Pearl kept her children on the beach until twilight. The receding tide took chunks of Mr. Tucker's remains with it until enough of his legs were gone that the rest of him fell over into the water and dispersed in the currents. Watching him fall, Naia realized the beach was a burial ground, the sand the ashes of all those who had given themselves back to the water. Ebb would be denied even this.

At dusk, Mayor Pearl sent Redley and Marts to recover Ebb's body. They dredged around by lantern light with a pole and a gaffe, and Marts even dived in with a waterproof flashlight, but they returned with an empty boat.

"You're sure you looked in the right place?" Mayor Pearl said.

"One hundred percent," Redley said. "The weight of the chain sunk him to the bottom, that's all."

"Better that way," Mayor Pearl said. "It will be as if he never lived."

"You should have let him give himself back to the sea," Naia said.

"No. It's a travesty when someone so young goes back to the sea," Mayor Pearl said.

"*This* was a travesty, mother," Naia said. "This... was..."

Her words trailed off. Outrage drove her from her place in the sand, which she had not left all day, and she slapped her mother.

Mayor Pearl recoiled.

Redley laughed.

Naia ran.

She crashed the surf, pushing in up to her waist, and then she screamed: "I'm here! Come for me! Take me! In the water life began, in the water life survives—I give myself back to the water! I give myself back! Let my life be renewed!"

Donal and Trak came splashing after Naia and dragged her back to the shore.

"What have you done?" Mayor Pearl shouted. "You have to get away from here, away from the water!"

"No," Naia said. "I'm going with Ebb."

She dug her feet into the wet sand and fought. Her brothers tried to grab her again. She dodged them, threw herself into the waves, and tried to swim but the water was too shallow. Her brothers surrounded her and pulled her out of the sea. Naia felt helpless—as if everything inside her was breaking to pieces and only Ebb could help her hold it together, but Ebb...

...Ebb was gone.

"Why?" Mayor Pearl said. "Why would you do that over a boy who lost his mind?"

"What Ebb saw was real." Her skin wet and slick, Naia slipped free from her brothers' hands then ran through the surf again, dodging them. "I want to see for myself. I want to believe! I don't want to be a monster."

"Monsters...," Mayor Pearl said. "The only monsters are fools. Now, let's go before the water takes you!"

"I want to be with Ebb," Naia said.

"Naia, stop!"

Naia's brothers dashed around, trying to grab her. She evaded them, working her way farther from the beach. Out in the sea, something splashed and churned, but Naia was too distracted by avoiding her brothers to see it. The disturbance in the water sounded as loud as a storm squall, but the sky remained clear and the wind calm. Naia slipped to her hands and knees. Water splashed her face. It soaked her from head to toe, her shirt and shorts pasted to her body. She struggled to rise, but she was so tired, and her body felt so heavy. Her brothers were only inches away from her, and then with shocking suddenness they became confused. Trak and Donal stumbled past her, almost knocked down by waves. Redley and Marts stopped dead and gaped around them. Even Naia's mother seemed affected. The surf lapped at her legs as she inched along it, hands reaching, calling Naia's name as if—

—*she can't see me*, Naia thought.

The darkness had come to them, but for Naia the beach brightened, and the water seemed electrified with fragments of starlight, the sea alive and vibrant with motion. Graceful forms sliced the dark surface. Dozens, swimming toward shore. Their faces rising and falling among the wave crests—the most beautiful faces Naia had ever seen.

"Ebb... I believe...," she said.

Her mother's voice came from the beach: "Naia? Where are you? Naia! Where did you go? Come back to me before it's too late!"

Naia ignored her. She could not look away from the water.

The mermaids were gathering. They were even more beautiful than Ebb had described them. More than she could count were coming together beyond the breakers, each stunning and luminous in the night, their perfect upper bodies riding powerful scaled fins that pushed them through the water. They watched Naia as if waiting for her to do something. Behind them, other shapes cut and jumped in the water. Dark shapes. Naia glimpsed gleaming black skin and scales, razor-edged fins, barbed claws, and shimmering eyes that reflected the stars—*the others.*

One of the mermaids—a woman with golden hair, green eyes, and pale, perfect skin—swam forward. "You have offered yourself to the water, but you don't really wish to return."

"I—" Naia said. "I miss Ebb."

"Who are you talking to?" Mayor Pearl said.

"She speaks to me, Pearl. I am Rogue," the mermaid said. "I am Ebb's mother, and you are the woman who tried to kill my son."

"No, no, that can't be. Ebb's mother died when he was born," Mayor Pearl said. "It's a trick. Who are you? Leave us alone!"

"You're so stubborn, Pearl," Rogue said. "You refuse to see so much. Worse, you deny it to others."

"Is... Ebb *alive?*" Naia asked.

"Yes," Rogue told her.

"Don't believe her, Naia. She's a liar like Ebb was," Mayor Pearl said. "Ebb's dead. He has to be."

"You're an ungrateful fool," Rogue said. "This world belongs to the waters now, and we rule the waters. You owe your existence to me. Every time your city seemed sheltered from the worst of the storms, every bountiful catch your fishers brought home, every illness that seemed to be cured by the sea breeze—that all came from my people. All we took in return were the lives of those who gave them to us. Ebb's father was one of you. He could not free himself from my song—but he never feared me. I sent our son to live with him because I hoped he would help you understand. You refused to hear what he said. You showed him only fear and violence."

A figure swam past the mermaids and stood in the shallows: Ebb.

He walked onto the shore and handed Naia the broken nautilus necklace.

"I snatched it out of the current," he said.

Naia embraced him and pressed her face against his neck and shoulder. "Ebb, I'm sorry I said the words. I was so angry. My life was collapsing, and I—"

"Shh, it's okay," Ebb said.

"Is this what you've always been?" Naia asked. "One of them?"

"Part of me, yes. But I never knew it until now," Ebb said.

"Oh, Ebb. I thought you were dead."

"Hey, at least you finally got to see them, didn't you?"

Naia looked surprised. Then she smiled. Seeing the mermaids filled her with joy, but when she looked at her brothers and her mother, the core of her being twisted with horror at the sight of monsters.

"Is this what you've always seen?" she asked Ebb.

"Yes."

"I'm so sorry."

"I'd rather see the world for what it is than be like them," Ebb said.

"Can you come back?"

"No, there's never any going back," Ebb said. "You can come with me, though. We can be together, but there's a price."

"What price?" Naia asked.

Ebb did not answer. He only waited while the dark figures lingering behind the mermaids moved past them and climbed onto the shore. The others were everything ugly in the sea. Shark eyes, and squid beaks, the shells and tails of horseshoe crabs, and joints like clustered barnacles. Fins like those of a manta ray, fingertips like blowfish spines, and hard, jagged scales that looked like rot. They thrashed the water as they came and revealed themselves to Mayor Pearl and her sons. Their screams froze Naia's heart. She tried to think of her family as monsters, as the things she had seen, but she could not—at least not entirely. Only Ebb's grip on her arm kept her from running to help them.

"It has to be this way," Ebb said. "They'll go back to the water. They'll become like the others, but at least their lives will have been renewed. And the city will be home to that many fewer monsters."

Naia wanted to bury her face against Ebb's chest, but she could not stop watching.

Water flowed out of her mother and her brothers. It spiraled in streams through the air to join the sea, where a black whirlpool swallowed it. Where the others touched her brothers and her mother, dryness spread through their bodies, changing them to sand, spreading outward from each contact until soon only sand remained. Satisfied, the others slipped back into the sea. The mermaids lingered awhile longer and then went after them.

Rogue was the last to disappear beneath the surface, but Naia sensed her still nearby.

Naia studied the five statues of sand. They looked like her mother and brothers as she remembered them from before tonight—from before she shared Ebb's sight.

Ebb clasped Naia's hand and wound the fraying strands of the nautilus necklace around their fingers. "You wanted to see," he said.

"Yes," Naia said.

"Let me show you," Ebb said.

Naia followed him down the beach, through the waves, and into the water.

Meet the Tuskersons

Someone once said show business is about second chances, but that's a lot of nonsense. Just ask Ernie McCabe. Remember him? That wiry, bobble-headed comedian from years back, had that corny catchphrase, "I got a million of 'em"? He laughed like a St. Bernard with the flu. Just a second-rate stand-up until he hit it big with that routine about the cheerleaders in the chewing gum factory. That's what landed him his top gig ever, starring on that old television show. You know the one—the show with that walrus family that lived in a Los Angeles bungalow, the Tuskersons. Used to air Thursday nights, and they did that Christmas special their first season.

Remember? Those happy, whiskered faces were everywhere back then. You could have been living in a cave at the bottom of the ocean with a metal box bolted on your head, and you still would have known about the Tuskersons.

Kids from coast to coast wore Tuskersons pajamas, played with Tuskersons action figures, and used Tuskersons breakfast bowls to eat Tuskersons breakfast cereal (corn pops mixed with walrus-shaped marshmallows). You could buy Tuskersons wrapping paper, greeting cards, and party favors; Tuskersons iron-ons and Underoos; Tuskersons three-wheelers (with plastic brake levers that let you spin out and handlebars that looked like tusks); Tuskersons Colorforms and Tuskersons coloring books; Tuskersons pens, folders, and notebooks; Tuskersons lunch boxes (with a Thermos!); and of course, Tuskersons board games. The Tuskersons even hit the recording studio for a few albums of pop songs and Christmas standards. If they could slap a picture of a walrus on it, they made it into Tuskersons merchandise.

No doubt about it, those Tuskersons were a talented bunch of sea mammals, and everyone loved them.

You remember, now, right?

Then you must remember Ernie McCabe. He played the Tuskersons' madcap next-door neighbor, that guy always popping in uninvited looking for Mr. Tuskerson's advice. McCabe worshipped the wisdom of the walri on everything from romance to stock tips, but in the end he always wound up right back where he started. Like that episode when Mr. Tuskerson told him he should serenade his dream girl, the cute local librarian he'd only admired from afar. So, the whole show, while the Tuskersons are carrying on like the Cleavers (only they're 600, 800 pounds apiece, all with whiskers and a healthy hankering for sushi before it was fashionable) McCabe is running around, sheet music flying in his wake as he pops in and out of the back door and practices his "do, re, mi"s and his "mi, mi, mi"s, while plucking at the nape of his throat.

Then at the end of the show, he gets down on one knee, lets out the shrillest, most hair-curling yodeling since Slim Whitman, only to discover that his designated sweetheart is stone deaf.

That was Ernie McCabe, all right, in more ways than one.

Ask Ernie about show business and second chances, he'll tell you what it's all about and none of it has much to do with redemption, not unless your self-resurrection can raise the dead presidents, too. Because it all comes down to cold hard cash and big fat bank accounts. Satisfy their greed and they'll beat a path to your doorstep. But comebacks don't come easy, and they don't come to folks who have already spent the whole of their talent and creativity. They don't come to worn-out comedians with new jokes that sound like old jokes the first time they're told.

Like the old saying goes, "Comedy is hard, death is easy," and Ernie McCabe wasn't much of a survivor.

That time when he could placate the network gods of avarice passed much too fast. A few more years on top and he might have been set for life. But it all turned sour one day and then the only knock that came on Ernie's door was the county sheriff there to escort his sorry, bankrupt soul out of a lovely seaside house that had become the property of a faceless bank. Ernie took his clothes and whatever else he could stuff into his Mercedes and left the rest behind. He didn't need the furniture and the decorations; he didn't want them.

They reminded him too much of Rita.

His faithless ex-wife wasn't a complex girl, but she had three things going for her: her looks, her sense of humor, and her razor-sharp instinct for self-preservation. Number one made sure she was never alone. Number three kept her comfortable in the style in which she had established herself as a punk kid (she preferred "ingénue," of course) straight out of some backwater, Midwest cow-town hell-bent on making her way in the City of Angels. Number two persuaded most people to forgive her for one and three.

Ernie never did, though.

He understood her, sure. He'd known from the day they met what kind of girl she was, but still he never forgave her for abandoning him. Three months after they cancelled Ernie's big show, the afternoon he came home from his fourth failed pitch for a new series, Rita kissed him hard on the lips, said goodbye, and then drove off in her Jaguar, her bags packed in back.

If she had only stayed a little longer, Ernie often told himself, his luck might have turned. If Rita had been there to love and support him through that first desperate year, he might just have found the inspiration he needed to land on his feet, but instead he sank, deep and fast, into obscurity, and in Tinseltown that meant he ceased to exist.

So, how do I know so much about some washed-up has-been like Ernie McCabe? Well, I'm the last person who saw Ernie alive the night before he disappeared forever from the real world and not just Hollywood.

"I loved them big, goofy walruses," said Ernie McCabe. "How could I not? They were like giant, wet teddy bears. Working with them day and night, training them to pull off the gags, watching them learn—it was great! Those guys had some sharp timing, let me tell you. Natural comedians. Hit a beat like Gene Krupa. They weren't just dumb animals. They understood! Not the whole television thing, no way, but they knew they were part of something, and once they saw where you were going they met you halfway. They loved it when the crew laughed, because then they knew they had done good, and, of course, then they got to chow down on a few fish. Best straight men I ever worked with. Cute as ribbons when they poured on the charm.

"So, yeah, I didn't mind sharing the limelight with the Tuskersons. Technically, I was the star of the show—that's what it said in the credits, that's what it said in my contract. My name was the only one that came up before the title. But the Tuskersons made people feel good. They made *me* feel good. Best damn years of my life working on that show. Only time I ever truly *loved* what I was doing.

"Who knew walruses could be so affectionate, so friendly, so *funny*?

"There was this one bit of business, let me tell you, this one routine, see, where Mr. Tuskerson and I snuck off to go fishing on the sly from Mrs. Tuskerson and the kids. So we're out on this dock on a lake, both of us decked out in fishing vests and caps pegged with lures, and I'm hauling around the poles and tackle. So, the gag is that when I put one foot in the rowboat, Mr. Tuskerson knocks the mooring rope loose and next thing you know I'm making like a cheerleader—doing a split and flapping my arms. Mr. Tuskerson is supposed to knock off his fishing hat, dive into the water, and push the boat back. Except—except it turns out a school of fish is going by and he swims off after them, leaving me hanging until—splash!—into the drink."

Ernie chuckled at the memory, and when his laughter faded to a dry crackle, he sipped some water from the glass beside his chair to soothe his tired voice. He straightened his shirt collar, primped his thinning hair, and winked broadly at the camera opposite him. "I look okay? Huh? You fellows be honest. I know it's been a few years, and I don't want to look like a slob for this. You sure you got film in that thing? It's awful small. All digital these days, I suppose. Well, that's all right, as long as the next word isn't 'exam,' heh-heh, right? Right.

"So, okay, we figured we'd shoot the scene all the way through a few times and edit the best takes together later. SOB, right? Standard order of business. Know what happened? Soon as we run through the first part, Mr. Tuskerson sees me flapping my arms as the boat drifts loose, and he knocks his cap off and dives in right on cue, but he doesn't come up!

"Stays down a good thirty seconds, while my thighs are getting homesick for each other, and then—surprise! He's back! And remember all of this is unrehearsed. This is a *walrus* ad libbing! Well, Tuskerson jumps out of the water right beneath me, and I take one look at those pointy tusks of his heading for my own private Idaho and you can guess what kind of look flashed across my face. But Mr. Tuskerson—he comes up soft as a pillow, lifts and balances me until he can nudge me back onto the dock. Then he swims out and pushes the boat back.

"Heh-heh, yeah, there you go," said Ernie. "Still good for a laugh today. Left me howling on the dock, the crew cracking up all over the place, and Mr. Tuskerson backstroking through the water like a champ who'd won the title in three rounds. The director loved it. Said we never could have staged something like that, so they wrapped it, rescripted the dubbing, and voila, a classic television moment was born.

"Oh, yeah," said McCabe. "Yeah, I got a million of 'em."

This wasn't too long ago.

I wandered into that little corner place down the block on a rainy Monday night. A high-class dive that place was, but I knew it would be warm and quiet but not empty and depressing, and that was what I needed. I'd been struggling all day with an article for one of the trade rags, trying to mold an interview with Miss Vapidity 2004 who had somehow convinced a bunch of producers that she was movie star material (and having seen those collagen-enhanced lips of hers, I could just guess how she'd pulled off that neat trick), and I had gotten tired of banging my head against the keyboard trying to make this woman sound fully brain functional.

So I sipped a whiskey, soaked in the gentle buzz of the place, and let the frustration melt away. The bartender, Tuba (and don't ask about the name because it is not a pretty tale), liked to keep the televisions mounted at either end of the bar on mute. That suited me fine. I watched images flicker by and made up dialogue that was, no question, far more entertaining than the real words. And the heat of the whiskey, the mellow mood of the bar, and its dusky atmosphere were working. I had just about figured out how to make next year's rehab-bound celebrity crash-and-burn case (no one was born as marvelously dense as this young lady; she had to be abusing some serious chemicals to achieve that) sound like a philosopher naïf when the door slammed open and in walked this big-headed, gangly guy.

"Oh, no," Tuba growled the moment he saw him. "You heard me last time, funny guy. You know the rules. Now get your butt out of my bar before I get physical with you."

"Sheesh," said the skinny man. "Keep your shirt on, Tuba, and your pants, too, while you're at it, and do us all a favor. Here. Look what I got. Okay?"

The thin guy raised a crumpled fifty over his head and snapped it tight between his hands. Tuba squinted hard like he thought it might be funny money, held the glare for a long few seconds, then went back to washing glasses.

"Keep it where I can see it," he said.

"Sure, sure. Got a million of 'em," the man said under his breath. "Don't I wish."

I knew right then who it was, but God did he look awful, like an accident survivor treated by a blind reconstructive surgeon. I could say the years had not been kind to Ernie McCabe, but the truth is that they had been *brutal*. Picture Father Time as a mob of baseball-bat wielding punks in steel-toed boots working out their "issues" on Ernie McCabe in a dark alley and that'll get you halfway there. He kind of smelled, too. He didn't stink. He wasn't dirty, but the air around him had a strange tang to it, kind of like very old, dry paper.

But his voice—man, that was still clear and full as ever, and that's what gave him away. That voice rocketed me back twenty-five years and all of a sudden I was a little kid in *Star Wars* pajamas sitting cross-legged in front of the television, laughing hard and listening to my parents laugh behind me, waiting for that famous line that, as clichéd as it was, somehow delivered the weight of all humor when Ernie McCabe said it just so.

"Got a million of 'em," I said. "I can't believe it—you're Ernie McCabe!"

Ernie raised an eyebrow and scrutinized me. "Huh, a fan," he said. "Well, I ain't who you think I am, so you just go on abusing your liver and leave me the heck alone, chucklehead."

He took a seat at the opposite end of the bar, putting his back to me so he could see the television. He dropped his fifty on the bar and waited for Tuba.

"Hey, put that money away, Mr. McCabe," I said, walking down next to him. "I'd like to buy you a drink."

He turned halfway around, made a "shoo-shoo" gesture with his hand, and gave me a loud, wet raspberry.

"No, really, I remember your show, and you were great," I told him. "How often does a guy get a chance to buy a round for his childhood idol?"

McCabe twisted back around. "Idol?"

Now I'll admit that I was a big fan of Ernie's when I was a kid, but he never really had been my idol. That honor went to baseball players and writers, but I wanted to get his attention—it surprised me how badly I wanted it, how eager I was to talk awhile with old Ernie McCabe. Why? Partly for the novelty of it, I suppose, and partly because it let me put off tackling "little Miss Reality Challenged and her inarticulate road show" for just a while longer, but mainly because I sensed that there might be a story in Ernie McCabe, one too good to pass up.

"Who are you?" Ernie asked me, his brow knit with suspicion.

I introduced myself, leaving out that I was a writer, and told him to put his money back in his pocket. This time he shrugged and did it, so I called Tuba, and when the burly man had filled our drink orders, I parked myself on the bar stool beside Ernie's.

"You really mean what you said?" he asked. "You idolized me when you were a kid?"

"Sure," I said. "Watched every episode of your show. My whole family looked forward to it every week. Great stuff. Funny stuff. Not like all this 'ultra-hip' sex stuff they show nowadays, all that melodramatic soap opera crap, and those whining comedians who just bitch and moan. Your show had class, Mr. McCabe. It had style. It had a heart."

Ernie nodded, taken aback by my sincerity, but I could see doubts still lingered. "Yeah, right, I'll bet you don't even remember the name of the show, smart guy."

My mouth hinged open; I drew a blank.

One of those rare but insurmountable failures of the recall system.

I knew the title of Ernie's show. It was on the tip of my tongue, but somehow I just couldn't bring it past my lips. I had watched that show every week, even the Christmas special, listened to the records, badgered my parents into buying most of the junk that went with it. The theme music, the sets, even the first names of each of the Tuskersons—all that was clear in my memory—but I just could not summon the exact name, and I could see in Ernie's eyes that I was losing him.

That's when I was saved by television: On the silent screen above the bar, a new program rolled, one of those entertainment insider nostalgia shows that dish up all the stale, behind-the-scenes gossip on popular old programs. It just happened that night's episode was about Ernie's old series, and with the corner of my eye I caught the bright-colored title logo from the opening sequence playing in a window above the narrator's right shoulder.

I leaned toward Ernie and said, "*Meet the Tuskersons.*"

Ernie's face beamed. "Yeah, that was it all right. Wow, you really do remember."

I pointed at the television. "Look, it's on right now."

Ernie bounced around in his seat, glanced at the screen then lunged across the bar and shouted for Tuba. "Turn it up!" he cried. "C'mon, Tuba, buddy, please, turn it up, pal, okay? I really need to see this. Been waiting three months! C'mon and do a guy a favor, will ya? This is important!"

Tuba shrugged and obliged, more to shut Ernie up than to accommodate him, I'm sure, but he aimed the remote, and then the narrator's baritone voice filled the bar and familiar theme music that I hadn't heard in years played in the background.

"...also starring Ernie McCabe, this oddball family of five captured the hearts of America for three seasons on *Meet the Tuskersons*. Tonight on *Hollywood Back Lots*, the behind-the-scenes story of how five wacky walri and one funny man turned a short-lived sitcom into an American legend."

The narrator faded out as the show cut to commercial.

"Oh, boy, this is it," Ernie said. "Finally! Ernie McCabe is going to be back on the map, baby!"

Ernie squirmed on his barstool and propped himself up in line with the television. He sipped his drink once and then seemed to forget it was there. His eyes stayed glued to the set, his lips twitched with impatience at the commercials, and when the show returned, an eager smile sprawled across his weathered face.

"So, right around the middle of the second season, we knew we had something special. We barely squeaked by for renewal after our first season, but now our audience was going up 20 percent every week. We were doing the best work of our careers then—me, the directors, the writers, even the Tuskersons. It was fabulous. It was unexpected. And people loved it!

"I was feeling so good, I popped the question to Rita at our favorite restaurant, and faster than she could say 'Yes' we were on our way to Vegas for one of the happiest nights of my life. We even hit the jackpot on a one-arm bandit on our way out of the Chapel of Eternal Union. That was a night to remember, let me tell you."

Ernie's excitement faded. He settled back into his chair, and a serious look swept his face as he drifted loose among his memories.

"Of course, it couldn't have lasted. I should have known all along, should have been ready for it, you know? But, hey, some shows go on for years and years, right? Look at *M*A*S*H* or *Leave it to Beaver*. Those aired for more than a decade, and I figured, why not us? Why not? Still can't say exactly why we were canceled in our third season, and just ten shows shy of a syndication package, too. I couldn't figure it out, then, and I don't understand it, now, but I know this: Once we were on top, things got ugly. Maybe that was the reason. People just got too greedy, forgot that our jobs were to make people laugh, not figure out new ways to screw another buck out of everyone else.

"I've never been very good with money, but I had dedication back then. I'd have done anything to keep our little show going. I ran ragged doing promotional appearances, putting in sixteen-hour shooting days, doing interviews, rehearsals, guest-shots, you name it, I did it. But I didn't mind! It was everything I had ever wanted from my career. And when I wasn't working I took care of Rita, took her out on the town shopping and went for weekend getaways. It was hard work to keep up with a young woman like Rita, but I held my own.

"I never fell back on drugs to help me, like the rest of them did. Never. They were everywhere, too. On the set, in the clubs, in the men's rooms at the restaurants, but I never touched them. Hardly even drank during the shooting season. Made me look Amish compared to everyone else, who were all on something. Coke, heroin, pot, booze, you name it, someone was taking it, and usually on the set. Hell, after a while, the producers were practically giving the stuff away like candy to keep people working without raises, but I always steered clear. I liked to keep my mind sharp for the show.

"It got worse toward the end of the season. One of the production assistants and a cameraman died in a car crash, both of them high as kites. Then the producers had a falling out that nobody could understand. Rumor was a woman came between them, but not one of their wives. They stopped talking to each other for more than a month. One day they trashed each other's cars in the parking lot—scratched them up, smashed the windshields. Crazy, crazy stuff. And then they fired our top director and two of our best writers when they pressed for better deals in mid-season.

"It wasn't fun and games, anymore, but it was still good. I was doing what I did best: being funny! I was living the dream that had kept me going through a couple of decades of stand-up working the clubs and variety shows. All that stuff going on around me? It just didn't seem important, at least, not until Rita got into it, too. See, once I was famous, we could walk into any place in town and get a table without waiting. People came up to us looking for everything from an autograph, to a loan, to a part on the show. I was flattered. I tried to be nice, but Rita could be a real snob sometimes, really nasty. I knew she was out there doing stuff I didn't like while I was working, doing stuff she shouldn't have been doing with people she shouldn't have been doing it with.

"Let me tell you, I never had any illusions about that girl, but, well, sometimes you have faith in a person even when you know you shouldn't. You hope maybe they'll do a little better by you than they do by everyone else.

"That's the real joke, isn't it? Hope?

"Yeah, I guess it is, but no one's laughing."

McCabe paused for a moment as he gathered his thoughts.

"That's when I started hiding out on the set and spending time with the Tuskersons. The producers had built them a custom habitat next to the studio. It's still there today.

Heard they converted it into a monkey house when that chimp craze hit, but back when the Tuskersons lived there, their manager, Clara Dobbs, used to let me in whenever I wanted. Dobbs told me the walruses loved me like one of their own, but then Dobbs could charm the skin off a snake, so I didn't pay much attention. Still, I liked hanging out there. A lot of nights, me and Dobbs sat on the rocks while the Tuskersons swam around their pool or basked under their sun lamps.

"The Tuskersons were the same at home as they were on the set: relaxed, playful, friendly. I felt good being around them, and Dobbs loved all my old material. Made me go through it over and over again, and laughed every time. Real laughter, not just going along with me. I mean, I must have done cheerleaders in the chewing gum factory thirty times for that gal, but every time she slapped her knee like she was hearing it new all over again.

"I missed that in those days. There were millions of people cracking up at home every week when I came on the tube, but I couldn't see them, couldn't hear them. And not even Rita laughed like Dobbs did. That gal was a genuine fan. Made me nostalgic for my club days when I was a nobody and all that mattered was getting a good guffaw out of the crowd. Not that I wanted to go back to that. I had too much to lose then, and I could feel how slippery my grip was. I was 'in,' but I wasn't '*in,*' if you know what I mean. Sure people loved old Ernie McCabe, but one hit show isn't enough to make them remember you when you're down and out. The distance between where I was and where I had been was pretty slim. I never wanted to be an outsider again.

"But that's life, right? Gives you hopes, fulfills them, and then takes it all away, and leaves you with…well, memories, I guess, only memories."

Hollywood Back Lots had done their research.

Mostly.

They covered all three seasons of the show and they spun all the old rumors in what felt like a new direction. The "documentary" started with the Tuskersons: five walri from nobody knew precisely where.

Well, that's not quite right.

Clara Dobbs, their agent/trainer, had known, but she never told. Dobbs was a cagey, old school showgirl from Cockeysville, and she knew better than to miss a chance to tease the public.

Dobbs claimed she found the Tuskersons in the far northern reaches of the Canadian wilderness where she had gone for solitude after a string of busted deals and lost clients. Out there in the frozen wilds, alone, destitute, desperate, Dobbs had thrown herself into an ice hole, and there she found her fortune. She hadn't planned on coming back up, but five walri that broke through the frosty crust had other ideas. They dragged her out of the Arctic water, fed her fish, and kept her warm by sleeping around her. It was her bulky, gray, down coat, soaked with water, Dobbs claimed, that attracted her saviors. The coat made her look like a sickly walrus.

More than a few scientists poked some fairly slackjawed holes into Dobb's account, but in show business, the story is mightier than the fact. It was all about the mystique, and Dobbs' tale was more dramatic than admitting that the Tuskersons were castoffs from some second-rate Seaworld that couldn't afford to keep five trained walri anymore, which was probably much closer to the truth.

No one lost any sleep over it.

The Tuskersons were America's mascots. No one wanted to spoil the parade.

Remember those T-shirts, the ones of the United States seal with the eagle replaced by a walrus? Ridiculous, yes, but they were everywhere. That's how popular the Tuskersons were. They verged on the iconic or, I suppose, the iconoclastic, depending on your perspective.

Whatever Dobb's eccentricities, she was one hell of a businesswoman. Got the Tuskersons booked on *Good Morning America*, Letterman, *The Tonight Show*, Donahue—you name it, the Tuskersons did it. They had cameos in summer blockbusters and guest roles on ailing sitcoms. By the third season (before anyone knew it would be the last) the walri craze broke the stratosphere. Happy Tuskersons fans could go on "The Walrus Diet" ("Fish fat: the secret to longevity!"), take walrus safari cruises, or unlock the secrets of human potential via the wisdom of walrus psychology ("Make your psychic blubber work for you!").

The entire viewing public was too busy appreciating the Tuskersons to care about whether any of it made a lick of sense. Watching those old behind-the-scenes clips of the Tuskersons waddling and frolicking in their on-set habitat, I could see where the crux of their success lay.

The Tuskersons, you see, were the perfect family—*the* perfect family. More *perfect* than any plastic television family unit, more together than any phony gaggle of smiling, attention-starved child actors bound for convenience store robberies, and their drug-addled, ego-tripping, sex-crazed maniac, grinning-like-fools parents.

The Tuskersons were rarer than gold when it came to television; the Tuskersons were *real*, a *genuine* family whose members loved and cared about each other in a simplistic but powerful, primal way that most human families found baffling but wished they could emulate. The Tuskersons lacked all guile.

The old clips rolled and soon I was sitting, head propped on my hands, leaning forward, rapt, just like Ernie. On screen the Tuskersons shambled their remarkable girths across a standard sitcom set with all the comic grace they could muster. When they talked their mouths flapped and smacked, a bit out of sync with their dubbed voices, but still firmly convincing. They delivered lines in a way no human actor could, with placid expressions devoid of presumption, their faces like happy masks, but real. It was enthralling, the special effect compelling in its crudeness, defined by some element, some quirk of editing or sound design that lent the Tuskersons a touch of extra credibility that set them squarely apart from their anthropomorphized animal star counterparts like Mr. Ed and Flipper.

Funny, but I had never noticed that before, had never even given it a thought.

Hollywood Back Lots said Clara Dobbs had trained the walri to flap their gums on command, but she had never revealed the secret of how.

A procession of talking heads went by, the voice actors who lent the Tuskersons speech, the writers and directors, the producers, the supporting actors, and each one reminisced about their days on the show, all the time they'd spent laughing, and how innocent the whole thing had been compared to today's sophisticated programming. They called it a magical time, and flashed cosmetically sublime smiles honed to feckless perfection as they oozed well-rehearsed zaniness and pretended they just might burst into a hearty knee-slap at their great memories. None of them could hide the dollar signs flashing behind their eyes when they mentioned the upcoming DVD boxed-set release of *Meet the Tuskersons: Season One.*

The narrator cut in with teasers for the rest of the show, and then the self-congratulatory sound bites gave way to more commercials.

Ernie looked at me and asked, "How long is this show?"

"An hour, I think," I told him.

"Huh. I must be on toward the end, then."

"They interviewed you for this?"

Ernie nodded vigorously. "Oh, yeah. About three months ago. They put me up in a fancy hotel for a weekend, sat me down in front of the cameras, and roll, baby, let it roll. Told them all about my days on the show, even snuck in some new material. Had 'em rolling on the carpet! Cameraman had to stop shooting while they got themselves together. Even got paid, except that fifty is all I got left. But I figure this is going to put me back in the game, get old Ernie McCabe's name on people's lips again, and then we'll see who takes my calls and who thinks I'm a washed-up has-been when America remembers how much they love me."

"Back on television after all these years," I said and slapped him on the back. "Must feel great, Mr. McCabe."

"You betchum," he cracked. "And this is just the start. I feel it in my bones, y'know, the way it feels when it's gonna click, when this rocket is about to take off—" Ernie swept his flattened hand across the space between us and thrust it over his head, "—and shoot the moon, baby! I tell you that new material is gold. Been working on it for ten years. It has to be good. Just you wait and see if you don't fall off that stool laughing when you hear it. And, you know, I got a million of 'em."

When he said it that time, desperation creeping into his voice and raw hope pooled in his lachrymose eyes, a sudden cold premonition filled my gut and then rolled and spun like a weather map hurricane. The narrator's slick face filled the screen. Ernie swiveled about, once more front row center, and I turned slowly, reluctantly, with him.

"Weirdest thing that ever happened to me on the Tuskersons happened one night after we wrapped for the day. This was around the start of the third season. I took a nap in my dressing room to rest up for Rita, but I was so tired I wound up sleeping past midnight. I'm passing by the set on my way out, and I realize how different the Tuskersons's living room looks without the studio lights blazing and the Tuskersons wobbling around. When we were shooting it felt like a real home, but not at night in the dark and the quiet. So, I decide to stop by and see the walruses. I figured I'd be on my own, but while I'm crossing the parking lot, I see Dobbs walk into the habitat ahead of me, and I think, 'Hey, great, it'll be good to talk to someone sane for a while.'

"Then I open the door, walk onto the landing, and there's Dobbs, thirty feet below standing buck-naked up to her waist in the water with the Tuskersons splashing around. I should have said something, let her know I was there, but I was too shocked to speak, and next thing I know, Dobbs dove under the water, and the Tuskersons followed her. Their shapes swam out and when they came up on the rocks on the far side of the pool, there were six walruses! Six! Not five, not five and woman, but six.

"Dobbs was really a walrus in disguise! At least, that's what I thought at first.

"Then I thought I was seeing things, but I was sure Dobbs hadn't resurfaced, and that meant either she was drowned at the bottom of the pool or she had become a walrus. Neither option particularly appealed to me.

"So, I climbed down the stairs to the pool level and took a seat on the rocks where Dobbs and I usually hung out. An hour goes by. Nothing happens. The Tuskersons are all off out of sight in the back of their habitat. So, I nodded off again, and then the next thing, I wake up and there's six walruses standing by the edge of the water, tusks shining, whiskers dripping, rolls of blubber floating. One of them waddles up onto the rocks, and I must have blinked or something, because one moment it was a walrus and the next it was Clara Dobbs, drying herself and putting her clothes on, and looking unbelievably casual about the whole darn thing.

"'How's it going, Ernie?' she asked me.

"I told her it was going all right.

"She buttoned her shirt and kind of combed her gray hair back with her fingers. Then she said, 'I can tell how much you love the Tuskersons, Ernie. They're special animals, all right. Simple, uncomplicated, peaceful. They're pretty fond of you, too, you know. They think you're pretty damn funny.'

"'Dobbs,' I said. 'Either I'm still dreaming or you're a walrus pretending to be a woman. Now, which is it?'

"'Neither,' Dobbs said. 'You're awake and I'm a woman, but I'll admit, I'm thinking about becoming a walrus. It's a fine life, Ernie.'

"So I explained to Dobbs that unless the laws of nature had just been repealed and I hadn't gotten the memo, she couldn't just decide to become a walrus.

"So she tells me, 'I know how it sounds, but it's true. The Tuskersons make it possible. Heck, you just saw me turn into a walrus and then back again, and you still doubt it?'

"I doubted it all right. I'd just seen it, but I was afraid to believe it. Maybe the stress was getting to me, making me hallucinate. Maybe I'd picked up someone else's Dr. Pepper by mistake and gotten a little surprise dose of something.

"Then Dobbs says 'You get used to it after a few times, Ernie, and then you find yourself not wanting to change back. There's the water sliding by when you swim. There's peace and quiet. No one clamoring for a pound of your flesh or dragging you into screwed-up headgames and power struggles. No biting your nails waiting for the ratings to come in. No worries about money or sex or how best to live your life. When you're a walrus, you just know how to do it. The hardest choice you make is which fish to eat, which rock to sleep on, and there are always others around you, your family, close-knit, always looking out for each other. It's the best, Ernie, no doubt about it. And I can see in your eyes that it appeals to you.'

"'Dobbs, you're crazy,' I told her. She just laughed.

"But, yeah, it appealed to me, I admit. Especially right then when I was running so ragged, and I knew I was already losing Rita. I think some part of me deep down knew the end was coming. We were still high in the ratings, then, but the show was splitting apart at the seams. People were at each other's throats. I should have known that it couldn't last, but I didn't want to admit it, and I sure wasn't going to say all that to Dobbs.

"'Consider it, Ernie. That's all I'm saying,' Dobbs said. 'Things change, and one day, you may be looking for a way out. You could still make people laugh. You could still do your job. Just promise me you won't tell anyone about this. The Tuskersons are kind of particular, you understand? They took me in when I was in pain. They see the same in you, and sooner or later, you will, too. Maybe tomorrow, maybe not for a long time, but you will and the offer will always be on the table. Just keep a lid on it, okay? Our contract is up for renewal next season, after all, and this getting out could complicate it.'

"I promised Dobbs to keep her secret, and then we left. We split up outside the door. By the time I got home, I had myself convinced that I'd imagined it all, that Dobbs was just some weirdo who liked to pretend she was a walrus. When things started to crash and burn, I forgot all about it, tucked it away in a mental junk drawer, until a year after the show was canceled and the Tuskersons moved into their permanent habitat.

"Dobbs had arranged for their earnings to pay for a private area at a local zoo, but she had disappeared by then, and no one knew where she had gone. I had an idea when I saw the pictures in the news and there were six walruses in the Tuskersons' new home. The papers said the sixth had been an understudy, but we'd never had any understudy. I thought of that strange night at the studio and I knew it was Dobbs. She'd finally become a walrus for good and wouldn't ever be changing back.

"Wait. Why are you stopping the camera? You don't believe me, do you? Can't say I blame you, but there's no other explanation. Trust me, I've spent years trying to think of one."

Hollywood Back Lots ended half-an-hour later. Ernie turned to me with bloodshot eyes brimming with imminent tears and blurted, "Well, goddamn it."

He clutched the drink he had been ignoring and knocked it all back in one gulp, then wheezed and slammed his glass down. He threw his crumpled fifty on the bar and hollered for a refill.

The *Hollywood Back Lots* theme played over the closing credits. There had been no sign of Ernie's interview, his contributions acknowledged with a montage of his best moments and the explanation that he had been too ill to make an appearance. Twice, other former cast members referred to him in the past tense, and then quickly corrected themselves. Ernie was in no prize shape, but I believed what he had told me about being interviewed for the show. He had been the only human star of *Meet the Tuskersons*. It was almost inconceivable that he might be excluded, but he had been.

Ernie stared out from beneath his drooping eyelids and looked so sad that Tuba spotted him his next drink.

I did not know what to say. My thoughts clashed as I looked for the right words, but before I could speak, Ernie reached out and put one of his knobby, shaking hands on my shoulder, and squeezed it.

"Don't sweat the noggin muscles, kid," he said. "You'll never guess. I got along fine with all of them, and I wasn't lying when I said I had a blast at the interview. The crew loved me. They all loved me. At least, that's what I thought back then, but maybe... maybe..." he said, and then fell silent.

Ernie's shoulders sagged even further. "You think, maybe," he whispered, "they all resented me? Because I was the star? Because I didn't go in for all the partying like they did? I never gave anyone a hard time about it. It just wasn't important to me. The show was important to me."

His breathing turned deep and then he lifted his head and looked me in the eye. "Dammit, I knew I never should have told them about that time Dobbs turned into a walrus!" he bellowed. "They cut me out because they think I'm loony-tunes."

I opened my mouth in time for my speechlessness to catch its second wind. This was part of the story *Hollywood Back Lots* would never touch.

Ernie told me the whole thing, just the way he had told it on camera for an interview that would rot on the backup file server of an archive somewhere if the producers hadn't already erased it. He couldn't explain exactly what the Tuskersons were or how they could help Dobbs turn into a walrus, but he was certain they had. He knew how it sounded, and except for having seen Dobbs change that one night, Ernie wouldn't have believed a shred of it. It was hard not to believe the old comedian when I heard the conviction in his voice. To him this was all real, and I wondered how long his mind had been so addled. Maybe as far back as when the show went off the air.

"They cut me out tonight, because they know," he said when he was done. "That must be it. They know Dobbs told me her secret, and they know the Tuskersons would never have any of *them*. So, they cut me! Ernie McCabe? Poof! Gone. Who's that? Who needs him? Maybe, if I hadn't talked about it, maybe if I had said things like those other people instead of the truth, instead of being honest, they would have let me back in, but after all these years, all the doors they've closed in my face, all the rejections, and the snickering behind my back—that has to be it! They're jealous because the Tuskersons chose me and not them!"

"Sure, Mr. McCabe," I said. "That must be it."

He nodded his head, and said, "Yes, yes, that's it."

"Mr. McCabe," I said, an idea blooming, "why don't we get your story out to the world? Look, I'm a writer. I get published all the time in all the big trade rags. We could meet tomorrow, go over the facts, get it all straight, and then I'll make sure everyone knows exactly what happened to good, old Ernie McCabe, the straight dope."

His eyes burned with the prospect. "Yes, yes," he said. "We should tell everyone. Get my name back out there. Maybe we can work in some of my new material. It isn't fair what they've done to me. Not fair, at all, how they've locked me out for all these years. I was a star!"

"That's right. A star. And stars deserve better than being tossed out like garbage. Let the public decide who's right and who's crazy," I said.

"The public always loved me," Ernie said. "You believe me, right? You do, don't you?"

It could have been the half-second pause before I answered or maybe my eyes diverted for an instant—I'll never know but something told him the truth, and when I said that I believed him, he knew I was lying. He was coming out of the haze of his disappointment. He sensed that all I was after was a hot story about a crazy old comedian and that maybe the folks at *Hollywood Back Lots* had done him a favor by not embarrassing him. I can admit it now—maybe what he saw were the dollar signs flashing in my eyes at the prospect of painting a washed-up a lunatic as a crazy outsider poised for a big comeback that would never materialize.

Who can say what was really going through Ernie McCabe's mind that night? I didn't much wonder until he missed our meeting the next morning.

I spent a week trying to find him before I gave up. Got as far as a cheap motel in a bad part of town, where he had stayed before the show aired. The manager hit me up for a hundred bucks, Ernie's outstanding bill.

After that I let it go. The story wasn't worth chasing, and I was feeling a little guilty about what I might have done to an old man who once made me and my family laugh, long ago, back in the days when we could still do that together.

I'd done some research that week, though, getting ready and boning up on *Meet the Tuskersons*, and a big chunk of Ernie's story held up. Clara Dobbs had disappeared after the show was canceled, and six walri, not five, had moved into the permanent habitat at the Barrymore Zoo, a small, private facility north of the city that had been built in the thirties by a rich movie producer. The drugs and the show's collapse were common knowledge. Ernie had been right about the Tuskersons's old studio living quarters; they had been converted into a monkey house for about eight years before the whole thing had been torn down to build a new soundstage.

One day after that night when I met Ernie McCabe I saw an article in the paper about a new arrival at the Barrymore Zoo. Yeah, you guessed it, a walrus, a new resident in the Tuskersons's private pavilion. Of the six original walri, four still lived, though they were improbably old by walrus standards, and that included the one that had supposedly been the understudy. The new addition was a guest that Clara Dobbs had made provisions for back when she was still managing the walri, an addition the zoo had been waiting a long time to receive, and once more there were five walri, and in a strange way, the Tuskersons were complete again, the perfect family they had been years ago, the perfect family they would always be.

I considered driving out to the Barrymore Zoo, thought about seeing for myself if maybe Ernie McCabe hadn't been crazy after all, if maybe he'd finally found his next big role, but I knew it was impossible, knew it couldn't be true. Right? And you know what? Even if it was true, so what? Who cares? Who wants to hear about some second-rate has-been finally finding happiness and getting the best of the world in the end?

I mean, where's the story in that?

The Kind Old Fellow

Hugh Carter, a much-admired old man, spent his days serving the destitute in the St. Francis Dispensary for the Homeless, located in the basement of the small Church of St. Francis beneath the shadow of the great stone monolith that housed the city government. People called him "a living saint," though this ranked as mere hyperbole, Hugh being, in the grand scheme of the cosmos, nothing more than an ordinary, kind-hearted and selfless soul. And anyway, Hugh didn't much believe in God. But the people of the city loved him. They knew him by his good works and his constant presence on CityNet, speaking on behalf of New York's poor and urging those of means to do what they could to help, the face and voice of the city's conscience. So, on the day the Reckoners arrested Hugh Carter for murder, the entire city ground to a dumbstruck halt, shocked as much by the raw incomprehensibility of Carter turned killer as by the fact that the authorities failed to execute his sentence the very moment they apprehended him. In fact, they failed to deliver any punishment whatsoever, a lapse intensely unsettling to the city's inhabitants, all twelve million of whom relied on the Reckoners's strict predictability to maintain order and civility on the overcrowded island of Manhattan.

Clad in black and gold uniforms, weapons at their hips, the Reckoners struck a familiar sight patrolling above the streets in small, dark hovercraft that flitted among the buildings like flies on a garbage heap. If you committed a crime, a visit from the Reckoners followed. No one could outrun or evade them, and no one could lie to them for they possessed the power to see within a person's soul and know the exact nature and degree of their transgression. Ascertained in an instant were the laws broken, your motive, the pain inflicted, and your state of mind. Immediate sentencing made it impossible to benefit from criminal behavior. Steal a piece of fruit and eat it before being caught, and they might force-feed you an emetic. Not necessarily an eye for an eye, but an equivalent eye for whatever the Reckoners decided measured up to your actions. No courts, no juries, no lawyers, no appeals, no judges, no writs of habeas corpus, no bail, no perjury, no showcase trials, no railroading the innocent, no star eyewitnesses, no exhibits A, B or C, no bailiffs, no stenographers…and practically no crime. What better deterrent than the knowledge that punishment for breaking the law arrives with swift certainty?

The Reckoners struck a balance.

Exactly how they achieved this extraordinary feat is not a matter of public knowledge. Some claimed they possessed highly developed telepathic abilities. Others extolled it as the grace of God at work on Earth, a form of divine justice. A Massachusetts Institute of Technology computer scientist once developed an almost impossibly complicated program to prove the Reckoners relied on technology. The program performed accurately 83 percent of the time. The Reckoners are correct every time. Fixated on solving the riddle of the seventeen percent gap, the scientist suffered a stroke from frustration and his experiments ended. He may have inadvertently proven, however, that the key element to the Reckoner's success lies in the human factor. A string of conspiracy theorists had claimed over time that the machinery of an elaborate cover-up backed up the Reckoner's decisions whether right or wrong. No investigation has ever supported this contention, which crops up most often in cases under appeal by the family of a convicted criminal.

Such protest is permitted; none has ever garnered a reversal of fortune.

What people *do* know about the Reckoners is that those men and women who place themselves in the service undergo lengthy and extensive training; they leave society behind and break off all contact with family or friends; candidates apply of their own free will and are accepted or rejected immediately and without discussion; and those accepted cannot decline an appointment once offered. The Reckoners became the regular police during the most chaotic period of the city's past. The exact details of their origin lie hazy beneath the grime of history. Consensus holds that Commissioner Piet Ruiz, the city's greatest cop, founded the agency, but few know much about him other than his outstanding arrest record and rapid rise through the ranks. When the first Reckoners appeared, crime had crippled the city and the assassination of a visiting world leader had sparked riots that spurred a savage crackdown by conventional authorities.

Yet Hugh Carter had killed a man in plain sight of at least six witnesses, and the Reckoners had done nothing but take him gently—almost deferentially—away in their sleek, quiet floater to the high reaches of the stone tower.

Three hours later a crowd had gathered outside the city offices. People had come from all parts of town, setting aside their shopping, their business, their recreation, gathering to clog the streets for ten blocks in all directions like hair clumps in a drainpipe. The Reckoners emerged in force, floating along the concrete passages of the city blocks, monitoring the crowd that remained calm despite its agitation and the blistering afternoon heat. The gathering itself might have been decreed criminal, except for an old law governing the people's right to peaceful assembly and the fact that many of the Reckoners wanted answers as much as the citizens.

At four o'clock the mayor's top aide, Jamal O'Henry, stepped onto a high balcony of the massive stone structure. His face flickered to life on the broad video screen mounted above the building entrance. At the same time, it flashed across CityNet screens on buses and subways and in the backs of taxis, in train stations and elevators, on street corner telecommunication kiosks, in offices and apartments and on personal cell nodes.

Jamal cleared his throat; a hush fell over the streets.

"This evening," O'Henry began, "at six o'clock, Mayor Randall Artemis will address the city regarding Hugh Carter. Thank you."

A disappointed sigh poured up in a hot wave from the unfulfilled multitudes. Boos and hisses followed. Some onlookers felt the urge to vent their frustration by smashing windows or mailboxes, but instead they clenched their fists and filed away beneath the Reckoner's careful eyes. They left not even a shred of litter behind them.

Inside the concrete buttresses of the nameless edifice, Hugh Carter released a defeated sigh of his own. He sat in a small chair, alone in an oversized storage closet hastily converted to a holding cell. A plastic pitcher of water waited on the floor, a paper cup beside it. An older man among the guards who had escorted him had demanded his belt and shoelaces and forced him to empty his pockets into a vinyl pouch. Then he slammed shut the door, leaving Hugh by himself in the bleak, gray room.

The situation baffled Hugh. He'd considered and reconsidered all the possibilities a thousand times. Every one of them led to his immediate execution on the street with a Reckoner's needle pressed to the back of his neck. None of them landed him in this makeshift prison. None of them predicted this stunning impasse.

The Reckoners had arrived within minutes of the murder. Hugh sat waiting on the warm curb, knowing well enough there was nowhere to flee. He unloaded his gun, handed it over grip first, and gave himself up. The first hint of the looming dilemma came when one of the Reckoners took Hugh's measure with her soft brown eyes wide with surprise.

She took Hugh by the arm. Her voice croaked from her suddenly dry throat. "I think you should come with us, sir."

The partners led Hugh to their hover unit, and dumbfounded, he followed. The eyes of the awestruck crowd traced their every movement, even as the craft ascended upon its humming turbines. Fifteen minutes later Hugh found himself sitting on the metal chair in the empty closet space, no closer to understanding where he had gone wrong. He had lost track of time when he heard a latch snap and echo, and the door swung open. Several Reckoners filled the hallway, crowded around a short, broad-shouldered man Hugh recognized as Mayor Randall Artemis. A line of assistants percolated behind him. Hugh straightened his back and thrust his jaw high with indignation. He had met Artemis in an official capacity on numerous occasions as he had many of the city's other mayors, but the two had never struck up a friendship.

"I know my rights," said Hugh. "Sentence me or let me walk free. *Action, reaction*—isn't that the Reckoner's motto?"

Mayor Artemis rubbed his chin thoughtfully with the thumb and forefinger of his right hand, a practiced gesture. Then, his rumination complete, he raised one finger stiffly and turned a stern glance toward Hugh. "If only it were that simple, dear citizen."

An assistant unfolded a canvas seat stretched across a metal frame, placed it opposite Hugh, and Artemis settled his girth onto it, squatting almost eye-to-eye with the prisoner. "Our side of this conundrum is there for you to perceive, wizened sir," he said, falling into the odd speech rhythm of politicians, calculated—by focus groups, expert linguists, and extensive market research—to offend the fewest people. "Can you simply be let free, you who have committed the ultimate crime? It seems not. Yet, no sentence allows itself to be passed by the officers who apprehended you. In fact, eight other Reckoners who have discerned your personage since you entered this facility all find agreement in their observations. Whatever punitive remedy they might decree can only ultimately reward rather than punish you. No here or there about it. The only choice that presents itself? Remain passive. Their nerves have taken quite a cold-water rattling."

"Well, how do you think I feel, locked away in this janitor's closet?" said Hugh.

"Your feelings? Immaterial. Only the sentiments of that guidance-seeking mob outside are of tangible concern."

"What mob?" Hugh asked.

Artemis gestured to another assistant. The wiry man wore a personal CityNet port and viewer harnessed to his chest. He swiveled the small monitor around and tickled the sensors of the keygloves wrapped around his hands. Images of the eager crowd flickered to life onscreen.

"Dear Lord," said Hugh, aghast. "They can't all be here for me."

"'Saint Hugh' they call you, or the 'Blanket Man.' Maybe 'Angel of Mercy,' or the 'Kind Old Fellow,'" said Artemis. "Surely their words have reached your ears over the decades. When they ponder their souls, where do they look, dear citizen? To you! For many you are a moral weathervane, free of judgment and hatred, full of tolerance and compassion, an ideal worthy of striving to achieve. When events stress the city to its breaking point, solace is often taken in your comforting image. You can be relied on to restore faith in humanity. But now the Kind Old Fellow has killed in cold blood, and worse, no punishment delivered. Such a course of events breeds only confusion."

Hugh accepted this silently. He led them all by example, however poorly they followed. He had never wanted it, but he had long ago made peace with his influence and embraced it. The notoriety helped him focus attention on those in need and get things done.

Artemis gestured again. The slender aide wearing the port retreated. A muscular young black woman in a dark suit emerged from the crowd of underlings and placed a gray envelope in the Mayor's hand. He slid loose a sheaf of papers and handed them to

Carter. They were photocopies of pages from books published in the last century. Hugh recognized the antiquated look of the type.

"These show that all our procedures in your case so far are on the up and up and quite legit if, in fact, somewhat primitive," said the Mayor.

Carter returned the papers unread. "I don't care about this. Execute me or let me go! I don't want any special treatment. You have to honor my rights."

"No, no, no. Sadly not an option, good sir. The apple barrel has been upset and now it must be set right and all the apples counted and weighed once again," Artemis said. "A murder has been committed, and the Reckoners claim they cannot execute, incarcerate, chastise or flagellate the culprit. So, if such a thing can be accomplished by a meek old man of your stature, the track of the work undertaken uninterrupted by this bureau for so many years thrown off, and the most successful law enforcement authority in the nation stonewalled, how long before others decide they might accomplish the same, too? And then? Chaos? Disorder? Unacceptable! Many might turn such events to their advantage, enemies of the established order, who wish to see our government crippled. A growing problem, this—agitators and dissenters, unhappy individuals fomenting doubt and stirring our habitually calm populace. Tensions run high."

Many who hated the Reckoners for truncating their freedoms had become increasingly outspoken in recent years. Speech remained free, so long as the speaker broke no laws. Censorship lost its value when no action it inspired could accomplish anything that lasted more than minutes. Some days Hugh saw the protesters lecturing on street corners or passing out flyers meant to rouse people and declare their hope of seeing the will of the citizenry overwhelm the Reckoners. But complacent people enjoyed their security. Hugh had dismissed the dissenters as a harmless symptom of the city's malaise, nothing more than an instinctive opposition to authority, their smoldering anger forever unable to ignite for fear of immediate reprisal. But if his case exposed a weakness among the Reckoners might that embolden them?

"A seemingly light chastisement would at least have preserved the way of things," the Mayor continued. "Questions would be asked as to why you were let off so easy, but the notion that you got away scot free would not be entertained, which is now, clearly, the impression of many. Thus, an example must be made by the only means available. You, elder sir, shall be tried in court by a jury of your peers. Confidence in the administration shall be restored. It shall be proven that the people may rely fully on their elected officials to protect their interests."

"You can't hold me here for that," Hugh said.

"The old laws were not cast away when the new ones were made, wizened sir. Tomorrow at nine a.m. sharp, your trial begins." Artemis rose, pausing in the doorway. He took the dark woman's hand and drew her forward. "This fine citizen is Belinda

Park. Your attorney." Artemis dipped in a cordial bow. "Good day."

At six o'clock the Mayor appeared on the high balcony, his shadow exaggerated to titanic proportions by the garish spotlights. Simultaneously, his visage blinked to life on screens in every part of the city. The roiling crowd grew silent.

"Good citizens," Artemis said. "Relax your tensions. Place your confusions to rest. Rely on your government to look after you. Such devilish crimes shall not be tolerated in the city. Tomorrow morning at nine a.m. sharp, the accused shall face justice in a trial by jury. Sirs and madams, please have a good night."

The Mayor returned inside, the sound of his achingly brief speech still echoing through the streets. For the second time that day, a hot, confused murmur ascended as one voice from the gathered throng that had sought resolution, but instead received chafing suspense. Again, the crowd dispersed, unsatisfied, but more than that, filled with the creeping sensation of unease that settles upon those poised at the brink of an abyss into which they fear they will be compelled to plunge.

In the barren utility closet high above, Belinda Park presented her first question.

"Where were you born, Mr. Carter?"

Carter pouted at her.

"Please," said Park. "Ideally, we should have several weeks to prepare your defense, but given the urgent nature of your case, the court has given us one night. Your cooperation is essential. Right now, my adversary is certainly meeting with his witnesses elsewhere in this very building and prepping them to testify."

"Can't they just execute me? Do we need this farce of a trial? Can't I just confess and plead guilty or something?" Hugh said.

"As your councilor I have to advise against that," said Belinda. "The trial will be no farce, Mr. Carter. I am fully qualified to represent you. I hold doctorates in anthropology, ancient society and customs, psychology, and contemporary law. The prosecutor will be equally qualified, and they have several eyewitnesses, so if you want to stand a chance of winning your case, you really should work with me. This whole event loses credibility if we fail to provide you with a spirited defense."

"Four degrees. When do you ever sleep?"

"A waste of time. I don't. A combination of hypnosis and Stimalert increases my productivity. I require ten minutes rest only every fifteen hours."

Hugh's eyelids fluttered shut. "We're all like that, now, hurrying and rushing about our lives, so distracted that we've lost true sight of the world. We push ourselves harder and faster, strive for higher standards, better productivity, grander triumphs to outdo those of the ones who came before us and did it all, and left nothing for us but to warp their achievements. And toward what? What does any of it gain us when in the end it changes nothing? I'm so tired of it."

"If you require rest, we could break for an hour, so you could nap."

Park began gathering her papers.

"That's not what I meant," said Hugh. "Look at me. I'm old and getting older. I've been doing the same work all my life since I was old enough to do it. Do you know how long that is?"

Park referred to her dossier. "Ninety-four years. You began working on your twelfth birthday."

"I was a child, and when I looked at the world through a child's eyes, I saw perfection—or at least it's glimmering potential," he said. "I saw what might be, what *we* might be, all of us if we could only get up on our feet and start running." Hugh glanced around the room. "Not even a damn window. But it's out there. We both know it. We feel it, even locked away inside these thick walls. Millions of lives beginning, ending, speeding by, colliding, falling apart, finding one another. Do you know what it was about human suffering that moved me most when I was child, Ms. Park?"

"No, but I don't see how that's relevant to your case."

"Of course, you don't," he said. "It was that the suffering seemed so unnecessary. Why should anyone go hungry when others ate more than their fill? Why should anyone sleep on the street while others owned houses with rooms they never entered? Not that I begrudged anyone their success or their possessions. If you worked for it, you earned it, and you deserved it. But the sheer evidence of abundance overwhelmed me. It seemed the greatest injustice that anyone should suffer the indignities on display each day in the streets. I knew my life's work would be trying to help those who needed it, facing the kind of 'crimes' the Reckoners hardly ever notice—the hungry left unfed, the sick left uncared for. And do you know what happened to me in ninety-four years of serving my fellow man?"

Park shook her head.

Hugh dropped his chin to his chest, lost for the moment in recollection, and then turned his stormy gaze on the woman's eyes. "I learned the truth. It can't be done. Never. The world, Ms. Park, does *not* change, not really, not fundamentally. On and on we go, living longer, getting smarter, growing stronger, becoming more sophisticated. But there are always those who have more and those who have less. Those who die in the streets from something as common as the flu and those who live for years beyond their time on the sustenance of machinery. Those who wander and become lost in the city's darkness and those who bleed it of its light. One man cannot share Atlas's burden. When I had seen the same sorrow-etched faces parade past me for the thousandth time, borne on by unanswered hope that lifted them like mismatched crutches, I knew all my work meant nothing, amounted to no more than a fleeting balm. That tomorrow and for all time the hungry and sick and unsheltered and forgotten would be there."

"Is that why you decided to kill Dr. Neusted? To vent your frustration over your failure to achieve your goals?" asked Park. "That might be the basis for a temporary insanity defense."

Hugh Carter ignored the question. He covered his mouth with one gnarled hand as he fought to hold back soft tears rolling down his cheeks and the gentle tremors shaking his frail body. He wept for a world lost to its fate, for the life he'd given to the world, for a child's vision—lost to brutal reality.

Belinda allowed him a courteous pause to gather his composure.

"No," Hugh said, as he calmed himself. "Mackie Neusted was a useless scoundrel lucky enough to be born *with* money but *without* an ounce of compassion, but I killed him because *I* wanted to die. I thought, if I killed Neusted it might remove a stain from the Earth and wake people up from their apathy, but mainly I thought it would bring about my execution."

"Immediate retribution has kept our murder rate in single digits for years," Park said. "Your case should have been no different."

"Then why did they spare me?"

"We'll know more about that soon. The prosecutor interviewing the Reckoners who picked you up is required to share his report with us."

"It could have been anyone, you know. Neusted or a hundred others like him, a thousand. I didn't hate Mackie, not really. I followed him to the street after our last meeting, and it just felt right. I needed to unload my despair. I wanted out of it all—my work, the city, the insanity of trying to break through in a heartless world. And killing Mackie was a fast means of dumping it. The Reckoners would never punish him for his cruelty. To them it wasn't a crime that he refused to make his company's medications for the 'hemorrhagic flu' available to those suffering from it the most. His greed cost peoples' lives. So, I chose to punish him. Isn't that what the Reckoners do to criminals? Then I waited to die."

Park typed notes on her computer, nodding occasionally to spur on Carter's confession. He let it pour out, the years of struggle and deprivation, the story of the path he had chosen only to have it wear him down year after year until it eroded his strength and hope. Then darkness had set in, and Hugh became another wandering soul among the millions that drifted each day through the city. He felt little of the passion that had once driven him like the churning steam engine of an antique locomotive, knowing he could not live forever or change the world quickly enough to satisfy himself.

Belinda questioned him from every angle late into the night, picking and choosing pieces to present to the court. She worked with the dogged air of an academic tackling a new intellectual exercise, eager to weave her arguments tighter and cleaner than her opponent's. Hugh doubted she very much cared what happened to him so much as how she performed. He was living on borrowed time if she lost—but she could put it behind her and go on to the next challenge.

Neither of them could have known she would never have the chance.

Something deep inside the stone tower rumbled like the hunger pains of a slumbering behemoth disturbed. The cell shook, and the light flickered. The clacking of Belinda's keyboard ceased. Hard mechanical noises erupted in the corridor. A body slammed against the entry. With a bright flash and a puff of acrid smoke, the lock evaporated, and the door flew open. Fluorescent light poured in. Through the lingering gray residue of the explosion, three men entered carrying guns, their faces slick with sweat and terror, an adrenaline-fueled mania in their eyes. One aimed his weapon at Belinda, who froze in her seat and emitted a tiny shocked sound.

"We're here for the murderer," the man shouted. "Stand clear!"

As they stepped forward, something glowed behind them. An electric sizzling buzzed through the room. The three men convulsed and shivered, becoming entangled with one another as their uncontrolled bodies collided and wriggled to the floor.

Four Reckoners appeared. A captain's badge adorned the uniform of their leader. The nearby sounds of fighting clattered through the smashed entrance.

"You're done here, Ms. Park," said the captain. Two of the others flanked Hugh and seized him. "We're taking Carter with us for his own protection."

"Mr. Carter's trial begins in the morning," Belinda said. "We have little enough time to prepare without these interruptions."

But the Reckoner's were already hustling Hugh toward the door. Belinda rose to intercede. The captain grabbed her by the throat, crushed a small device against her flesh, and she collapsed, unconscious. He cradled her falling body gently to the floor. The others sped down the corridor. Their leader rushed after them. The Reckoners silenced Hugh's attempts at protest, flashing a stun gun in his direction to make it clear he would go with them, willing or not. They took him through reaches of the government offices few people ever saw, along back corridors and service tunnels into the deepest arteries of the monolithic building. They passed vacant offices and a darkened cafeteria lit by the cold glow of a coffee dispenser, twisted and turned past rows of blank doors shut tight, scuttled down dim stairways and through access passages crosshatched with wires and pipes. The ruckus of the melee faded behind them until they continued forward in an unnatural quiet, interrupted only by their footsteps and the noise of their breathing. Hugh struggled to keep up with the young, fit Reckoners. His lungs ached. His pulse pounded.

Soon the group reached a small, dark passage that led them to flashing lights and open air. Cold, dry wind swirled around them. Hugh gasped to catch his breath. Overhead hung the diffuse haze of cloud-reflected city lights like a pale copper canopy. The four Reckoners gazed skyward, searching. A cluster of lights appeared, defining the silhouette of a hover ship as it banked around the corner of a once magnificent skyscraper long dwarfed by the shadowy edifice of the tower. The ship buzzed low and close to the buildings, a red signal light blinking at its nose. The craft descended, throwing up a backwash of air that swept the tiny platform clean. The Reckoners pushed Hugh toward the hatch. A moment later sudden silence and regulated warmth shrouded them in the vehicle's interior, and as quickly as it had come, it rose back to the darkness.

The captain removed his headgear. His chiseled, bony face appeared ghostly in the glow of the cockpit lights. "My name is Suez," he said. "You'll be safe with us."

Hugh surveyed the serious faces of the others, who regarded him coldly.

He's old, they seemed to think, *but he's a killer. Caution is advised.*

None of them were older than thirty, except for Suez, clearly in his sixties. One was the woman who had arrested Hugh.

"What do you want?" asked Carter. "Are you going to kill me?"

Suez shook his head. "Reward you for murder? Deliver what you most desire?"

"We've been waiting years for someone like you," said the woman. "We've been preparing. You have no idea how fragile the order we impose on the city is, Mr. Carter. There are powerful people who want to break our authority and let corruption and crime creep back into our society. Tonight, they believe their goal is finally in sight."

"What does this have to do with me?" Hugh asked.

"What Lucy means is they want to prove the Reckoners can be wrong," Suez said. "Your trial is meant to restore faith in the old methods of justice, turn the city against us, and erode the established order. We can't let that happen."

"Six people witnessed me kill Mackie Neusted. I confess!" said Hugh.

"You've led a peculiarly righteous life, old man," Lucy said. "That balances much of your crime. Plus, you killed to gain release from your despair, to profit by your death. You also intended to make an example of Mr. Neusted and inspire others like him to give more to the causes for which you advocate. Another benefit to you. That we cannot permit. The only rational sentence is to assure that you go on living and suffering, a hard concept to convey to masses that have been conditioned to scream for blood. For years the media has made us out to be righteous avengers in the biblical tradition, a depiction influenced a great deal by our enemies. These days most people can only understand justice in terms of violence. If you stand trial, you'll be convicted and sentenced to death. The public will ache for your blood to be spilled. But in this case that does not serve justice."

Hugh felt fear for the first time since he had pulled the trigger that ended Mackie Neusted's life. What torture did the Reckoners plan? He had never guessed that these agents who supposedly saw the world in stark black and white, clear-cut rights and wrongs, could ever fabricate something more than simple retribution.

76

After a few minutes of flight, the craft banked, and Hugh noticed through the front windshield that fires burned on the steps of the city offices. People scurried around in every direction. Groups of armed men attacked the front door. Weapons raised, they launched useless sorties against the stone façade of the monumental structure and urged the flames to grow with defiant screams even as Reckoners swooped down on each of them and brought them to their knees.

"The dissenters," said Lucy. "Little better than a mob."

"Some have said the same about you," Hugh said.

"Not everyone understands what's happening in this city, Mr. Carter, but they're going to find out. Don't let what you see down there disturb you. It's a diversion. They pretend to fight for you while we know that their true objectives lie elsewhere."

An apartment building eclipsed the scene of mayhem as the ship turned sharply earthward. The plunging sensation tied a knot in Hugh's stomach. Moments later the craft leveled out and dropped gently to a rooftop platform. Hugh and the Reckoners disembarked beneath the shelter of a makeshift canvas hangar. Two other hovercrafts stood nearby. A dozen Reckoners moved about the work area. Hugh's captors ushered him from the heart of the activity, down a metal staircase, and into the building. Along the way they passed other Reckoners, all of them alert and on edge, each armed and in full uniform and patrol gear. The escort brought Hugh to an expansive room furnished with a long, wide table bordered by rows of high-backed chairs. A line of CityNet pods ran along the table's centerline. One wall of the space was given over entirely to windows, and the lamps were kept dim to allow a spectacular view of the city. Its lights glittered like jewels, and the black skin of the East River snaked along beneath graceful bridges. A tall woman in a tailored black uniform stood before the glass. She faced the captivating view, and, without turning, said, "Please sit down, Mr. Carter."

Carter chose a seat and noticed that except for Lucy and Suez, his escort had withdrawn. The woman by the window glanced at the time on her wrist display, then turned, locking eyes with Hugh as she approached him with self-assured strides. She took his hand in her warm palm and shook it. Her dark uniform bore no insignia of rank.

"My name is Ciara Donatello. I'm honored to meet you. I wish the circumstances were better. I've always respected your dedication to our city," she said.

Hugh studied her face and spied hints of softness long ago driven out to leave behind only sharp lines of tough muscle and the permanent ghost of cynicism lurking beneath her expression. A burned patch of skin around the left corner of her mouth had healed over with grayish scar tissue. But when she smiled, as she did in greeting him, a glimmer of hope shone through, undoing much of the harshness and ruin displayed there. That light stirred something within Hugh. He faced no simple cop doing her job. Wisdom brimmed in her eyes.

"We haven't much time, but I'll do what I can to help you understand what's happening and what role you must play," Ciara said. "Most people trust our deterrent, but to some we're the enemy. They believe we rob them of their freedom, but they're quite careful not to break any laws even though they conspire against us. Or at least they have been until tonight thanks to the interference of some in the city administration who see us as an obstacle to be removed. They despise the limitations we impose upon them as much as they covet our authority. They are powerful and possess the resources to undo our achievements. Randall Artemis is among them.

"They've been waiting for an apparent crack, however slender, in our effectiveness. They've been fueling the futile rage of the dissenters for years with money and promises, assuring that when the moment arrived, they could unleash that pent-up fury on their own city and turn it against us. That opportunity has come. They hoped to catch us off-guard, but we have sources of information they don't know about."

Ciara gripped Hugh's arm to guide him from his seat to the window. Across the room Lucy shut the lights. The glass seemed to vanish. To Hugh it almost seemed they floated, intangible, above the city.

"When Piet Ruiz established our group, he swore it would always uphold the law, and so we have done. But we don't make the laws. Those who do have managed to create the loopholes they needed to prepare for tonight and seize the power they believe should be theirs. We've been forced to wait for them to act. Do you see that building on 40th two blocks from the river?"

Hugh strained his eyes to pick out the one, a square brick structure set back from the street behind a parking lot. He recognized it. One of his missions stood opposite it and he passed it often.

"One of our headquarters. Seven hundred people work there," Ciara said.

A blinding amber sphere of force erupted from the site. It expanded in microseconds and stung the night as it rolled outward to swallow the whole of the building. The bubble of flame burst, sparks shooting forth. A pillar of black fog spewed into the sky. Hugh watched in horror. The sound barely reached them. He felt the faint tremor of the concussion in his fingertips pressed against the quivering glass.

Hugh gasped. "My God."

"No one was hurt. The building was evacuated earlier. The dissenters didn't know that when they attacked."

Another ball of flame burst to life across the river in Queens spitting fire and soot into the air. Far downtown a third ignited, and Hugh imagined other explosions tearing through the darkness all around them—the Armory uptown and the barracks in the Bronx, the Battery in lower Manhattan, the Navy Yard in Brooklyn, all the facilities used by the Reckoners. Their offices and command centers, their motor pools and lunchrooms, auditoriums and training centers, vanishing in sudden conflagrations. Ciara's calm demeanor suggested amazingly that none of it worried her.

"*All* of our buildings were evacuated," she said. "All our records have been transferred and all personnel secreted away to other locations in the city like this one. The dissenters are lashing out at empty shells, but they've left themselves vulnerable and exposed. Now we can bring justice to them."

Already Hugh saw tiny silhouettes cutting past the flames, the black hovercrafts and patrol units dropping to the burning ruins as the Reckoners responded. The sky sprang to life with flashing lights and the glint of gold trim as thousands of officers swarmed over the city and descended on their enemies. Hugh's position left him too high to see the activity at street level, but he could picture in his mind the black-clad men and women corralling the perpetrators, chasing them until they could run no further, stilling them. He turned away, weak and overwhelmed, and stumbled to a nearby chair. How could his act of selfish desperation have become the catalyst for such destruction? Both sides had been waiting for someone like him. Did it matter which one succeeded? Either way, he believed his city, his people—the ones who looked up to and trusted him—would suffer and lose.

"Our opposition will be eliminated by morning," Ciara said. "The fires will be extinguished. No innocents will have been harmed. Even Artemis will be in our custody. We will have taken control of the city."

"The people won't know who to trust, who to turn to," said Hugh. "They'll be living in the fear you've bred, terrified of their own protectors and their leaders. What good can you possibly think you've accomplished?"

"That's how it will be for a little while," said Ciara. "But order will have been maintained. In time we'll be stronger and more trusted than ever for it. The people are going to accept us because you're going to help us reclaim their hearts and minds. This will be your penance."

Understanding descended on Hugh like a torrent of icy water. He had given so many years of his life to serving the city, and they would have him continue when he was least capable of doing so, when he wanted only to lay down, defeated, and rest forever. Despair had hollowed him out. They sought to fill him up again with their own purpose.

"You'll get no help from me. I'll kill myself like I should have in the first place," Hugh said. "All my life I worked for them. They're no better off than when I started. And you and your kind have done nothing to help. *Action, reaction* is all you are. You work to change nothing."

"Are you certain?" said Ciara. "Maybe you didn't give enough, Hugh. Maybe after everything you let them have, every part of your being you gave to their service, they still wanted more. Maybe they wanted you to believe they could change. But you never did. Not really. You thought it would be easy. You thought you could fix things by crying alone in the wilderness and pleading for compassion. When it proved impossible, you gave up.

"Each year more and more people apply to our ranks. We refuse many suitable candidates. Fewer and fewer people attempt to commit crimes. The gift we Reckoners have is very special, Hugh. I can't explain it to you in conventional terms. It's awareness beyond the five senses upon which most people rely to construct reality. Understanding of how humanity fits together. The number of people who bear the seed of that knowledge is growing. Before long there will be more of us in the city than those without it. Consider it, Hugh—so many people living with an utter clarity of vision for right and wrong, a comprehension of justice embedded in their souls rather than their minds. All the things you've been working your whole life to eliminate—hunger, apathy, poverty, avoidable sickness—will cease to be an issue when the traits that permit those things to exist are burned away. We can spread that knowledge to the world. Piet Ruiz led us here. Now our mission must be reborn with another lone man. I know you feel it, Hugh. You would have made an excellent Reckoner had you chosen to join our ranks."

Hugh could not bring himself to look into Ciara's eyes. They glowed with belief. Could it be true? Could this be the source of the Reckoner's power? Or was it a fairy tale meant to draw him into their machine? People still trusted him despite his crime. He had realized that when they gathered in their numbers to witness his fate, when they hoped that all would be restored as it had been. If he reached out to them, they would listen.

Suez crept quietly to Ciara's side. "We haven't got much time."

Ciara activated one of the CityNet pods on the table. The screen flickered to life. A few keystrokes summoned a split-screen view of the lower floors. Armed men fought their way through a corridor and up an emergency staircase. Groups of outnumbered Reckoners resisted.

"Someone leaked to them that this should be one of their targets," Ciara said. "We discovered it only a few hours ago. Their spy has been punished but it was too late for us to bring in reinforcements. We're spread too thin as it is. We need your decision quickly, Hugh. The way I see it, you only have three options."

Suez placed a gun on the table in front of Carter, a stark gray unit of steel, loaded, Hugh could see by the indicator, and prepared to deliver death.

"You're of no use to us if you're unwilling," said Ciara. "So, choose—join us, or wait here for the dissenters to find you, or give yourself the release you desire. For how many years did you hope one man could change the world, Hugh? That the world could be better than it is? That humanity could be better? Now is your chance to lead them."

Hugh peered out at the smoke blotting away the city. The building on 40th continued to burn, but as best Hugh could tell from so far away, his mission had gone unscathed. He lifted the gun, its grip cold in his sweating palm, and tested its heft. He struggled to quiet his inner turmoil and make space for the sensation Ciara described, the feeling of knowing what lurked beyond his senses. Was something there? Enlightenment or void? He probed the darkness of his own heart, the regions he had long ago shut off and forgotten. If it were to be found at all, it would be found within him.

Gunshots cracked in the corridor. On the monitor screen, the dissenters closed in on the wide oak door of the conference room.

"We have seconds," said Lucy. Ciara raised a hand to silence her.

She knelt before Hugh and placed her fingers on either side of his face to direct his eyes toward hers. "I can help you."

Hugh stared into the depths of her eyes. He barely heard the rising commotion beyond the door. He floated downward through the black clouds of depression that had suffused him these last few years, swam past the pain that had driven him to lash out in violence. The mists parted lazily and beneath them lay more darkness, solid, unyielding, icy. A gentle force urged him on. Ciara.

A heavy object slammed against the entrance. Lucy and Suez drew their weapons and dashed across the room. Other Reckoners clambered in from a side passage, bracing themselves for the assault. The door bucked on its hinges.

Hugh tested the barrier that contained him. His weakness left him stunned. The barrier felt rock solid and immovable, like the weight of all history pressing the doors of hope shut tight day after day, week after week, year after year for decades and centuries, its weight measured in the tragedies and failures of every man and woman who had ever lived.

Ciara leaned close. "Stop lying to yourself, Hugh. You know it's there."

She was right. He knew. So far away that he could hardly discern it, a tiny spark flickered in the black field that consumed him. He gravitated toward it.

The door crashed down and dissenters poured in. They screamed and fired an indiscriminate wave of projectiles into the room. They had crushed their rage for too long, fought too hard for this moment, and they meant to make their fury known. Lucy and Suez led the defense, closing with the intruders to beat them back and stop them. Better armed and trained than their attackers, they stalled the onslaught, but they could hold only until sheer numbers overran them.

Hugh seized on the flickering will o' the wisp that had never left him, but that he had long suppressed. The darkness eroded as the light radiated outward, warmed him and flowed through every part of his being until it had seared clean the last remnants of the despair to which he had succumbed and the anger he had permitted to take root. It singed away all doubt. Once again, he looked out on the world through a child's eyes, innocent and full of desire for perfection. He had tried to discard that light many times over the years. Every time he made excuses for the failures of others. Every time he accepted less from someone he knew could achieve more. Every time he made allowances in the name of mercy for greed or sloth or envy or myriad other sins. He had pushed it away time and again, but it had never abandoned him. His denial had held him back from understanding the power of people's connection to him, obscured how deep ran the voids they used him to fill.

It had been locked away inside him for years, his secret conviction he was better than those he helped, superior to those who gave any less than he did. That belief's power flooded through him. For the first time in years, he felt might accomplish what he had set out to do. Punishing Mackie Neusted had been a first faltering step toward a new destiny, for him, for the Reckoners. Hugh opened his eyes, his face afloat with joy he had not felt in seven decades. Ciara's stark, infinite expression offered confirmation of everything he experienced.

Then a shadow fell across her.

Could this be his punishment? The distortion of all he had lived for. Sentencing him to their service in whatever unimaginable plans they harbored for the city? Could they intend to degrade him and all his work until they declared him redeemed and let him die? For a moment Hugh existed in perfect neutral balance, poised between crumbling doubt and precipitous belief, his soul exposed.

Something dark blasted through the air in a blur.

Ciara's head snapped sideways. Dark fluid sprayed from her shattered skull. It stained her long, light hair and sent a warm splatter into Hugh's face. She collapsed onto the floor. As Hugh watched the unimaginable glory fade from Ciara's eyes, all his doubts leapt into overwhelming clarity. His perception of the world transformed, ripping away his uncertainty and fear, roof shingles torn loose by a hurricane.

He saw the stains of corruption infesting the dissenters—savage men who would hold back the world, forever clouded by the shadows of their fear, primed to lash out at any who dared otherwise. He perceived the absolute wrongness of Ciara's death at their hands. He recognized the undeniable need to answer it.

He lunged to his feet, raised the gun at the dissenters, and squeezed the trigger.

Shots exploded like thunder erupting from every part of his thin, weary body.

Outside, pyres flickered, flashing lights battled darkness, and weapons sparked. Their illumination etched apt prelude to the new dream Hugh Carter would bring to the world.

Brides of Fire

"I won't marry the volcano! Too smoky, too hot," Queo said.

When it came to choosing a husband, my sister had an answer for everything.

My mother shook her head and frowned, her deft hands shucking corn, building a mound of husks on the dirt floor of my family's thatched-roof *ruca*. "You're almost eighteen. You aren't getting any younger. All the young men will be snatched up. Then the volcano will be your only option if you don't want to be a man's second wife and have no say in your household."

"What about Huenu?" My father stood by the door, late sunlight gleaming in the sweat painted on his skin by toiling in the fields, where my older brothers remained, working the last of the daylight. "He's kind, and his family owns many goats."

Queo glanced up from slicing greens for our stew. "And Huenu resembles them. No, he is not for me."

"Maiten, then, a good hunter," mother said.

"Who always smells like blood and wild hogs."

"Antiman likes you, and his family has good land," father said.

"Did you forget Antiman once threw a snake at me when we were children? He's cruel, and I don't like his laugh."

Mother sighed. "Then it must be Pehuen."

"An imbecile who gets lost whenever he's out of sight of our village? Never."

My father sighed. "No one's perfect. You have many suitors, but if you don't pick one you may spend your wedding night sleeping on a bed of hot lava. Nothing you can do about it."

"Not nothing!" My grandmother's voice crackled with age. She sat warming herself by the *kutral* with a blanket of bright fibers shawled across her shoulders. She had looked asleep, and she startled me so much I spun in a circle three times, slapped my feet together, and then landed with my legs crossed. Grandmother showed us her wrinkled, gap-toothed smile. She lifted her knobby hands, made a ring of her index finger and thumb with one, and then poked in and out of it with her other index finger. In a sing-song voice, she said, "Volcano only likes *maidens*."

"Enough of that! You're awful," mother said.

"Would you ruin our family honor? Queo must become a respectable wife so she can care for us when we are old and useless like you," said father

My grandmother snorted and slapped her hands together.

With only ten summers to my name, I took the circle of my grandmother's fingers for the loop of a rope snare, and her pointing finger a husband or the volcano spirit. I didn't understand how using a trap to solve my sister's problem might taint our family honor, but I didn't question it. After all, we lived in troubled times.

Mount Antu stirred again, a new and frightening experience for anyone my age.

The ground beneath our village trembled almost daily, and the volcano's burning throat spewed a pillar of chalky smoke into the ashen sky. These objects of terror obsessed everyone in my village, especially the maidens like my sister Queo. Our *machi* said the volcano rumbled and roiled because it desired new wives to end its loneliness. Our people renewed offerings to its spirt, the *cherufe,* granting it goats and crops, dancing and singing in its honor, even spilling precious metals and gems into its fiery crater. We hoped to soothe it but kept our expectations low. My people may have held off an Incan invasion, but volcanoes always seemed to beat us. Before my birth our village sat in the shadow of the mountain's north side until the volcano—unhappy with past sacrifices— vomited hot ash and lava to ruin it. The Mapuche who lived in our region prayed to *Ngenechen,* the lord of the people, to make the *cherufe* more grateful this time, but like pent-up anger, fire and heat sometimes spewed out uncontrollably.

"Ignore your grandmother," mother told Queo. She threw a sharp glare at her tiny, old mother. "She envies your youth or she wouldn't make such a ridiculous suggestion."

"There is Quidel or his brother Yaco, whose fields produce the finest corn. Or Nahuel, who pulls many fish from the river. He's quite handsome," said father.

"Then you marry him if you think so! Quidel is bowlegged. Yaco is missing two fingers. Nahuel stinks of fish and his hands are always covered with fish scales. I don't want my husband to touch me with fish scale hands."

Exasperated, mother ceased shucking. "Be reasonable, tiny flower. The *cherufe* has taken three brides yet still the mountain growls and fumes. You were one of the lucky ones when we chose number four yesterday, but will you be so lucky next time or the time after that? You think after Piro was picked to marry the volcano, her family expected her sister Ipi to be the very next chosen? Bad luck happens. Wait and see if the *cherufe*'s new wife doesn't satisfy him, and then you can take your chances again. Is that what you want?"

Queo jumped to her feet and slapped her hand on the low table. "Stop asking me to settle for bow-legged dirt-diggers and fish scales! I will marry only the perfect husband. My family should want nothing but the best for me."

"Please, Queo, the volcano," father said, but Queo's shriek of frustration cut him off.

Queo fled our *ruca*, leaving my parents speechless. My grandmother made the loop-and-poke gesture again and laughed until it became a loud, hacking cough.

I ran after Queo. "Where are you going?"

"To see the *machi*. The perfect husband exists, maybe as close as the next village. I only need time to find him. I have to make sure I don't marry the fire before then."

"There are many maidens in our village. Maybe you'll never be chosen," I said.

Queo stopped and held my shoulders. "But I will. And soon. On the first night a hot glow creased the mountaintop, I went to the *machi* and traded chores for a prophecy. She told me if I don't soon marry, I will become a bride of fire. Do you want that to happen to your own loving sister?"

I shook my head, jogged in place, and waved my arms. "No, no, no!"

"Then don't try to stop me."

"I'll come with you. I'll help you."

I ran to keep pace with Queo. Her legs, longer than mine and fueled by determination, carried her swiftly across the village. At the *machi*'s hut, we waited, silent and anxious. I tried hard to stand still, but after only a few seconds I found myself hopping in place and spinning around twice on every fourth hop. After a little wait, the *machi* emerged and grinned at us from the shadow of her shaman's post, carved with steps and shelves for offerings. She invited us inside her *ruca*, where we sat on the cool dirt floor.

"You want a husband," the *machi* said to Queo.

Queo bowed her head. "The *perfect* husband. I want time to find him."

"The man of your dreams? He exists. You won't find him going from village to village, searching high and low. You aren't a chief's daughter who must marry a certain way."

"How will I find him?"

"When you understand the nature of perfection, you will know where to look."

Queo groaned. "How long will that take? I need the perfect man now. The village might marry me to the *cherufe*."

The *machi*'s brow creased. "A difficult problem, especially since your time *is* coming. Ipi shall become *cherufe*'s fourth wife tomorrow. You may not be chosen next, but soon. *Cherufe* is stubborn and will demand many wives in exchange for sparing our village. There's only one thing you can do. I've offered this to other maidens, but none have been brave enough to try it."

"Anything! What is it?" Queo said.

"Hmm, no, you may find it too frightening."

"No, I won't. I promise! Please tell me. Please!"

"You know what *cherufe* does to brides who displease him?"

"Yes," Queo said, her enthusiasm fading.

I shuddered, slapped my knees, and then wrapped my arms around my shoulders and shook three times. My mother had told me the stories. "If *cherufe* doesn't like a bride, he shoots her flaming head into the sky on a streak of hot lava and returns her to her village. Horrible!"

The *machi* nodded, "Horrible, indeed, but also an opportunity. If you catch the head of a spurned bride of fire, it may tell you the *cherufe's* secret desire. Then you will know how to quiet the volcano. Do that and you'll have all the time you want to find a husband and your pick of grateful men too."

Queo gasped. "I can't! I'll be burned up."

"That could happen. If you're brave enough and sincere about trying, though, I'll help."

"I'll do anything to get the perfect husband. I'm fearless."

The *machi* weighed my sister's words. "Very well." She walked to a shelf and grasped a water skin, which she handed to Queo. "Rub this oil onto an animal hide, and the hide cannot burn. Catch the flaming head in the hide. Put the oil on your hands to protect them. But do not drink it. It's serious poison."

Queo stared at the water skin in her hands. "Is this truly possible?"

"Anything is possible if the gods favor it," the *machi* said.

"Thank you," Queo said.

She stood and bowed. I somersaulted then sprang up beside her with a twist and a hop.

"When this is done, I'll come and clean for you," Queo said.

"No. You did plenty for me last time." The *machi* looked at me. "But *you*, boy, *you* must come see me soon about your belly frogs."

At age three I swallowed two young frogs, who grew up in my stomach and produced more frogs. All of them bouncing around inside me made me jump and dance, so I could never sit or stand still for very long. The *machi* tried for years to trick them out of me, but they seemed quite content in my innards. I hopped three times then danced in place.

"Okay. Yes. I'll come."

"Good." The *machi* gestured toward the door. "Now, go. Be brave!"

We left the *ruca*, and soon Queo stopped and gave me a fierce look.

"You cannot tell mother and father about this. They won't like it," she said.

"Will you really try to catch a fiery head?"

"I must if I am to wed the perfect husband."

Queo's determination frightened me. I imagined the fiery head of a rejected bride soaring through the air, growing giant sized, its wide, gaping mouth full of glowing teeth spread apart to devour my sister. I couldn't let her face such a terror alone. "I'll go with you."

"No, it's too dangerous."

"Ayah, ayah, ayah," I shouted.

I danced in a circle around Queo, clapping my hands, twisting like a swimming lizard. My sister walked again. I followed, dancing and shouting.

"Stop that," she said.

I ignored her. "Ayah, ayah, ayah," I cried, even louder.

"I said, 'Stop that.' You're bugging me."

I raised my voice and danced harder, having long ago learned to use my frog restlessness to get what I wanted: People agreed to almost anything to end such an annoyance.

She stopped. "All right, all right! You can come. Just be still."

"Yay!" I threw myself on the ground, tumbled head over heels, and bounced up facing her. "What's the plan?"

"Tomorrow Ipi marries the volcano. After dark, we take an animal hide, prepare it with the *machi*'s oil, and hope the *cherufe* spits out Ipi's head."

"Ipi is a bossy loudmouth, almost as bad as her sister. That's why the village chose her to marry the volcano. *Cherufe* will be eager to get rid of her."

My sister smacked the side of my head. "What if the volcano likes bossy loudmouths? Hmm? You think of that? Volcanoes *are* bossy loudmouths. Maybe they like their own kind."

"Oh, no, do you think that's true? It would be bad for you."

"Oh. Yes, it would," Queo said, as if she hadn't thought of that. "Let's hope Ipi is too much, even for a volcano."

That night excitement drove sleep from me. Several times, I paced around the *ruca*. My mother shouted at me to go back to bed. My father threatened to work me in the field until I tired so much I would sleep for a week. My brothers threw rocks at me. Even grandmother piped up, reminding us all that if I simply swallowed a large snake, as she had often suggested, it would eat my belly frogs and end my dancing and jumping. She never told us what would become of the snake afterward, though. Afraid it would stay and make me slither, I ignored her advice. When I finally slept, I dreamt of the burning heads of maidens squawking like parrots and flitting around a black-orange sky on fiery wings. Queo flew with them, eyes burning, still seeking her perfect husband.

At dawn I woke up sweating and ran outside to pee.

Ipi's wedding occurred that morning. The whole village turned out, and the *machi* banged a rhythm on her *kultrung* while she performed the ceremony. We sang and danced out of a sense of duty and fear, and I longed for more joyful gatherings, like *Nquillatun*, the festival of the land. Before noon, the *machi* and a group of elders escorted Ipi up the volcano. Everyone else returned home or to the fields and tried not to think about her. Queo's plan weighed on my mind, making the day drag on forever. The evening and the night passed painfully slow. After dark, I lay on my mat and waited for my family to fall into a deep sleep. Only when they all snored loudly did Queo come, clutching the *machi's* water skin and one of my grandmother's dusty jaguar hides.

"Grandmother will be mad," I said.

"She'll never notice it missing," said Queo.

The ground outside our *ruca* shivered, probably because Ipi and the volcano were already arguing. I worried no flaming head would fly for Queo to catch. Spirits behaved in unpredictable ways, especially hot-tempered ones. So far the *cherufe* had not declined any of his new brides. We climbed the steep slope at the foot of the volcano then ascended the incline toward its distant, glowing peak. Night creatures filled the darkness with chirping, buzzing, and hooting. Ghostly illumination brightened the land, lava light reflected by ash clouds spreading across the sky. Without warning, the ground shook hard. Queo and I grabbed onto trees to keep from falling down. When the tremors calmed, we continued, hoping only to get close enough to the volcano to catch Ipi's head before it burned out. Several times the ground jolted. I couldn't tell if my wild dancing came from my belly frogs or the bouncing, rocking earth. A third of the way up, the earthquake grew so severe Queo and I stopped dead.

She spread out the jaguar hide, and rubbed the *machi's* oil onto it, keeping plenty on her hands. Then she shoved the water skin at me to hold.

"This spot is as good as any to wait," she said.

The top of the volcano brightened with pulsing white-orange light smeared with streaks of ash. Little eruptions and the hiss of steam drowned out the animal voices. A terrifying tremor shook screams from our throats, then all other sounds ended. Startled birds fled into the darkness. A rain of fire pelted us. Queo and I clutched each other until echoes of the awful sound faded. A high, whiny shriek replaced them.

"That sounds like Ipi! Do you see her?" Queo said.

She stared at the sky, swirling with orange and black streaks, brightened by shooting stars of smoking lava. I wanted to douse myself with the *machi's* oil, but I feared its poison.

"There!" Queo shouted.

She ran, and I dashed after her.

Ipi's voice grew louder, closer, but I couldn't see her among the flaming debris ejected by the volcano. I focused on following Queo as she cut right and bolted up a hill.

"There, there!" she said.

Ipi's fiery head plunged from the petulant sky. Her mouth hung wide, her teeth seethed like windblown embers, and a piercing shriek fled her lips. Remembering my dream, I feared she might eat Queo, but then my sister leapt into the air, unfurling the jaguar hide. Ipi thumped into it and then collided with Queo, knocking her to the ground. Queo tumbled but held tight, wrapping the hide until only a little light from Ipi's fire leaked out.

"You got her," I said.

"I got her," Queo said.

I spun around and danced. Queo danced with me as best she could with her arms full. A little blob of lava streaked along my back and I yelped. Fire still fell. We fled, but no matter how fast we raced or what direction we ran, we couldn't escape the firestorm. At a trail I knew, I grabbed Queo's arm and led her down the path to a cave, where the fire could not reach us.

"That was close," I said.

"I'm glad you remembered this cave," said Queo.

She placed her bundle on a rock ledge then undid the jaguar-hide wrapping. Ipi stared at us. Dancing fire replaced her hair, and her face burned with inner heat. Her eyes gleamed, hot coals beneath lashes of sparks. Wisps of flame spurted from her nostrils and mouth, and curls of smoke leaked from her ears. Her head had been severed mid-neck. Veils of heat shimmered from her, making us sweat.

"Who do you think you are to smother me like that?" Ipi said. "This old jaguar hide is soaked with something stinky. Take me back and put me where I belong. You can't go around snatching people's heads in the night. My husband is unhappy with the Mapuche people. You're ruining his message to them."

"That's why we caught you, Ipi. We want to make *cherufe* happy. The *machi* said you can tell us his secret desire. Then I won't have to worry about marrying him like you," Queo said.

"*You* marry *my* husband? Don't make me laugh. You're not good enough for him. He would spit out your head after one look at your skinny legs and stringy hair."

"Why did he spit *you* out, Ipi?" I said.

Ipi glared at me, and her fire brightened. "My sister! She turned him against me. She saw he would love me more, that I would be his most honored wife, but she wanted that for herself. She tricked *cherufe*, and he sent me away."

"I'm very sorry. If you tell us what the *cherufe* wants then we can save the village and our families," said Queo.

"Why should I betray my husband's secrets? What's in it for me?"

Queo and I looked at each other, at a loss for what to offer.

"What do you want?" Queo said.

"Go into the volcano and bring my sister here to me. Then I'll tell you. I can live apart from my husband if my sister is with me. It's only fair she pays for betraying me."

"Go into the volcano? No, no, no," I said.

I hopped across the floor, clapping my hands, and bounced myself off the cave walls.

"Stop that! Why are you doing that? Stand still, you crazy boy," Ipi said.

"Don't you yell at my brother. He can't help it. He has frogs in his belly."

"It's very irritating," said Ipi.

"If we retrieve your sister, you promise to tell me *cherufe*'s secret desire?"

Flame trickled from the corners of Ipi's smile. "Yes, yes, I promise."

"Then I'll do it," Queo said.

My sister wanted to go alone, but I refused to stay behind by myself with Ipi. I couldn't let Queo sneak into the volcano without help, especially not after she stood up to Ipi for me. Ipi told us a secret way into the *cherufe*'s cave so we would avoid the climb to the volcano's peak. More aftershocks rippled the ground as we walked, but at least fire and lava had stopped raining down. We came to the hidden entrance of a cave-tunnel sloped down into the mountain. Hot air scented with the stink of char and warm soil wafted from it. Orange light flashed deep within its throat like the door to the *nag-mapu* itself.

"Let's go home," I said to Queo.

"Have you turned against me? I said you didn't have to come."

"No, but it looks dangerous and very fiery, like the entrance to the underworld."

"No doubt it will be. But I told the *machi* I would be fearless, and the *machi* doesn't help liars. Would you make me into a liar because you're afraid?"

"No."

"Then let's go."

Queo entered the cave and started the descent.

I hopped from one foot to another, clapped my hands, and then dropped to my knees, frog-hopped twice, and ran into the tunnel to catch up. The secret entrance provided a true shortcut. Soon we stood at the edge of a vast, steamy cavern speckled with lava pools and red-and-white-hot rocks. Slicks of sweat coated our skin and dripped into our eyes. The *cherufe* slept on a bed of coals, a fearsome, powerful giant, even lying down. Embers and puffs of gray smoke blasted from his nostrils when he snored. Near him a row of rock shelves carved into the cave wall overlooked a smoking pit. The flaming heads of the *cherufe*'s brides filled the shelves. The cloud rising from the pit veiled them with gray mist. Every so often it shot up in powerful blasts. When its heat touched the wives, they screamed and yelped, making strange, melancholy music, an old tune of the people, passed down through generations, sometimes sung late at night by the elders. Missing notes matched gaps on the shelves, where the *cherufe* reserved places to add brides and complete his chorus.

"Is that why he takes so many wives? Is he looking for the voices that make the right note? Is *cherufe* a music lover?" I asked Queo.

Queo didn't answer, awestruck by what she saw. Then the *cherufe* huffed and rolled over in his sleep, revealing his fiery manhood.

Queo gasped and paled.

"Whoa, Cherufe could pee a river of fire," I said.

Queo smacked my head. "Shut up. Wait here while I get Ipi's sister."

Queo picked a clear path across the cavern, winding between bubbling lava and burning stones. The brides of fire watched her clamber over a pile of fallen rocks, and as she scrambled down the far side, they called to her.

"What are you doing? Who are you? What do you want?" they said.

"Be quiet. Do you want to wake the *cherufe* and get me burned up?"

"Why shouldn't we wake our husband? Why are you here?"

"Piro's sister sent me," Queo said.

"Ipi!" said Piro, third head in on the fourth shelf up from the bottom. "I thought I was rid of that jealous cow. What does she want?"

"To see you again. She's sorry she was mean and wants to apologize," Queo said.

Piro scowled. "How do you know?"

"She told me. My brother and I found her head when it fell."

With the jaguar hide stretched before her, Queo stepped toward Piro.

"What are you doing? Stay away from me!" Piro said

Queo threw the hide over Piro, wrapped her snug, and yanked her from her shelf. The other brides shrieked. The smoke pit boiled. Jets of hot moisture streaked up from it. All the fires in the brides fattened, brightening the cavern.

The brides cried out: "Now we will sing. When our husband hears Piro's note missing, he will wake up and burn you. Thief! Thief!"

Queo stood at the foot of the rock pile when the brides wailed. Their ancient tune, sad and haunting like the whispers of wandering ghosts filled the cavern. They missed many notes, including Piro's now. At the silent beat her voice failed to fill, the *cherufe* stopped snoring.

"Run, Queo!" I yelled.

Queo dug into the crooked places among the fallen stones and pulled herself toward the top of the rock pile, moving at a crawl with Piro's head tucked under one arm. She would never make it. The *cherufe* rose. Steam and smoke blew from his shoulders. His body shed scales of semi-cool, molten rock as he stretched. Standing over us his heat birthed a harsh wind, and his burning manhood seemed even larger and more monstrous. Squinting against the light and heat, Queo scurried down the rock jumble, keeping to the shadows the *cherufe's* light created.

91

He looked groggy, but it didn't take him long to spot Queo. He watched her as if amazed to find an intruder in his home then raised one lava-cracked hand to grab her.

I sat on a low stone and rubbed oil from the *machi*'s water skin onto the soles of my feet. Then I jumped up and slapped my belly to wake my frogs. Soon they had me dancing all over the place, but even if I landed on a hot rock or splashed the edge of a lava puddle, my feet did not burn, thanks to the *machi*'s very potent oil. I aimed myself toward the *cherufe*, singing nonsense words.

"Wu, wu, waponi, wu!" I called out.

I threw a rock at him. He forgot Queo for a moment and stared at me. His eyes widened and flickered as he crouched for a closer look. I danced harder, slapping my tummy to rile up the frogs. They went wild. I hopped and bounced like a flea, jogging everywhere, leaping stones, dancing across lava spills. *Cherufe* didn't know what to make of me.

"Wu, wu, wu, big wu!" I yelled.

From the corner of my eye, I saw Queo descend the rock pile and rush back along the clear path. I whirled and skipped, made animal moves, squawked and howled like beasts. The *cherufe* must have thought he dreamt or hallucinated me. He rubbed his head.

Queo was by the entrance to the shortcut. I danced my way in that direction, and when I came close enough, I bowed to the *cherufe*. Then I ran.

Queo and I made it halfway up the shortcut before the *cherufe* roared.

The mountain shuddered with his massive footsteps.

The light in the tunnel intensified.

The *cherufe* chased us.

Queo and I raced out from the mountainside and ran. Queo hugged Piro's head to her chest with both arms. The mountain shook, making it hard to stay on our feet, but soon we returned to the cave trail, and before long found ourselves hidden in the cave with Ipi.

"Is that Piro? Piro, are you under there?" she said.

Piro's muffled voice replied from within the jaguar hide.

Queo unraveled the wrapping and set Piro beside her sister.

"Now," Queo said. "Tell me the *cherufe*'s secret desire."

Ipi couldn't answer. Piro let loose with a string of scolding insults and complaints so loud they made it impossible for her sister to speak a word. I had never heard such ugly words so full of venom. They came so fast from Piro's burning mouth that she spat little jets of fire with them. Queo tried to shout her down, but Piro wouldn't stop. Ipi frowned. Her expression deepened with each new insult, until she burst out with a shriek and spit nasty words back at her sister. Their fires jumped and flared and filled the small cavern with flashes of light and heat. Queo could not get through to them. Not even my hopping and nonsense shouts could get their attention. Then Piro stretched her mouth as wide as she could and tried to hit Ipi with her steaming, bubbling tongue. If they'd still had bodies, they would've been thrashing each other in a flaming catfight. At this rate, they wouldn't stop until they burned out. Then Queo would never learn what the *cherufe* wanted.

"It will be morning soon. Then mother and father will know we've been gone," I said to Queo.

"I have to separate them." Queo took up the jaguar hide. It was nearly dry; the *machi*'s oil had boiled away from being wrapped around Ipi and then Piro. "Give me the water skin."

I handed the almost-empty skin to Queo. The cave shook. Dust and bits of stone rained onto us.

"What was that?" I said.

"The *cherufe* is almost here." Queo said.

Another jolt rocked the ground. Queo and I fell over, and Queo dropped the water skin. She scrambled to retrieve it, but the cavern filled with light and heat. From the cave entrance, the *cherufe* roared, quaking the air with a blast of hot lava breath. Queo clutched the water skin in one hand, while she used her other to spread the jaguar hide.

"He's coming! Look!" I shouted.

Lava trickled into the cave, a creeping stream of it.

"I need more time!" Queo said.

I felt sad for Queo, but I grabbed her hand and dragged her deeper into the cave. Again, the *cherufe* roared, and everything trembled. Ipi and Piro stopped fighting and fell silent. I led Queo to a craggy cave wall, where we climbed to a ledge near the ceiling and huddled like nesting birds. The *cherufe* crammed his huge body into the cave. Lava flowed from between his toes, covering the floor and rising. It sent the old jaguar hide up in flames. The heat rose fast, and it became hard to breathe. Queo and I sweated so much we looked like we'd just walked out of the river. Queo opened the water skin, poured some oil onto her hands, and then handed me the skin. She spread the oil over her arms and legs, down to her feet, and up beneath her dress, all over her body.

"There's only enough. Use it, quick," she said.

I poured oil into my hand.

I was afraid it would poison me, but I knew *cherufe* would burn me up.

I rubbed the oil all over then took the skin and tipped it, pouring the last drops onto my hair. At the same time, the *cherufe* shrugged and twisted, bumping the cavern, jarring me, and I poured five drops straight into my mouth.

"Ahh! Poison!" I said.

Queo stared at me, horrified. She snatched the skin away.

"Why did you do that?" she said.

"I didn't mean to," I said.

Right away, a twisting, bubbling feeling churned my stomach.

I groaned. Queo gestured for me to keep quiet.

The *cherufe* looked in our direction. We flattened ourselves against the wall. He inched closer. One huge, burning hand reached up. Its red fingertips scraped the lip of the rock ledge. He could almost reach us. I clamped a hand over my mouth. My stomach ached, and my body tingled as the poison worked through me. I wanted to scream or cry, but if I made a sound, then *cherufe* would find us. Even if I died, I wanted Queo to escape. The ache in my guts overwhelmed me. I doubled over. As I bent, a loud blast of gas blurted from my rear. *Cherufe's* fingers hesitated then crept toward me. I wanted to throw myself over the ledge to distract him from Queo, but I couldn't move. Nausea and pain filled up my body. The inside-out feeling in my belly wracked me. I dropped to my knees to throw up with a wriggling, tickling sensation rising up my throat. Something large and solid squeezed into the back of my mouth, wiggling over my tongue. My mouth stretched wide, and a full-grown frog pushed its way out between my lips. It hopped onto the stone in front of me. A second one followed it. My body convulsed, and then there came a group of small frogs, one by one, until the entire frog family vacated my belly. Right away, my stomach settled, and I felt better. The frogs squatted in front of me, making frog noises, and hopping over each other. Queo stared at me, astonished. Then *cherufe's* hand stretched closer to us. In seconds, he would grab us. I slapped the ground behind the frogs and blew on them. Queo did the same. We goaded them toward the edge, dodging *cherufe's* fingers, and then the frogs hopped into the air. They spiraled down in an awkward stream that landed in the *cherufe's* left eye. Each frog vanished in the fire with a puff of frog smoke. The *cherufe* snatched back his hand and rubbed his eye.

Piro's shrill voice came from across the cavern: "What are you doing with those frogs? Are you a child? I didn't marry a child. I married a husband. Get over here and act like one."

Ipi joined in: "We're cooling off too much in this filthy cave. My neck is sore. We have work to do, a household to run. How do you expect anything to get done when you let us be stolen away then play with frogs instead of taking us home?"

The *cherufe* crossed the cavern. Queo and I collapsed against the wall, relieved.

I didn't understand everything that Piro, Ipi, and the *cherufe* said to each other, but I didn't need to. The sisters' voices grew louder and shriller while the *cherufe's* roar became lower and weaker, until the cave barely trembled when he spoke. Despite their arguing, the two sisters didn't want to be separated. They demanded the *cherufe* take them *both* back to the volcano.

"How can they want to go back to that cave?" Queo whispered. "How can they want to be with him?"

I shrugged. "He's their husband."

"How can they be happy with him?"

"What choice do they have?" I said. "They're married. Nobody's perfect, right?"

Queo gave me a funny look then and said nothing more.

Cherufe and his brides argued a long while and the cavern rumbled and echoed with their voices, but in the end, the *cherufe* relented. Lifting Ipi and Piro in his fiery hand, he carried them away. Queo and I hid until we heard his footsteps fade out. We fled the cave while the *machi*'s oil still protected us. Lava puddled everywhere and splashed up onto us, but we reached the trail unhurt. The horizon lightened as the sun prepared to rise. We raced home, arriving at our *ruca* only minutes before our parents awoke.

After that, Mount Antu settled. Its black plume and night brightness died out.

Four days later, Queo married Nahuel, and never mind the fish scales.

I never went back to see the *machi* about my belly frogs.

My sister spoke to anyone who would listen of all I had done for her, and years later when my time to marry came, I had my pick of brides.

Super-Villain Showcase #53: "Enter the Deep Loa"

"All life springs from the *Deep* Loa." Steadying himself with the Staff of Carrefour, a seven-foot length of gnarled cypress, Doctor Bocor nodded at the four-story memorial statue of Omni-Guardian. His faded Haitian accent lent his words a lyrical rhythm. "The simple truth is the *Deep* Loa be the ones who write our fates and draw our destinies. Everything in life comes from them."

Dodger, Omni-Guardian's grieving partner, shook his head. "Sure, Doc, those Loa of yours are powerful. That's why I hired you to resurrect Omni again," he said. "But they aren't everything. There are other gods. And there's *science*—and that trumps everything."

They stood on a scaffolding stage erected for Omni-Guardian's memorial in Goodman Park. Opposite them, lit by red, white, and blue floodlights, the statue jutted from a parade of funereal wreaths twined with silk ribbons and glittering condolences. Every detail of the fallen hero's features and iconic costume lived in the sculpted granite, capturing not only his likeness but the raw bravado of his classic salute: right fist raised overhead, left arm bent ninety degrees, left fist poised beside his chest as he gazed upward. A familiar pose whenever Omni-Guardian leapt into action. Frozen forever in stone. For the fifth—or was it the sixth, or maybe seventh time? Doctor Bocor had lost track. He laughed, blending amusement and contempt.

"Don't speak to me about science and gods. I have Ph.Ds in applied theology, quantum physics, and xenobiology. You best listen when I tell you all the different worlds and universes spring from the *Deep* Loa. I learned that truth by my Gran'mama's knee in a Port-au-Prince slum when I was younger than you look." Doctor Bocor squinted. "And speaking of youth, that three-piece suit hanging off you makes you look even younger than those silly armored tights you wear on patrol."

"Hell's wheels, Doc, the tights are part of my uniform. People expect it," Dodger said. "And I'm *not* young. You know that."

"I said 'look,' didn't I? Quit griping. Most folks would kill for immortality and eternal youth."

"Not if they were trapped being fifteen forever."

Though worse fates came to mind, Doctor Bocor said, "Maybe. But that's talk for another day. Time I did what I came here to do."

He unbuttoned his overcoat, unveiling a diamond-eyed, gold skull on a silver chain above a line of fetish pouches hanging from his neck. He positioned each pouch over his black silk suit and tie. His magic sparked. Impatient, like him. He had bristled in the shadows, waiting for the service to end and the crowd of mourners to clear the park, and then as if they meant to torture him, the heroes—Omni-Guardian's best friends—had lingered afterward for a private wake. The fliers, the powerhouses, and the runners. The men with iron skin, and the women with starfuel in their souls. The alien athletes and extra-dimensional wizards. The physics experiments gone improbably right. The living machines and cyborg psychics.

And, of course, Shadow Hand.

The night champion.

Omni-Guardian's oldest friend had stayed longest.

Only a mere man—and yet so much more than all the others and their powers combined because of what he embodied: the ultimate human potential fulfilled.

Doctor Bocor had faced and fought every one of them over the years, failing only when they ganged up against him—which they always, inevitably did. Had they known he lurked so near while they bid their final farewells, they'd have come after him in an angry, united wave. But the Loa had concealed him. The power of the traditional Loa had been enough for that, as it would suffice for the work ahead. He only need call on the *Deep* Loa when he required real power. The time for that would come soon enough. He clapped his hands, stamped his staff on the stage boards, and spit out a burst of Haitian Creole and mystical patois that baffled Dodger.

The air around Doctor Bocor swam with tiny flares of light. A hum rose from behind the stage curtains. It grew to an urgent whine before becoming a low roar like a dozen industrial fans blowing, reaching a manic pitch when a cloud of robot drones streamed into sight, their Frisbee-sized bodies blinking green, mystical energies. They jerked through the air like frenzied bats then glided out over the empty folding chairs and litter left by the crowd. Deploying vacuum hoses, infrared sensors, and magical receptors, the drones scanned the seats… the ground… the trash. They dipped down to snatch up bits and pieces, like kingfishers diving for food, hoovering the detritus into waiting compartments.

Dodger eyed the drones with suspicion. "Those gadgets really work? I mean, the last time you used actual zombies."

The furrows of Doctor Bocor's brow deepened. "Of course, they work. Did you call me because my juju might *not* work? Hell, no. You call me because my juju *always* work, bless and thank the Loa. Baron Samedi, lord of cemeteries and night, got no fear of technology. A single zombified brain—blessed by the Baron, divided among my drones—makes them work together with one mind. Their cybernetic sensors tell them where to find fallen scraps of hair, or dried-up tears and saliva on blades of grass. Or even DNA traces in flakes of dead skin. All the people's grief sprinkled there like morning dew for me to collect and weave into a potent fetish to do the thing you're paying me to do." Doctor Bocor tipped the Staff of Carrefour at Dodger and flashed a broad smile full of aged but bright teeth. "That be, if you don't stiff me again."

"Stiff you—? Twisting tornadoes, Doc, it only happened once. In 1968! That was only because Knuckle Duster tried to heist my armored car. You still got your dough, only a little late. Haven't you ever heard of forgive and forget?"

"Forgive, maybe. I forget nothing."

"Ah, don't sweat it. You'll get your green. Omni Corp is flush. It's all electronic any—" Dodger recoiled from a buzzing drone. He shifted to a defensive stance. "What in Sam Hill?" The voodoo robot hovered eye-to-eye with him, then vacuumed a wisp of hair from his shoulder before it flittered away.

"You're not off limits, are you?" Doctor Bocor cocked an eyebrow.

"You should've warned me is all."

With a dismissive hiss, Doctor Bocor said, "No harm to you."

Dodger sighed then sat and dangled his feet over the edge of the stage.

"I shouldn't complain," he said. "It should be me buried down there. If I hadn't followed Omni onto that airship in 1932, I'd be nothing but dust by now, and maybe that's how it should have been. If I'd died on Radu Island, none of this would be necessary."

"Radu is long gone," Doctor Bocor said. "Obliterated by nuclear testing."

"Doesn't matter. The Zenith Stone was a one-time deal. When its rays struck me instead of Omni, *I* walked away immortal instead of *him*. So unfair. The world needs him. Nobody needs me."

"Omni-Guardian needs you," Doctor Bocor said. "Who'd be president of Omni Corp if not you? Omni got no time for licensing deals and spinning his image, no time for lawyers and contracts. True heroes can't be about the money."

"Even without Omni Corp, he'd still be a hero. But without him, I'm just an average slob. If I don't bring him back that's all I'll ever be until the dang-blasted sun burns out."

Dodger dropped to the grass and approached Omni's statue.

Limping a bit, leaning on his staff, Doctor Bocor followed. He wheezed, stifling a cough, feeling his age, the cold, and the fatigue of controlling his drones. He sensed their work nearing completion. Good. He wanted to go home. Pray to the Loa—the *Deep* Loa, who existed beyond the Loa of his childhood, the gods above gods, the gods the traditional Loa entreated when their power fell short. First, though, he needed rest. The night had drained him, leaving him bitter with memories of when this work came effortlessly and he could channel the Loa's power for days at a time. Like so many other super-powered beings, he'd expected his youth to last forever. Age caught him off guard when it came and brought illness creeping through his body like a thousand lethal spiders spinning black webs of poison. At least they hadn't touched his mind. Bless and thank the Loa. They had allowed him that much. He intended to make it his final salvation.

Light flickered from video screens embedded in the statue's pedestal, playing a loop of Omni-Guardian's greatest moments. Grainy black-and-white photos of his earliest days during the Depression. World War II newsreel footage. Then the first rare color images of him in action from the pages of *Northgate News Magazine*. Clips from his past memorials played in sequence, each generation honoring their fallen hero, right up to his latest last battle—against Stone Killer. Already days past, preserved by ubiquitous video cameras and smartphones. Half of Northgate's financial district reduced to rubble during the fight—then a last blow from Stone Killer even as he crumbled to pebbles beneath Omni-Guardian's assault. In the electric reality of the video screens, Stone Killer's boulder fist outraced the shockwave rending his body, leaving Omni-Guardian no time to roll clear or meet the Killer's fist with one of his own. The moment before Stone Killer caved in Omni's chest, the scene cut away to commercials for iPads and Omni Corp brand gourmet coffee.

Only the weakest of the *Deep* Loa had been with Omni that day. The uninspired ones, the ones who favored cheap shots and false drama despite the creative power they possessed. Doctor Bocor had made sure of that. The *Deep* Loa didn't realize how much he influenced them now. Whenever they touched him, he touched them back. He crept into their minds and nested *his* ideas there. Little by little, he was writing his own fate now even sometimes choosing which of the *Deep* Loa drew his destiny on the cosmic tableau. It had taken decades for him to accrue the power, but, unlike Omni-Guardian, he never feared to use it.

"How will you explain Omni's resurrection this time?" Doctor Bocor asked. "Purple ray? Ultramight serum? Global delusion caused by dark particles?"

"Does it matter?" Dodger said. "The public will be so excited to have him alive they'll buy anything I tell them. They always come rushing back no matter how much they wailed and gnashed their teeth when he died."

"Does anyone even remember his true origin?"

Dodger shrugged. "A few."

"They never tire of the cycle of loss and reunion, over and over. They worship him as if it's the first time every time. It's all okay as long as—*officially*—voodoo spun by Doctor Bocor got nothing to do with it."

"That's about the size of it. Omni can't be connected to *you*. I mean, you've done hard time, Doc. And even if Jimmy Carter flopped in the White House, people haven't forgotten how you tried to stage a zombie coup against him. That's a lot worse than stiffing someone on a bill."

Doctor Bocor rubbed his bristly chin. "So it is, so it must be."

The drones returned then and circled until Doctor Bocor opened a leathery sack the size of a grocery bag hanging from his belt. Icy air wafted out, making Dodger shiver. One by one, the drones entered, filling the sack beyond its visible capacity, until their humming faded.

Dodger chuckled. "Tight squeeze in there."

Doctor Bocor snapped alert and scanned the park shadows.

"What is it?" Dodger asked.

"One of my drones is missing. Someone's interfering."

Dodger stiffened. "Who'd have the brass to sneak in here on a night like this?"

Doctor Bocor traced spirals in the air with his staff and whispered a prayer to Grand Bois for heightened senses. His call answered, he studied the shadows flowing with soft movement and discerned someone there. Then as if the interloper sensed Doctor Bocor taking notice, the body leapt into motion, releasing the final drone, which hummed over the empty chairs and into the open sack.

"Who's there?" Dodger yelled.

Doctor Bocor spiked his staff to the ground. Indigo light sparked from the soil, coiled up the cypress wood, and then burst from its tip, illuminating the stage and empty seats. Across the field, the figure darted into the dark of the tree line, outracing the expanding light, revealing only a flash of midnight blue leather before vanishing.

"Who the—?" Dodger said. "Couldn't quite see but something… seemed familiar."

Doctor Bocor sensed a measure of his magic missing from the last drone. A grin creased his lips. "Only a souvenir hunter," he said. Then as the light faded, he tied the sack closed, then buttoned his coat, covering up his fetishes.

"If I didn't have bigger knots to tie right now, I'd teach him not to snoop." Dodger slammed a fist into his open palm. "So, what's next?"

"Now I court the Loa. Let the energy grow," Doctor Bocor said. "Meet me here next month, the night of the new moon, midnight."

"You got it. I won't let Omni down," Dodger said. "See you in thirty, Doc."

Dodger pulled strings to close Omni-Guardian's memorial to the public on the night of the new moon, rendering Goodman Park empty. He met Doctor Bocor by the statue of Omni-Guardian. The voodoo man wore a poncho woven with mystical sigils and colorful images of the Loa over his signature black silk suit. He clutched the Staff of Carrefour, radiating a dim light. Raccoon skulls, snake skins, and chicken feathers dangled from a bandolier strung across his chest. Half a dozen fetishes hung from his neck. A top hat adorned with a ring of panther teeth and a human skull bereft of its lower jaw topped his head. Power borrowed from the Loa made him seem younger and stronger than he was. In contrast, Dodger looked childish and out of place in his skin-tight, red-and-yellow body suit, glittering with armored plates and chainmail patches. His cowl, covering the top half of his face, emphasized the softness of his juvenile jaw-line.

"Expecting a fight?" Doctor Bocor said, eyeing the outfit.

"Seemed appropriate since Omni was entombed in uniform," Dodger said. "Is it ready?"

From within the folds of his poncho, Doctor Bocor produced a large fetish pouch. Infused with a pulsing red light, it resembled a human heart.

"As they say, your check cleared."

"Told you so," Dodger said. "So? What now?"

"What do you mean? Ain't you paid me to raise the dead?"

Poncho swirling as he turned, Doctor Bocor rounded the statue's pedestal by the gloomy light of the Staff of Carrefour. He studied the back wall of the immense stone block then tapped three places on the smooth granite with the staff's tip. Within the pedestal, levers clicked and gears turned. A heavy slab swung outward, exposing the top stairs of a flight descending into utter blackness.

"How'd you open that?" Dodger asked. "The Silver Key designed it to be impregnable."

"Ain't no secrets from the *Deep* Loa. One invents the Silver Key's secret of how to do a thing. Another make up the secret of how to undo it—*and then tell it to me.*"

The stairs wound deep beneath Goodman Park, into a sepulchral stillness and a viscous dark that bled the Staff of Carrefour's light, leaving them to find their way in a persistent gloom. The stairs ended in the antechamber of a vault sealed behind a door of steel and grandium alloy. Doctor Bocor bent to one knee, bowed, and prayed to the Loa.

After a while, he paused and glanced at Dodger. "You going to let us in?"

Smirking, Dodger said, "What? Did the Silver Key stump the mighty Loa?"

Doctor Bocor shook his head. "Need to conserve our energy to do this terrible thing."

Dodger rolled his eyes then punched numbers into a keypad mounted beside the door. He turned wheels and pulled levers, working the secret combination—parts of which called for precise pauses. After several minutes, during which Doctor Bocor prepared to let the old Loa ride him, priming his connection to the *Deep* Loa, Dodger completed the combination and yanked the door handle. The giant vault opened. Buttery light greeted them from within it.

"Last chance," Doctor Bocor said on the threshold. "Once we plea for this boon, the Loa won't release their grip till it's granted."

"Good!" Dodger said. "Let's bring back Omni."

Inside the tomb, Omni-Guardian's corpse—dressed in full red-and-white uniform—lay in a glass, hermetically-sealed coffin atop a wide dais. Strong, noble, lifelike even in death. Decay delayed by his residual power and his sterile casket. Only his face appeared hollow, his gray eyes sunken in their sockets. Above the coffin floated a glowing sphere, a parting gift from Alice Wotan, a fragment of her home dimension that would never dim.

Dodger touched the glass casket.

"It's going to be fine," he whispered. "Like it always was."

Around the coffin, Doctor Bocor poured a circle of salt and lime then inscribed its edges with the signs of the Loa. He arranged the skulls, skins, and feathers from his bandolier along the circle, interspersing candles among them and igniting each sooty wick. He chanted. His words came in urgent bursts as he struggled to steady his breathing and hold his troublesome cough at bay. The circle complete, he pointed his staff at Dodger.

"Open the casket. Stand by Omni's head," he said. "From this point, do everything I say exactly as I say it, or the Loa may deny your desires."

Dodger worked secret controls. The lid popped with a hiss and a faint stale odor. He stood by Omni-Guardian's head, hands gripping the coffin edges.

"Papa Legba, Mait're Carrefour, open the ears of the Loa to us," Doctor Bocor said.

Candle flames flickered as he danced, his body whirling faster and more surely with each circuit around the coffin. The ghost echo of drums and ecstatic voices drifted into the tomb as if from another world. Doctor Bocor's voice resonated with a sense of will, an entreaty across time and reality.

"Damballa, Nibo, Samedi, look 'pon us with favor, honor our petition. Maman Brigitte and Brave Ghede, grant to this burial place passage to the Loa's power."

The air sizzled. A thunderous boom snapped, shaking the tomb walls.

"Legba, Damballa, Samedi, let my plea reach the ears of those who dwell above, let my words speak to the *Deep* Loa."

Crimson light pooled in Doctor Bocor's eyes. He laid the red fetish—its energy bleeding from it—onto Omni-Guardian's chest, above his heart, then shifted behind Dodger. Whispering to Nibo, to Samedi, to the ones beyond them—to the true gods, the *creators*—he yanked back Dodger's head. From within his poncho, he drew a bone-handled knife and slid the blade into the crease where the collar of Dodger's armored suit met his cowl.

His wrist tensed, preparing to draw the knife across Dodger's throat.

"Be calm, now. Fight your reflexes. You'll recover," Doctor Bocor said. "It's necessary to make a sacrifice. Blood comes only from blood."

Dodger stiffened. "Quit flapping your gums and do it already!"

"Let it be done," Doctor Bocor said.

Before he could make the cut, though, a dark object whirled over the coffin and struck Doctor Bocor's wrist, opening his fingers by reflex. The knife fell.

"Stay away from him!"

Shadow Hand entered the tomb, the midnight blue of his leather costume blending with the shadows. A black fist insignia marked his chest. He snapped his wrist and another ebony dart lanced through the air, biting Doctor Bocor's other arm, breaking his grip on Dodger's forehead. He doubled over, clutching his wounds.

"Shadow Hand?!" Dodger said. "Twisting tornadoes! What are you doing here?"

Shadow Hand leveled a tranquilizer pistol at Doctor Bocor.

"I've been tailing you since the memorial, Dodge—since I saw you with… Bocor," he said. "I didn't tell you because Omni swore me to secrecy. He had a premonition he would die again, and he asked me to look after you." Shadow Hand slipped a leather-bound book from a pouch on his belt. "He asked me if he died to find this and bring it here."

"Bless the Loa," Doctor Bocor said. "The Tome of Souls!"

"How'd you get that?" Dodger asked. "I mean, Ice Spy left that thing in the Nomad Dimension and froze the portal shut decades ago."

"Omni-Guardian knew if anyone could figure how to bring it back, I would. He wanted me to use it to save his soul." Shadow Hand stepped up to the casket and brushed the red fetish aside, replacing it with the Tome of Souls. "We're holding his soul here, Dodge, keeping him in limbo. We have to set him free, write "The End" and let his soul be rewritten for another life—or with Omni's level of power, maybe even other *lives*. I know you want him back. We all do. But this is for the best."

"No!" Dodger said. "Omni-Guardian *has* to exist—*always*! The world needs him just like he was. *I* need him!"

"Dodge, it's hard to hear, I know," Shadow Hand said, "but Omni-Guardian doesn't *want* to come back. How many times has he escaped death? He told me how you hired Doctor Bocor to revive him every time he fell. Deal after deal with the devil. At first, he appreciated it. Then he tolerated it. But now his time is past. This isn't his world anymore. Omni's body might never have wavered, but his spirit did. Omni Corp keeps him like a living relic. Nobody wants him to ever change. But the ideas that made him are spent. We need new ideas. Omni wanted to make room for them. He told me if he had to give his famous salute one more time, he was going to weep. Let him have peace. We'll keep his memory alive. You can come work with me."

"I don't understand… Wait!" Dodger said. "What the heck are you talking about? Ideas? Rewriting his soul? That's nonsense!"

"It'll be all right, Dodge. Here, cover Bocor." Shadow Hand tossed a second tranq gun to Dodger, who caught it and pointed it carelessly at Doctor Bocor.

Sliding a silver pen from his belt, Shadow Hand wrote the Omni-Guardian's name on a page of the Tome of Souls then below it added "R.I.P." and "The End."

The book flared. Its pages riffled forward and backward. The air grew icy. An electric crackling sounded. The book flared then slammed shut.

Shadow Hand lifted it from the corpse.

"It's done," he said. "Dodge, you and I, we'll stick together. You're... you're like a son to me."

"*A son?*" Dodger let the tranq gun drift away from Doctor Bocor. "Damn it, I'm forty years older than you! I'm twenty years older than Bocor! Hell's wheels, why does everyone treat me like a fucking child?"

He fired both barrels of the tranq gun into Shadow Hand's face.

The tiny darts clustered together beneath his right eye, needles plunging deep through his mask into flesh. Shadow Hand dropped faster than his shock could register.

Dodger snatched up the Tome of Souls then whirled on Doctor Bocor.

"Do it!" Dodger said. "Bring him back."

Doctor Bocor shook his head. "Omni-Guardian's soul entered the Tome. I felt it *wanting* to go. It moved on. You understand? I bring him back now, he'll be a true zombie. Mindless. No self will."

"Good," Dodger said, exasperated. "That's how I want it."

"You want Omni-Guardian... a zombie?"

"See? Even you think I'm still a dumb kid who can't manage his money or be a real hero. Do you know *I* saved the world three times!? *Me!* Without Omni-Guardian or any of the others. You know what I got for it? A fucking pat on the back and an 'aw, ain't he cute' kiss from Lady Aphrodite. You have any idea what that woman's lips do to a fifteen-year-old body?" Dodger said. "I turned 107 last week. I need some security. Omni turned all wishy-washy when Kira Karnes died on the Moon. He shuttered up the Floating Guardroom. Started whining about the burden of carrying the weight of the world on his shoulders. Going on about how he wasn't sure half the people he saved were even worth it. That's not how Omni-Guardian is supposed to act. He makes everything *okay*! That's his job! He was going to kill his brand with all that soft talk, undermine Omni Corp. And, worse, he wanted to quit earth and go wander among the stars like some Richard Boone Paladin in space."

"Richard... who?" Doctor Bocor said.

"Paladin. *Have Gun Will Travel*," Dodger said. "Twisting tornadoes, didn't you have television in Haiti?"

"That show's... more than sixty years old."

"Don't change the subject! Finish what you started. Bring Omni back. Place him under my control. I know who the world needs him to be. I'll restore him, and I'll never have to worry about him leaving me in obscurity like some... some... hapless boy sidekick!"

"It would not be wise."

"It's not your choice."

"Nor yours," Doctor Bocor said. "It's up to the *Deep* Loa, as all things are."

"Fine. Get them on the horn and do what I paid you to do." Dodger poked Doctor Bocor in the chest. "Or you can give me back my money."

Doctor Bocor considered this for a moment then nodded and rolled aside the unconscious Shadow Hand. He sent Dodger back to the head of Omni's corpse. Raising his voice to Legba, to Carrefour, and to all their fellow spirits, he re-opened himself to the Loa and let their power flow back into him. Chanting, lifting his spirit, summoning the strength to dance the circle, he whirled and snatched up his bone knife. Its blade flickered dully. The Loa rode him now—and he rode them back. As he became their presence on this earth, he sensed them opening to him. He pushed through them, grasping for the *Deep* Loa, reaching higher, into their world, eavesdropping and invading their thoughts.

It's like he writes himself, thought one.

Such a compelling character, I love drawing him, thought another.

He's taken on a life of his own, thought a third. *Like he lives beyond the pages, larger than life. Keeps pushing his way to center stage.*

Doing a definitive run. Hope the editorial kangaroo court buys into this. Deadline breathing down my neck. Shit, go with it. Doing great work here. Sales are through the roof. Don't screw it up now.

Doctor Bocor fed them, tweaked them, nudged them, urged them to send more power to him, to make him the brightest light in this world—and they listened, not suspecting where their ideas came from. They were making it happen, making him the star. Soon he'd have the power to leave this universe, ascend to the *Deep* Loas, and become one of them. The ritual struck a fever pitch. Doctor Bocor spun, grasped Dodger by the hair, stretching his neck, as he cried out, "Damballa! Legba! Writer! Penciler! Editor! Grant me this power and bend this world to my will!" Then he struck in a lethal blur, opening Dodger's jugular with the bone knife and releasing his blood onto Omni-Guardian's corpse.

Gurgling, Dodger braced himself against the coffin. His blood flowed onto Omni. He shivered then toppled to the floor, dropping the Tome of Souls.

A searing wind swept the tomb.

Doctor Bocor trembled, his eyes ruby coals burning with the spirit of the Loa.

A whoosh of breath parted Omni-Guardian's lips. The corpse sat up.

"You got no faith in anything but the status quo," Doctor Bocor said. He looped the rope of the glowing red fetish pouch around Omni-Guardian's neck. "You really want something in this life, this world, you got to make it happen. If you don't have the power to do it, you find the ones who do and make them do it for you."

Dodger dragged himself to his feet. His immortal nature closed the wound in his throat almost all the way before it ripped open again, fresh blood spilling out, even as it began healing once more. Frightened, he gaped at Doctor Bocor, who plucked up the Tome of Souls then slid it away under his poncho.

"I told the *Deep* Loa how to make sure every little piece fell right into place— *for me*. They thought it all was their idea," Doctor Bocor said. "Omni-Guardian sad, defeated. Shadow Hand swiping a bit of my magic at the memorial to open the Nomad dimension. The Tome of Souls returned. All the time, I kept the good Loa away from you and made sure only the lesser spirits wrote your stories. Did you think I'd give a stunted, deathless head case like you control of the most powerful being that ever lived? That honor is *mine* alone. I cut your throat with an enchanted knife keyed to DNA from a wisp of your hair. Your wound is trapped in a localized time loop. It'll never stay healed. You'll never speak again, and I'll never have to listen to your whining. So, *Hells wheels*, how about all that?!"

Doctor Bocor touched his skull medallion to the red fetish pouch on Omni-Guardian's chest. The glow suffused the skull, turning its diamond eyes ruby red.

"I control Omni, thank and bless the Loa. A few weeks preparation, and I'll send my soul from this dying body of mine into his. I'll have enough power then to rip a hole from this world into the world of the Loa, to slip my mind into one of their brains. Who knows what power will come when I'm writing the fate of this whole world and everyone who lives here? Who knows what other universes I might find to amuse me?"

Dodger shook his head, splattering blood. From a pouch on his belt, he slipped a small signal device and activated it. Doctor Bocor slashed it with the Staff of Carrefour, cracking it apart. The pieces landed near Shadow Hand, who moaned and started to rise. At Doctor Bocor's order, Omni Guardian climbed from the coffin and knocked Shadow Hand back down.

"Let your friends come," Doctor Bocor said. "I got the strength now and soon, *I'll be one of the Deep Loa*. I'll pull all your strings. Let them come. Let them witness to the birth of a new god among gods."

Mother of Peace

They prowled the ghost city by night and hunted the thoughts of dead machines. Dr. Bell told them it was the only way to win the war. Find the old weapons and reactivate them. They had all heard it before, but she repeated it when they moved out of the jade moonlight into the shadows of a crumbling tenement row. Her way of saying "Be careful" as they detoured around a dirty bomb hotspot leftover from a battle fought before any of them were born. Dr. Bell hoped Calypso's contact did not lie inside the high-becquerel zone. The sievert count there was more than the thin-skin suits they were wearing could deflect.

As they neared the next avenue, Sergeant Tanner ordered the squad to stop and sent two soldiers to scout the intersection. His voice came over Dr. Bell's earpiece. "Can your mutant give us a location yet?"

"How many times must I remind you he's not a mutant?" Dr. Bell said. "Why don't you ask him yourself?"

"Figured he already knew I was wondering."

"He gave his word he won't peek into your head without permission."

"How would I know if he did?"

"You wouldn't," Dr. Bell said.

She missed Sergeant Williams, whom Tanner had replaced two weeks ago, but she reminded herself it had taken almost three months for Calypso to earn Williams' trust. It would take Tanner time too. Leaders did not like telepaths. Dr. Bell considered it fortunate that most of their squad had been together so long now that they treated her and Calypso as equals. Despite the growing number of telepaths appearing in the population, most people still considered them outcasts.

"If this duty doesn't suit you, Sergeant," Dr. Bell said, "I'll support your request for reassignment."

"No, ma'am," Tanner said. "The brass handed me this job. I intend to do it."

The two scouts returned, crouched low. Dr. Bell thought they looked nervous, but it was difficult to read expressions through their faceplates. Her earpiece went silent as Tanner switched to another channel for their report. The men gestured high and low at the intersection then separated and took new cover.

"Hey, Calypso," Tanner spoke over the squad's open link. "You got a hard twenty on our contact yet?"

"Narrowed it to two blocks," Calypso said. "We're on the wrong side of the hotspot. Shortest route is south at the next avenue, thirty blocks downtown, then cut over on 14th Street and loop back uptown about five blocks. Should be somewhere around there."

"Can't take the next avenue," Tanner said. "Enemy presence there."

"How many?" asked Dr. Bell.

"Three locations for sure. Two ground level. One high, probably a sniper. Six men minimum. Could be more."

"Let me feel it out," Calypso said. The comm link went quiet for several seconds, and then Calypso came back. "There are eighteen, at least. All Chinese. Calm thoughts. They don't know we're here."

"Thank god for small favors," Tanner said. "Okay, let's turn back before we blip their radar."

Dr. Bell shuddered. Calypso had made no stronger contact than this one since she taught him how to recognize the brain waves that identified a Centry warcraft. She did not want to lose it. She had searched for missing Centries across North America for two decades and found only rusted-out wrecks littered on old battlefields. The cybernetic machines, built to end the war, were meant to last a hundred years, but after thirteen months in the field the entire system had collapsed. Many units fell in battle; most vanished and their tracking units went dark. But despite the quixotic nature of Dr. Bell's commitment to finding a live one and reigniting the program, the top brass had not yet lost faith in her.

Dr. Bell thought at Calypso, *Will you make this contact again if we don't find the source tonight?*

To allow for instantaneous communication, she had given him standing permission to scan her surface thoughts, keeping anything personal behind a mental barrier. She did not like the hesitation in Calypso's reply.

Maybe, he thought. *But you know how it is. We've been through this city before, no contact like this. Things are how they are right now, today. It feels good. We should go for it.*

Dr. Bell had watched over Calypso since she found him hiding alone in a bombed-out school, a terrified eight-year-old. That was ten years ago, and he had helped her ever since then. He wanted to end the war as much as she did. He would have run out front of the squad, leading the way to the contact if only she allowed it.

Dr. Bell braced herself and then told Tanner, "We can't turn back."

Tanner unleashed a string of profanities, but he stopped short of demanding a retreat. Dr. Bell rode out his tirade and explained that they could not risk losing the contact. She had full authority for such decisions. She did not have to justify them, but she did not want to antagonize Tanner.

After Tanner calmed down, she said, "Find another route."

With a mumbled curse, Tanner clicked off comm. He scrambled across the street to where his second-in–command, Corporal Dolan, crouched behind the blackened skeleton of a city bus. The two officers conferred, and then Tanner's voice came over the open link.

"Subway entrance off the avenue. Uptown side of the intersection. If the tunnel isn't blocked we can walk under the ambush points and come up six blocks south of our target then double back. Should cover us."

"Assuming no one's waiting in the tunnel," said Dolan.

"I can give a warning if anyone's there," Calypso said. "They won't get the drop on us."

"Fine. Down there, you and Dr. Bell bring up the rear," Tanner said. "Ladies and gents, weapons ready. Let's go."

Following Tanner's lead the squad spread out and edged toward the avenue. Moonlight tinged faint green by a haze of dust and ash fell like water over their thin-skins. The transparent suits reflected their environment, blurring the soldiers and giving them a sort of shimmering camouflage. Dr. Bell checked the magazine in her rifle while she waited for Calypso to fall in ahead of her. She knew if anything blocked the tunnel Sergeant Tanner would insist on turning back, and rightly so. But the unfairness of it would tear at her, after searching so long, coming so much closer than ever before, and with so much at stake. More than any other contact she had traced in recent years, she felt this one promised to deliver the thing she had spent so long seeking, the one that would lead to all the others.

As they neared the intersection, Tanner ordered everyone to drop to their bellies and snake-crawl through the rubble. Ahead of them waited a gap in cover. Beyond a burned-up delivery truck, an explosion had left a shallow crater and scattered away the rubble from a space of about fifteen feet. For the time it took them to round the corner and descend into the subway station, they would be exposed.

"Don't like that blank spot," Tanner said.

"I see it," Dr. Bell said. "We'll have to be fast."

"You and Calypso go first. With me. Get you down the stairs before they can take a shot if they see us."

Dr. Bell thought the plan to Calypso, who agreed, and then the two wormed their way to Tanner's side. The squad surveyed the avenue. Through night-sights, the enemy positions were visible by turquoise splotches that marked the half-hidden faces of the hostile soldiers. Otherwise the cracked street appeared desolate.

"Can you figure their locations?" Tanner asked Calypso.

"They're not far, between us and the contact," Calypso said. "Sorry, I can't be more specific at this range."

Tanner put Dolan in charge of bringing the rest of the squad into the tunnel. Then keeping low, he darted like a ghost across the gap and disappeared into the deep shadows of the entrance. Calypso went five seconds later, a blur flashing through the gloom. Dr. Bell followed him, moving fast on the cybernetic, prosthetic legs that let a woman in her fifties keep up with the others. Tanner directed her down the stairs, where Calypso scanned the subway station with an LED lamp. Clear except for old litter. Dolan came next and relieved Tanner at the entrance. Then the rest of the squad rushed into the gap.

Dr. Bell froze the moment she heard the whistling sound coming from the sky. It howled like a fierce wind, but she recognized the signature noise of an anti-personnel, fragmentation mortar, a glorified grenade, but nasty, like the one that had stolen her legs and left arm, and condemned her to rely on prosthetic limbs. It had taken the life of her unborn child too. She grabbed Tanner with her cybernetic arm and dragged him downstairs. Dolan bolted down the steps from street level, shouting over the comm for everyone to take cover. Bell thrust Tanner into the darkness then clutched Calypso by the waist and leapt after him.

The whistling became a clipped shriek.

Then the missile hit.

The subway station trembled.

Flame and smoke and shattered concrete flooded down the stairs. For a moment Corporal Dolan became part of it, a twisting, tumbling ragdoll, and then the cloud enveloped him, and he vanished. The shockwave rolled through the station, cracking the information booth windows and slamming Dr. Bell to the floor. Calypso's voice stayed in her head, reassuring her he was all right. She shouted for Tanner, but the rumble of the explosion drowned out any reply. Dr. Bell rolled until she bumped up against something hard. She curled into a ball and covered her head with her cybernetic arm. After awhile, the concentrated chaos faded away to a plastic stillness broken by dripping bits of stone and ceiling tile.

Through the dust cloud, Dr. Bell found Calypso against the iron bars of the turnstile gate. She tried to raise Tanner on the comm. He came through, faint to Dr. Bell's explosion-deadened ears. She and Calypso located the Sergeant and helped him to his feet. They found Dolan dead at the bottom of the stairs, half buried in a frozen sluice of rubble that had sealed the station.

"We're trapped," Tanner said. He pulled Dolan's dog tags from his neck and stuck them in a pouch on his belt.

"I'm so sorry." Dr. Bell would miss Dolan. Twice he had saved her life.

"Most of the others are still alive. I sense them," Calypso said. "Enemy soldiers came on foot after the missile strike. Now it's a firefight."

"Not a damn thing I can do to help them," said Tanner. "Can't even raise them on the comm link."

"It's the radiation." Dr. Bell gestured toward the ceiling. "Or the old pipes and wires in the ground. Communications are always sketchy in the city."

"Sarge," Calypso said. "If you want, I can convey your orders to Private Rasmussen. He gave me permission to talk to him thought to thought. At this range, I should be able to pick him out of the crowd."

Tanner frowned. "Tell them we're alive. Tell them to fall back and withdraw. Return with reinforcements to wipe out those enemy installations."

"What about us?" Dr. Bell said.

"Unless you can clear half a ton of rubble from this exit, we're going down the tunnel, like we planned."

Dr. Bell raised an eyebrow.

"You said it was a good contact, didn't you?" Tanner said.

"The best we've ever had."

"Yeah, well, I want to see this war over as much as anyone, so let's do our job. To hell with whoever tries to stop us."

They clipped LED lamps onto their chests then jumped the turnstile. Tanner led them to the end of the platform and down the steps to track level. The tunnel yawned ahead, empty and deathly still. The war had hit city so hard that Dr. Bell doubted even rats remained down here. Not enough people still lived in the city to support them, and unlike cockroaches, they could not live in the irradiated places. Tanner went first and Bell took the rear with Calypso between them. After they traveled only a few yards, the station behind them fell away to darkness. Walking the railroad ties like steps, they settled into a steady pace along the center of the downtown track, progressing in a bubble of icy light. The gray concrete walls caked with dirt and soot never changed. The faded remnants of red and yellow warning signs provided the only color.

Coming around a curve, they entered the next station and found an abandoned subway train. Calypso detected no one inside. Tanner led them onto the platform, and they flashed their lights through the grimy windows as they walked the length of the train, spying on the mostly empty cars. In a few, broken skeletons sat dressed in rotting clothing.

"What do you think happened?" Tanner said, as they left the dead train behind them.

"They probably came down here to hide from the fighting," Dr. Bell said.

"Not with the people on the train. With the Centry program. You've been after this longer than I've been in uniform. Figure you must have some theories."

Sooner or later, Dr. Bell had this conversation with almost everyone who came into the squad. They had all grown up with the mystery of the Centry program and its shattered promise of victory and peace. Warcrafts, like flying tanks with human intuition and responsiveness, piloted by the brains of mortally wounded soldiers implanted in them. They coordinated via a satellite link, now believed defunct, and from the day they hit the field, they had succeeded in halting the enemy advance and pushing it back. For one year, victory loomed in sight. Now Dr. Bell thought the brass kept her going only to stoke the embers of that hope. After two hundred years of fighting, every day came like a hard crack in the face. Resources so depleted that some battles were fought with swords and pikes. A food supply clinging to subsistence levels. The prospect of ending the war in a day, however improbable, helped a lot of people get up in the morning. Dr. Bell remembered that whenever she answered a question like Tanner's.

"A lot of things might have gone wrong," she said. "I think it was a flaw in the cybernetics programming. If I can correct it, maybe I can revive the sat-link and fix the others. The Centries were built to be self-sustaining for a hundred years, so there's a chance I can bring back online any machines still intact."

"You work on the original program?"

"I was twenty-one when Centry began. If you entered the sciences then, you contributed to Centry. That's what I did for more than ten years until it all went live. Then a year later, the Centries disappeared, and the only work left was this. These days I'm the only one who hasn't given up the ghost."

She did not tell Tanner the real reason she kept looking or why she kept coming back to search this same city. She shared that with no one. She suspected Calypso had pieced it together, because he knew the last reported coordinates for each Centry as well as she did. He knew the three Centries that had gone down in this area. But he would never dare ask her. Anyway, better to hide the personal element or risk people seeing her work as a crusade. If she was right about why Centry failed, if she could find one live Centry craft, even if not the one she most wanted, she really did stand a chance of ending the war, and then no one would care about her motives anyway. In the end, her reason for doing what she did—personal or not—was the only real reason that truly justified fighting in the first place.

The station closest to their target location came up clear, but it hedged the boundary of the hotspot, so they kept moving. Two stops later, they entered the 14th Street Station on its lowest level, and then tracked up the stairs behind Tanner. They went slow, with weapons ready, even though Calypso told them he sensed no one ahead. On the station's main level, they found part of the ceiling caved in by something that had left an enormous cavity filled with layers of wreckage. Faint moonlight poured through gaps in the rubble. The scale of destruction suggested a crashed vehicle or an unexploded missile. Dr. Bell walked to the edge of the debris and pushed aside a chunk of concrete. She grabbed a length of broken rebar and used it to pry away large pieces, working with the strength of her prosthetics until she exposed an edge of blue-gray metal.

Calypso and Tanner helped her. The three of them heaved away broken concrete and chunks of shattered tile until they uncovered part of a pitted hull painted with call letters and the American flag. Beneath the flag, embossed captain's bars and the name "McCardle" decorated the metal. Dr. Bell flashed her lamp around the debris then leapt halfway up the mound and scrambled on top of the pile. She forced another chunk aside, her cybernetic legs giving her the power to shift it until it tumbled away. She pushed another and another, eliciting a warning from Tanner to watch where she threw rocks. The debris mound proved too unstable for him and Calypso to climb, and they could not jump atop it like Dr. Bell.

"Get off there before it collapses," Tanner said.

Dr. Bell ignored him and continued excavating. The scales of a dead subway station tumbled off the pile. When Dr. Bell did leap down, her face beamed.

"It's a Centry," she said. "It's hard to tell under all this wreckage, but I cleared the top of the hull, and there's no mistaking it. The cockpit is intact."

Tanner moved back to the metal hull and placed his hand on the painted American flag. Then he set down his rifle and shoved more rubble away from the craft. Calypso and Dr. Bell worked with him, shoving away hunks of fallen street and ceiling, rolling the pieces too big to lift, until they cleared a recognizable section of the warcraft.

"Sonofabitch," Tanner said. "Exactly like the pictures."

"Didn't you believe me?" Dr. Bell said.

"That these things existed? Yes. That we'd find one intact after twenty years? Guess I figured they were all lost. Alright, let's call in a recovery crew."

"Not for this one. Not yet, at least."

"Why not?"

"This isn't the contact," Calypso said. He stared at the uncovered patches of the warcraft then placed his hand on the hull like Tanner had done. "I get no thought activity at all."

"He's dead," Dr. Bell said.

Calypso nodded. "I think so."

"How can you know?" Tanner said.

"He's been down here a long time, covered in rubble, cut off from the sun. The machinery may still work, and maybe the nuclear battery is still charged. But the nanites that kept the brain alive can't be. They were fueled by chlorophyll, and without sunlight, they wouldn't have lasted more than a few months. The brain plugged into the cockpit would have withered and died only a few days after the nanites stopped repairing its cells and manufacturing oxygen and nutrients. I'm sorry to say Captain McCardle has been dead a long time. I've found seven others like this over the years. Intact but dead."

"The contact is stronger here," Calypso said. "We're not far."

"It has to be topside somewhere," Dr. Bell said. "Exposed to the sky, but not in the open."

"Not getting out through here to look." Tanner nodded at the rubble-choked exits.

He jogged across the station to check the other stairways and found only the southwest stairwell passable. The trio climbed it to the street and surveyed the neighborhood. Although Calypso sensed people in the area, no one felt close enough to pose an immediate threat. They spread apart, and Tanner led them, following Calypso's directions. The creamsicle glow of fires burning somewhere on the avenue mingled with the sky's brackish hue. In a few hours it would be dawn, and the sun would cook off the night haze.

The contact grew stronger. Calypso, restless, wanted to go faster. Tanner tried to hold him back, but Calypso's excitement spread contagiously, and before long the trio jogged together. They crossed another block. Then ignoring Tanner's warnings, Calypso sprinted away.

"Down here!" he shouted.

Dr. Bell and Tanner raced after him.

"This way," Calypso said.

Tanner hollered for him to slow down and wait, but Calypso kept running. He vanished through the broken front doors of a high-rise office building.

Wait! We can't see you now, Dr. Bell thought at him.

Calypso thought back, *Okay, okay, but it's here, in this building, right on top of us. It's here! So let's go, slowpoke.*

Dr. Bell edged past Tanner, who yelled at her to slow down. Tanner tried to keep up, but Dr. Bell's prosthetic legs outpaced him, one of the few times she felt grateful for her machine limbs. Calypso was right. Now was the time to act.

Thirty yards from the building entrance, something like an invisible wasp buzzed by her head. Another came right after it. Time seemed to grind to a crawl. Calypso's voice exploded through her mind.

Get down! Get down!

All around Dr. Bell the pavement spit up asphalt dust like a deep puddle splattering under a sudden rain. The air filled with humming, zipping sounds. As Dr. Bell crouched and then leapt toward the building's broken entrance, hot stings drilled through her upper body. She cleared the distance on the power of her cybernetic legs and tumbled into the shelter of the pitch-black lobby. In an instant Calypso reached her side, his thoughts a wild jumble of apologies for being distracted, for not sensing the sniper, for not warning her sooner. The raw emotion pouring out of him overwhelmed her. For all his courage, in that moment, Calypso was only a boy convinced the woman who was like a mother to him was about to die. Dr. Bell gripped his hand and tried to soothe him.

Not your fault, she thought. *He was too far away for you to know he was dangerous. Don't blame yourself. Please. Not your fault.*

She thought it over and over, coaxing Calypso back from the edge of panic. When she had helped him regain his focus, she asked him about Sergeant Tanner.

Calypso edged to the open doorways. *He's pinned down behind a dumpster. But I don't think he's hurt*, he thought.

How many of the enemy? Dr. Bell asked.

Only the sniper.

Then you have to take him. I know you don't want to, but you have to. Or Tanner might die.

She felt the fragility of Calypso's spirit. She hated the burden she forced on him, but she saw no other way. Calypso withdrew into the darkness.

You need my help, he thought.

Help Tanner first. You have to. Please.

Dr. Bell welcomed the darkness, afraid of how Calypso might react if he saw her torn up and bloodied. She needed him to act. She could not leave him alone out here. If her wounds were as bad as they felt, only Sergeant Tanner might remain to get him home.

Please, she thought. *Trust me. You do trust me, right?*

Of course, I do. You've done everything for me. I trust you more than anyone else.

Then do what I say. I know what I'm asking. I know you can handle it. I wouldn't ask if it weren't the only way.

Calypso's thoughts churned in the blackness between them. Then he extricated himself from Dr. Bell's mind to protect her from what he needed to do. The abrupt break startled her. Calypso crept back to the entrance, becoming a shadowy scarecrow in the gloom. The gunfire had died down, but a fresh shot came every few seconds— the sniper letting Tanner know he still had him in his sights. Calypso planted his feet. What happened next happened in stillness and without a sound. A gunshot plinked off the dumpster. A few seconds passed. Another round shattered the glass off a lamppost behind Tanner. A few more seconds passed. The next bullet gouged concrete far from its target, and the next struck a window in a building on the next corner. Seconds passed. No other shot came.

It's done, thought Calypso. Then speaking over the comm link, he said, "All clear, Sergeant Tanner. Come in now. I'm sorry I didn't warn us. I won't let down my guard again. Please hurry. Dr. Bell is wounded."

Sadness burdened Calypso's voice. Dr. Bell knew the dying thoughts of the sniper now echoed through his mind. They always would. To think someone dead, as Calypso had done, required staying connected with the target's psyche until the very last moment, rewiring brain patterns for a suicide circuit. The dying impressions were too powerful to ever forget. But she believed Calypso strong enough to live with what duty had called on him to do. When Tanner entered the lobby, he guided him to Dr. Bell.

"How bad is it?" Calypso asked.

Tanner flashed his lamp over Bell's body. "Pretty damn bad. Time to evac."

"No," Dr. Bell said. "We're too close. The contact's here. Pack my wounds. I can make it."

Tanner pressed field dressings over Dr. Bell's wounds. "Out of your mind if you think I'll let you go anywhere other than home."

Dr. Bell pushed herself onto her knees.

"Shit. Don't move. You're hurt." Tanner tried to ease her back down.

With her cybernetic arm, Bell jolted Tanner aside and then forced herself to stand. Her breathing worked only in shallow gasps, and her heart raced, but her mechanical legs held steady.

"We have to hurry," she said. "We might not find it again."

"You need a medic," Tanner said.

"Or what? I'll die. Like how many millions of others in this war. We don't have a lot of true choices in our lives, Sergeant. You're not taking this one away from me. I swear to you if this contact turns out to be a Centry, this all will have been worth it. And if I die then so be it. I've outlived too many people to care about that now. So, please, follow Calypso's directions."

Dr. Bell thought Tanner might face her down. Instead, he nodded and then followed Calypso to a staircase at the back of the lobby. They climbed it. Dr. Bell, weak from blood loss, set her legs to automatic and let them carry her behind Calypso and Tanner.

They passed the fourth floor, then the fifth, and kept going. Dr. Bell expected they would have to climb to the roof, the only place that made sense for the contact's location. It took them about an hour to reach the access door. Tanner broke the lock. Then they stepped back into the moonlight with a view of the dark city in every direction. The fires on the avenue burned bright.

"Where?" Dr. Bell asked Calypso.

Spikes of pain drove through her chest. Her vision grayed for a moment. Breathing came harder with every breath. She suspected she was bleeding into her lungs. Calypso looked frightened, and she knew she must look awful, covered in blood.

It's okay, she thought to him. *Believe in me. Where?*

At the center of the roof rose a bulky ventilation unit. The Centry lay on the other side, covered in thick dust. It looked peaceful, sleeping. Dr. Bell, Tanner, and Calypso approached it.

"Incredible," Tanner whispered.

Calypso brushed dust from the hull to expose the call letters, American flag, and the name "Bowman" painted over captain's bars. Dr. Bell swallowed a sob. She had not realized that seeing him would resurrect so much of her grief. She realized then that even after all the years she had searched, she did not know if she had ever really expected to find him. She circled the craft, which aside from scrapes and dents, looked undamaged. She opened a panel near the cockpit and accessed the diagnostic interface. Running off the nuclear battery, it lit right up and set to work. Dr. Bell checked the cockpit environment. The numbers for oxygen, nitrogen, temperature, and protein count all came up good. She cycled through the next batch of data then initiated a full system check. Two minutes later the display reported all systems, except the satellite link, running but they had not been activated outside of drill mode since the Centry program crashed.

"You're alive," she said. "Why won't you work?"

The machine did not answer.

"Calypso," she said. "It's time to use your training."

"It's not safe," he said. "I sense others in the building. They're hunting for us."

"How many?" Tanner said.

"Half a dozen."

"Sniper must've alerted them," Tanner said. He checked his weapon and jogged toward the roof door. "Only one access point. I can hold them off, but not forever."

"We'll be quick. We have to be. If they find the Centry they'll destroy it," Dr. Bell said. "Now, like we practiced, Calypso, okay?"

Calypso nodded and then sat down in the shadow of the machine and closed his eyes. Tanner watched. "What's he doing?"

"Entering the Centry's brain. He's going to link me to it, so I can see what went wrong."

Dr. Bell sat beside Calypso and held his hand. His mind touched hers and then guided her toward the Centry. Once he eased her in, he backed off, leaving her connected to Captain Bowman's brain. It amazed Dr. Bell how easy the connection came, and she wished she had known about telepaths when she was helping to build the Centries. The soldier's mind—stripped down, full of combat information, and packed with Centry programming—opened to hers. She connected to memories of battles and an intense, fiery vision, the fight that had put Captain Bowman on the Centry roster. He had come in at the end, one of the last units to go online, and Dr. Bell remembered how it had crushed her to see his broken body in the operating room before his brain entered the machine. She had not even known then that she carried his child.

She dug through scattered recollections and impressions. The Centry process struck a fine balance between removing enough memories to make a century of existence bearable while leaving enough to preserve the soldier's humanity. Dr. Bell wanted those memories.

Everything flickered. Calypso strained to keep the connection open. Dr. Bell pushed deeper, moving her awareness past banks of codes and concepts that she had helped create. She forced her way down to the central core of Bowman's mind. There she located the memory she wanted.

A remembrance of her herself.

She was smiling, and sun glowed through her hair.

She felt the softness of her skin the way Bowman had felt it the last time they had been together. His mind cycled that moment like a loop. It had been designed that way to keep the Centries sedated when they went offline for repairs. A programming error had set the clocks running wrong, making it seem that a century had already passed when only little more than a year had gone by. The Centries had defaulted to maintenance mode, but because the glitch existed only in one part of the programming, they could not complete the routine and return to their bases. Instead they had simply shut down wherever they were, trapped in pleasant memories designated to sustain them through a prolonged state of inactivity. The simplicity of it made Dr. Bell furious. Someone's carelessness had allowed the war to persist long after it should have ended.

Dr. Bell sharpened her focus. The strain dragged on her in her body and mind. Drawing on Calypso's help, she scanned Bowman's cybernetics programming until she located the error. She noted the code and the proper fix and thought them to Calypso, so that Bowman could be repaired when reinforcements recovered him.

I can do that now, thought Calypso.

What do you mean? Dr. Bell thought.

I can fix him. So much of the coding is embedded in his mind, it's like an open book to me. Calypso paused, and then thought, *I wish you had told me about him and you. I consider you my mother. Perhaps I could have thought of him as my father.*

Think of him that way now. Remember, not everything is meant to be shared between parent and child.

I understand, Calypso thought.

If you can fix him, please do.

I already did.

Dr. Bell felt the change flow through Bowman's mind as Calypso drew her out of it. She hated to lose the connection. It had been so long since she had felt so close to anyone. The attack that wounded her and killed her child had come only six months after the Centry program launched. She had been alone since then. Before she could protest, she was out of Bowman's psyche and back in her own.

Gunfire rattled the air.

Calypso dragged her around the Centry for cover.

"They're at the door," he said.

Dr. Bell crawled to the diagnostic panel and checked the readings. They had switched from drill mode to duty mode. Even more amazing, the satellite link showed as back online. Bowman came to, fully functional again, and plugged into every other surviving Centry.

Can you do what you did for the others? Dr. Bell thought to Calypso. *Go through his mind like I went through yours, via the satellite link? All at once?*

Calypso did not answer right away.

Captain Bowman began to vibrate. He lifted off the ground, raising a blast of stale air.

He knows you're here and what you did, and he's grateful, Calypso thought. *He misses you, and he's…happy…to meet me.*

Stay with him as long as you can, thought Dr. Bell.

And, yes, Calypso thought, *I can do what you're asking.*

Do it, please do it, don't wait, and don't worry about me, and don't miss me too much, Dr. Bell thought. *Only you truly understand what we've done here, and it's up to you to see it through, to win this war, for me, for us, for our family.*

The enemy broke through the door then, forcing Tanner to fall back, and then Dr. Bell saw Captain Bowman's shadow as he rose higher into the air. Her thoughts fell back inside her mind. She was only herself, shivering from a cold wave spreading outward from her chest. She imagined the other Centries, left alive all around the country, rising like Captain Bowman, the awakening of a ghost army—then Bowman opened fire, cutting down the enemy soldiers in seconds. The roar and flash of gunfire filled Dr. Bell's senses. Calypso would stay safe and protected by what he could do as she had so long protected him. It pleased her to leave him with the prospect of victory and freedom and a better world than she had ever known. The echo of gunfire faded. Bowman's shadow darkened Dr. Bell's sight as he set down beside her.

After that, she knew nothing more.

Grilg Friendly

Ted Willis winced at the pale, corn-colored china cup rattling against its saucer, as his wife, Katrina, handed it to Agent Franks and did her best to ignore the horrific rabble beyond the living room bay window. When Katrina spilled tea onto the silk coffee table runner, Ted drew the blinds against the nightmare scene outside. It helped a little. The blinds did nothing to diminish the braying coming from the front yard, but Katrina was able to pour tea for Doctor Brandt and Mr. Noe without any further spills.

"Thank you, Mrs. Willis," said Agent Franks.

"We should have known something was wrong," Ted said. "How could we have been so dense?"

"Don't blame yourself, Mr. Willis," said Mr. Noe. "What's happened is beyond your control. Even had you recognized it for what it is, you couldn't have stopped it. There's no way you could've known to call us. That's why we monitor these things."

"Charger just wouldn't settle down," Katrina said. "He caught the scent of something and sat up all night growling and barking by the front door. Wouldn't budge an inch. I thought it was probably just a squirrel or that big gray cat from down the street. Now he won't come out from under our bed."

"Please, Mrs. Willis," said Dr. Brandt. "If you work *with* us, we *can* smooth all this over."

"This morning, I saw something out of the corner of my eye every time I passed a window. Like shadows bobbing around. I thought it must be a flock of sparrows in the yard," said Katrina.

"Definitely not birds," Franks said.

"The kids were up all night, Bessie with nightmares and David just not being able to sleep. He wanted to go outside, but I wouldn't let him. Not at that hour, of course not."

Ted moved behind his wife's high-backed chair, placed a firm hand on her shoulder. "Katrina, please. These people want to help. Let's listen to what they have to say."

Katrina looked up at her husband, mustered an anxious grin, and nodded. "I'm sorry. Go ahead, please."

Agent Franks cleared his throat. "I know this is overwhelming, the kind of thing you've never seen outside of bad dreams or half-baked science fiction movies. It's a shock, but I assure you there are many good reasons for why all of this is kept secret. Your family's reaction is one of them, Mrs. Willis. Imagine a thousand or a hundred thousand people feeling exactly what you're feeling now. It would create a highly volatile situation. Luckily, we're very good at our jobs and ordinary folks like you rarely have to deal with these circumstances."

Outside a boy cheered and yelled, "Follow me!"

A murmur of throaty bleats echoed him, and a stampede of pattering feet chased his laughter. Katrina shuddered at the small, flitting shapes crackling the laurel bush by the side window.

Noe sneered. "You waste time, Agent Franks. The Willis' are not interested in the rationale behind our business. They need to understand so that they can make a decision on how to proceed."

"I know, Randolph, but one step at a time, all right? We're asking them to absorb a lot of information very quickly."

"Agent Franks," Ted said. "How is it no one else can see all this? People have been passing by all morning, and not one has reacted as if anything were out of the ordinary."

"They see your house as it would appear on an ordinary day. The illusion is part of our containment procedures. We've been monitoring your place since the event to make sure no one came or went from your property."

"But you were able to pass through."

"Of course," said Noe. "We're professionals. This is our job. We know what we are doing. Now forget all these meaningless details and let's get to the point."

"Randolph," Brandt said. "Control yourself."

"I'm sorry, but the strain is wearing on me." Noe rose and bowed to Mrs. Willis. "Excuse me, but I think I would like some fresh air. Agent Franks, I suggest you expedite matters before I grow too fatigued."

The slim, thin-haired man crept by the coffee table and disappeared into the kitchen. Seconds later the back door creaked open then slapped shut. A round of guttural exclamations cheered the sharp sound.

"More tea?" said Katrina.

"No, Mrs. Willis." Agent Franks stood and peered out at the side yard. His sharp jaw and square nose cut an imposing profile in the hazy brightness of the window. "Mr. Noe, Dr. Brandt, and I all work for a special department of the government. It's a top secret, joint effort maintained by several agencies such as the CIA, Homeland Security, NASA, and the NIH. We mainly carry out research, but we also run several active field operations. I really can't say more, but given the circumstances, it's unavoidable that I confide in you to some degree. I want you to trust us. We're experts, and we've been doing this a very long time."

Katrina snapped upright in her seat. "Did you hear that? That was Bessie calling."

"No, dear, Bessie's sleeping," said Ted.

The Willis' daughter had lapsed into silence earlier, submerged in a defensive shell against the morning's surreal and intolerable events.

"Our work began several decades ago," Franks told them. "For the most part, we've been able to keep what we do under wraps in accordance with an executive decision made when our group was founded. That decision has been proven right time and again. Things run smoothly this way. But, every so often, something does go wrong. After all, chaos is pretty much what the Grilg are all about."

"The Grilg?" said Ted. "Those things have a name?"

"Everything has a name," said Dr. Brandt. "Grilg is the most convenient equivalent to what they call themselves that our linguists could devise."

"You mean they're intelligent?"

"Very much so. What we do wouldn't be worthwhile if they weren't," Franks said. "That's the whole point of our interaction with the Grilg. Mutual benefit between two intelligent species. Communications were rough in the early days, but they've improved drastically."

Katrina bolted to her feet. "That was Bessie! I'm sure of it. She needs me." She dashed across the living room and scurried up the stairs, calling her daughter's name.

"She's not taking this very well," Ted said. "Can't say I'm doing much better."

"That's natural," said Franks. "We have people to help you adjust."

Katrina's warbling scream cut through the house, and for a moment, even the feral, outdoor squabbling deadened in response. "Ted! Help! They've come through the window!"

Ted crossed the room in two strides, only to slam into Agent Franks blocking his path. "Stay here, Mr. Willis. We'll take care of this."

Dr. Brandt bounded up the steps, her black hair swinging like a pendulum. "It'll be all right, Mr. Willis," she hollered. "We're trained for these kinds of occurrences."

"My wife and daughter are up there."

Ted tried to shove past Franks, but the agent forced him back and drew his automatic from its shoulder holster. The sight of it squelched Ted's resistance. Franks held the gun barrel pointed downward and off-target a few inches, reluctant to use it.

"Don't make this something it doesn't need to be, Mr. Willis. I will not let you upstairs. Dr. Brandt can handle it," he said.

"You pull a gun on me in my own house? Stop me from defending my family? Who do you think you are? What do you want from us?"

Franks exhaled in resignation. "I'd hoped to have much more explained before it came to this, but Randolph is right. I'm wasting time. Mr. Willis, we're here for two reasons. One is to clean up this mess with the Grilg. The other is to recruit your son to join our organization."

Ted's face blanked. "Recruit David? For what?"

Footsteps pounded along the upstairs corridor, mingled with hurried voices, a startled yelp, and long, snarling squeals. A door slammed. A window thudded shut. Katrina screamed a second time, her voice rising and shredding the limits of her disgust.

"Coming your way," Dr. Brandt shouted.

Three Grilg collided in a surprised pile at the top of the stairs, their intended escape route cut off by Agent Franks. The sight of them sent a wave of revulsion through Ted, but he could not avert his eyes. The flesh of their trowel-shaped muzzles rippled as they breathed, and the slithering tendrils that flanked their mouths wriggled like sea worms. Their bulbous eyes were like black marbles polished with a shimmering film; they widened at the gun in Franks' hand. Frightened screeches erupted from their throats, and the three beasts stumbled over each other, looking for another way to flee. Brandt and Franks had them trapped.

"Down the stairs and out the front door," Franks said, gesturing with his weapon.

The Grilgs' eyes narrowed to almonds as they considered Agent Franks' order, and then the three of them loped forward down the stairs, their arms and legs pumping. They stood a little over three feet tall, and their soft, golden fur shimmered. One by one they passed between Ted and Agent Franks, each one turning its crimson face toward Ted with bald curiosity. He looked at the floor. He could not stomach the way they moved, hunched on all fours, one pair of limbs gripping the ground as the torso flipped forward like a domino and the next pair took root. Their joints swiveled like those of a doll whose rubber band ligaments had snapped. Magenta tongues lashed behind their ruby lips. A thick musk wafted from their bodies.

Ted found his mental picture of the Grilg easier to bear than the actual sight of them. Somehow, memory diminished their repellent nature. They weren't all that different from animals he had seen a hundred times on television, but not only their appearance disturbed him. It was *them*. That they *existed*.

As if reading his mind, Franks said, "They're not all that ugly, really, but they don't belong here. They just look wrong in our world. Technically, they shouldn't exist, not according to *our* natural laws, anyway."

"Do you ever get used to it?" Ted asked.

"No, but we're taught to cope. We can teach you."

Franks held the front door open as the three Grilg exited. A handful of others, lounging on the front steps, peered into the house, indifferent in the morning sun.

"All clear up here," Dr. Brandt called down from the second floor. "The ladies are shaken up but no one's hurt. I'm going to stay with them. Mrs. Willis wants to be with her daughter."

"Good work, Dr. Brandt," Franks said.

The agent ushered Ted back to the living room and the two men sat. Franks holstered his weapon. "I'm sorry I had to do that, Mr. Willis, but I couldn't let you run up there in a panic. You might have hurt one of the Grilg, or worse, killed one. Most of them aren't inclined toward violence, but they will defend themselves if they feel threatened. I also had to consider the political bombshell an accidental death might have created among our resident Grilg population. They have no intention of hurting your family. Your son has been playing with them outside all morning, hasn't he?"

"We couldn't stop him. We tried to keep him in, but he had some kind of seizure that only let up when he went outside."

"That's to be expected. David is what we call 'Grilg friendly.' It's a rare trait, but it exists in people like Mr. Noe or your son. Friendlies have a connection to the Grilg that we don't fully understand. The Grilg maintain a sort of communal consciousness among their clans and social groups. Without it, they can't live, so they rely on 'sensitives' among them to sustain it. Think of them as wizened elders with a pronounced empathic facility. Our Grilg friendlies help them replicate that here in an alien environment, while the sensitives work through the shock of adjusting. Friendlies generally have other talents crucial to our operations, too."

"And you want David to work for you? To be a Grilg friendly? But he's only a boy, only twelve," said Ted.

"Almost too old for training. It's good we found him now."

"What would happen to him?"

"He'd come with us to our facility about ten miles north of here. There's a vacant lot surrounded by shopping centers and strip malls. It used to be an old racetrack. Not an obvious choice for the kind of work we do, but it happens to have prime coordinates for Grilg arrivals. Most of it is underground. If you walked onto the field, you'd experience the illusion of having crossed it, but really you'd be transported instantly to the other side, courtesy of the same technology the Grilg use to reach Earth."

"Where do they come from?"

"Another place. Call it whatever suits you: a different dimension, a parallel universe, an alien planet at the far end of a wormhole. I don't understand the physics. That's for the lab boys to sweat over. In the end it doesn't affect my job, which is to help the Grilg enter our world and contain their presence here."

"Why bring them here in the first place?" asked Ted. "If you're so determined to hide them, why not leave them where they are?"

Franks sighed and hesitated before answering. "It's not that simple. Many of the Grilg have specialized abilities and knowledge in chemistry and physics. Dimensional/spatial travel is a semi-natural skill for them. They're helping us master it. In about a decade or so you're going to see a flood of miraculous new products reach the public, all a result of our collaboration, though that fact will be kept a secret. The complication is that the Grilg world is ruled by a corrupt government who leaves the population to live in squalor and has individuals killed at its pleasure. We can accommodate only so many refugees, though, so the Grilg underground helps us screen candidates. Sometimes a desperate group bribes or fights their way free, bucks the system, and we wind up with what we have here. Unauthorized asylum seekers. Not necessarily the Grilg's best and brightest. They hitched a ride on the official transportation event that occurred last night, homed in on your son, and here they are. We detected them as soon as they branched off the established continuum."

"Send them back," Ted said.

"They'd all certainly be killed if we did."

"Then get them the hell off my property, at least."

"We intend to, but if we simply load the Grilg into a bus and cart them away, it would have a bad effect on David."

"What affect?"

"Arriving Grilg bond closely with the first Grilg friendly they meet, in this case, your son. They lock onto the friendly while they're between worlds and use his or her mind to navigate their way here. This group took a big risk. If the sensitives among them hadn't located David, all of them would have been trapped between worlds. Not an unheard of fate for rogue travelers. When we registered the breach, Randolph added his abilities to your son's raw faculties to boost them enough to keep the Grilg from leaving your property, and then we raised a camouflage field. Your son is anchoring the Grilg. Without him, the shock of an alien environment would be a thousand times more powerful. It would kill many of them. The sudden break in contact could drive David into a permanent catatonic state."

"You're saying David has to stay with them?" Ted whispered.

"Yes, Mr. Willis. We'll teach him to fulfill his role and he'll have a life and a career with our organization. We're prepared to offer your whole family a new life so that you won't be separated from David."

"David didn't choose this. He doesn't want this. I won't let you steal my son."

Agent Franks leaned forward, his expression sober and hard. "We'd like to have your cooperation, Mr. Willis, but we don't require it."

Ted's response sputtered on his lips as window glass shattered in the kitchen and a series of high-pitched growls rumbled through the yard. The back door clattered open, and Randolph Noe yelled from the entryway. Dozens of tiny claws scrabbling against kitchen tile drowned him out. A throbbing mob of Grilg spilled into the dining room; their gibbering filled the house. Golden flashes danced through the air, and Grilg appeared clinging to the walls, hanging from light fixtures, perched atop the china cabinet, clambering across book cases. More swarmed in, tracking mud and wet grass across the beige carpets, ripping floral patterned upholstery with their pointed nails, even overturning Mrs. Willis' delicate tea set. Dark liquid stained the ivory table runner. The Grilgs' ultra-black eyes spun like tops in their sockets. Vermillion tongues flashed and licked pulpy faces that undulated and panted.

Agent Franks leapt forward, gun drawn again, as two Grilg mounted the arms of his chair and expelled waste products from translucent appendages tucked into the folds of their underbellies.

"I don't understand this. They've never attacked before," Franks said. "Brandt? Noe? What's your status?"

A heavy object slammed the floor upstairs. A woman cried out. Brandt's voice floated down the stairwell. "We're being overrun. They're breaking the windows!"

The tinkling of shattered glass punctuated her statement. Katrina screamed. Bessie shrieked. All of it filtered dimly through the ceiling to Ted and Agent Franks.

Noe staggered into the living room, his clothes torn and his face bloodied. One eye had swollen shut and his lips were thick and red, marring his speech. Grilg hopped all around him.

"There's a spy," he said. "A spy among them told them we plan to kill them!"

Half a dozen Grilg grappled Noe's back, and he toppled, his face cracking against the hardwood floor. The little creatures hissed and writhed. Their bodies shook with primal rage, and their limbs flailed in a savage dance. Two of them stood atop Noe's shoulders, their gazes fixed to the back of his neck, and emitted terrifying growls as every hair on their bodies turned rigid like filament blades. They swung their arms, pinwheeling them as they scythed Noe's neck and back, slicing cloth, lashing skin, and drawing blood. Noe cried out with each blow.

"Dammit!" said Franks. "If Noe dies, the empathic field holding the Grilg will weaken, and they'll run free. He has to stay conscious." The agent seized a fireplace poker from the hearth and tossed it to Ted. "Defend yourself, but try not to kill them."

Franks leapt across the room and kicked the two Grilg from Noe's back. Others lunged toward him, but they shrank away, spitting and seething, when he waved the automatic in their faces. Ted swung the poker with awkward care, sweeping clear the area around him. The Grilg climbed the walls, slithered along the molding, and curled into hardened spheres of golden spikes falling and rolling toward him. The ceiling shook with a sudden scuffle upstairs, the shock knocking loose several clambering Grilg. Their bodies twisted in the air, limbs dropping forward while their torsos remained horizontal. They landed on their feet, unfazed.

"What do we do?" Ted shouted.

"Find the spy! The Grilg ruler sometimes sends agents through to cause trouble. There must be one in this group. He's got them convinced we mean to kill them," Franks said.

The Grilg grew bolder in the face of Franks' still unfired gun. The agent kicked them away but a threatening ring formed around him.

"How do we find the spy?"

"David can tell us. Get to your son. Make him understand." Franks squeezed off two rounds into the kitchen floor. Ceramic tile erupted in puffs of white dust. The chittering and snorting Grilg scattered. "Now! Before they regroup," he yelled. "I have to stay and protect Noe or they'll all get loose."

Franks yanked a radio from his jacket and snapped orders into it, calling for backup.

Ted plunged forward, wielding the poker to clear his path, knocking aggressive Grilg right and left, swinging madly at the ones hurling themselves at him from the kitchen cupboards. His feet slid on Cheerios spilled from a box upended on the edge of the countertop. He blocked out the Grilgs' cries of pain as he whacked them and hoped he wasn't killing them.

Ted kicked open the back door, squashing several shocked Grilg against the porch rail. The wicked things filled his yard with a riot of bouncing, running, tumbling, swinging blobs, some moving so swiftly he could discern only the blurred brightness of their coloration. Others hung from the trees and hedges. A crowd of them had opened the hood of his Volvo and were picking apart its engine. Another group squatted around a small fire they'd made in an empty birdbath, roasting a pigeon. A band of them marched up and down the grass, blowing into tiny flutes and plucking at little stringed instruments to make discordant music. Half a dozen miniature Grilg chased each other in circles, children playing a game.

Beyond the hedgerow at the edge of the lawn, the neighborhood stood in the unremarkable stillness of a clear, spring morning. Wisps of cloud crossed blue sky. Light breezes shook fresh leaves in the treetops. A car rumbled down a nearby street, and somewhere a lawnmower buzzed and a leaf blower hummed. Ted felt as if he had never seen this place before, this town where he had lived for more than fifteen years. To cross the sidewalk now would be as monumental a journey as the one the Grilg had made.

"David!" he yelled.

Three dozen Grilg spun, watching him.

He ran down the side yard, pausing to look up. Dozens of Grilg covered the sides and roof of his house like ants exploring a peony. Three upstairs windows had been smashed, and Grilg skittered in and out in hurried lines.

Ted yelled for David as he plunged toward the front yard. His son sat on the lawn, cross-legged, his back resting against the maple tree in the shade of its deep green leaves.

He seemed entranced by a row of Grilg gathered at his feet, as though holding council. The Grilg bounded upright and hissed as Ted approached. Their shining hair turned sharp, their intentions clear.

They would not let him approach his son.

Ted tried to explain over the ruckus, but his words proved useless. He could not verbalize all the strange and implausible things Agent Franks had told him. He could not stop thinking about Katrina and Bessie, their terrified pleas still ringing from the upstairs bedrooms. Gunshots boomed in the front hall, and he wondered how much longer Franks could keep Noe conscious. Ted's head spun with the dizzying entropy of the Grilg herd whirling and popping around him. The creatures approached him and pawed at his legs. The more Ted spoke, the more confused David appeared, as if every word his father uttered widened the gap between them.

Three Grilg huffed and screeched at David, and in response, the child belted out a hearty guffaw that shook his sandy, unkempt hair. It fueled Ted's frustration.

"You're lying Daddy," David said. "You want to hurt my new friends. Well, you can't!"

David laughed at him, laughed along with the beings that had invaded the Willis' quiet house. Ted had restrained himself long enough. This was his home, his property, his family, his son—and it was up to him to defend it.

He swung the poker with deadly accuracy.

Two of the six Grilg fell to the lawn, their ruptured skulls guttering violet fluids onto the grass. A third followed when Ted again wielded the poker, and the remaining three snarled, their hair rising as Ted bore the metal rod down over and over and twice more, until all six of the sickening creatures that had hijacked his son lay dead and broken on his front lawn. He choked back a cry of anguished victory.

A school bus rumbled along the street, windows down, the voices of children drifting through the air as it passed, none of them aware of the carnage only a few feet away. Then everything turned quiet. The Grilg made no sound. Each one of them stood rooted in place, their ridiculous eyes bulging with shock, their dangerous fur now flaccid.

The front door burst open and Agent Franks emerged, lugging Mr. Noe by the armpits. "You did it, Ted," he said. "You stopped them."

Then Franks saw the six dead Grilg sprawled out beside the front walk like deflated balloon animals, and his face blanched with horror.

"I'm sorry," Ted said. "I'm sorry, but they wouldn't let me reach David. They were turning him against me. I had to protect him."

"They were the Grilg sensitives, Mr. Willis," Franks said, indicating the dead bodies. "One of them must have been the spy, inciting them through his empathic link. You stopped the spy, but you killed all of their sensitives."

"Then, it's over," Ted said.

"No," said Franks.

A brown van lurched to a stop by the curb and men in uniforms jumped out, rushing toward the house, Franks' backup, arriving seconds too late.

Ted wheeled about and called to David. The boy seemed adrift on a wave of shock, his mind reeling as he sought sure footing. If Ted could just draw him back, maybe Agent Franks wouldn't want to take him away. David's eyes focused on his father for a few seconds, and Ted's heart leapt. He was reaching him! Then David screamed, folded to his knees, doubled over with pain, and clenched his hands to the sides of his head.

"David!" said Ted. "Listen to me!"

Agent Franks approached father and son. "The Grilg can't live without a sensitive, Mr. Willis," he said.

Ted lifted David from the ground, cradled him in his arms, oblivious to the Grilg withdrawing from his house and gathering in the yard. Their chattering resumed in hushed, nervous vocalizations. Ted betrayed no reaction to the plaintive cries of his wife whose screaming continued even after the creatures fled her bedroom. Behind him, serious men with glaring faces filled the front yard.

"With proper training, a Grilg friendly can be taught how to fulfill the role of a sensitive without sacrificing his humanity," Franks said. "He can then properly interlock with the Grilg. Done incorrectly, the Grilg friendly is left unable to live apart from the herd. In effect, he becomes one of them."

"Is my boy dying, Agent Franks?"

"No," Franks said. "The Grilg will sustain him. They need him as much as he needs them, now. I'm sorry."

Long, suffocating seconds passed before David stirred. His entire body trembled as though an electric shock rippled through him and he broke free of his father's embrace. Ted reached for his son, but the boy retreated until his back struck the trunk of the maple tree. He clambered up the limbs and crouched on a thick, low-hanging branch, glaring down at the men watching him from the lawn. Countless Grilg around him mimicked his posture, aped his every gesture, and then in unison, led by David, they craned forward and hissed their defiance to a world that was not their own.

I Am the Last

"Do your people even remember this world exists?"

Carter Brennan thought he saw a faint flicker of reaction in the Regent's holographic projection. Holoflect dyes painted on the walls allowed the holojector bubble mounted on the ceiling to project any desired setting on the visiting room, but the Regent and Brennan never bothered with it. Brennan found the utilitarian gray of the unadorned space—the only one out of hundreds of Markworth Station's visiting rooms used for more than a decade—soothing. He remembered when people booked the rooms solid for months in advance and submitted custom settings to make their visits memorable. Days long gone.

"Some remember." Regent Angunda shrugged. "Most don't want to. More to the point, they don't need to. Your world has become our Garden of Eden, a place the old tales tell us we came from, but our reality exists in the Ether. We live in it every day, like you do in yours. You believe your world is real, don't you?"

"My world *is* the real world," Brennan said.

"You've always been such a literalist." Angunda smiled. "As were all your predecessors. Must be part of the job description. The Committee doesn't favor men with imagination outside the design department. Do you realize you're the seventeenth liaison I've known? Think about that. I've been here almost nine hundred years while all your predecessors have died and become fertilizer. You don't have to leave Earth, you know. You could transfer your consciousness in here. You and your family would be most welcome to join us."

Angunda made the offer almost every time they met. Brennan found it tempting.

If not for the Orion Explorer Program, he might have accepted, but that represented the safe choice, the easy choice, one a great many people had already made. He wanted his family to live a real life and experience real things, to explore the universe. He wanted their existence to matter in the real world.

"Thank you," Brennan said. "But my wife takes my boys to watch the rocket launches almost every day after school. There's nothing they want more than to go into space. They live for that day. How can I deny them that? Especially when I want it, too."

"The lure of new frontiers," Angunda said. "A thousand years ago, Markworth Station was the new frontier. Today, we're a curiosity."

"No." Brennan shifted in his chair. "You're part of humanity. Won't you reconsider coming with us? The Committee built a section of the fleet to contain everyone at Markworth Station. We can transfer you. It will be almost like you never left."

"Almost. That's the catch," Angunda said. "I've studied the programming specs for the Ether fleet. So have a hundred thousand or more others inside Markworth. We haven't taken your offer lightly or for granted. In some ways, the fleet specs are more sophisticated and elegant than what we have here—but they're also more limited. They provide only 60 percent of our current environment. You don't know what you're asking us to give up. The bottom line is we simply don't wish to leave."

"You'll be alone," Brennan said. "Only criminals and Earthbound for Life enclaves are staying behind. Even the Earthbounders's ranks are thinning since the launches started. There won't be enough people left to maintain the population. The latest calculations show that within three centuries of the last rocket's departure, there won't be a living man or woman left on this planet."

Angunda frowned. "We are eight billion living men and women."

"Yes, of course," Brennan said. "I misspoke. Apologies."

"Forget it. I see your point. Flesh and blood humanity will be gone."

"No one will be here to carry out maintenance or refuel the generators. If anyone in Markworth Station should change their mind, you'll have no one to transfer you out or adjust your programming."

"I understand the situation," the Regent said. "We all understand."

"So, your people are in agreement, one hundred percent?"

Angunda gave a joyless chuckle. "Among eight billion, disagreement is a given. All the same, though, we'll stand together. We gave anyone who wanted to leave a chance to do so, and no one came forward. Life in the Ether is hard for you to understand. In here, we're not so much apart from one another as flesh and blood people are. We're bound by the neural network, and we share connections your people can't experience. We've discovered unexpected dimensions to our lives, and the possibility—"

Angunda hesitated.

Brennan nodded, urging him to continue.

"I've never brought this up before because people outside Markworth consider the idea antiquated, if not outright misguided. You may not understand it. Most of us in here felt the same way when we first came over, but experience has taught us something different."

"Taught you what?"

"The possibility," Angunda said, "that there is a god in the machine."

Tension coiled in Brennan's gut. "If you have any gods, they're the programmers who created your world."

"Absentee gods—long dead gods, in fact," Angunda said. "The god we experience is living and present with us."

"How do you know that?"

"Of course, we don't know. We have faith," Angunda said. "But we fear any change in fundamental programming—if we were to join the fleet, for example—might leave us cut off from its presence."

"It?"

"In the Ether, 'he' or 'she' is a choice."

"Right." Brennan rubbed his eyes. "Maybe," he said, "maybe it's better you don't come with us."

"It is." Angunda nodded. "Not for the reasons you're thinking, but it is."

"This is our last meeting then," Brennan said. "Maintenance will continue for three more weeks. Then the generator stations will be calibrated and set to run on automatic. The Committee has put a lot of effort into preparing for this and layering in redundancies. The reactor cores are full. You should have a solid million years, probably more, barring the interference of accidents or natural disasters. It's the best we can do. It's not forever, but it's a long time."

"Nothing lasts forever. Who can complain about a million or more years of life?"

Life, Brennan thought, *is out here, where we breathe and bleed.*

"Please thank the Committee for me," Angunda said. "Thank you for all you've done for us, for caring enough to try once more to persuade us to go with you. I'll miss you, Brennan."

"Good luck to you, Regent," Brennan said. "Good luck to your people."

"To you and yours as well."

A faint click came from the holojector, and Regent Angunda vanished.

Brennan shivered in the sudden silence. In that instant, Markworth Station seemed more than ever like a tomb.

Collecting his coat and attaché, Brennan made his way to the exit, passing rows of darkened visiting rooms that would remain forever unused, unlit. As he crossed the vast lobby, the wind howled outside. It buffeted him when he opened the door, bringing the first cold drops of a looming rain to his face. He rushed to his car and slid behind the wheel. Inside, the quiet clung to him as it had in empty Markworth Station, but different—almost comforting. The rain squall broke open and smeared the windshield. Brennan switched on the wipers and hoped it would rain enough to break eight months of drought. Not that it mattered. Everyone leaving Earth would depart within a few more weeks. He lingered in a last look at the monolithic installation nestled into a crook at the base of Markworth Mountain. Then he drove two miles to the gates and let the car's autodrive take over.

He saw the protesters first thing when he returned to Calper. His route took him past the entrance to the launch site on the outskirts of the city. About a dozen Earthbound for Life members stood there with flash signs and portable holojectors displaying their slogans. Behind them a rocket sliced upward atop a plume of white and blue flame. Another stood ready on the next launch pad, three more lined up behind it. Brennan couldn't hear the protesters' shouts, but he knew their positions well enough. It boiled down to the beliefs that humanity would wander lost among the stars in suicide machines disguised as rockets in an exodus meant only to reduce the population so the elite could start over with the Earth for themselves. Conspiracy nonsense. The Earthbound still believed the planet could be repaired.

An impossibility, Brennan thought.

As if backing up this conviction, the earth rumbled and shook. The car jerked to an emergency stop in response. Brennan trembled inside it while the quake lasted. The fourth he'd felt that day, it came with lightning and thunder, and an uneasy sense of chaotic energy waiting to be unleashed. It lasted only minutes, and afterward, Brennan's car restarted. At the sound of the motor, one of the protesters threw something against his windshield, spilling a viscous, white protein stew sold by street vendors over the glass. The rain washed it away. Brennan saw the protesters shout and point at him, shaking their fists. They had spotted the Committee insignia on his car.

It doesn't matter what they believe, the Earth is spent.

He pitied anyone who couldn't see that and grasp the miraculous opportunity the Orion Exploration Fleet offered. He ordered his car to accelerate away from the protesters. Late for his appointment now, he activated his Committee security clearance. The car shot forward and sped through Calper, forcing other vehicles to slow down and let him pass, cutting through traffic, tipping traffic signals in his favor as he neared them. He reached the medcenter in record time, sent the car to park itself, then hurried into the lobby. An elevator brought him to the 117th floor, where he met his wife, Layna, and his sons, Callon and Bruce, in the lobby of the psychiatrist's office.

"There you are," Layna said.

"Sorry, got held up by that ground tremblor. How'd it go with the boys?" Brennan gave his sons a mock serious look. "Any deficiencies?"

"Not a one, Dad," Callon said.

"We're cleared for liftoff!" Bruce said.

"Excellent. I'm proud of you," Brennan said.

Layna kissed him on the cheek. "You'd better get in there if you don't want to lose your appointment."

"Right," Brennan said. "Get us a table at that café on the 63rd floor. I'll meet you when I'm done."

Brennan saw his family into the next elevator then hurried to Doctor Avery's office. He found the doctor waiting for him behind his desk, positioned in front of a giant wall mirror in a gilded frame carved to resemble entwined grape vines and flowers. He wore a pair of interface spectacles and tapped away on keys they projected onto his desk.

"Sorry, I'm running late." Brennan tossed his coat over the arm of a leather wingback chair and set his attaché beside it as he sat. "I crossed paths with an Earthbound protest on my way back from Markworth Station."

"Hmmm, two entirely different groups, yet neither want to leave Earth." Avery stopped typing and pushed his spectacles up on his forehead. "There's a lesson there, although I can't imagine anyone is much interested. All they care about these days is psych evals for spaceflight. Understandable, I suppose."

"I ran into my wife on my way in. You've already cleared my family."

"I'll clear you too, Carter. I can ask you the questions if you like, go through the motions, but it's a waste of time. You'll be fine," Avery said. "Up to you."

"Let's skip it, then," Brennan said. "Even if you red-flagged me, there's no way I'm not getting on one of those rockets."

"So be it. Cleared for liftoff."

Avery pushed his glasses back down on his nose, typed some more, and then took an ID chipcard from the top drawer of his desk. He stared at it for several seconds, allowing infrared light from his spectacles to authorize it. Then he handed it to Brennan, who took it, stood, and reached for his coat.

"Wait, Carter, sit," Avery said. "We have our time. I was hoping you'd indulge me."

Brennan returned to his seat. "How so?"

"I want to know about Markworth. Why won't they come with us?"

"I really shouldn't say," Brennan said.

"I know, I know, it's classified and privileged and blahblahblah, but we're only going to be on this rock a few more weeks, and the curiosity is killing me. I understand the Earthbound for Life folks. They're scared, and they're contrarians. A lot of them are too dim to think for themselves. They've been duped by their crackpot leaders. At the end of the day, probably half of them will wind up on a rocket. But the eight billion in Markworth? They took in, what, about half a billion new consciousnesses from opt-outs? So little would change for them if they came with us. Their world would get smaller, maybe a little less exciting, but they wouldn't be on their own."

"The programming changes are part of it," Brennan said. "Even if we could replicate their entire system in the fleet, I think they still wouldn't go. They believe

134

they've found... well, something unique in the Ether. They're afraid it can't exist anywhere else."

"What's that?"

"I haven't even given my report to the Committee yet."

Avery smiled. "Humor my scientific curiosity. Anything you say is protected between doctor and patient anyway. I can't tell it to another soul in this world. What did they find?"

"God," Brennan said. "They believe they're not alone in there."

Avery leaned back in his chair. "A god that exists in there with them or a god for all of creation?"

"Don't know. Didn't ask," Brennan said. "Whichever it is, it's enough to convince eight billion people to stay where they are. Maybe it's no more than a programming glitch."

"Very interesting," Avery said. "You don't believe, I take it."

"Who does anymore?" Brennan gestured vaguely upward. "The only heavens I aspire to are the ones out there."

Brennan stood and gathered his coat. He waited for Avery to emerge from behind his desk then shook hands and said goodbye. They might see each other again someday on a rocket or another planet, but the chances were slim. Brennan left Avery standing in front of the mirror, studying his reflection. He made it halfway to the elevator before he remembered his attaché case. He rushed back, knocked on Avery's door then pushed it open. The attaché rested right where he'd left it, and Avery still stood before the mirror—except a faint glow now surrounded him.

"Doctor...?" Brennan said.

Avery didn't acknowledge him. He leaned toward the mirror until his forehead touched it. A glimmer of light pooled where his skin made contact with the silvery glass. Then came a faint click, and Avery vanished into the smooth surface. Brennan rushed across the office, confused. He stopped short of the mirror, saw no sign of Avery. In the abrupt emptiness, Brennan felt like he'd jumped back to Markworth Station, alone, to a decommissioned visiting room.

Doctor Lester Avery blinked. The ambient light of the lab hurt his eyes.

He sat up, yawned, and accepted a mug from a nearby technician.

He sipped. The cool drink soothed his throat and replenished the nutrients he'd lost while downline in the Grid. The monitor above his couch read 36:23:09. He had been in for a day and a half—the equivalent of a month's worth of Grid time.

"Orange." Avery took another sip. "Not my favorite. Got any cherry?"

"Sorry, doc." The technician shook his head. "Military crew came in yesterday for a battle sim and drank it all."

"I'll survive. Hate the aftertaste, though."

Avery slugged back the rest of the drink. He swiveled his legs off the couch and stood, feeling a touch dizzy, a normal side effect. He left the lab, went to his office, and logged in. His window afforded him a view of the spaceport. Cargo crafts and transports lifted off in a steady stream. From a distance, they looked like paper models rising on the wind instead of high-tech ships set free by gravity interference drives. Avery smiled at the sight, so much more beautiful and accomplished than what the people in the Grid had achieved. No matter how well Avery's team refined the Grid programming, reality still ruled.

A knock came at his door. Bureau Director Lorenzo pushed into Avery's office.

"You're back," he said. "Good."

"You don't waste any time," Avery said. "I haven't even logged a report yet."

"I'm impatient. Give me the highlights."

"The new modules are working well. The safeguards we put in place are doing their job. I don't think we'll ever get locked out of the system again like last summer," Avery said. "It's all humming along now, catastrophe averted. The evacuation is proceeding. We've barely had to nudge anyone in the right direction. Given the opportunity to advance, they seize it. Barring another crash in the sub-programming—almost impossible at this point—all should remain well."

"What a huge relief," Lorenzo said.

"I only hope the crew over in world-building has some scripts and modules ready to go soon, because the first rockets are flying, and a couple thousand years passes fast in Grid time."

"That's something I wanted to see you about but tell me the rest first."

"Not much else. It's all pretty much as planned," Avery said. "Except for one interesting bit. The Markworth Station folks think they've discovered God."

"What do you mean?"

"Carter Brennan tried again to convince them to go on the rockets. They declined, again, but this time they said it's because they believe there's a living god in the Ether with them, and they don't want to leave him, her, or it behind. I'll have to gather more data next time I go in."

"A creator-god?"

Avery shrugged. "They know the creators of their world were programmers."

"Unexpected." Lorenzo looked thoughtful for a moment. "Someone slipped a bit of code in on the sly. Delgado in sociology, maybe. He's always trying to run little experiments without anyone noticing."

"Wasn't him. You fired him last month, remember? Even if you hadn't the new security protocols would detect anything like that," Avery said. "I don't think this is one of us messing around. It's spontaneous. Our projections for unsanctioned, in-system deviation have always underestimated the true degree of spontaneity in there. Or it could be a bug. You should go see for yourself. When's the last time you went downgrid?"

"I'm a busy man, Lester. This Bureau doesn't run itself," Lorenzo said. "I'll send my son downline and let him bring me up to speed. He's itching for a project with more responsibility."

"Suit yourself," Avery said. "The good news is the environment is holding its integrity. For better or worse, the people in the Grid have forgotten that they all started out in our world before mapping their psyches down there."

"That's welcome news, at least. If they ever decided to come back, we'd have body riots on our hands again, and what the hell would we do with a few billion new citizens anyway?" Lorenzo shuddered. "Okay, I'll let you get back to work. I want your full report by the end of the day."

"You got it," Avery said. "Didn't you mention something about world-building…?"

"Oh, right, yes, when you have a minute, go see Lois. They're hung up on fauna designs for one of the Sirius worlds. She wants your input. It's slowing the whole damn project down, so make sure you see her today."

"Consider it done," Avery said.

After Lorenzo left, Avery banged out his report. He struggled to sum up the development at Markworth Station. Programming allowed a lot of leeway for social evolution but only within planned parameters—and no one had ever programmed for a god in the machine inside the machine. Markworth Station itself had begun only as a lark to see what would happen if the people in the Grid were permitted to create a Grid of their own: the Ether. Worlds like an infinity image, endlessly reproducing and reducing itself. The people in the Grid had all begun life in the real world, but over time they'd come to think of their world as the real one; and the eight billion who'd entered Markworth over the last millennia in Grid time did so unaware it was the second time they had bumped their consciousnesses into a simulated environment. What occurred inside there to convince them they'd found god? The question stumped Avery. Finally, he surrendered and wrote: "Further study required to properly analyze divinity developments in Markworth Station." He logged in his report and then went to the world-building facility on the next floor.

Lois smiled when Avery entered her office. She threw her arms around him and kissed him. "Mmmm," she said. "Glad you're back. I missed you last night."

"I missed you for a month," Avery said.

"You poor thing, we'll just have to make up for lost time tonight."

"If you went into the Grid with me, we could spend two weeks together anywhere in the world you want to go and be back for breakfast."

"Sounds lovely," Lois said. "But no vacations for me till I get things back on track here."

"Right. Lorenzo said you needed help."

"I do." Lois let go of Avery and straightened herself, all business now. "Let me walk you through it."

They spent the next two hours reviewing the latest selection of wildlife Lois's division had designed. Avery saw little wrong with them except that most had an unnecessary whimsical flare, and some possessed strikingly fierce characteristics. Unpolished, unfinished. Lois's division needed to perfect them before handing them off to coding. Bad fauna could devastate a colony or sink an entire world. Avery offered suggestions, which he and Lois then debated until they both grew too hungry to continue and decided to call it a day and grab a late dinner.

"You saved me two weeks of kicking these back and forth with design until they got it right," Lois said. "Brewster's crew is burning out. We've populated nine new worlds in three weeks. That's enough to deplete anyone's inspiration."

"Glad to help," Avery said. "I guess even gods need an assist now and then."

Lois crinkled her face. "Gods? What's that about?"

"Isn't that us?" Avery said.

Lois gestured for him to explain.

"At least as far as the people in the Grid are concerned," he said, "we're building their universe and populating their worlds with plants and animals over which we shall grant them dominion. We create their fates."

"Not entirely," Lois said. "We've left them free will."

"That's because we want to be gods, not dictators."

Lois stared at Avery like she couldn't make up her mind if he was joking or not.

Avery laughed. "Don't strain yourself," he said. "I'm only kidding around."

Later while they ate dinner, Avery explained his findings about Markworth Station. Lois appeared fascinated and laughed at his earlier jibes retroactively, but now that he'd made the points, he found them hard to dismiss. It wasn't much of a stretch to paint themselves as gods to the Grid. He thought of an article he'd read before his last trip downline: more than 70 percent of the world's population and resources worked in a meaningful way toward servicing the Grid. He glanced around the cafeteria full of bureau employees and abuzz with wait staff, cashiers, and cleaners, and realized that being gods made for good industry. Creating a reality kept people working. It filled another essential component of society too: it gave them something to have faith in.

Vestiges of traditional religions still existed around the world, but most people these days tended toward atheism. *Except when it comes to us,* Avery thought. *We have all the faith in the world in ourselves and that we're doing the right thing no matter how it affects those in the Grid. If we ever get it really wrong, then they're on their own down there.*

"We really have made gods of ourselves," he said.

"What's that?" Lois asked.

Avery stared at her. For a moment, Lois seemed utterly unreal, like a ghost. Avery experienced a moment of certainty that if he touched her, his hand would pass through her body, and she would blink out of existence. He shivered.

"Are you all right?" Lois asked.

She took Avery's hand. At the feel of her warm skin, Avery's senses settled.

"Fine, yeah," Avery said. "Lost in thought for a moment, that's all."

Later that night in bed, as Lois neared climax, she gave Avery a wicked grin, and then cried out, "Oh, god, yes, oh, god, oh, god!"

Avery couldn't help it: He burst out laughing.

Afterward, Lois fell into the deepest sleep Avery had ever seen. In the morning, he awoke to the sound of a faint click. His alarm he thought at first, but he'd woken early and turned it off before it sounded. He could barely rouse Lois. She remembered little of the previous night's conversation, so Avery refreshed her memory. Lois said it came back to her then, but he had the nagging suspicion she said so simply so they could move on with their day.

Keela McCormick unplugged from the control suit and shook off the residue of being Lois. She sat in the lab for a time, thinking nothing, letting the impression of being In-world fade away. The hum and tick of the machines and the steady thrum of the geothermal generators below the surface filled the otherwise silent lab.

She liked Avery; she really did.

She told herself that's why she kept going back as Lois.

That missed the whole truth, though. She also found Avery's connections down the Grid and into Markworth station fascinating. One of only a handful of people with direct contact that deep into the system, only Avery seemed to ever gain any insight or perspective from the experience.

"We want to be gods, not dictators," he'd said.

What an outrageous idea, Keela thought.

Avery wasn't a god. He could never be a god.

No one in In-world could.

God is here, Keela thought. *I am God. Everything they do in In-world, everything on the Grid, everything in Markworth Station—worlds within worlds—I control.*

Keela yawned and her stomach grumbled. She left the lab and ambled to the upper level kitchen, where she foraged through the pantry and the freezer until she found what she liked. She cooked it and then took her meal to a table and chair by the windows, where she ate and studied the view. To the west stood a mountain range, its jagged peaks frosted with snow. In the south a lake churned in the wind with gray waves that reflected the overcast sky. Dark at noon. Always dark, always a shade of winter. Keela had never seen anything else, though she had read of warm days and sunshine, had seen stored video of lush green forests and blue oceans. A fantasy world, a world still in its prime, not like this one on its deathbed.

She tried to see the beauty in it.

Rhaj had always insisted it existed, but she never saw what he saw.

She missed him. She'd lost track of the days since he'd died. Her loneliness made it hard to care about the passage of time.

Through the window, she made out part of the road to the lab site, its surface cracked, pitted, and cluttered with dead weeds. A section of fence along the perimeter twitched in the wind. Had it been bent over like that yesterday? Surely not.

It's going to be today then.

She finished her meal and then hurried down to the lockers and suited up to go outside. She stopped at the armory and strapped a pair of pistols to her belt and grabbed an energy rifle.

Outside, the cold ate through her suit and mask.

She hiked downhill from the lab, crunching crusts of ice and ignoring the chill that sank deeper into her bones with each step. Out by the fence, she saw recent footprints in the snow. It had snowed this morning, but none of the fresh fall clung to the pushed-down section of fence or filled the depressions of the footprints.

More footprints led up the barrier from the other side, the outside.

The intruder had come from there.

It's true. Someone else is here.

Impossible.

She had hoped for days that the figure she saw moving around the foothills and rushing across the grounds at night existed only in her imagination. She couldn't guess who it could be. Everyone she knew was dead or in In-world. Only she remained, left to run the systems, adjust the programs, and balance the fuel stores. She had buried the rest of the team under a veil of ice and snow as each one died, Rhaj last, and so it couldn't be any of them. How could someone turn up now, so near the end of everything?

She knelt and traced the contours of one of the footprints.

Real.

Unless…

A horrible thought came to her: What if a spontaneous presence had sprung into existence like the god in Markworth Station? One arisen from her need to feel less alone in existence and help her through her last days? She didn't think so. She wasn't part of In-world. Things didn't simply leap into being in the real world.

The end of her—the end of everything—gave her no fear. There existed only the universe of matter and energy, no more, no less, and within it existed In-world, which she oversaw like its god, making her the god of the Grid and the Ether too. She could destroy it all if she chose to, or damage it, or secure it, or render it a utopia or a hell, or leave it to itself.

Its creators had died long ago; only she remained—its divine balance.

The footprints led in from the wasteland and trailed into the grounds.

Keela followed them.

"What are you?" she said.

A voice inside her answered: *It's you.*

It wasn't, though. It couldn't be.

She wasn't losing her mind or sleepwalking or blacking out and doing things she didn't remember. The medications prevented it. She had checked the security cameras to make sure. Unless, did the voice mean the intruder was like her, dipping down into this world from one above how she dipped down into In-world, how Avery dipped down to the Grid?

The idea enraged her. No world existed above this one.

She was God, no one else. Before she died, she would pull the plug on In-world and all the worlds it contained, and humanity would end with her. She wouldn't send them soaring to new worlds in rockets. She wouldn't pack fuel into the generators so they could run a million years. She wouldn't transfer down and live forever. She couldn't even if she'd wanted to—the tumor in her brain made it impossible. Everyone on her team had suffered some similar anomaly that kept them trapped in reality, a trait that doomed them to stay behind and die while the rest of the world got to live.

No, Keela thought. Now no one else from her team still lived; she realized the cruelty and unfairness of that.

There was no other real world than hers. If there was, wouldn't they intervene? Wouldn't they heal her? Pull her up to their level? Wouldn't they try to save all the people over whom she held power? That's how it went in stories with heroes and villains and the world at risk, but in real life, all life ends only one way.

The footprints led Keela to a service entrance that hadn't been used in years.

Something had wrenched the door from its hinges and left it askew in the snow.

"Shit," Keela said.

She inched into the darkness inside and listened while her eyes adjusted from the snow brightness. *Tweak the code*, she thought. We used to tweak the code to make ourselves stronger or faster or more attractive and then screw with the In-worlders. Sometimes it happened on its own when the interface got glitchy, or a bug interfered, or the admin systems locked up. *Is that what this is? Someone from above messing with my head? Or trying to… help me?*

Impossible. There's no one above, no other world.

I am the last—I'm God.

Keela followed a sound coming from a room down the corridor.

Nothing above.

Nothing.

She adjusted her grip on the rifle and turned the corner.

A faintly glowing figure stood in front of her, turning, gesturing, speaking, pleading for something, for life, a message Keela refused to acknowledge.

She screamed and fired.

A lance of blue-white light crackled out from the rifle and hurled the figure against the far wall. The scent of burning cloth and flesh filled the air, overpowering the filters of Keela's hood. The residual crackling of the energy faded. Keela heard a faint click. With one foot, she rolled the smoking corpse over to see its face. She couldn't tell if it was a man or a woman. The rifle blast had destroyed its features and most of its torso. It carried no weapons, no telltale gear. She could undress it to find out, but she didn't care.

The intruder should never have been here in the first place.

She dragged it outside and buried it in a snowdrift with the others—not hers, not her team, but…the others? *No, there were no others, there couldn't be any others; there was no one else at all.* Keela's head spun. A sharp pain spiked through her skull and down her spine. Her vision blurred for a moment then cleared, and she saw bodies, all dressed in the same type of suit, all charred and devastated, their faces erased by the blast of an energy rifle—her energy rifle. *Others.* She knew that couldn't be right. Then she blacked out and collapsed.

She shivered when she woke. The cooling body lay beside her.

She stopped herself from looking past it into the irregular drift of snow crusted with ice.

She scrambled away, staggered to her feet, and ran back to the lab. She doffed her outside gear then made a warm drink and sat by the windows in the kitchen. Pain lingered in her head. It grew worse every day. She felt weaker and more adrift each morning. The tumor ate away at her cognition, making her hallucinate. Her time running out—all time running out. Outside, a shape moved along the distant ridge. A black speck, but even at this distance, she could tell it moved like a person.

A person who couldn't be there, who shouldn't exist.

I am God, Keela thought. *I am the last.*

She reached for her energy rifle then thought better of it.

No point going out there again or going on. She would simply have to prove it.

Creator. Destroyer.

In-world, the Grid, and the Ether—billions of lives—would end when she did, and the time approached.

When she finished her last cup of coffee, she would retreat to the lab, and do her duty.

He Who Burns

It's Thursday night, and I'm inside a burning warehouse, using every ounce of geomancy I can muster to avoid being burned to a crisp. At the same time, I'm flapping my arms and screaming over the roar of the fire to get the attention of a 24-foot-tall dragon, who's gulping down barrels of rocket fuel like Jell-O shots and belching out huge balls of flame. Meanwhile, half of downtown New Alexandria is going up in smoke in the biggest blaze the city has ever seen, and everyone's counting on me to put out fires that have been burning for three days.

Next time my neurosurgeon girlfriend bitches to me about job stress, I think you know what I'm going to say.

Right now, though, I'm only concerned with the dragon. Except he's not exactly a dragon; he's a salamander, and he's the biggest one I've ever heard of, let alone seen. That's because salamanders thrive on fire. They grow when they bathe in it, but it should take days, months, or even years for them to reach this size. This one grew so fast because all of this fire is alchemical in origin, which makes it like Miracle-Gro for salamanders. It also makes it almost impossible to extinguish with standard fire-fighting tools like water or chemical sprays, which means the best way to get rid of it is for the dragon…sorry, salamander…to soak it all up. The trick is convincing him to do it, but when I finally get the salamander to see me, the first thing he says is, "Why aren't you burning up?"

Fair question.

To him, I'm an ordinary-looking guy in a mildly fire retardant police jacket, who's standing at the heart of a burning building, but all around me there's this bubble, maybe arm's length deep, where the fire simply isn't, and the air is clean and cool. Even for a salamander, that's not something you see every day. While he's staring at me, though, his breath washes over me like the heat from an open blast furnace, so hot that I feel enough of it through my bubble to start sweating bullets. Sweating makes me nervous. That makes me sweat even more, and now that I'm sweating, I'm jumpy, and the salamander is staring down at me with eyes that look like buckets full of molten steel, and so I do the first, knee-jerk thing that comes to mind.

I offer him my card.

My business cards are printed on high-quality, textured stock the color of sand in the morning light, and they always make a good impression. They say: Maximilian Toth, Forensic Alchemist, with the elemental symbol for earth beneath it.

Squinting at my snazzy business card, the salamander says, "Is that paper?"

Another burst from the blast furnace. His breath hisses and resonates. His voice makes my body vibrate, along with the floor, and the walls, which reminds me I'm in a building rapidly hemorrhaging structural integrity to the destructive power of fire— alchemical fire, no less—and it takes me a half a second to realize what he's getting at.

"Oh, right," I say. "That'll burn right up."

"Why don't you read it to me?" says the salamander.

So I do.

"That would explain your not burning, if your field of expertise were fire. Did it not occur to you to send a fire-based alchemist to converse with me?"

Now he's poking a sore spot, because he's absolutely right. Our fire guy, Nicolas Simms, should be the one doing this. He should be worrying about keeping the ashy mess that is *half* of downtown from becoming the ashy mess that is *all* of downtown. It should be him walking into burning buildings to chat up creatures whose natural element is fire. I know that. Everyone knows that. But there is, of course, a chain of events that led up to this moment.

There's always a chain of events.

That's alchemy; that's life.

In this case, though, maybe I should say that's death, because Simms was murdered the day before the fires started, and forensic alchemists simply cannot be replaced overnight.

It takes us months to get in tune with the elemental energies of our jurisdiction. So with Simms returning to the clay from whence he came, that leaves New Alexandria with only me and two other forensic alchemists. There's Antonia Blanco, air, and Michaela Gilmore, water, and right now Gilmore is occupied with containing the downtown burns.

That's where I should be too, and Antonia should be here, because she helped convert this warehouse for its current use as an aerospace technology laboratory for Velocitech Inc., particularly in engineering its most special feature. That's something the salamander really needs to know about so that he and everyone in New Alexandria and a 75-mile radius don't wind up incinerated tonight. Antonia *should* be here explaining all this, and she would be too, if she hadn't decided to turn right at the same moment three firemen rushing a ladder down the street outside headquarters decided to turn left. The sound Antonia's skull made when the ladder connected with it was one of the defining moments of my life. Before Antonia even hit the ground I knew it meant I was in for a hot time in the old town tonight.

I tell all this to the salamander.

He says, "Simms? Stocky guy, bald, a scar along his cheek?"

"That's him."

"Sorry to hear that. And I do hope Ms. Blanco makes a full recovery."

The thought of being down two alchemists if Antonia doesn't bounce back sends visions of navigating canyons of paperwork while pulling triple shifts through my head, and I shudder. "If she doesn't get better, I'll kill her."

The salamander smirks. "Right. Like that'll help. But you are very brave to come here."

"I'm a hometown boy. Got to represent for my city. But, tell me, what can I call you?"

"I won't tell you my name."

"No, obviously not." In alchemy, possessing an elemental's name gives you power over it. Not absolute power, but enough to be really annoying. Thus, most elementals keep tight-lipped about their name. "But I can't keep thinking of you as salamander or dragon. What would someone call you at a cocktail party?"

"I don't go to cocktail parties. Not that I wouldn't if I were ever invited. If I did folks would call me He Who Burns All Flammable Items."

"That's a mouthful," I say, thinking some days you really can't catch a break.

"I have a nickname my friends use."

"Elementals have friends?"

"That surprises you, but you simply assumed I go to cocktail parties?"

"Good point. Sorry."

"If you explain how it is you're not burning up, which is the first question I asked you—and I have been exceptionally patient for a hot-blooded creature in awaiting your answer—then I shall tell you my nickname. If I like your explanation, that is."

I agree, but the terms make me a little queasy. Letting He Who Burns know how I'm doing what I'm doing is giving something away, and other than that he hasn't so far tried to burn, crush, or eat me, I really have no reason to trust him. Also the more I think about it the harder it is to do what I'm doing. Talking about it means thinking about it, and I'm getting tired. I thought I'd be out of here by now, message delivered, crisis resolved, but these things always take so much longer than you expect them to when you plan them out at headquarters.

"I have some charcoal and asbestos in my pockets. I'm using them to ask the ground beneath the building to absorb the flames and smoke in my immediate vicinity," I say. "It's working like a filter. There might be some toasty cockroaches down there, but better them than me."

"As above, so below. Reverse the environment. Clever," says the salamander. "How long can you keep that up?"

"Oh, indefinitely. Piece of cake. Do it every day."

"Because you look tired to me."

"Been a long few days."

"I hear you. The decade I've been having, you have no idea."

"So, nickname?"

"Oh, right. That."

"Hey, come on, we had a deal."

"You know that you not being a fire-based alchemist means I'm permitted to burn, crush, or eat you as I might any ordinary human, and it wouldn't be a breach of protocol or etiquette?"

"It's like that? I thought we were having a meaningful conversation here. Trust me when I say it's not in your best interests to do any of those things to me until you hear what I have to say."

"I wasn't planning on harming you, unless you laugh at my nickname."

"I promise I won't laugh."

"Then you may call me Frizzle."

It takes a lot of effort and my best poker face, but laugh? No, not me, not with being burned, crushed, or eaten on the table. Besides, growing up on the streets of New Alexandria, I heard kids in the neighborhood calling each other much worse. So, I nod and act like I'm honored, which really I am, given the alternatives. But because fire and salamanders are unpredictable, I need to keep the conversation moving.

"Frizzle," I say. "Do you know who summoned you?"

"I assumed it was Simms who called me."

"To burn up half the city?"

"I did not start those fires."

"You sure spread them around."

The Velocitech complex is near the waterfront. Frizzle's walk across the city left a fiery trail you can probably see from space. Frizzle doesn't answer. Instead he does the salamander equivalent of raising an eyebrow, and then he snorts a cloud of fire in my direction.

"Then you don't know why you were summoned?"

"Obviously, I do not."

Right then, the heat gets to me. Everything in sight ripples with it and it looks like the world is melting. My head aches and my throat goes dry as sandstone. I close my eyes and rub my temples. Then I look up at Frizzle, trying to meet his gaze, despite how terrifying it is, but I can't. I'm wearing down.

At all times I wear four pieces of earth on a leather strand around my neck. Tonight it's a piece of chalk from Stonehenge on the Salisbury Plain, a chunk of volcanic rock from the ruins of Pompeii, a knob of gold from the deepest mine in Africa, and a shard of granite from my home neighborhood on the west side of New Alexandria. I switch it up depending on the task at hand or my mood, but that's my power combo. It energizes me and boosts my confidence. I wear it whenever things get serious. I reach under my shirt and rub the granite between two fingers. It's dry and smooth, and it steadies me.

I look Frizzle in the eyes and deliver the shocking news: "Someone summoned you so they can kill you."

Frizzle squints. His lips curl back and forth, and his forked tongue flicks out as if he's licking the flame.

"That's not funny. I thought we were getting to be friends, and you make a joke in such poor taste. Hmmm. Burn, crush, or eat, I wonder?"

"No joke. A crazy guy plans to torch the whole city, and you're the flamethrower."

"Do you know how hard it is to destroy an elemental?"

"It's almost impossible."

"It is completely impossible. We are forces of nature. Elemental."

"Not to be contrary, now, but when you answer a summoning, you bring your form into the material world. Here, you really are more dragon than salamander, and that means you're subject to the laws of chemistry, alchemy, and physics."

"So, what?"

"You need fire to live. In this world fire needs three things to exist: fuel, heat, and oxygen. Take one away, no fire. No fire, no Frizzle. What happens then?"

"If what you say were to happen, then I would disperse into my fundamental form, causing a fiery blast of several hundred degrees Fahrenheit and scorching to cinders everything within, perhaps, a 60- or 75-mile radius."

"See? That's why I'm so concerned about your welfare."

Frizzle smirks. "Fuel, heat, and oxygen are all in abundance here. No elemental of any kind has been destroyed in the physical world for centuries."

"Okay, then, let me ask you this: Where are you going?"

"Do you mean right now? Or in general with my direction in life? Because I've been having some doubts and feeling rather isolated lately."

I've summoned precious few elementals in my time as an alchemist. They really don't belong in the physical world, and you can borrow their power without having to bring them here. Plus, being elementals, they tend to be one dimensional. Because they have no soul, they have no morality. They're the ultimate rationalists, and that makes them challenging to deal with. Earth elementals live in a geological timeframe. You could ask one a question then walk the dog, go out for coffee and brunch, read the paper, and still get back in time for what at best might be a one-word answer. Never have I met an elemental as curious, talkative, or metaphysically inclined as Frizzle. Salamanders like him must have inspired the legend that dragons are wise.

"Listen, you need an ear to bend or a shoulder to cry on about your path in life, hey, I'm there for you on any other night," I say. "Tonight I'm preoccupied with right now."

"What are you getting at?"

"The fires brought you here, right?"

"Yes. Their rich, alchemical combustion was irresistible."

"Those fires were planned in the shape of the dragon-fire sign to make sure you wouldn't miss them."

It took me two days to figure that out because the pattern was invisible from ground level. Only when I plotted all the fires on a topographical map, hoping for an earthy way to extinguish them, did I see it. That was when I knew they added up to more than mere arson. By then, though, it was too late to stop Frizzle from materializing.

I explain everything to Frizzle. He raises a fiery eyebrow when I tell him I even rushed an alchemical autopsy of Simm's corpse. It's standard for another alchemist to examine the body of any deceased alchemist ahead of the coroner, because you can't always be sure that dead is dead when you're dealing with alchemists. Sometimes dead is a transition, a pause, or a cocoon-like hibernation without the cocoon. You'd be surprised how many alchemists were buried alive before the new policy took effect. Once I found the pattern in the fire, it seemed likely Simm's murderer and our firebug might be the same guy. He probably killed Simms to stop him interfering with the fires, and that meant the body might hold some clues.

My exam confirmed that Simms was in fact dead; three bullet holes in his chest and three large, bloody exit wounds in his back left no doubt about it. Also, Simm's link to the region's natural fire energies had been severed before he died, which meant he'd been so weak and sickly that he was easy prey. An alchemist's bond to natural energies grows stronger with time, and when it's broken without proper planning the separation takes a heavy toll. That meant the killer had probably stolen some of Simm's power before murdering him.

The corpse's biggest clue, though, came when I discovered that a small bone or section of bone had been removed from each of Simm's limbs, his torso, and his head. A coroner's exam would've missed that, but even after death, the body retains a low-grade electromagnetic field, and I could read that. It was hazy, but the gaps acted like pointers for the stolen bones. They meant I was dealing with someone very in the know, because the power inherent in an alchemist's bones is one of those deep, dark, secret-handshake kinds of secrets that no alchemist would ever blab about to an outsider. I was certain our firebug had used Simm's bones to help light his fires.

Frizzle's only comment as I lay all of this on him is to say, "Fascinating."

I can see he's waiting for me to connect all the dots, so I tell him how the autopsy findings narrowed the suspect list. There are only so many licensed alchemists in New

Alexandria, plus a handful of unlicensed alchemists, who think we don't know about them, but that's because they're not very good alchemists. Also on the scene is an unknown number of crackpots, wannabes, and almost-rans, who don't have the skill, intellect, wisdom, or physicality for alchemy. Most become alchemist's assistants or conventional scientists. Some go it alone. There's not much you can't find on the black market, but alchemy is hard, but not impossible, to learn without a mentor. After autopsying Simms, I figured our firebug for a local loner, because igniting so many alchemical fires in such a short time meant he knew the natural energies of New Alexandria. No one had wandered into town on impulse and started burning up the place.

The NAPD started pounding the pavement and checking out alibis. In nine hours they had cut down the list of people who could've started the fires. In another five, they had reduced it to those with a motive, and then to our lead suspect. That came from a lucky break: Some bureaucrat in human resources had jotted down something actually useful on the civil service application of a man named Chandhi Mason. Ten years ago Mason had applied for a technician's position in the NAPD forensic alchemy division. His education, skills, and experience made him a perfect candidate, but he wanted to train only in Simm's group. Only fire interested him. That's a red flag.

Alchemists can't choose the element with which they have the strongest affinity. There's a process for determining that, and if you want to be an alchemist, you take what you get. It's too dangerous otherwise. Once you've mastered your element, you have a degree of power over the others, but you'll never be as strong as a specialist. Mason's tunnel vision got him tagged for an interview with a shrink, who learned that Mason's entire family had died in a tenement fire when he was a kid. The firemen got to Mason's bedroom before the fire did; his family wasn't so fortunate. Thus his obsession with fire, but that wasn't why he didn't make the cut.

The real reason, which the paper-pusher who processed Mason's rejection letter noted at the bottom of his application, was: "Believes he saw a dragon."

Frizzle wrinkles his nose and rolls his eyes at this part. "What precisely is wrong with that?"

"Nothing," I say, "if the dragon was real."

"Well, real is so relative."

There's some truth to that, but any elemental knows as well as I do that most mythical creatures *are* mythical. Some are real like, say, salamanders, but don't waste your time looking for a manticore.

Dragons are a special case.

Pretty much no one believes they exist now in the classical, living-under-a-mountain, sleeping-on-a-hoard-of-treasure sense. Whether or not that type of dragon ever existed is hotly debated. I have an opinion, but I *know* some types of dragons, like salamanders, are real. Other alchemists argue that salamanders are elementals, not dragons, but to me it's a fine distinction, because everyone agrees that salamanders contributed to the origins of our legends about fire-breathing dragons. It's all a bit technical, but regardless of where you stand in the dragon debate the bottom line is that if you believe a fire-breathing dragon burned down your apartment, you're probably not playing with a full deck.

"The point is," I say, "this guy's a rogue with an axe to grind over you burning up his family while he was still wearing footie pajamas."

"How does he know it was me?"

"There aren't a lot of salamanders native to New Alexandria. If he included something burned in the fire that killed his family in his summoning process, then it would've implicated you."

I give Frizzle the details of the fire. The New Alexandria Fire Department had no problem digging them up from their records. They considered Simms one of their own, and nobody knows how to get a job done faster than a bunch of pissed-off firefighters.

"I was there," Frizzle says. "The fire began with faulty wiring. What a wonderful little tinderbox! It blazed quite fast, and I feasted on its flames. I was smaller then, but to an imaginative child, I would have seemed very much like a full-grown dragon."

Minus the feasting on flames part, that's pretty much what the NAFD report said.

"So, it's a trap, get it?" I say. "Mason wants revenge."

"No matter. Properly summoned, I must answer. I will explain when I see him that I did not cause the fire, and because I have enjoyed myself tonight, I will offer him a bag of gold in compensation for frightening him when he was a child."

"He wants vengeance for his family burning up and for New Alexandria rejecting him. He's probably spent years planning this, learning the alchemical processes to do it, and steeling himself to kill an entire city because he flunked a psych test. I really don't think a bag of gold is going to smooth it over."

"Alchemists crave gold above all else," says Frizzle. "What about *three* bags of gold?"

That's the soulless rationalist speaking. The notion of senseless, emotionally driven vengeance is hard to parse when you see existence only in terms of processes and transactions. Matter becomes energy, energy becomes matter. There's no particular attachment to one state or the other. Alchemy is all about transformation. Elementals don't like to get in the way of transformative processes, even the unpleasant or hazardous ones. While Frizzle might think of self-preservation, the idea of his destruction isn't very real to him, because all of his elemental energy will go back into the natural pool to be reconstituted sometime in the future. Unless every mentor I've had since I first began studying the Emerald Tablet has been wrong or lying to me, the deaths of millions of people who won't ever be reconstituted means little to him.

Unless I can convince him otherwise.

"We seem to be getting along pretty well, right?" I say.

"We do."

"You trust me?"

"I do not think you are lying to me."

"Great. Here's what you need to know: Mason is luring you into a chamber inside this facility. If you enter that room, he'll destroy you. Turn back now, and you save yourself."

"How exactly will he destroy me?"

"With a vacuum."

Frizzle scowls and his eyes brighten. Tendrils of flame drift from his nostrils and the corners of his lips.

"Explain," he says.

"Velocitech, the company that owns this facility, builds planes that go Mach 4 and rockets that put satellites in orbit. And, yeah, it occurred to me and a lot of other people how foolish it is to have a rocket lab inside the city limits, but the mayor was hell-bent on attracting new business. You should've seen the alternatives. All I'll say is hazardous waste storage. But Velocitech does aerodynamics design testing here. That rocket fuel you've been guzzling down is part of their latest round of product development."

"It is a most worthy and flammable vintage. I have tasted nothing so fine since Krakatoa last erupted."

"Glad to hear it. What you need to know is they have a vacuum chamber here big enough to fit a full-size rocket. That's where Mason is waiting for you. Once you're inside, he's going to slip out the back and activate the vacuum. Goodbye air, goodbye fire, goodbye Frizzle and New Alexandria."

"You are certain he can do this?"

"I am."

Antonia helped build the chamber, using a touch of air alchemy to ensure its seals would hold. She had no doubt about what Mason planned or that it would work. She explained everything to me, the mayor, and the police commissioner right before she got knocked on the head.

"Then tonight shall be a sad and fiery occasion," says Frizzle. "I have been summoned, and I must go."

"No!"

"No?"

"You can't. Everyone will die!"

"How many are there in your city? A few million out of the billions on the planet? That's hardly everyone. Of those how many would mourn my destruction were it not linked to their own? How many would speak to me as an equal like you have done rather than flee in terror? It matters not. I was summoned. There are proprieties to observe, obligations to fulfill."

"If you mean rules, Mason summoned you illegally. In this city that right belonged only to Simms."

"Irrelevant. What's done is done. I would offer you a head start to escape, but I do not think it would help."

Frizzle turns and moves across the burning space. Parts of the roof fall in, a singed and chunky rain. No part of the building remains un-ignited. The heat rises. My protective bubble weakens, and so do I. As he crosses among the giant tongues of flame licking at the walls and equipment, Frizzle looks imperious and majestic. It saddens me to imagine him going stoically to his destruction. But it saddens me a lot more to think of dying and of all the other people who'll die if Frizzle enters the vacuum chamber. It hits me hard that my time on earth is about to end. I really wish I could be with Lucy, my neurosurgeon girlfriend. But I'm going to die alone, apart even from the city that is as much a part of me as I am of it, because the fire is heating up the last few barrels of fuel Frizzle didn't drink. It's only a matter of minutes before they explode. I'll die before everyone else. Even if I could somehow buy only those few minutes more, I would, and as soon as I think about the fuel, the answer comes to me, and I wonder: *Why not?*

"Frizzle," I call. "Wait."

Frizzle's head rises high on his sinuous neck. He looks down at me across the length of his body. The red light in his eyes is so bright and deep now that his face seems to glow.

"Yes?"

"Forget what I said about self-preservation and preventing the death of millions. Life becomes death, death becomes life, right? We all gotta go sometime. What if I made you an offer?"

"What kind of offer?"

"A bargain. You agree not to go into the vacuum chamber. Instead, you suck up all the flames, put out all the fires in the city tonight, and then leave here and go back to your elemental home."

"In exchange for what?"

Frizzle's curiosity gives me a second wind. My idea will work. It *has* to work. Everything will be fine. By tonight the fires will be out, and I'll be sleeping with Lucy in my arms. By Monday morning, I'll be back in my lab with my alembics and my fluid condensers, and I'll be sifting through a bucket of crime scene dirt to solve an ordinary homicide. And the whole time I'll have the AC on full blast because I don't ever want to be hot again.

Frizzle leans down, and I spell it out for him. My proposal makes him quite happy. He grins, releasing a sheet of flame that spreads over us like a canopy.

After that, the fires begin to go out.

The warehouse is extinguished first. The flames flash and swirl, seeming to run like water down a drain right into Frizzle. Pretty soon, enough of the building is clear and cooling that I can let up asking the earth to protect me. My bubble pops. I'm surprised at how dry the air feels, how pure it tastes, as if the fire cleansed and rejuvenated it. Frizzle works his way back along his path from downtown, drinking in the fires as he goes and leaving a swath of smoky, blackened buildings and vehicles. I follow him.

It's the weirdest thing I've ever seen: fire flowing into a red, three-story-tall dragon, who seems as happy as can be and hums as he goes. By the time we reach the heart of downtown, others are walking behind me, an ad hoc parade, all of us deeply relieved that our city will burn no more.

Soon the last of the fires go out.

After that, Frizzle vanishes. I don't even see him leave.

Later a SWAT team raids the ruins of the lab. They find Chandhi Mason in the vacuum chamber, dead as a doornail. The fire-proofed, rocket-testing chamber isn't burned up, but the only way Mason could keep the heat and fire out while he waited for Frizzle was to close the seals. Apparently he didn't know that doing so automatically flushes all the air from the chamber. No one sheds a tear.

The mayor, though, isn't too thrilled with me.

He's overjoyed that I got the fires put out and sent Frizzle on his way, but he doesn't like how I did it. He thinks it'll cost too much. He thinks it'll be dangerous and bad for the city's reputation. He thinks the people who live outside the city will bitch and moan, and of course, they will, but I don't care. I tell him not to sweat it, pun intended, because this is the best deal anyone could've possibly gotten, and that it works out great for everyone involved, especially all of us who avoided being burned to a crisp.

What I offered Frizzle in return for taking his fire and leaving was simple: a cocktail party, once a year, every year for ten years, up in the mountains outside of town. The folks of New Alexandria supply ten barrels of the best vintage our local jet-propulsion scientists can cook up, and Frizzle can bring a few friends. I even promised to call him He Who Burns All Flammable Items the next time I see him. That's the thing about anyone who comes to New Alexandria expecting the worst: Show them a good time, make them feel at home, and they feel like they've lived there all their life.

Even to a soulless rationalist that was a better deal than being dispersed to his basic components, although I wonder now exactly how much danger Frizzle was in by the time we struck our bargain. The coroner couldn't pin down the exact time of Mason's death, but he didn't last long once the lab was ablaze. The moment he died, his hold over Frizzle ended. There would've been nothing compelling Frizzle to enter the vacuum chamber then. He could've left anytime. Maybe I got played a little, but then salamanders are unpredictable, and you never know. I don't think about it. I'm happy to be alive, and a year from now, I'll be happy to drive a truck full of rocket fuel into the mountains and deliver a high-octane happy hour. Mostly, though, I'm happy because by then we'll have a new fire alchemist on duty, and this will all be his problem because dragons…sorry, salamanders…simply aren't my jurisdiction.

The Star Gazers

Khate winced at the six-inch, steel fragment protruding from her thigh, welling blood onto her flight-suit. She should've grabbed the damn first aid kit when she wriggled free of the wrecked lifeboat. Retrieving it now meant crawling back over Jarn's corpse.

At least her mother's field pouch and its contents remained strapped to her waist thanks to her single-minded refusal to part with it. From the look of her wound, though, she needed the first aid kit more. The gash seemed deep enough to require spray flesh but probably not life-threatening if she stanched the bleeding. The balance of her bruises, cuts, and burns hurt like hell but would heal well enough on their own. She wished Jarn had also come through the crash as relatively unharmed as she and choked back a deep sob.

Plastic-and-electric humming alerted her to the return of the hover-assassins that had downed the boat.

Groaning, Khate lurched beneath an immobile fold of the nearby Star Gazer's robe and toppled into the enormous structure's shade. Salton metal in the Gazer would hide her from the HA's sensors. Jarn had sighted on the figure before the salvo that had blasted them from the sky, and the boat had come down only thirty meters away. She landed on her knees, skidding to cover. The shrapnel in her leg twisted, blasting agony through her adrenalin rush and tipping her into a gray fog. She lingered there, bleary and light-headed, until the squad of HAs, having detected no signs of life, departed.

Khate opened her eyes to empty sky.

Bracing herself on the warm base of the Star Gazer, she struggled upright.

Endless meadows of sere grass swayed around her in warm, half-hearted breezes. To the south awaited the planet's only city, Salton's Rig, her destination. To the east and west, lines of Star Gazers at thirty-seven-kilometer intervals encircled Salton's equator. To the north, past the smoking wreck of the lifeboat, a sea of grass she knew gave way to desolate taiga near the pole, a haunted land filled with the ghosts of spent mines from her mother's first expeditions.

The decimated lifeboat slouched like an oryx chewed apart by jackals. Khate eased from the Gazer's shadow, watching, listening, but detecting no sign of the HAs. Every motion added fuel to the bonfires of pain burning in her body. The stink of machine blood and burned metal seared her nostrils. As she neared the boat, her body refused to take another step, overwhelmed by the fierce smell of her husband's charred flesh, by raw, sensory grief. She exhaled an apology to Jarn, her words warped into a keening dirge as they crossed her trembling lips. She had brought him here only to die as would countless others if she failed. She compartmentalized her despair the way her mother had taught her, the same way she had so many other losses on her path to this moment and saved it for mourning later—if later ever came.

Shutting her eyes, she crab-walked through the misshapen hatch. Radiant heat enveloped her. She covered her mouth and nose with one hand as the greasy, sour odor of Jarn's still-sizzling flesh flooded her nostrils. Touching him as little as possible she fished for the first aid kit. Each second of groping the ruined console passed like a thousand days of torture until her fingers found the hard, plastic case and nudged it free. She pressed the kit to her chest and backed out, gagging, desperate for open air. Midway back to the shelter provided by the Gazer, she folded to her knees. Fresh agony flared in her thigh. She dry-heaved before she collapsed and rolled onto her back, every limb buzzing with hurt.

High and far above, a nuclear blaze churned on Salton's mesospheric fringes, remnants of the transport ship that had brought her and Jarn here.

Its entire crew, all its passengers, except for her, sacrificed to bring her to Salton's Rig.

Hot tears spilled down her cheeks. Her mother's ways failed her, and she wept. Whether for Jarn, her pain, the dead and all those soon to die, or for all of it together, she couldn't say.

Beside her the 400-foot-high Star Gazer remained unmoved, poised eternally skyward. Its many eyes peered longingly at the heavens. One of its right limbs reached toward space, sleeve peeled back from a coiled appendage bristling with wiry tendrils. Motionless swaths draped from its knobby joints and slithery lashes, more like wings or fin membranes than robes, though that's what people called them, imparting a sort of reverence. Iridescence limned the enormous figure. Colors coruscated in its Salton skin. Waves cycled through the tall grass in rhythm to the shifting hues. So ripe with a sense of motion yet forever unchangeable, encapsulating the mystery of Salton metal. Power source. Weapon. Building material. Energy given form and substance. An enigma to which Khate possessed the answer no one wanted to believe. From here, the Gazer appeared to reach toward the burning scar of her dead transport, stretching to catch a dying ship that would never fall—or perhaps to deflect its unwanted intrusion.

Khate choked back a fresh wave of sobs, sat up, and snapped open the first aid kit.

Using the scissors, she snipped away part of her suit. The wound looked clean, but rich, burgundy blood still bubbled from it. She grabbed the spray flesh can in one hand, gripped the shrapnel with her other, and clenched her jaw. She eyed the strong analgesics in the kit but didn't dare ease her pain at the cost of dulling her reflexes. After a silent count to three, she yanked the sliver loose and released an anguished wail. She sealed the wound with spray flesh, antibiotic vapor cooling her skin then tickling as it dried and closed the gash.

She watched until the bleeding stopped, and then she crashed back on the grass.

Her pain dimmed to a constant, throbbing ache. She drew an energy bar from the kit and ate it, washing it down with a shot of electrolyte tea.

After a while, the sweat on her brow dried, and the persistent reek of death sickened her.

She unzipped her mother's pouch and confirmed it still contained the data chips of half a dozen Riggers who'd taken the flight to Endless. Each had come from a lost corpse drifting in its forsaken ship through one of the many debris clouds the war with the Infinite Empire had left scattered around the galaxy. Each held a razor's edge of truth, a testament to hubris. And each justified the lives she'd used, the fortune she'd exhausted to obtain them—but only if she could reach Salton's Rig before morning and show them to her contact. If only enough time remained for the people who held power to act on their truth.

Jarn had intended to land them midway between Rig and the nearest Star Gazer, only twelve klicks away, but the hover-assassins drove them off course 100 kilometers out. Khate had no idea how far from the city her boat had crashed.

She zipped the pouch closed then rose and hobbled south, her gait steadying with every step. On the grasslands' western edge, twin suns hung low, emphasizing the urgency of her task. Night fell quickly on Salton. She walked until the stars emerged then used them to gauge her position. Rather than a dozen klicks to Rig, more than seventy lay ahead of her. On foot she could never reach the city in time. The realization gutted her.

To come so close only to fall so short.

Someone had betrayed her to Alann Thanh, and Thanh had responded as he'd sworn to if she ever returned. He hadn't yet killed her as promised, not directly, but if she couldn't make the city before dawn, she was as good as dead. She may as well retreat to the wrecked boat, lie down beside Jarn, and wait to die with everyone else.

Instead, she pressed southward, thinking of her mother a century ago.

Afloat in interstellar space, sustained only by basic life support, her ship's engines, comm systems, and weapons dead, Mina Salton had hurried through repairs, racing against starvation, dehydration, or asphyxiation that would almost certainly claim her before she completed them—when she drifted across the enigmatic empty ship made of Salton metal. The first discovered. She'd used it to get home then tracked down its abandoned origin world—the only known source of the metal—and reaped a fortune.

Hope never fails us, her mother used to say. *We fail hope when we release it before it's done with us.*

She died never knowing her discovery also handed humanity the keys to its extinction.

Night fell and the wind turned chilly. A fog of stars speckled the sky. Against the distant glow the lights of Salton's Rig daubed onto the clouds, ships danced.

Khate's leg throbbed. Her stomach grumbled.

The rhythm of grass and earth crunching underfoot mesmerized her.

When a cruiser buzzed out from the west, the proximity alarm in her bio-monitor warned her before she spied its approaching lights.

The tall grass offered only shadows for cover, so she flattened her body to the earth and hoped the cruiser pilot didn't see her. But the ship didn't fly over and vanish as she wished. It hovered for several seconds before the clank of landing skids deploying announced its descent less than fifty yards from her position.

Khate struggled to her feet and then ran, bolting south.

She ignored an amplified voice ordering her to stop. Grass and soil padded underfoot. Clicking, beeping, buzzing sounds followed her, until two hover-assassins floated in front of her face, their glaring sensor beams outlining the guns aimed at her. The drones rattled off further demands for Khate to stop. She shrieked and swung the first aid kit, knocking one of the HAs to the ground with a crack and a shower of sparks.

"Hey! Watch it!" an amplified voice called. "You know how much it costs to repair those?"

Footsteps drum-rolled after her. Khate spun to confront a figure whose face hid behind the lowered visor of a flight helmet. Beyond, the cruiser idled, its engines bright with Salton metal glow. The pockmarked hull indicated the flier belonged to a bounty hunter, scavenger, or another class of outcast, none of whom could mean Khate any good.

She snatched up the damaged hover-assassin and aimed its gun.

The figure skidded to a stop and raised its arms. "Whoa, whoa! Okay, okay, don't sweat the damage. I can probably fix it myself. Just point that another direction, will you?"

Khate ignored the request. "Open your helmet, slowly."

The visor rose to reveal the soft face of a young man with delicate Asian features, hair shaved to the scalp, pilot's anti-glare smudge rimming his eyes. Khate detected an odd mix of fear and hope in his expression.

"I'm Slinnmath Raychan. You can call me Slinn," he said. Unamplified by his helmet, his voice sounded warm and young. "Are you Khate Salton?"

"Don't worry about who I am. How old are you?" Khate said.

"What? What the hell does that matter?"

"You don't look old enough to fly the Gazer trail, let alone own a cruiser. Who's in your flier waiting to jump me?"

"Oh, I get it. No one." Slinn shrugged. "I may be young, but I fly better than most people twice my age. So why not fly the Gazers? I inherited the cruiser."

"Is that so? I'm going to have to take it from you," Khate said. "I need to be in Salton's Rig tonight."

"Yes, I know. That's why I came for you. I'll take you to Rig."

Khate pulled back. "You came looking for me?"

"The Gazers told me you'd be here. They said Thanh would try to kill you and fail, and I should look for you in the grasslands tonight."

"What do you mean the Gazers told you? No, forget it." Khate menaced Slinn with the damaged drone. "You're lying. Key card, now. I'll fly myself."

The *click-hum* of a weapon to her left her gave her a chill and she froze.

"Shoot me, my other HA shoots you." Slinn nodded to the second drone which floated above Khate's shoulder, its gun-barrel eye focused on her head. "You realize I could've killed you without even landing if that's what I wanted, right?"

Khate hated to trust any stranger on Salton let alone a boy, but if he could bring her to Rig she didn't want to turn her back on hope rewarded. She lowered the damaged HA. The other ramped down its weapon and backed off.

"Fine, then, you drive."

She tossed the broken drone at Slinn's feet and stalked toward the cruiser. Slinn retrieved his property then caught up and ushered Khate onboard. They soon lifted off to an altitude which offered a clear view of the lights at Salton's Rig and the eternal glow of the Star Gazers east and west of them. Slinn piloted with skill equal to his claim.

Khate studied his sincere eyes intent on flying, his narrow lips and soft cheeks, the face of a painter, poet, or musician but not a pilot flying the Gazers, fighting other scavengers for the meager bounty of erosion-shed Salton metal scales.

"How'd you inherit this ship?" she asked.

"My uncle left it to me. I dropped out of university and came here to accept it. He's the one who taught me to fly. I've been flying the Gazers almost a year. The dreams started right away."

"What dreams?"

"It's how the Gazers talk to me. Well, not *talk* exactly. They send me impressions or put me into other, ah, consciousnesses to experience. It's hard to explain. I kind of assumed you had the dreams too. I mean, you know more about the Gazers than anyone else. They're not what we think, are they?"

"No," said Khate.

160

A satisfied grin brightened Slinn's face. "I knew it!"

"What do you think you know?"

"They're alive, right? Salton metal, this whole planet is sentient."

Khate sighed. "You don't even know what you don't know."

"Yeah, well, I know how to fly, and I know to thank someone who picks my ass up from the grasslands and gives me a ride."

Khate rested her head on the seat back. "Thank you for the ride, know-nothing Slinn."

Engine thrum filled the silence between them.

They passed the next Gazer en route to Rig. Its monstrous face and myriad eyes regarded them with unblinking indifference, reflecting multiples of distant flickering fire. Khate glanced upward to the wreck of her transport, an extra star in the night, burning hotter and brighter than Salton's rising moon.

"How do you know your dreams come from the Gazers?" Khate asked. "Couldn't they be from your subconscious?"

"Collective subconscious, maybe. I'm not the only one who dreams them. A dozen of us dream pieces of the same dreams then decode them collectively, piece together all the separated things. We dream fragments of cities with towers and great halls that defy geometry. Streets that entwine infinitely on themselves. We visit sunken places where light doesn't exist, yet we can still see. I was in art school before I inherited the cruiser and came here so I draw. Others write, make music, or sculpt. The planet wants us to understand it."

"The Gazers tell you that?"

"Why else would they communicate? They need us to explain them to others."

"Assuming I even buy that, how do you know you can trust the dreams?"

"They brought me to you, didn't they?"

"There are other ways you could've known to look for me," Khate said. "People in Rig know I'm coming. I've already been betrayed once on this journey."

Slinn shrugged. "I guess."

Rig drew closer, brighter, an unchecked tumor of metal, glass, plastic, and commerce. It remained so much smaller in Khate's memory, no more than a cluster of temporary shelters, and steel, building skeletons, and roads that existed only on maps. She knew it best that way, at its beginnings, her childhood home where her mother led the Salton mining efforts, and ships of all kinds brought workers and equipment and took away tons of Salton metal. Mined day and night, and bound for shipyards orbiting Cluster, Nyad, Galapagos, and other worlds. All for the war effort. Every ounce of cargo still increased her family's fortune. Khate had spent her share as fast as she accrued it until she'd stooped to borrowing from Jarn to make the last leg of her journey back here.

"You can't dock at the port. I'll be found," she said.

"The Gazers showed me it'll be fine. Thanh thinks you're dead."

"I don't care what you dreamt. Set down by the eastern market near the med plaza. It'll be desolate this time of night."

Glittering lights and shifting shadows expanded to fill the view screen. Constant motion. Boundless energy. Ships rising and falling by the immense spaceport she had never seen before. So much had migrated to the realm of pure memory. Khate wrung her scarred hands.

The cruiser slowed for approach.

She squeezed Slinn's arm. "Didn't you hear me? Approach from the east."

"Relax. This is the best way."

"No, turn this thing around now!"

Slinn shook his head. "My cruiser, my choice. Salton wants it this way."

Khate grabbed Slinn's wrist and yanked, trying to pull it from the control board and force a course change, but he proved stronger than she. Status lights flashed when Rig's flight control system locked onto the cruiser, and the small ship's flight computer defaulted to autopilot. Any change now would draw immediate pursuit from manned security patrollers. Khate weighed her options. Fight Slinn, seize the cruiser, and run. Hide on board and try to slip into Rig unseen. Or place her trust in Slinn and his dreams and hope for the best.

The cruiser entered the landing zone, drifting to a docking platform quicker than she'd expected. She decided on hope. It had brought her this far.

Outside, a standard flight crew converged on the craft.

No sign of HAs, city police, or of Thanh's Special Mining Guard.

"See?" Slinn said. "We can walk right in."

Khate waited a little longer. Nothing out of the ordinary appeared on the dock.

She and Slinn barely merited notice from the bustling crew when they debarked to the flight way and entered the spaceport.

"I have to go to the Okama Building in the med plaza," said Khate.

"We can get rail transport down here." Slinn directed Khate to a fork in the corridor but then hung back as she rounded the first curve. "The thing is, Ms. Salton, the Gazers have given us so much we have to trust them now and do what they want, and they don't want you to go to the Okama Building."

"What?" Khate heeled around. "What do you mean?"

Ahead a scuffle of feet pattered. Men in Mining Guard uniforms rushed at them. Khate swore at Slinn then shoved past him, heading back toward the dock, but guards came from that direction too and blocked her way.

She punched Slinn in the chest, knocking him against the wall. "Idiot! Liar!"

"Trust the Gazers," he said. "Everything will be fine. Better than fine. Wonderful!" The guards encircled them. Slinn joined two officers who pressed through the ranks.

A familiar and unwelcome voice boomed down the flight way. "I swore to kill you if you came back here. You've been gone so long, I never expected I'd have to make good. Why'd you do it, Khate? Why return?"

The guards parted for Alann Thanh.

The gray-haired man stood nearly a head taller than the others, his face textured by years of worry and sunlight. He had lost nothing of his strength or posture to age. The sight of him unwound Khate to her ten-year-old self. Playing with dolls in the grass. Lifting her head to watch him walk in from the mines with the setting suns at his back after a day running the northern rigs. Mother calling from inside their housing module, hushing her away until he shucked his mine suit and washed up. An ocean of time between them that seemed to have passed in a sudden torrent. Only his hair's deep gray streaks and the faint droop at his left eye's corner broke the spell.

"I came to stop you killing every human in the known universe, Father," Khate said.

Her stature grew as she spoke, strengthened by her words. Rifles wavered in the hands of a few guards. Her father frowned.

"You've been crowing disaster since before I exiled you, yet we continue mining, living, thriving, despite all your Cassandra's tears. Your mother would—"

"*She* would be proud of me. Would've looked at the evidence and decided on the facts. She never would've shunned me for asking questions and pursuing the answers, no matter how much she didn't like them or how improbable she judged them."

Thanh sighed. His gaze moving over Khate, lingering at the pouch strapped to her waist.

"That belt belonged to her," he said.

"One of the few things of hers you let me keep."

"I've missed you all these years, Khate. Not a day passes I don't think of you and wish things were different. It's good to see you. I doubt you'll believe me, but it troubles me deeply how worn and tired you look. Whatever keeps us apart, I'm still your father. I sent you away to avoid hurting you or anyone else for that matter."

"Tell that to the people on the transport you destroyed. Tell it to my... my husband's burnt corpse lying in wreckage on the grasslands."

Thanh shut his eyes and exhaled deeply. "I'm sorry, Khate. So very sorry. Their blood is on your hands, though. Along with those of the men and women you were to meet tonight at the Okama building. You knew the cost of returning to Salton, yet you chose to rope these people into your delusions. I must protect the trade. I must supply the war effort. Many more lives than theirs are at stake."

"They were already as good as dead." Khate fought hot tears and tried to believe her own words. "All of us are if you don't listen to me."

"Then speak now. I'm listening."

"You're opening six new mines. Don't! Keep them offline. You don't know what you're really digging into. I promise you that. You *don't* know. But I can show you."

"I knew you returned because of the mines." Thanh rubbed his forehead. He glanced at the guards, all hanging fire with nervous expressions. "If I keep them offline what of the fortune our mines provide which funded your years running from star to star? What of our struggle against the Infinite Empire if the Salton metal supply ends? How many will die if our defenses are weakened? Millions? Billions?"

"It'll be far fewer than if you bring those mines online."

"An outrageous claim! Where is your evidence of such a calamity, Khate? Where are the answers you say you've spent your life seeking?"

Khate unzipped her mother's pouch, scooped out the data chips, and showed them to her father. "Here. From half a dozen veteran pilots who flew a mission to Endless."

A quiet, collective inhalation passed through the guards, the officers, even Slinn. Thanh studied his daughter's face. Khate saw a crack in his façade, a glimmer of curiosity she had not seen there since childhood. She clutched tighter to hope that no longer seemed entirely futile.

"Pilots who fly to Endless never return," Thanh said.

"I went searching for them."

"They never return *for a reason*, Khate. Prolonged exposure to Salton energy in a flight configuration affects one's mind. The mission to Endless is the last act of heroes before they turn dangerous to those they're sworn to protect. Whatever is recorded on those chips you ripped out of their brains isn't likely to even make sense."

"They're heroes, true. They protected us. Not from what they'd become but from what they feared they would set free."

"Stop being obtuse, Khate. Make your point."

"Look at them. Decide for yourself. That's all I ask."

"If I do and disagree, I'll have to keep the promise I made. It's my duty to protect the mines. If you don't convince me, you'll...well, I'll bury you beside your mother."

"Do you promise to act as decisively if you do agree?"

Thanh nodded. "You have my word."

Khate spilled the data chips into his open hand. He signaled for the guards to stand down then offered Khate his arm. She took it reluctantly and walked beside him to a waiting car with Slinn and four guards. A childish urge to hold his hand summoned dusty memories of walking with him to scout new mines and camps on the grasslands, and her nostrils filled with the scent memory of drying sweat and grass pollen. Her mother's laughter echoed faintly in her thoughts, and her father's young smile flashed across her mind's eye. She unhooked her arm and slid into the car.

After a short trip, Thanh ushered Khate into a gallery at the Mining Commission. The guards waited outside. A replica Star Gazer dominated the large art hall. A dozen men and women sat on loungers and chairs in its shadow. All eyes turned toward Khate and her father. When Slinn took his place among them, Khate guessed they were his fellow dreamers.

The gallery included an entire wall dedicated to Khate's mother's artwork. The sight of it nearly stole her breath. It seemed her father had gathered almost every piece her mother had ever created, even some Khate had last seen in museums on Earth, or Mars, or Navroxen. Scintillating colors glittered from neo-organic canvasses and nanometer-thin sheaves of copper and platinum, the first Salton metal art ever created. Khate had never seen so many of her mother's works in one place. They bored a small, cold hollow within her, not only for the sense of loss they amplified but for their collective echo of all she had seen on the salvaged data chips. It occurred to Khate her mother had known—or at least intuited—much more than either woman had understood.

The other walls showcased newer, less beautiful art. Relief sculptures. Cultured biofilms. Stardust collages. Dendral wood mosaics. Even handwritten pages of poetry and prose. The work of Slinn's dreamers Khate guessed, puzzle pieces created from fragmented dreams, glimpses of awareness too large for any single person to decipher.

"Slinn told you about the dreamers," Thanh said.

Walking the gallery wall, Khate nodded. "He didn't tell me they're working with you."

"The planet communicates through them. It communicated with your mother. She didn't comprehend it, but it manifested in her art. No one knew it back then. Now people have lived here long enough to make sense of what they experience. We're learning the planet's language. It guides us, Khate, through the dreamers. The new mines are right where it asked us to build them. They're not going to harm Salton. All will exist in a new type of harmony. We're partners now, humans and planet working together."

Slinn pointed to a triptych of paintings on ferrous glass. "These are my contribution."

"This planet is not alive," Khate said. "It's not even a goddamn planet."

Shocked silence blanketed them. All the dreamers stared at Khate with the lacerating pity reserved for those who have lost their senses.

"Khate, be reasonable," said Thanh.

"View the data. Look at the proof. I still have friends in the Mining Commission. I know the mines come online at dawn so there's time left to make the right choice."

"All right," Thanh said. "Let's get this over with."

Thanh and Khate moved to a room off the gallery. Thanh thumbed the chips into a tray where they glowed when connected to the system. He keyed in several codes.

Darkness spilled around them transforming the room into empty space, twinkling stars everywhere.

"Khate, as long as we haven't looked at these, I can spare your life. We can send you to a psych facility to restore your senses. No one will begrudge me an act of mercy for my daughter, not while I control the Salton metal trade. Reneging on a vow will make me look weak for a while, but my reputation will recover. If we look at your data and it changes nothing, though, you'll have tied my hands. It will have been a tacit attempt to interfere with the war effort under false pretenses. I'll have to…You'll have to be executed as a traitor. Khate, I don't want that."

Khate laughed.

"The universe doesn't care what you want," she said.

"All right, then. Show me."

Khate punched a final command into the viewer. The room melted. The walls dripped and folded around them and gave way to the vastness of space. A montage of flashing stars and far-off, pastel planets plunged them into a kaleidoscope. The walls and ceiling resolved into six discreet feeds unraveling the lives of six fighter pilots, all accelerated to the point of subliminal impression. The projectors scanned Khate's and Thanh's eyes and brains. Algorithms optimized the display for maximum comprehension in the shortest length of time. Years of experience danced across the screens, a mash-up of spaceflights, military bases, and combat missions. Short-lived explosions of enemy and friendly ships alike blotted out the stars. The perceptions of six men and women committed to duty, their mission punctuated only by infrequent revelry in officers' bars and furtive couplings between sorties; their lives burned like flares, hot, bright, and fast; their minds loaded with stubborn rage for the Infinite Empire, the endless adversary—and then space around them changed.

Thanh recoiled to the center of the room. One after another each display embarked on the flight to Endless. Pitch black space gradated to an oily, colorful sheen swirling in vortexes. Holes formed and widened, pressed stars aside, and devoured planes of empty void with the creeping vibrancy of Salton metal. Reality fragmented into geometric absurdities. Planets swelled, burst, and then contracted. Stars exploded and their pieces floated in fractal clouds of kinetic potential. Six times over, the universe tore itself down, reordered itself, and created something new.

Khate had seen this all before and couldn't bear to see it again. She focused on Thanh.

His mouth hung open. Tears poured from his eyes. Colors painted prismatic snakeskins on his face.

Convergence arrived. The moment when each pilot—altered by Salton metal—truly saw the universe, glimpsed the metal's purpose, and sensed the malevolent presences it held in check. A sub-audible cacophony invaded the room, a rabble of chaos unheard but felt in Khate's bones, accompanied by deathful whistling. The things the pilots saw reached into their minds softened by exposure to Salton metal to sway them to help them, to free them, to open their way into a universe they wished to devour—and the warriors fled to Endless to resist. They sacrificed themselves to prevent the things from using them.

Blood thundered in Khate's head. Her heart lost its rhythm.

Thanh stumbled. Gasping, Khate touched his arm. He shrieked and threw himself against the control station, killing the display.

The room returned to normal.

Unable to look his daughter in the eye, Thanh asked, "What are they?"

"They're what's inside Salton. This planet isn't alive, not even a real planet. It's a prison built to contain them. All these years, we've been chipping away at it. It's not the planet sending dreams but its prisoners. The more we dig, the easier it is for them to reach us. Like the pilots who flew the Endless. The Salton metal softened their minds so these things could reach in and manipulate them. They resisted, thinking they'd cracked up from trauma. If the dreams sent by these things showed you where to place the new mines then that's where they want them so they can break loose."

Thanh knelt before Khate and grasped her hands. He tried to speak. His lips trembled for several seconds before he found his voice. "I'm so sorry for not listening. For not trusting you. For making things worse."

Khate helped her father to his feet, his body shuddering beneath her hands.

"There's time to fix that now," she said.

A scream came from the gallery, followed by a thunderous crash. Khate and her father shared a questioning glance, and then Khate opened the door onto a dozen dreamers gone berserk. Several tore down the artworks they had created, while others fought and choked each other. One lay dead on the floor, her head a puddle of blood and bone and muscle debris as if her skull had exploded from within. Slinn clambered over the replica Star Gazer, hammering its eyes with a length of steel scrap.

Thanh grabbed his daughter's hand and rushed her from the gallery to an adjoining room with a view of Rig and the nearest Star Gazer to the east.

"My spies tracked you all the years you were gone, Khate," Thanh said. "They told me everything you did and hoped to accomplish. Oh, god, I'm so sorry, but I couldn't risk letting you make trouble here. I couldn't endanger the war effort or risk the new mines."

The building rumbled and shook.

"I knew you'd try to stop us," said Thanh.

Outside, the nearest Star Gazer shifted. Its enormous bulk rose, split apart, then shed itself in glowing chunks that rained down on the grasslands. Its many eyes and limbs, and the folds of its membranous robes disintegrated, spewing a cloud of color toward the night, gathering with polychromatic bursts from other Gazers. The aurora they made flowed as if every Gazer on Salton had cracked and now divulged its toxic colors upward, obliterating the starlight and the burning stain of Khate's lost transport. The kaleidoscope sky swirled and bubbled then lacerated the night blackness.

A gargantuan, inhuman eye peered through. The gash widened. A second eye joined it, then others. Khate felt child-like, lost, and adrift. His eyes stark with fear, her father looked like no one she knew.

"Oh, no, no, what did you do?" Khate said.

Thanh held her by the shoulders as the world quaked. She focused on memories of her mother's voice, whispers from better days, on boxing away her terror, and holding her hope close.

"I brought the new mines online three days ago. They've been drilling non-stop."

As gravity broke and maddening colors swarmed her, Khate clung to her father amidst a world, a universe becoming a new thing. She wondered, if faced with this new reality, would her mother cling to hope or release it. Then the thoughts of the things freed from gazing at the stars pierced her mind with prismatic electricity, and the question ceased to matter.

A Cat's Cry in Pluto's Kitchen

The fleeing boy hurdled a pile of rotting trash then dashed toward a hole in the brick wall at the end of the dank, theater district alley. Darting ahead of Detective Daniel Matheson and three of New Alexandria's finest, Morris Garvey leapt after him, skidding on slick garbage as he landed, almost falling, but then racing faster when the boy dove for his escape route. Garvey, a man who acknowledged few limits, poured it on then skidded to a crouch and snatched the boy's feet before he passed all the way through the hole. He yanked him back and lifted him. In the boy's tight grip dangled a burlap sack stuffed with cash, plucked only minutes ago from a crack in the foundation of the Fullerton Street Burlesque House—ransom placed there this hazy Sunday morning in hopes of recovering Brazilian virtuoso Felipe Sandeman's stolen violin.

One glance told Garvey, who'd handled rough street children before, that the struggling, kicking boy, about twelve years old, was not the thief they were looking for, only a simple courier, or worse yet, a naïve patsy. Now he needed the boy to gather his wits and focus on what he had to say before Matheson's coppers caught up and put the fear of God into him. A trusty group, the detective's hand-picked squad, but they believed intimidation was the only way to deal with children.

"Boy," he said. "Look at my face. Do you know who I am?"

The boy glanced at Garvey but kept struggling. When awareness lit up his eyes, he took another look. The fight bled out of him.

"You know me? Yes?" Garvey said.

"You're the steam sweep man. Everyone knows you."

In New Alexandria people said that if you built a better chimney sweep the world would beat a path to your door. That was because Morris Garvey had made a fortune by building a better chimney sweep, enough money, in fact, to create the city's most profitable and best-known business: Morris Garvey Steam Sweeps and Machinations Sundry. Steam-powered, automatic chimney sweeps only marked the beginning for Garvey, who'd grown Machinations Sundry into every field of mechanical and magical endeavor, garnering an international reputation for embodying the height of modern ingenuity, all before age 30.

"Then you know my reputation for dealing with alley rats like yourself," Garvey said.

"Yes, sir. I do, sir."

"Good." Thudding footsteps warned that the police were approaching fast. "Under no circumstances will you leave this alley with that bag of money. I trust you accept that. But you may still choose where you wind up today, either locked in The Tombs or sitting down to a hot meal and a chance for a future. So make the best decision of your life, now, son. Trust me. Go along with everything I say. Can I count on you?"

The boy nodded.

Garvey stifled a laugh at the frantic blend of awe and confusion in the boy's face. Given the child's involvement in the ransom pick-up, Garvey suspected his world had been turned upside down more than once in recent days. He only hoped the boy possessed wits enough to seize the opportunity being offered him.

"Excellent. What's your name?" Garvey asked.

"Andy Parker, sir."

"Nice to meet you, Andy."

Detective Matheson reached the end of the alley in a thunder of footfalls and a flapping bluster of overcoat.

"Damnation, Morris, but you run like a jackrabbit," Matheson said, catching his breath. Then with a sneer at the panting police officers arriving behind him, he added, "At least someone in this lazy urban blight can still stretch their legs, all right. Here I am, a fifty-two-year-old cowboy outrunning three of New Alexandria's finest, and our little rabbit would've been down his hole if not for you."

The broad, Texas drawl in Matheson's voice made everything he said sound much larger than life, even "Homeric" as Garvey had described it the first time the two met. That Matheson had appreciated the reference had secured in an instant the friendship between the two very different men. Where Garvey had grown up on the streets of New Alexandria and built a fortune through his wits, intelligence, and hard work, the older Matheson hailed from a cattle ranch in Texas, where he had at times carved out a living as a sheriff, a gunfighter, a blacksmith, a sportswriter, and even a schoolteacher. He had come north to New Alexandria to study modern police techniques and risen to the top of the city's police force.

"The money is secure," Garvey said. He stood Parker on his feet and dusted him off. "If you would do the honors, Mr. Parker."

With only a moment's thought Parker handed the cash sack over to Matheson. "Not a cent less than when I snatched it, sir."

Garvey was pleased to see his snap judgment of Mr. Parker as cleverer than not had been correct.

"Now, don't try playing on my good nature, son," the detective said. "Thievery and ransom aren't pursuits to be taken lightly, no matter how young you might be. I'll be sure and tell the judge how you turned this in *after you were caught*, but I'm afraid you'll be bedding down in The Tombs tonight."

"Detective," Garvey said. "I can save you a lot of trouble and work in that department. You see, Mr. Parker here is, in fact, a member of my Sundry Troubleshooters. In training, of course, and still wet behind the ears, which is why he didn't recognize me right off and ran. It was only last week I gave him his first probationary field orders to find mischief, get mixed up in it, and report back to me. He was headed to my offices, directed by his inflated sense of loyalty to turn this money over to me rather than take his chances with your uniformed colleagues. I'm certain he can give us valuable information about who put him up to grabbing the ransom. We both know it was no common street wretch who engineered the theft of Felipe Sandeman's violin. Consider our good fortune that the perpetrators recruited one of my lads for this exercise."

"Our good fortune, you say." Matheson removed his hat, wiped sweat from his brow, and let out a long breath. "What say you, young Mr. Parker? Is that how it really is?"

"Yes, sir," Parker said. "Like Mr. Garvey tells it."

New Alexandria held in common knowledge Garvey's reputation for rescuing lost children. Born after he hired many of the young chimney sweeps his steam sweep machines had left jobless it had bought him much good will. Since then he often recruited capable boys and girls from the streets into his Sundry Troubleshooters, giving them a chance for a future doing everything from lab work to serving as his eyes and ears out and about in the city. More than once Garvey's Troubleshooters had lent Detective Matheson a helping hand.

"Really, now?" Matheson said.

"Most definitely, sir." Parker dug his dirty hand into a tattered pocket and pulled out a handful of shining coins and a gold pendant on the end of a silver chain. "The coveys what put me up to grabbing the money gave me these, sir. That's evidence there, right? They gave me my instructions in Pluto's Kitchen, sir, down where all them cats run wild. I can show you where it was."

"Can you now?"

"Yes, sir," Parker said. "I'd be doing my civic duty and living up to the chance Mr. Garvey's given me."

Garvey swallowed another laugh and felt his esteem for Andy Parker double. The boy fell into the role of Troubleshooter as if born to it. He had handed Matheson what amounted to a fortune for a street urchin, exchanging it for a chance at a better life. Mr. Parker, Garvey decided, was even sharper than he first estimated.

Matheson took the coins and pendant. "What were you to do with the money?"

"Keep it, sir," Parker said. "They said they didn't need it. If I got away, it was mine for services rendered."

"You were right, Dan," Garvey said. "The thieves have no interest in profit. This was a snipe hunt."

"One we couldn't ignore," Matheson said. "Sandeman surely runs hot-blooded for a music man. I believe he'd have popped a gasket if we hadn't at least tried to buy back his fiddle."

"His fiddle," Garvey said. "Indeed."

"Now we know the truth, I like this business much less than when we only had a hunch," Matheson said. "This here episode was meant to send us chasing the wrong herd. Hell and damnation, the whole morning wasted. It's not like I haven't got my corral cracking already what with the Expo closing and that Egyptian exhibit drawing crowds over at the Nestor Museum."

Garvey grasped the detective's frustration. Time was short. Sandeman, set to perform tomorrow night at the closing of the World Expo, refused to play with any violin other than his own. Sandeman invited his fame not only for his musical skills, but for his stamina in intense performances that often lasted several hours. His concert would close a month-long conference dedicated to improving international relations amidst rumors of assassination plots afoot against foreign leaders scheduled to attend. The Expo had stoked the city's underworld activity to a fever pitch in the past weeks, making the violin theft seem too opportune to label mere coincidence.

"Maybe not wasted," Garvey said. "What's that bauble Mr. Parker brought us?"

Matheson dangled the pendant by its chain. A finely wrought piece of gold, fashioned with delicate, intertwined flourishes around its edges, it glittered in the alley's misty gloom. Its engraved face depicted the bust of a fierce, cat-faced woman dressed in a loose, flowing gown clasped at the shoulders with an Usekh collar: the ancient Egyptian goddess Bast.

Detective Matheson squinted as he studied the pendant. "Feel as if I've seen something like it only the other day. Don't you?"

The carving resembled a cameo on a bracelet worn by the Irish opera singer Maureen McCalla, Felipe Sandeman's wife. Garvey had noticed it when Matheson introduced him to the couple two nights ago. He reminded the Detective.

"One cat-headed lady is chance, two a mystery," Garvey said. "Perhaps Mr. Sandeman has been less than honest with us."

"Could be," Matheson said. He tucked the pendant into a vest pocket, and then he offered his hand to Parker, who stared at it for a second before he shook it. "Well done, Master Parker. You're off to a dandy start as one of Mr. Garvey's Troubleshooters. Make sure you stick to the straight an' narrow, and you ever think about giving real police work a go, you come talk to me, y'hear?"

The path to Morris Garvey's laboratory gave visitors a calculated tour of Machinations Sundry's most impressive features. It led them through the vast steam sweep factory room, where a hundred men and women assembled and shipped the machines that had made Morris Garvey famous. From there it cut through the railroad and street car engineering studio, then along a corridor that passed open rooms where workers built many of the gadgets and appliances Garvey had invented, and finally up to the company's rooftop hot-air balloon port, which offered a stunning, 360-degree view of New Alexandria. A brass and glass elevator brought visitors down to Garvey's lab, a complex of indoor and outdoor research stations and offices built within the facility's expansive courtyard. The Machinations Sundry building occupied a full city block, and Garvey's lab took up half that space, an area filled with the constant noise of industry and experimentation. By the time Detective Matheson, who knew the route well, guided Felipe Sandeman and Maureen McCalla there, sweat gleamed on the big Brazilian man's forehead, and his delicate wife stared around, wide-eyed and dazzled. A bearded elevator operator escorted them into the car and down to the laboratory level.

"Brilliant though Mr. Garvey may be, how can a tinkerer such as he help us?" Sandeman asked while they descended. "Why do you not have all of New Alexandria's police force combing the streets and cracking some heads, as they say in the dime novels?"

"Cracking some heads, you say?" Matheson lifted his hat and smoothed his hair. "Well, now, Mr. Sandeman, I'll surely take that suggestion to heart, right after clue-finding and fingerprinting."

The elevator car jolted to a stop and the gate clanked open. The operator led Matheson, Sandeman, and McCalla through the maze of Garvey's lab. The clang of metal striking metal, the hissing of steam, and the occasional crackle of electricity drowned out Sandeman, who carried on explaining to Matheson—for possibly the hundredth time in two days—how if he did not recover his violin in time to play at the World Expo finale then Argentina and South Africa would almost surely go to war over the Antarctic dispute. The more he talked, the more Sandeman sweated and reddened, becoming almost inarticulate by the time the elevator operator ushered them into Morris Garvey's office.

"Where on earth is Mr. Garvey?" Sandeman cried in a burst of spittle-laden breath. "We are international musical stars. He should be here to meet us!"

"I'm right here, at your service," Morris Garvey said.

Detective Matheson sighed in relief. Sandeman and McCalla stared in disbelief at the elevator operator who had seated himself behind Morris Garvey's desk. Garvey removed his operator's cap, pulled away the false beard he had stuck to his face, and unbuttoned his uniform jacket.

"It's enlightening to hear conversations when people think I'm not present," Garvey said. "You, Mr. Sandeman, speak far too much for someone with so little to say."

"How dare you?" Sandeman said, his already cherry-toned face brightening. "You have insulted my honor, sir."

"Any insult to your honor has been inflicted by your pomposity. I recommend you don't now compound your error with arrogance or stupidity, not if you wish to recover your magic violin and protect your life and that of your charming wife."

"I will not listen to this!" Sandeman shouted.

Ms. McCalla stepped between the two men, took her husband's hand, and massaged it, effecting an immediate change on the virtuoso. Ms. McCalla captured her husband's attention and soothed him. The beautiful woman had said little since Garvey met her, but she carried herself with the grace and confidence of royalty, and her composure seemed unassailable. Garvey wondered what hidden qualities of Sandeman's commanded her affections for the match seemed entirely unjust to him. He envied the obvious dedication she shared with her husband.

"Felipe," she said, working Sandeman's hand in hers. "Don't be foolish, my sweet. The man said he's going to get your violin back and save our lives. Why not listen to what he has to say?"

Sandeman calmed as if the storm inside him had given way to its eye, and his face resumed its natural blush. He kissed Ms. McCalla's hand then bowed to Garvey.

"I apologize, Mr. Garvey, for allowing my emotions to run away with me," Sandeman said. "Passion is the great fault of those of us who have given our lives so fully to music. I am a lucky man to have a good woman to bring me back to earth. If you can forgive my outburst, I would be most grateful for your aid."

"No forgiveness is needed for such a natural reaction to your situation." Garvey stood and exchanged the elevator operator jacket for his own, which hung on a coat rack behind his desk. He straightened his hair and checked his appearance in a mirror. "I should apologize for my deception. It was necessary because until this moment I suspected you and Ms. McCalla of lying about the nature of the crime committed against you. I now realize you are only lying about your magic violin."

"You have called it that twice," Sandeman said. "My violin is not magic."

"Then why will you play no other?" Garvey said. "And why is it desired by the Cult of Bast?"

"Whoa, hold on there a second," Matheson said. "A couple pieces of cat-lady jewelry doesn't necessarily mean the Cult of Bast is back in town, does it?"

"I'm afraid so. Our morning was not as misspent as you thought," Garvey said. "One cat-headed lady is chance, two a mystery, indeed, but three? Or four? That's a pattern, a trail to follow."

Garvey led the others to a cluttered worktable beneath a row of tall windows where he had arranged several recent newspapers. The open articles covered several events: the opening of the Egyptian exhibit at the Nestor Museum, the theft of a ceremonial cloth from the private collection of the city's foremost scholar on ancient Greece, and the sudden preponderance of cats in Pluto's Kitchen, a downtown, waterfront neighborhood. The last played to its headlines' comic effect, but it remained unexplained why every free-roaming feline in the city seemed drawn to the Kitchen. Also on the table were a record of a title exchange for the purchase of an old apartment building in the same neighborhood and a shipping manifest.

"You see? It's quite obvious," Garvey said.

Sandeman and McCalla regarded him with bafflement. Matheson pushed his hat back on his head.

"Obvious to you, Morris, but for those of us without the time and resources to track and study every last worm that turns in this city, it might yet be a bit of a leap," Matheson said. "How in the hell did you get that title record on a Sunday?"

"Called in a favor," Garvey said. "Let me explain. The Egyptian exhibit opened last week at the Nestor. Here is a copy of the shipping manifest, which includes three unusual canopic jars, ceremonial containers used to store human organs for burial. These jars bore the effigies of cats and were dated to about 200 A.D., long after the fall of the Ptolemaic dynasty, the last Egyptian empire. They never reached the museum. The stolen Greek cloth was known as the Shroud of Ailuros, the Greek's name for Bast, and was said to have been woven in Bubastis on the Nile River Delta. Lastly, there is the purchase of a decrepit property in Pluto's Kitchen by the Sistrum Company at the same address where Andy Parker was hired to collect the ransom. A sistrum is a rattle favored by Bast. Since its sale, the property has become the epicenter of the Kitchen's present feline infestation."

"I confess it does paint a particular picture," Matheson said. "But what has the cult got to do with Mr. Sandeman's magic fiddle?"

Sandeman gasped, then said, through clenched teeth, "My *violin*, sir, is *not* magic."

Garvey held an open hand toward Ms. McCalla. "Ma'am, may I borrow your bracelet? You can guess which one."

Ms. McCalla slipped a gold bracelet from her wrist and handed it to Garvey. "It can only be this one."

Garvey displayed the carved ivory and alabaster cameo inset into the gold band, a depiction of Bast similar to the image on the pendant Andy Parker had provided.

"Where did you get this?" Garvey said.

"In Egypt. It was a gift," Ms. McCalla said. "Sent to me a few months ago when I concluded my last tour of Europe and the Near East."

"A gift sent by whom?" Garvey said.

"The wife of the mayor of Cairo."

"Well, there, you go. The mayor of Cairo has been a widower for two years now. I was with him, consulting on a steamship program for Nile shipping, when his wife succumbed to a fever."

Garvey crossed the room to a workbench where a brass tank was mounted on a wooden stand. He opened a porthole door, placed the bracelet inside, and then clamped it shut. Working the device's intricate control panel, he said, "Please watch the lamp on top. The brighter the light, the stronger the magic."

The mechanism vibrated and hummed. It clicked and whirred and puffed out weak blasts of steam from its release valves, and then the lamp came to life with a faint bronze light. Garvey checked his pocket watch, noting the time, counted down a few more seconds, and then switched off the device. The lamplight lingered then faded out. Garvey removed the bracelet and returned it to Ms. McCalla.

"Ma'am," he said. "Your bracelet is imbued with a weak magical field, sufficient for someone to locate you with a properly attuned scrying device."

"I had no idea." Ms. McCalla stared at the bracelet as if she'd never before seen it.

"My magic detector doesn't lie," Garvey said.

"So you finally got that thing working," Matheson said.

"Even better, here's the prototype for something to make life easier for you and your men." Garvey picked up a tool that resembled a hammer forged from brass tubing, tiny gears, and pieces of gemstones. A smaller version of the magic detector lamp occupied the claw position. Garvey waved it over Ms. McCalla's bracelet and a faint light flickered. "Ms. McCalla, I believe you were given that bracelet by the Cult of Bast so they could track you until they saw an opportunity to steal your husband's violin."

"But why?" Matheson said.

"Only its owner can tell us that. My guess is it has to do with the Thirteen Cats of Bubastis. Am I correct, Mr. Sandeman?"

Sandeman flopped into a nearby chair. A rivulet of sweat ran down one side of his face, and after meeting the three expectant stares directed at him, he shrugged and dropped his gaze to his feet.

"I have never heard of these cats of Bubastis," he said. "I don't know what to tell you."

"The truth ought to do," Matheson said. "We'll sort out the rest."

"Felipe," Ms. McCalla said. "I am certain we can trust Detective Matheson and Mr. Garvey to be discrete. Is that not correct, Mr. Garvey?"

"Most correct, ma'am," Garvey said.

"All we're looking to do," Matheson said, "is get back your fiddle, make sure your show goes on as planned, and keep y'all and everyone else at the Expo safe. Unless you've committed a crime, what you tell us won't go beyond these four walls."

Sandeman emitted a resigned blast of air. "Then I have no choice. I must take you gentlemen at your word. I have not lied. My *fiddle* is not magic—but its *strings* are. The spell has nothing to do with my musical ability. They only give me great endurance, allowing me to perform for many hours without fatigue. I keep it a secret because it would be very difficult to explain that distinction to the public. What that has to do with cats, I do not know."

Matheson said, "Fiddle strings are made of catgut, ain't they?"

"Not literally," Garvey said. "The intestines of goat or sheep are most often used. But where magic is involved, the necessary materials are often unorthodox and sometimes quite literal. Mr. Sandeman's violin strings may be made of actual catgut taken from one of the Bubastis cats."

"Sonofagun, doesn't anyone ever just rob a bank in this city?" Matheson said.

"I have told you everything, gentlemen," Sandeman said. "I know nothing of these cats or their cult. I do not see how this will help recover my violin."

"It won't," Garvey said. "Not if we sit around here talking. Now, we must act."

"In Bubastis, the legends say, the goddess Bast often dwelled for a time among the many temples and shrines consecrated to her honor," Garvey said.

He sat pressed in the back of a speeding coach with Detective Matheson, Sandeman, and McCalla. The horses' hooves tapped out the rhythm of their urgency. They raced toward the Sistrum Company's building in Pluto's Kitchen. Matheson had summoned a police squad to meet them there.

"She guarded and nurtured the town as if its people were her children. Whenever the spirit moved her, she blessed random cats there with immortality and imbued them with magic. She did so thirteen times, creating a pack of cats endowed with enough magic power to have made Bubastis the seat of a new empire if only the townspeople had understood the nature of the enchanted animals among them. Alas, they did not, and soon the thirteen cats wound up scattered around the world by chance and Bast's enemies. As centuries passed, they died, one by one, because Bast had not made them invulnerable to accidents or violence.

"Only one is believed to remain today, sheltered by Bast's cult. They seek the remains of all the others, so they can resurrect them through magic. They can only do that while at least one still lives. If they believe the violin strings are the remains of one of the cats, then they want them. They may have stolen the Egyptian exhibit's canopic jars for the same reason. It's rumored some of the Bubastis cats were mummified. I'd wager the Shroud of Ailuros factors into the ceremony they plan to undertake."

"If they succeed, what could they do with the magic cats?" said Sandeman.

"Damn near anything they want to," Garvey said. "But don't worry yet. They need the remains of *all* the cats for the resurrection ceremony, and they'll want to do that in Bubastis, anyway. So we only have to stop them leaving the city with your violin strings if they haven't already."

The coach tilted as it took a corner and then jolted over cobblestones, marking their entry to the Kitchen. The police had cordoned off the Sistrum Company's building, and Garvey had assigned a handful of Troubleshooters to neighboring rooftops and sewer tunnels to monitor the less obvious exits. When the coach stopped, Matheson instructed Sandeman and Ms. McCalla to wait inside, and then he and Garvey stepped into the street.

Cats roamed everywhere. Black, brown, and gray. Calico, Siamese, and tabby. They wandered around and rubbed against the legs of police officers. They came and went from adjoining alleys and strolled in and out of the Sistrum Company building. They mingled with the police, purring and indifferent to whether or not they were in the way. Garvey, who was allergic to them, sneezed three times and kept clear of the largest clusters, while he waited for Matheson to choose half a dozen men for the raid.

The detective then led the way into the run-down building. Still more cats roamed the gutted, decrepit first floor. The black gaps of missing steps riddled the stairs to the upper floors. Gloom filled the space, lit only by daylight creeping in through the grimy windows and cracks in the walls. Matheson halted Garvey there and ordered three men to investigate upstairs and three others to take lanterns and check the cellar. Garvey tried to follow the cellar group, but Matheson held him back.

"No need for you to take unnecessary risks," he said, raising his voice to be heard over the din of mewling and hissing cats.

"Simply setting foot in this building is a risk," Garvey said.

"If it weren't for the Cult's involvement and time a-wasting," Matheson said, "I'd have ordered you to wait in the wagon with our favorite fiddler. But I may need your expertise on the spot. So, stick close to me, now, y'hear?"

An alarmed shout came from the basement.

Matheson and Garvey rushed there, Matheson pushing ahead on the stairs. The detective lit a small lantern he carried on his belt, and the two men followed the police officer's beckoning cries. They entered a large room, where three officers stood, their lanterns illuminating a grisly scene. Four men lay dead on the floor, each with their throat slit deep across the width of their neck. Blood dribbled from the wounds; the smell of it hung rich in the air. Cats circled around the bodies, eyeing the intruders with hostile curiosity.

"Those wounds are fresh," Garvey said. "The killer may still be here."

"The entire cellar is only this room and the other," an officer said. "No one's down here."

"Not in the open at least." Matheson sent an officer upstairs to put the others on alert for a murderer, and then he asked Garvey: "What do you make of it?"

Garvey crouched beside one of the bodies and lifted its dead hand. A ring gleamed on one finger: a silver oval engraved with the cat-faced likeness of Bast.

"Dead cultists make no sense." An uncharacteristic edge of anger sharpened Garvey's voice. "None of this does. They took the violin two days ago. Why stay in the city? Why bother with the phony ransom? What kept them here? These men wouldn't be easy victims for a common cutthroat. Either they were taken by surprise or by trained killers."

"Assassins," Matheson said. "Damnation, I'll have to warn Ridley at Expo security."

"Shh," Garvey said, rising. "Do you hear that?"

"What?" Matheson said.

The sound came again, almost inaudible: a faint mewing and the twang of a single violin string, like water plinking into a tin cup. Garvey paced the room, seeking its source, but Matheson pinpointed the hollow section of the wall before he did. Closer inspection by lantern light revealed a series of discolored bricks, which operated a secret door. It swung open onto darkness. A cat leapt out and raced for freedom. The plucking sound grew louder. The men lifted their lanterns and shed light on a fifth cultist, who lay on the floor, curled into a ball, with a violin clutched to his chest. Smeared in blood from knife wounds, he lingered on the edge of consciousness. The police dragged him beside his dead brothers. The cultist's eyelids fluttered. He mumbled through quivering lips.

"That's Sandeman's fiddle," Matheson said. "But what's he saying?"

Garvey knelt beside the wounded man. "Sounds like, 'Betrayed.' Who? Who betrayed you?"

The man's glassy eyes met Garvey's intense stare. He released the violin and drew a finger across his neck in a forceful slash. Then he fell unconscious.

"We've stumbled into the middle of a double-cross," Garvey said.

"They were working with the assassins?"

"Or the assassins were using them, taking advantage of their surveillance of Sandeman. The question is why? In either case, at least we've got the violin."

Matheson ordered an officer to go upstairs and blow his whistle. In minutes the entire building shook with activity as police conducted a top-to-bottom search. Several carried axes in anticipation of finding further secret rooms or hiding places. While they worked, Garvey wiped the blood from Sandeman's violin and carried it outside to the coach. Garvey traced his fingers over the strings; they felt smooth and perfect, as if they would never wear down or break. He plucked random notes and was immediately refreshed and energized, but he also felt a dark undercurrent in the tone that reminded him of the source of the strings' power. A hundred feet from the coach, Garvey stopped.

Purring, mewing cats surrounded and stared, none of them daring to come closer than a few feet. The animals gathered from every quadrant of the neighborhood. The violin possessed a measure of Bast's magic, a power that even New Alexandria's most contentious alley cats respected. The cultists' clumsiness puzzled Garvey. He had driven them out of New Alexandria once before. They would have known he would keep watch for their return. He could not understand why they hadn't, like the cats, shown proper respect for a greater power. The trail to the violin seemed too straight now, as if events had been manipulated for the illusion of challenge rather than the genuine experience. The cult never would have returned the violin. Thus, the staged ransom must have served someone else's purposes, someone who wanted the violin returned, but not too easily. Garvey felt a nagging sense of having missed some small but important thing.

From inside his coat, he produced his prototype portable magic detector and passed it over the violin. The light bulb flared to brilliant life, flickered, then brightened and popped in a spray of glass. The cats scattered with startled cries. Garvey reeled from the sudden blast but steadied himself. A haze of dusty light surrounded him. The instrument possessed much greater magic than Sandeman had described. Fragmented thoughts gnawed at the back of Garvey's mind.

McCalla's bracelet.

Andy Parker's cat-faced pendant.

The dead cultist's ring.

He recalled that on the second day of the World Expo, France had hosted a Night of 1,001 Gifts, a festive twist on the traditional exchange of goodwill tokens among diplomats. Garvey had read the list of presents in the paper; the Egyptian deputy ambassador had given the other diplomats jewelry carved with images out of ancient Egyptian myth.

Garvey stared at the violin.

Felipe Sandeman must not play this.

Then people shouted warnings at him. Garvey spied a dark flash of motion on a nearby rooftop in time to drop to his knees and roll before two gunshots cracked the air.

Something bit into Garvey's shoulder and injected pain through his body. The street came to life with policemen rushing in every direction, firing on the shooter. Garvey saw some of his Troubleshooters dashing into the fracas too, converging from neighboring rooftops. He tried to stand, but his strength deserted him. He held onto consciousness—perhaps even his life—by a tenuous grip, as if a force outside him bolstered his constitution.

Matheson's hand clamped onto Garvey's shoulder and rolled him onto his back. Garvey drifted through a cloud of agony. Matheson tried to take the violin; Garvey refused to let go. Still, he felt it inching from his powerless fingers.

He shook his head.

"Sandeman must not play," he whispered. He clutched uselessly at the violin. "The 1,001 gifts hide a death trap."

Then the instrument left his grasp, taking the world with it as Garvey blacked out.

The shocked nurse leapt from her seat when Garvey snapped awake and shouted that Sandeman must be kept away from his violin. When he realized his situation, and the nurse regained her composure, Garvey asked, "How long have I been out?"

"Eighteen hours, sir," the nurse told him.

"Then there's still time."

"Now, sir, please, lie back and rest," the nurse said. "You're injured."

"Best do as she says," Detective Matheson said. He was sitting in a chair by a window, half-hidden in shadows. "Nasty poison on the slug that clipped you. Good thing it was only a flesh wound. Seems the rejuvenating power of Sandeman's violin saved your life. So, of course, like a greenhorn, I took it away from you."

"The violin!" Garvey said. "Dan, listen, keep Sandeman away from it."

"Calm down," Matheson said. "It's all rounded up now. I'm capable of solving a case or two without your inspired intervention. But I'm grateful for your ingenuity. After I saw your magic-finding doohickey pop, I confiscated Sandeman's fiddle—which, of course, gave me no pleasure whatsoever—and I turned it over to the thaumaturgy squad. Turns out more than the strings were magicked up. Sandeman swore he knew nothing about it, and I believed him, so I put that together with what you said about the gifts. I arranged with Ridley to have them all checked and found a magical match: a pocket watch engraved with the face of Bast, given to the ambassador from Argentina. If Sandeman had played within a hundred yards of it, the magical backlash from the violin itself would've killed everyone in the vicinity. Damn ambitious bunch of assassins we're dealing with. The one that shot you poisoned himself soon as we caught him."

"They used the cult of Bast to get the violin so they could rig it with magic. If they'd simply ransomed it back to us, it would've been too easy. It would've tipped us off."

"They were planning for us to find it like we did, but we got there early, thanks to you. I figure they were trying to take you out of the game to even the odds," Matheson said. "The Egyptian contingent claims someone slipped the pocket watch into their bag of gifts without their knowledge. Ridley doesn't believe them, but he'll never prove it. There must be someone else involved, but I can't suss out who."

"You've got a hell of an investigation ahead of you."

"That's no lie."

"So, that's it? No show for Sandeman?"

"Hell, no, that ain't it. Sandeman huffed and puffed all the way to City Hall, so we got his fiddle strings cleared out of evidence. He's putting them on a new violin, and the show must go on."

"Good news, I suppose."

"Better news is you pulling through." Matheson stood, removed something from his pocket, and set it on Garvey's nightstand. "Ms. McCalla came by to thank you. I told her I'd deliver the message. She said she didn't think she'd have a chance to see you again before she leaves town, so she left you a gift. Get better, now, y'hear."

Matheson tipped his hat and left.

Garvey settled into his pillows and stared at his gift from Ms. McCalla. He frowned. She had left him the magic bracelet given her by the Cult of Bast.

Long the Night and Low the Flame

1

Alice Atropos seated herself at the senet table, and silence fell in the gaming hall.

Roulette wheels clacked to a stop and remained still, blackjack dealers ended their counts, and at the craps tables, players clutched dice, uncast. Even at the arcane challenges such as mehen, nine men's morris, tafl, and the game of Ur, play paused while servers, including me, froze in their tracks, drink trays in hand, and behind the bars the clink of glass and ice ceased.

All eyes shifted to Old Jack Chance and the dais at one end of the hall. More beard than body, Jack sat at his post, overlooking the sprawling casino pit, ready with his alabaster senet board. Unchallenged most nights, he hadn't played a match in recent memory, but he betrayed no surprise or reluctance as my sister, Alice, shrugged free of her leather jacket and draped it on her chair back. Her campaign badges and warrior's rank insignia—the colors of a Thread-Cutter—ran vibrant from wrist to shoulder along the weathered black leather of her left sleeve. The gaming hall forbade weapons in the casino, yet Alice wore her military standard issue knife and handgun on her belt, a courtesy extended to veterans—and for a Thread-Cutter such as Alice, acknowledgment of how little sense it made to disarm one capable of killing half a dozen enemies bare-handed in less than a minute.

Everyone in the pit sensed her awareness of us, her preternatural, intuitive assessment of her surroundings, her calculation of our fascination, fear, and curiosity. Her gaze never swayed from Old Jack, but her body language betrayed her surveillance when she tilted one ear toward the crowd, and when she tied a length of her gray-streaked black hair into a ponytail, careful not to expose her neck. The short distance between us and her seemed reckless and exciting, like standing inches from a tiger without the bars of a zoo cage to separate us.

Old Jack opened the drawer of his gameboard, a rectangular box 18 inches long, six wide, and four high, with thirty squares delineated on the playing surface. He removed the pieces then lined up the dark ones along the left side of the board, the light ones on the right, five each. He set the black-and-white dice sticks in front. A mirror mounted on the ceiling above Old Jack's table provided onlookers a view of the action.

183

With a nod to Alice, he said, "Is it your true and honest wish to chance with me a journey beyond the river of mortality and behind doors locked by Keres and Thanatos, by Hel and Camazotz, by Maat and Baron Samedi?"

Alice's reply carried across the hall: "It is."

"I accept your challenge. Once we begin, we must, by law, play all nine rounds. Should you win more games than me, I'll add one year to my term as this city's Old Jack Chance, and in recognition of the game's demonstration of the gods' favor for you the city shall grant you any boon you desire within the bounds of the law, such as property, financial reward, or clemency for yourself or another for a crime. Should you lose you must, by law, accept the journey decided by the matches. Lose up to six, and you may return to your life, unchanged. Should you lose seven, you must follow the Journey to Penae, forfeiture of all your worldly possessions; eight losses require you to Journey through the Passage of Xipe Toltec, loss of rank and status followed by social rebirth; and with nine losses you pay the ultimate price, the Journey to Erebus, exile into the deep darkness outside the cities. Do you accept these stakes?"

"I accept them," Alice said.

"Please state the boon you wish to obtain."

"Clemency for Noralissa Apedemak and unconditional release from Van Waal Prison."

Noralissa Apedemak. A warrior from a rival city. Named for a lion-headed god of war with three faces and four arms, Apedemak. I didn't understand what hold she possessed over Alice, who'd captured her in battle. Despite being enemies, Alice always spoke of her with warmth and respect and condemned her imprisonment as unjust but never explained why or told me anything that justified her risking so much at the senet table for her freedom.

"Very well." Old Jack scribbled on a notepad, sighed, then nodded twice. "Through senet we glimpse what the world beyond this one holds for us in the afterlife and what the gods wish of us in this life. Do you also have a question of Fate in mind?"

"I do."

"Keep it clear in your thoughts when you choose light or dark. In this way the gods will understand what you ask and choose to grant your boon or deny it if your fate lies elsewhere."

Alice poised her hand above the senet board equidistant between the rows of playing pieces. Coins jingled and gamers murmured as they placed hurried bets on which she would choose. I wanted to scream for her to stop and step away from the game, but the law prohibited interference with anyone who challenged Old Jack. The curl of a smirk appeared on Alice's face as she held us in suspense, our gazes glued to the mirror. Then with a swift snap of her wrist, she snatched a piece and placed it on the board. Dark. Acknowledgement of death's inevitability, the expectation of its proximity, and a confession of one's desire to enter whatever fate this life held. I prayed Alice made her choice only from a sense of irony. The thought of her bearing an actual death wish saddened me.

Old Jack and Alice set their pieces upon the board.

Each space marked a stage of the journey to afterlife. Players cast the dice sticks with the objective of moving their pieces first into the final squares, which represented the waters that flow between the worlds of the living and the dead. Crossing them symbolized divine union. Exiting all one's pieces from the board first left an opponent metaphorically stranded in limbo, a serious comment on their standing in the eye of divinity. Many people played unauthorized senet for prophecy, prayer, or augur, but Old Jack—chosen by his predecessor from among the city's poorest population—ran the city's only official game.

Alice cast the sticks, and the match began.

She moved her first piece several spaces on the board. Old Jack took his turn, receiving a higher number; his first piece passed and blocked Alice's. She cast the sticks again and moved her second piece along a different path. Again, Old Jack surpassed her, and so game one continued, the sticks favoring Jack on every roll. Gamblers bet on each turn, each throw of the dice, even on which spaces a player might choose, all other games forgotten. Soon all Jack's pieces led Alice's, and several turns later, as she caught up, he moved his final piece across the river and off the board, winning the game. The crowd released a collective sigh. I hated to see Alice on display like this, but no one, including myself, dared look away as Jack cast the first roll for game two. Alice took an early lead, moving several pieces deep onto the board, but then the fickle sticks showered Jack with luck and sent his pieces ahead. Two of Alice's remained on the board when Jack's final piece crossed the river.

Between rounds, the unnatural quiet of the gaming hall made my skin crawl. Gamblers didn't care if she won or lost beyond how it affected their wagers. Old Jack claimed rounds three and four, the sticks giving Alice no relief. My sister then led through most of game five. It came down to a single space between each players' last piece. Again, the sticks turned on her. The loss eliminated any hope of Alice freeing Noralissa Apedemak. Now she played for fate.

She held her own through game six, but lost, and when she lost game seven and drew the Journey to Penae, anticipation electrified the crowd. My heart sank for my sister, but if her losses ended there, I could help her get back on her feet.

Of all the rounds so far, Alice came closest to winning game eight, her warrior spirit on display in her determination with each casting of the sticks and the selection of each space. But the sticks did not favor her, and she drew the Journey through the Passage of Xipe Toltec.

By the time Alice and Old Jack set the board for game nine, whispers raced through the crowd about how a Thread-Cutter might act with nothing left to lose. Would Alice consent to the loss the game dictated? Or might she fly into a rage of denial? Other warriors had gone berserk for lesser defeats, their combat instincts aroused by humiliation. If Alice vented her frustration, how many people would die before casino enforcers subdued her? An insulting question to ask of my sister and a Thread-Cutter honored by the city many times over for her service—yet the apprehension in those around me felt almost tangible. As the final round commenced, Alice and Old Jack rolled the sticks in turn and moved their pieces on the board.

They played the closest game of senet I've ever seen. Alice's pieces controlled the board then Jack's, then Alice moved her first piece off, then Jack moved off two. And on it went until only a single piece remained for each player, and both stood at the edge of the river. In the end when Alice required any roll above a three to win, her dice sticks came up two.

The crowd gave a collective, shocked gasp.

Money changed hands as gamblers settled bets.

Somber, Old Jack moved his last piece across the river, and said, "Thank you for the game. I wish you good fortune on your Journey to Erebus, the fate the gods have delivered to you. May you travel safely through the darkness." He gathered his pieces into their drawer.

Alice stood and loomed over the crowd. Gazes shifted from her inscrutable expression to the weapons at her waist to the stillness of her hands at her sides. When she snatched her jacket and slid it on, the crowd gasped again. Then she undid her ponytail and shook her hair loose. A sign, only I understood, that she intended no violence. If she had, she'd have kept her hair back out of her eyes. Everyone held their breath as she left the dais. The crowd parted as she strode to the exit. For several long seconds, only her confident footsteps sounded in the casino. With a last glance at us, she left.

As Alice stepped out of sight, I abandoned my drink tray on a baccarat table, ignoring the dealer's protests, then rushed after her.

2

In the cold, muddled gray of the noontime dark, Alice surrendered.

Casino officials backed by a police overseer ripped her patches and rank insignia from her sleeve, leaving only remnants of colorful threads. Alice proffered her service credentials, the keys to her house, and her identity cards, all her property and wealth now split 50/50 between the city and the gaming hall. The law allowed senet losers to keep anything on their person at the time of the game and, for those fated to make the Journey to Erebus, their transportation, a motorcycle in Alice's case.

186

After the officials left, Alice lifted her helmet and straddled her bike.

Before she could hide her face, I said, "Why the hell did you do that?"

She frowned at me as I shivered and zipped my coat. "I could only do what the dice allow, Brennan."

"No, I mean, why play at all?"

"Little Brother, please, I don't need you biting at my heels right now."

"Oh, no, you're not pulling that crap on me. You come in when you *know* I'm working and play this out in front of me, that means you wanted me to see it. So, you don't get to ride off into the gloom without telling me why. You can't ditch me without a word like you did when I was a kid and you enlisted."

"Come on, Bren, that was years ago."

"Yeah, when I was too young to do anything about it. This time, I'm not letting you off the hook. Why does Nora Apedemak matter so much to you?"

Alice slouched on her motorcycle seat.

"No warrior as honorable as her should be locked up."

"She's your enemy."

"Cities have enemies. Warriors have opponents, and some opponents share more than combat, Bren." I gaped at Alice, but before I could speak, she said. "I did it because if I can't see right by Noralissa and my fate doesn't lie with her, then I want to know what's really out beyond the last cities."

"Out there, it's darkness, Alice. That's all there ever has been. Apep, Ahriman, Erebus, and Nyx. Our entire world, endless dark. You know that better than me."

"It's said the gods dwell on the far side of the dark, isn't it? That the dark is the river that separates us. They live in the Houses of the Gods in light we all once enjoyed until they stole it from us. Don't you ever wonder about that?"

"Children's stories. We made up the gods so frightened people can sleep better."

Alice shook her head. "What if the stories are right?"

"So, what if they are? If the gods are sitting somewhere in their Houses at the end of the Journey to Erebus, what difference is it to us who never see or hear from them? What changes even if daylight isn't a myth and the gods stole it all for themselves? You think you can steal it back? If they're powerful enough to take it in the first place how can you best them alone?"

"I'll cross that bridge when I reach it."

"Why play Old Jack, then? You could've bargained for Noralissa's freedom or made the Journey to Erebus with half the army on your side."

"Any bargain for Noralissa's freedom would require her to renounce the oath she took when she earned the name Apedemak. She'd never agree to that. And who could I ask to take such a risk with me going into the deep dark? We each have our own fate. I wasn't sure this was mine until Old Jack won that last round. If he'd lost, I'd have given up the idea of making the Journey, but senet speaks the mind and will of divinity."

"It speaks the luck of the dice sticks. It's a game the city uses to check anyone ambitious and bold enough to play. What would you have done if you won?"

"Freed Noralissa because that would've been the will of my divine fate."

"Fate? You always told me we make our own luck."

"We do. Luck and fate aren't the same. I wouldn't waste my time at the roulette table, but senet is sacred." Alice squeezed my shoulder, her grip crushing. "I've thought this over for a long time, Bren. What more can I accomplish? I've won every battle I've fought. I've led our people to victory time and again. I've cut the threads of so many of our enemies I've lost count and earned the title of Atropos of the Moirai. When I close my eyes or look in the mirror, I see the faces of the dead. I hear their screams before I fall asleep, as if I'm killing them all over again. When you've lived with death as much as I have, it stays with you, woven into your being. I will always be a killer, the role fate delivered me."

"The role you—and *only* you—chose."

"Fate deceives us into thinking we have a choice, Bren. What's left for me here if I must think about Noralissa rotting in a cell for the rest of my life? Aging out of service? Living with all the horrid things I've done? Waking up every morning to wonder why I go on living while so many of my brothers and sisters in arms have died?"

"There are medications, psychological conditioning, ways to cope with trauma. You can do so much more than you realize."

"That's not the fate the gods assigned me. If they wanted me here, I'd have defeated Old Jack. At least, this way, I'll see what's really out there and, maybe, bring that knowledge back."

"If you survive. Who says you can even come back?"

"I've survived many terrible things, little brother. By law, I must make the Journey to Erebus. The law stands silent on what I may do once I've completed it."

"That's because no one ever has."

"Well, I'm going to try."

"You won't try alone then. I'm coming with you."

"No, Bren, no, this is my fate, no one else's. I couldn't contemplate asking even the hardest, battle-tested warriors to follow me so far into the dark. I won't ask you."

"You're not asking. I'm choosing."

Alice scowled. She raised her helmet then lowered it onto her head.

"Little brother," she said, voice muffled. "Make a different choice."

Her motorcycle engine revved, and then she roared off and vanished into the maze of city streets. Anxiety electrified me, a neurosensory memory of the day I woke to find

188

Alice gone into the military and me on my own in our tiny apartment facing a future as blank as our walls. The bustling city that sprawled around me as far as the eye could see abruptly felt as empty and meaningless as those walls. Without even poking my head into the gaming hall to quit my job, I ran to my own motorcycle in the employee parking lot, shoved on my helmet, tugged on my gloves, and then sped after my sister.

<h1 style="text-align:center">3</h1>

I caught up to Alice on the Hell Gate Bridge.

Older than me by several years and warrior without compare, she never matched me for knowledge of the city streets. She took the busy, main route north, but I sped along winding back alleys and narrow side roads that avoided most traffic and halved the travel time. I rode up beside her before we passed the bridge's middle, where frigid wind swept against us. Alice glanced at me before her engine gunned, and then she flew ahead on her military-issue bike, more powerful than mine. I used every trick I knew to keep up as she fled through the city's northern reaches. Whenever she thought she'd lost me I caught her in the distance, never losing sight of her for long. After an hour of cat and mouse, she gave up and slowed, conceding our wordless argument, and we crossed the Sedna River Bridge together. I would follow in her footsteps as I so often had in childhood, perhaps for the last time.

We rode all afternoon, guided through deepening darkness by amber streetlamps and the vehicle lights of city traffic. All who saw us pass stopped what they were doing and stared. Even the street people nested in crumbling doorways and trash-strewn alleys roused to watch us. None of them needed to know Alice to know her purpose. The bright scraps of threads fluttering along her left sleeve told her story. A few people blessed us with signs of one god or another. A few cursed or mocked us. Most watched, indifferent, or perhaps wondering what waited at the end of the Journey to Erebus.

By early evening with the ever-dark sky's slate luminosity deepening to impenetrable black, we reached the northernmost outskirts of the city and stopped to fuel up. Each of us added two full gas cans to our cargo, and a short time later, we passed the city limits and embarked on the road in between places.

Desolation lay to either side. The ruins of houses and shops, once vital and well-tended, now somnolescent and neglected, most of the people long since relocated to the relative safety of the city. Out here, between cities, sprawled the wild land of those who refused allegiance to any authority but their own. In the wildest days of my youth, I'd ventured this far from home a few times with friends, daring each other to ride one more block, pass one more burned-out house or shuttered shopping center, to venture into the hollowed-out buildings—until fear overcame our boldness and sent us racing back to the city streets.

Alice knew these lands far better than I. She had fought in them many times, crossed them to put siege to the cities of our enemies, lived and slept in them for days and weeks during campaigns. Whatever fear they might once have held for her she had shed years ago.

I silently thanked her for her calm when the thunder of half a dozen motors filled the air.

Behind us, a brigand gang rolled out from an enormous shop building that once had held uncountable treasures, an unimaginable bounty open to all, long abandoned to chaos. They came in pickup trucks, men and women crouched in the beds with rifles and clubs. Alice gunned ahead of me. I kept pace as best I could. The trucks still gained. I felt guilty and inferior as I realized I held Alice back from outrunning them alone on her powerful bike.

I shouted for her to flee without me. Instead, she waved me onward, then hit her brakes, and dropped to my rear. I glanced over my shoulder as the front wheel of her bike rose from the road and she whirled around on her rear tire and drove head-on at our pursuers.

I glimpsed the rest of the action in my rearview mirrors.

Relying in her military-grade gyroscopic balancing system to keep her steady, Alice drew her gun and fired. Its muzzle flared four times. The windshields of the two lead trucks shattered. The silhouettes of their drivers slumped away from the steering wheels. The trucks caromed to either side of the road, spilling their passengers as they jolted against the curbs and flipped. People tumbled into the air then crashed to earth. Alice's other shots had blown out the tires on the second pair of vehicles. Both spun out of control, collided, and ground together into a tangled mess of steel and plastic that clogged the road. The brakes of the last two trucks squealed. Smoke spewed from their tires, but they couldn't stop before they skidded into the wreck ahead of them. Alice sped past the wreckage then made a tight arc behind it and circled around for a second pass at the smashed trucks. Her gun barked again as the less-injured attackers raised weapons. None fired a round before Alice killed them with a single shot each.

I had never seen my sister in action. In all her stories, she had held back the worst details. Her unerring skill. Her apparent fearlessness. The ease with which she killed. These things I had never known until that moment. The Thread-Cutter's fate. To achieve a level of skilled lethality so great as to know in the moment a battle began who'd live and who'd die. To *see* each fighter's lifeline and know whose to cut to reach victory and whose she might safely ignore. The faces she saw in the mirror, the screams she heard in the night became real to me then. Did my big sister, the one who'd once cried all night about how badly she'd broken the noses of three bullies who targeted me in the third grade, about how much blood covered their faces, still exist?

All this in long, frantic seconds, and then Alice fell in beside me, and we left the carnage behind. Smoke rose from the ruined trucks, gray against the black sky. Screams drowned in the growling waves of our engines.

My stomach twisted in knots. My nerves jangled from the unaccustomed fight-or-flight reaction. I gestured for Alice to pull over. She shook her head. Her voice spoke in my memory, from years ago, the brutal field trials where I washed out in my second week when I came of age and applied for the service, following in her footsteps then too: *Shrug it off, Little Brother. While you catch your breath, your enemy improves their position. Victory laps are a waste of time. Keep moving, keep alive.*

We rocketed down the road into the pit of night. A knot of tension ached in my head. Alice truly had my best interests at heart in trying to leave me behind. She knew this world and all its dangers with an intimacy unattainable to me. She had always been braver, more capable, swifter to act rather than overthink. Two things bonded us together, the stony loyalty of sister and brother and my unshakeable faith in her to protect me, the flipside of her commitment to never let me down.

I hoped nothing ahead of us would ever truly test that bond.

Far down the road, the light of a massive fire turned a patch of the barren sky orange.

<h2 style="text-align:center">4</h2>

A church to the old god burned.

Alice and I stopped on the edge of the firelight illumination.

The flames reached thirty, forty feet into the sky. Dense smoke rolled off the structure in a pillar that smudged into the night. Old timers talked about days when flickering stars filled the night sky and a moon hung above us like a cosmic eye. I suppose, if such things still existed, the smoke would've blotted them out. Instead it twined into a churning stem that linked the black expanse above to the fire below until it became possible to wonder if the church now rose to the sky in ashes or if it had fallen, burning, from it.

A group of people on a hilltop south of the conflagration watched the flames feast. They sat inside a semi-circle of torches. I assumed they'd set the blaze, and I wondered why. Anger or disillusionment. Bitterness. Acceptance that their god had forsaken them. Maybe only setting the record straight. Outside the cities, pockets of the old faiths remained, but who could keep faith in an old god, who never showed its face, when new ones had, as our leaders claimed, cast us in the everlasting darkness and accepted each sacrifice we sent them along the Journey to Erebus? Had the gods taken our light to punish us for putting faith in a false divinity? Or had the old god died, and its children inherited the universe? I wasted no time asking Alice because she wasted no time wondering about such things. For her the answers lay at her journey's end. For me, the questions only equaled tales for children and dreams for the disillusioned.

I felt affinity for that group on the hill, though.

Setting torches to the past to free the present.

Fire consumed the peaked roof until the great cross fixed there toppled and fell.

Like them, Alice and I sought our own churches to burn.

In the name of what, I couldn't say, but whatever we learned on our journey, our lives could never resume their old shape. Alice risked reducing the church of her beliefs to smoke and ash, and I suppose I, who'd burned my own long ago, risked learning I had done so in haste and foolishness.

At Alice's signal, we pressed on and rode for several hours more, until the city's ambient light, which had tinted the blank horizon behind us, faded entirely, and thrust us into utter dark.

For now, only the glow of our headlamps showed us the way.

At double zero twenty, by my watch, we pulled off the road into a grove of trees.

Alice dismounted and removed her helmet.

"I'm tired, and if I'm tired, you must be exhausted," she said.

Adrenaline still charged me. Tired, yes, but my mind was wide awake and racing.

"It's best we rest. Our journey from here won't be as easy as it has been."

"Easy?" I said. "We were attacked as soon as we left the city."

"By untrained gang rollers. I went soft on them. Another minute's effort, I could've left them all dead," Alice said.

Two minutes, dozens dead. My imagination failed to conjure the scope of such violence.

"It's safer not to travel in the darkest hours. There are things that come out to hunt only then. Our road gets rougher from here with every mile."

Sliding off my bike, I said, "How far north have you been?"

"Farther than most, not as far as some. We've got a day's solid riding before we strike territory I've never seen before. Another day, maybe two after that to reach Hierophantia."

The City in the Voices of the Gods.

The last city before entering the northern reaches and the final leg of the Journey to Erebus. The only neutral city in the world. No other city dared threaten it for fear of how the gods might respond. It seemed such a journey should take much longer than mere days, that the territory of the divine ought to lay beyond finite measure.

Alice grinned. "You're thinking it's closer than you ever imagined. That's only to Hierophantia, though. No one knows how far the road runs on from there."

By the light of our headlamps, Alice opened her cargo bin and dug out two shimmery silver cubes, about four inches square, and handed me one.

"Thermal blanket," she said. "It gets cold out here. It also provides heat camouflage to hide us from the prowling things."

My body had already started shivering. I unfolded the cube into a ten-foot-by-ten-foot blanket and wrapped it around my shoulders. Alice handed me two nutrient bars, took two for herself, and then we settled into the root mound of the largest tree and ate.

"You really think we'll make it back home after this?" I said.

Alice shrugged. "You ever hear of anyone returning from the Journey to Erebus?"

"No, but I hardly ever heard of anyone making the trip either. Old Jack Chance sits alone almost every night. The ones I've seen play against him had better luck than you."

"Not luck, fate. They had different fates than me."

"Sure, okay, but I got to thinking the Journey to Erebus was so much bullshit. A grown-up version of the stories Mom told us as kids to scare us off doing stupid things." I bit off more of my nutrient bar, a sweet flavor I couldn't name. The food eased me from my adrenalin high. I spoke with my mouth full. "Not that we ever listened, or you would never have enlisted."

"True. Those awful yarns about Dad's time in the service fighting in the Western Night Wastes."

"She realized her mistake when you asked her to tell them again every night for a week."

"That's the thing, Little Brother. We each have our fate. Doesn't matter how we come to it. One way or another, we get there. Have you given any thought to how you're going to explain running off with me like this to Chloe?"

My heart skipped a beat. I hadn't thought of Chloe once since following Alice, and that, I suppose, said everything about what she really meant to me.

"You know about her?"

"I have eyes and ears everywhere, Little Brother. I always watch out for you."

"We aren't a serious thing. Or *weren't*, I suppose, after this."

"Afraid she won't understand you disappearing for days if you ever make it back?"

"Certain of it. She'll have moved on before we reach Hierophantia. Chloe's a delight in many ways, but loyalty isn't one of them. If we never return to the city, it won't matter."

"I'm sorry, Bren. You can go back anytime."

"I chose this. Chloe and I would've ended soon enough. She made no bones about wanting more out of life than I could ever provide for her."

"You could find someone else, settle down, have a good life."

"I have a good life as long as I have my family."

"You and me against the world, huh?"

"How it used to be."

Our blankets crinkled softly in the silence. Alice ate the last of her nutrient bars, crumpled the wrappers, and then tucked them into a pocket.

"What's Noralissa Apedemak going to think when she never hears from you again?"

"I hope she'll think I died in battle."

"You defeated her, captured her, and delivered her to the military court. If you wanted her free, why didn't you let her go when you could've?"

"I did my duty," Alice said. "After I captured Noralissa, we relied on each other to survive in the wastelands until I got her back to friendly territory. For a time, the wars didn't matter. That's all I'll say about it."

"Okay. Then tell me, could you really see the fates of those gang-rollers?"

"I see their life-threads. I see which ones are ripe to cut."

"Can you see your own?"

Alice's voice softened. "No. I wouldn't have needed Old Jack's game if I could."

"Can you see them when you're not fighting? Can you see mine?"

No answer came. Alice's breathing fell into a steady rhythm, asleep, as if she could change gears with her body the way she did with her bike.

I laid awake. Whirling thoughts pelted me like hailstones. Whenever I neared slumber, another one shocked me alert. Fear about what I'd left behind and what waited ahead. Questions I'd never asked about things I'd believed my whole life. A stray wish to see our mother again so potent it tightened my chest. A wish that she had never taken ill and died. Excitement and awe at seeing the world so far from the city. Eventually, I whispered myself calm, but as I teetered on the edge of sleep, a primal, bone-drilling screech ripped through the darkness.

A chorus of horrible, yearning voices replied. I saw nothing of what made the sound, but the screeches came from above, as if their source floated in the air or walked on giants' legs.

Alice's hand dropped onto my arm, and I jolted.

"Stay still," she whispered. "Don't move or use your light. They'll pass soon enough."

"What are they?"

"Screechers. I've only ever heard them. I know a few people who saw them and survived. They all describe them differently, but every version sounds awful."

The screeches ripped through me to the bone, like the shriek of metal ripping or the buzz of a million angry wasps gathered at my ear. The ground trembled. A gust of wind carried a sour, garbage stench across my face. After a time, though, the darkness settled back into stillness, and the air cleared.

"How the hell am I supposed to sleep out here, Alice?"

"Pray to Hypnos or Tutu, and sleep will come."

The next moment, she dropped back into slumber. I took her advice and recited the Prayer to Hypnos our mother had taught us, over and over, until it lulled me to sleep as a last thought passed through my mind: "I never heard of anyone coming back from Erebus, Alice, but none of those who made the journey were you."

5

The next morning, the sky vomited rain.

It fell in thick, aggressive rushes, borne by wind that sent the icy wet creeping into every seam and crevice of our clothing. The storm swallowed much of the sky's ambient light and left us in a gloom little brighter than the night. It transformed the roadside landscape, buildings and all, into smudges of shadow that reminded me of a backlit cityscape painted on one wall of the gaming hall. Intended to create the illusion of an outdoor patio, it looked morose and abandoned because its lights had died, leaving only the suggestion of the illusion. In the downpour, the world seemed equally unreal, a false impression that only dissipated when the rain relented.

We rode then through a windy drizzle. Head hunched over her handlebars, Alice relied on her bike's gyroscopic balancing system to steady her on the slick road. An ordinary bike like mine required white-knuckled, jaw-clenching effort to stay in Alice's wake and let her break the brunt of the wind and water rushing at us. She rode slow for my sake; without me, she would've ridden much faster. She seemed comfortable traveling through the inclement weather. I expected she'd done so in the past on campaigns that required covering great distances fast to strike hard at our enemies' cities. As a result, our city commanded the respect of much larger, stronger metropolises that had experienced the pain inflicted by our Thread-Cutters; our Water-Takers, who steal the water of life; and our Morrigana, who wash the clothes of warriors in blood.

Out here on the desolate road, none of that mattered, had ceased to matter once Alice sat at Old Jack Chance's table. New doubts troubled me as we rode now. Had I made an impulsive, selfish mistake when I chose to go with Alice? What if I distracted her and she never completed or returned from her Journey to Erebus because of me? Once we reached Hierophantia I could stay behind and free her of the burden of looking out for me. Let her ride at full speed without looking back, how she did now, to see if I still followed. Had a similar calculation motivated her years ago to enlist and leave me on my own? My resentment at her abandonment had blinded me for years to the possibility that Alice had removed herself from my life to allow me the room to emerge from her shadow.

Deep in thought, visibility clouded by wet gloom, I hadn't noticed the rain pick up again. I almost missed Alice's taillights when they flared crimson. I braked too hard, and my rear wheel commenced a frightening skid on the wet pavement. I kept calm as adrenalin flooded my nervous system. My heart pounded. My throat locked, cutting off my air. Time nearly froze until my eyes picked out single, fat raindrops as they bulleted across my line of sight and splattered my helmet visor. I eased up on the brake, turned into the skid, goosed the accelerator, all just in time—and my bike righted itself. Quivering from shock, I rolled up and stopped beside Alice.

"You okay?" she said.

"Fine. Just got distracted for a second."

"A second is plenty of time to get you killed."

"I hear that. How do you do it, Alice? How do you stay so focused? You ride through this mess like you're a part of the bike."

"I've ridden through much worse. Imagine, not water, but bullets and firebombs coming down, and smoke so thick you can't see your partners six feet away except for their lights, but you can hear their screams over the radio when they take a hit. I hardly notice this rain."

"Shit, Alice, the stuff you've seen," I said. "Why'd we stop here anyway?"

Alice smirked. "Something I saw." She gestured at the road ahead where a woman stood in the murk.

"Company," I said.

"Ride my six. Watch your rearview like a hawk. We get jumped, haul ass down the road. I'll hold them off while you drop ground between us, and then catch up, and we'll find a place to wait out the storm. I want to avoid fighting in this pissing rain."

I fell in behind Alice as instructed, and we closed the distance to the woman.

She stood in the middle of the road, no rain gear, her clothes slicked to her figure, hands at her sides, with her palms outward to show she held no weapons. Long hair lay matted to her skull. Windblown strands of it crisscrossed her face. She looked childlike despite her age.

Alice halted ten feet from her. The woman stared at us. Though I found it impossible to tell in the rain, it seemed to me tears filled her eyes. Then I noticed the dilapidated car at the side of the road. Two other women hunkered down behind the car's rear driver's side door, the only one left, and peered out at us, their expressions equally fraught.

"Help us, please," the woman in the road said.

Alice surveyed our surroundings while I kept one eye on my rearviews, which reflected nothing but a water-streaked blank. The woman didn't move. The rain came down hard and icy. She lowered her hands in resignation and repeated her plea.

Alice raised her visor. "What help do you need?"

"We're going to Hierophantia. Our car died. One of my sisters is sick."

"Yeah? What can we do about it? Your car is scrap from the looks of it."

"That's not our car. We walked the last fifteen miles from where it died. Found this wreck and got in to escape the rain for a while."

"Wait it out. It'll pass."

"My sister's fever is too high. She needs a doctor. There's a roadside clinic fifty, sixty miles ahead. If we wait out the rain and walk, that's a day or more. You could get her there in a couple of hours."

"Why would I do that?"

"To save her life."

"What's your name?"

"Donia."

"Donia, my name is Alice Atropos. You know what that means?"

"You cut threads."

"That's right. No missions of mercy for me."

"You're making the Journey to Erebus, aren't you? I can tell because your patches are gone. An Atropos with no badges means you forfeited all you had. That's a chance to make something new of yourself, isn't it? To reinvent the killer you were? To show mercy?"

"One who has killed is always a killer. But you have a point. My duty has changed. What city are you from?"

Donia named a city southwest of our own, an allied metropolis, whose military had taken part in at least two of Alice's campaigns. Alice gestured me forward. I wheeled next to her and opened my visor.

"What do you think, little brother? Help them?"

The woman looked fragile and bare, as if the rain had stripped her naked, and left her no scrap of propriety, and yet I saw strength in her too, power that had brought her and her sisters this far, and a stubborn will that had enabled her to release her fear and dignity to beg for help in the road. The other sisters impressed me the same way, although the younger of the two looked feverish, her face flushed and her eyes glassy.

"Of course, we help them," I said.

"My bleeding-heart kid brother."

"What choice do we have, Alice?"

Alice flashed me a wry expression. "Are you saying it's fate that we help them?"

"No, that's not what I'm saying."

"Uh-huh. We can't take them all, though."

"You don't have to," Donia said. "Take our sick sister, leave her at the clinic. She can stay there until we catch up."

Alice shook her head. "These clinics, Donia, they aren't what you may have heard. A sick, young woman alone there won't be any safer than on the road. One of you must go with her because I can't waste time there waiting for you to catch up. Choose who goes, who stays."

Donia summoned her sisters from the car. The sick one looked twenty-one- or twenty-two-years old at most, the other in her late twenties, compared to Donia's mid-thirties and gray-streaked hair. Donia pointed to the middle sister then the youngest.

"This is Greta, and this is Talia. Take them. I'll make my way on foot."

The sisters protested, terrified to leave Donia on her own, but in the end no other choice made sense. Even with Alice's high-end bike we couldn't risk riding with passengers in the rain. We piled into the ruined car to wait out the storm. Alice napped, her right hand resting on her gun, her left on her knife. The sisters and I eyed each other in the cramped space, all of us too nervous to sleep or speak. After more than an hour, the downpour faded to a mist. I roused Alice. Talia shivered like leaves in a high wind as Alice helped her onto her bike. Greta saddled up behind me. As we left, the sisters waved to Donia, who vanished into the gloom before we rode twenty yards.

I hollered over the wind to Greta, "Why the hell do you three need to get to Hierophantia so bad you're walking there?"

Greta shouted back, "That's a long story."

6

"Talia has visions," Greta told me.

We sat side-by-side in the clinic reception room, waiting for Alice who'd gone with Talia for her examination. The nurses understood the threat Alice represented. Alice wanted to make sure the doctor did too. Half a dozen people sat around us. A father and son, both dirtied in mud and ash, slept with their heads reclined on their chair backs. A teary-eyed, middle-aged woman coughed into her coat sleeve every few minutes, the resonant, hacking pertussis of a deep-rooted sickness. A man and woman held each other, lines of existential fear etched on their faces, and I guessed they must have brought an ill child here. Across from them sat a solitary man, dressed head-to-toe in black, a black watch cap covering his head; he read a paperback book and looked carefree compared to the others.

"What do you mean visions?" I said.

"Dreams, but they occur while she's awake," Greta said. "Nightmares really. They come on like a trance. She narrates them as they happen. We used to think of it as a gift. When she was a kid, one time she dreamt of our dad having an accident while riding to work with a friend. We made him stay home. The accident happened. The friend died. Our dad was okay. We've taken Talia's visions seriously ever since."

"It had to be a coincidence. No one can see the future," I said.

Greta laughed without a touch of humor. "What about your Thread-Cutter sister?"

"Alice sees fates, not the future, and only in combat, and that's all the result of incredible sensory training and experience not psychic hoodoo. Unconnected events occur. People see a pattern in them and believe what they want to believe."

"You can stop right there. I've heard it all before. I don't care what you think. I could give you a dozen more examples like the time she saved my dad, but only one thing convinces people: seeing it for themselves. Anyway, you asked."

"No, I asked why you're going to Hierophantia. You still haven't told me."

From the back corridor, a doctor approached the terrified couple, and a wary hush fell over the waiting room. A few words and his expression converted their terror to grief. Powerful tears flooded their faces. They clutched each other tighter. Across from them, the man in black stood, tucked the paperback into a pocket, smoothed his clothes, and then walked into the rear of the clinic. An undertaker, I thought, until stories Alice had shared of body harvesters and human traffickers outside the cities rushed to mind. I jumped to my feet and followed him.

Eight exam room doors lined the back corridor, four on either side. At the far end a steel door to the exterior hung ajar, creaking in the wind. Motor hum came from outside. Four of the doors stood open, the rooms empty. From behind one of the closed doors, I heard Alice's voice. Unfamiliar voices from behind another. The last two, at the end of the hall, stood shut. I opened one and found an empty room. With a deep breath, I opened the other.

The man in black stopped in the act of swaddling a baby with the exam table blankets. He flashed surprise and anger at me. The infant, who wore a pink, knit cap, squirmed, and whined as he pressed it closer to his chest, untucked blankets dangling.

"Who the fuck are you?" he said. "You don't belong back here."

"Doesn't matter who I am. Put down the child and leave."

His eyes narrowed. He crushed the little girl against himself with one hand, drew a gun with the other. "Get out of my way."

"No," I said. "You shoot me, everyone will hear it."

"Yeah? What will they do? Nothing."

Footsteps and voices filled the corridor behind me, one of the nurses shouting at someone not to go back there, Greta's voice arguing. I poked my head into the corridor, and yelled, "Get Alice!"

The man in black moved fast, taking advantage of my moment's distraction.

Alice's voice in my head: *A second is more than long enough to get you killed.*

The man plowed into me with one shoulder, cradling the girl from impact, body-checking me with his full weight. I stumbled, but as he pushed past me, striving to reach the back exit, I grabbed the collar of his coat, yanked him around, and slammed him against the wall. The baby wailed. The man pointed his gun into my face.

Time slowed. My world became fragments of a fractured whole, each sliver processed one at a time in astounding detail by my racing brain.

Down the corridor, the nurse screamed, "Oh, shit!"

Voices clamored in the waiting room.

A doctor shouted.

Outside the clinic's back door, the motor revved in the rain.

The stink of its exhaust filled my nose.

The wind-nudged door swung, clicking as it struck the frame.

Greta screamed for Alice. A new door opened on the corridor.

The baby girl bawled. Tears glistened on her face.

The man in black snarled and cocked his gun with a click.

The odor of gun oil chased away the exhaust fumes.

The man glared at me with violence and fury.

Hardly a second had passed. My hands moved before my consciousness understood their actions, fingers grasping, palms pushing, focused on the gun barrel.

Light and thunder filled my senses. My orientation evaporated except for where my body collided with the man in black. The world turned silent. Pure physical struggle defined my existence, not with a person but with a mass of muscle and energy, all resistance and violence, and me reduced to the will to overcome, to live. The struggle seemed like it would never end, and then something lifted the threatening weight from me. All pressure vanished. I dropped to my knees, braced against a wall. My eyes itched and burned. They fought for focus. Shadows took blurred shape.

Alice held the man in black to the floor with his arms yanked behind him. Greta cradled the little girl, red-faced and still howling, but safe in her arms. Alice kicked open the back door. The waiting car sprayed dirt and leaves as it fled. My hearing returned by slow degrees. I spotted a neat hole in the wall and realized I'd spoiled the man's aim but suffered the senses-shattering effects of his gun firing right in front of my face.

Alice shouted something I couldn't understand. Then the nurse helped me to my feet and into one of the exam rooms. She treated my eyes with a wash, and my vision cleared as the pain abated. I heard her well enough to understand she couldn't do anything for my ears. She tapped her watch. *You have to wait it out.*

Everything caught up with me then. Excess adrenalin sickened me.

I leapt from the exam table and threw up into the sink. Greta brought in the baby girl's parents. They held their daughter in their arms together, afraid to break contact with her, with each other, and looked at me like something I wasn't: a hero. I barely heard their thanks.

Raising a hand, I asked, "What's her name?"

My voice sounded cottony and muffled in my head.

"Marjorie," said the mother, sounding small and faraway.

I smiled then let Greta help me into the corridor.

Alice returned through the back door. She slammed it shut and threw the locks.

I knew better than to ask what she'd done with the man in black. We gathered in Talia's room. So much color drained from the faces of the nurse and doctor that they resembled figures in an unfinished painting, blank canvas in place of features.

My head throbbed. I leaned on Greta for support. I heard enough through my deadened senses to follow Alice ordering the doctor to give Talia antibiotics and whatever other medicine she needed then stock us up with a supply. Talia and Greta would come with us.

On our way out, we passed an open examination room. The two men who'd been asleep in reception stood there with a woman, their wife and mother, I guessed, wide awake now and alarmed. The reception area had cleared out, no sign of the coughing lady. Alice stopped to tell the nurse at the desk to give a message to Donia when she arrived, the threat clear if the woman failed to deliver it. Then we all stepped outside, where the rain had stopped.

The family thanked us again. I couldn't hear them, but their faces spoke the message as they climbed into their rusty pickup and then drove away.

Alice took Talia on her bike. The medicine kicked in fast, pepping her up.

Greta joined me. As I poised my foot to kickstart the engine, I said to her, "Still didn't get the story of why you're heading for Hierophantia." I sounded to myself like a man shouting from the bottom of a well, and if Greta heard and replied my battered ears didn't catch it.

7

The road led into darkness more complete than any other I'd ever experienced.

In the city, even in the heart of the darkest hours, streetlights burned, shopfronts cast neon glows, and cabs and busses sprayed light on the roads. Out here, only our motorcycle headlamps cast light, and that illuminated no more than the empty space directly ahead of us. Past that narrow, bright cone lay solid blackness. Dark sky and lightless earth joined to create an illusion of absence. We continued inside our tiny bubble of life. No world, no universe beyond it. Existence on hold. Reality paused. Offline due to technical difficulties. Like dead air on a phone or a screen with no signal, lapses that spread outward until they consumed all but you and the people around you.

I lost track of time. We rode for minutes, hours, or days, and nothing changed.

Settled tight against my back, her arms clutched around my torso, Greta slept, I think, or, a bizarre, horrifying thought, switched off and inactive while I couldn't interact with her.

At times, my eyes played tricks on me. The road shimmered or rippled like water. Alice's headlamp pulsed and shot forth orange and yellow bursts. The infinite darkness swirled like the famous fantasy painting of a starry night by that Dutch artist, except colorless, delineated only by coiled tones of black. Across those whirlpools of void, giants crossed, like mountains walking in the night or cloud creatures that spanned miles descending to earth.

When Alice guided us off the road to camp for the night, I trembled as I climbed off my bike. I grasped Greta and turned her to face me, relieved at the sight of her features, reassured by the apprehension in her expression because I'd startled her. From the edge of our headlamps' glow, I stared at the nothingness through which we had ridden, unsure if the surrounding silence resulted from my still-recovering hearing or an actual lack of sound.

Alice approached me silently and laid a gentle hand on my shoulder.

"The darkness deceives," she said. I heard her better now but still tinny and muffled. "You can't trust what you see out here. We're as far away as we can get from a city, from any remnants of the in-between places. The land out here doesn't belong to us."

"Who does it belong to?" I said.

"To things that thrive in darkness. There are humans out here, but I wouldn't call them people anymore. The full, unbroken darkness changes you. They trained us in the service to cope with it for extended times, but even the best-trained and most resilient of us wouldn't spend more than a week out here."

"How long will we be in this?"

"We rode for almost sixteen hours today."

Shocked, I said, "No, that's impossible. It felt like…"

"Like what? Minutes? Days? Hours?"

I tried to figure it but couldn't. "All of the above."

"The darkness messes with our senses. Or the electromagnetic energy does. Out here are pockets of radiation and places where the atmosphere itself changes. It's best to keep your eye on your clock and your odometer. You can trust those."

"How far will we ride tomorrow?"

"If all goes well, we're twenty hours out from Hierophantia. We might reach it tomorrow. The next day for sure."

"What else is out here? You said humans. Screechers, too?"

"Those are everywhere. What we might find this far out in the dark, I don't know. No one has ever seen the things that live out here. What we know of them comes from survivor's reports, and they never got too close. It's assumed anyone who got closer didn't survive."

"I never knew the world outside the city was so different."

"People in the cities don't like to think about it."

"Better that way, I guess, to live in ignorance and pretend we understand the world."

"Whatever gets you through life."

"What else don't we know?"

Alice laughed. "That, Little Brother, is more than I care to tell when we both desperately need some sleep. Another time."

We returned to the campsite, a low depression against the base of a hill of gravel and dry earth, softened a touch by the remnants of desiccated wild grass. The bikes lined up in front of us provided a little shelter. Greta and Talia played senet with a miniature board one of them had set up, their pieces arrayed in an augury configuration.

"Come play," Talia said. "Pray with us. Ask the gods for their wisdom."

Alice stared at the board for several seconds, a fierce gleam in her eye, before she shook her head, and reclined against the hill.

"Brennan?" Greta said.

"I've heard enough of the gods' so-called wisdom."

The sisters gave me a curious look as I took a place by the hill. I nodded off, too fatigued for worry to keep me awake. A while later, her senet game finished, Greta rolled against me, and we shared our thermal covers, provided again by Alice. Her body pressed against mine in sleep felt no different than the road. At one point, screechers woke us all, and I tried to comfort Greta, but she didn't need it. She and Talia knew the dark's terrors better than me.

Other things passed our camp. At times, the ground trembled and the road rumbled. Hot winds buffeted us with grit and pebbles. The air overhead filled with a mammoth shape I sensed but couldn't see beyond swirling shades of darkness. My mind tried to make sense of them but concocted impossible forms too harrowing to exist.

Distant voices carried clear across the empty land, human words that confirmed Alice's assessment that these humans no longer counted as people. They spoke of vile acts, and their wish for fresh victims, and I sensed Alice's body shift to alertness, watching until silence fell again, and we heard nothing more from them.

After sleep, we returned to the dark road and the path of our headlamps.

I watched my odometer and clock, as Alice had suggested. It gave me focus that stopped my eyes from reading patterns into the emptiness. I fell in sync with the road, with the growl of our engines. The ride, Greta's weight against my back, and Alice and Talia on Alice's bike ahead of me became everything. My senses focused so intently that it took a long, shocking moment to process it when Alice and Talia and their bike blinked out of sight. One moment, they rode ahead of us, silhouetted by the glow from Alice's headlamp, the next darkness consumed them. Greta's grip tightened around my waist, confirming she'd seen them vanish too. I cried out Alice's name and accelerated, thinking she'd only pulled ahead of me but caught up to nothing.

In the middle of the road, I stopped and removed my helmet.

Silence everywhere, except for the residual ringing in my ears. The tickle of a freezing wind brushed my face, and I shivered.

Greta and I rode back the way we'd come, convinced Alice and Talia had stopped, and we'd passed them, but we found no sign of them. I recognized a hole in the road and knew we'd gone back past where they vanished. We turned around and drove the stretch of road again. Greta took a flashlight from my kit and scanned the roadsides.

When she spotted a turn-off, she signaled me to stop with a squeeze.

Her flashlight revealed a cracked and narrow lane off the main road. Fresh tire tracks marked its coating of dirt and grit. In silent agreement, we rode down the path until a small light appeared far ahead. Speeding up, I raced toward it and found Alice's bike, headlamp still lit. The path continued, but the tracks ended there.

Taking off my helmet, I called, "Alice!"

Greta shouted for her sister.

The chilling wind kicked up and rattled sand and dirt against us.

An odor like days-old garbage and rotten meat tainted the air.

A shape flashed across Alice's headlamp. The ground shook.

Greta screamed. She rose into the sky, into the dark, and then winked out the way Alice and Talia had. I ran to grab onto her, too slow, and, though I leapt for her, I landed on my knees, empty-handed. Another scream came from behind me, and as I turned to face it, Alice appeared in the headlamp's glow, running hard, her knife in hand, blade dripping black liquid. She sprang onto the seat of her motorcycle, used it as a springboard, then arced into the darkness. She lashed the emptiness with her knife blade. A horrifying battle shriek passed her lips, fierce, determined. For several seconds, Alice blinked out, but I heard her, above me, screaming amidst an invisible thrashing. The wind swirled, knocking me down each time I tried to stand—then Alice and Greta dropped from nowhere and landed hard between our bikes. Alice scrambled to her feet, and then ran out of sight, and returned moments later with Talia.

"Back on your bike, now," she cried. "We need to reach the road. Go, go."

The wind rose and punished us, hammering down, slowing us, filling our faces with grit and the horrible scent of rot, chilling our throats and lungs with every breath. I fought my instinct to lay down and take cover, the urge to gag and vomit from the stench. I pushed Greta toward my bike. Alice looped an arm around Talia's waist and carried her. She threw her onto the seat then swung on herself. We pulled on our helmets and raced back toward the road.

In the hounding wind, dirt and sand shifted on the path. Faces formed in its patterns. Some human, some not, with murky features tormented by expressions of hatred, rage, despair, and envy. Each face broke apart and scattered as quickly as it coalesced, replaced by another. Alice hunkered down, her head almost between her hands on the handlebars. I imitated her, and the wind blew over me with less fury. An enormous thud shook the earth, bouncing the road grit inches into the air. A second followed and jolted my bike, but I righted it.

One more powerful impact came. Alice swerved, her bike tilting side to side. I fought to keep mine upright and steady. The wind attacked like a hundred pushing hands trying to knock us down—and then we reached the road, turned north, and sped away.

The bone-aching cold, the horrid stench, and the ferocious wind fell behind us.

Back on the road, we traveled through the expansive dark for several more hours without speaking, frightened to stop, afraid to talk about what invisible thing had attacked us or what the faces formed by sand and dirt meant. Above our engine noise, we heard screechers overhead, and we dared not slow until we put distance between us and them.

8

Fires burned on the outskirts of Hierophantia.

Mounds of dirty snow covered the ground, and treacherous, icy roads threatened to wreck us at every curve and slope. The town itself stood far in the distance, a dome of light rising from blocky shadows that tinted the solid black sky above. Beyond it lay the Psychopomp Road, the last leg of the Journey to Erebus, a trail into what the old-timers called *terra incognita*. Others called it limbo, or the anteroom of endless night, or the big black nothing, or the highway to hell, or even nirvana, depending on your outlook. Alice referred to it only as the next stretch of road ahead of us, and I chose to think about it as little as possible.

With Hierophantia in sight after so many hours traveling, the reality of our purpose struck hard with the realization that, like so many others before us, we might pass into the darkness and never return. A need to confront the gods and know the truth drove Alice. My instinct to help my sister drove me, and doubts about how much help I really offered nibbled away at my conviction.

We passed the first of the roadside fires, a bonfire flaming in a shallow pit. People sat around it amidst a handful of tents and makeshift camps. A few tossed more fuel onto the blaze as we passed. Most stared at us with naked curiosity and, to my confusion, with bold envy, as if they wanted to move on into Hierophantia but couldn't. I wondered what stopped them when at each site sat cars, trucks, and bikes that all looked in working order.

The answer lay at a place where the road sloped down through a short canyon, confined by icy rock walls on either side, where a checkpoint blocked the way.

Alice stopped her bike at the canyon mouth. I halted beside her.

The sisters looked over our shoulders. Talia had bounced back fast with her medication, no fever for hours, and Greta had remained so quiet behind me for the last long stretch of riding, I thought she'd fallen asleep. Spotlights illuminated the checkpoint, a high, chain-link fence on rollers and a handful of cars and trucks parked on the other side. Armed men patrolled the line. Alice removed her helmet and scrutinized the canyon. Her gaze lingered on its high walls. I followed her line of sight and saw snipers up top.

"What the hell? You ever hear of Hierophantia being closed up like this?" I said.

Alice said nothing, only continued surveying the way ahead.

"We heard rumors," Greta said.

"Of what?" I asked.

"Dark times up this way. Bad people taking over."

"I saw them in my visions," Talia said. "They all have guns and knives, and they come at their targets with blood on their lips and teeth. They peel the skin from the bones of the dead and carry people into the dark. Hierophantia is full of violence."

I kicked out my bike's stand and dismounted to stretch. "Why didn't you warn us?"

"I was sick, and I didn't know for sure," she said. "Sometimes I'm wrong."

"What else are you holding back? I mean, even if you're not sure, you may as well share so we can be as well prepared as possible. What rumors did you hear anyway?"

Greta untied her hair and shook it loose. "Rumors along the road. People warning us to stay away from Hierophantia because blasphemers had taken over, and they use their power to prey on the weak and the needy and those who come here out of hope."

Out of hope.

I gazed back along the road at the scattered fires and the sick and weary faces they lit. It had never occurred to me hope might drive a person this deep into the darkness, but when all else fails only mystery remains to offer opportunity.

"They'll want us to pay to get in," I said.

Now Alice spoke: "No. They'll want us to pay for our lives."

"How so?" I asked.

"This checkpoint is a classic ambush. Once we're in the canyon, we surrender any defensible position. I guarantee men are posted on either side of the road, ready to close off our retreat. There will be a cash price to enter. It will be so high very few can pay it. There will also be a cash price to let us leave when we tell them we can't pay. It will be lower, but still more than most could offer. Pay one or the other. If we try to run without paying, they'll shoot us all down. So, there will be another option. Barter with goods or services. They'll offer Greta and Talia the easiest solution, payment with their bodies, maybe a tour making the rounds of their brothels, and when they've used them up, then maybe you become a citizen of Hierophantia, or leave town, or they'll kill you to control the population. For you, Little Brother, servitude will be all they'll accept. That could mean you pay with your body too or you become someone's slave. Once they realize who I am, they'll demand I fight for them, maybe take a post on those canyon walls to victimize those who come after us. If you're lucky, Bren, they'll treat you okay to keep you as leverage against me. I've seen this set up in the cities of our enemies or run by brigand gangs along the road. It's how dictators control people. They won't make any deal that benefits us, only them. We'll belong to them. The people we passed on the road are the ones who realized that before they entered this canyon."

"Why are they still here? Why not go back where they came from?" said Greta.

"Maybe they have nothing to return to. They came here out of desperation, and at least here they're closer to the gods, and their prayers might be heard sooner," I said.

"How horrible and sad," said Talia. "Hierophantia is a sacred place. It's meant to be a neutral city, a *human* city, not one run like a prison."

"Every place is a prison to some degree," Alice said. "What differentiates them is how well people get along with the jailers—even when we ourselves are the jailers."

I thought of my city life, of my strictly regulated work hours, of the restrictions and rules that governed how I used my apartment, what I did on the streets, what shops and public places I entered, what I ate, what water I drank, how I acted in public, what lights I used, how the city's bureaucracy filtered my earnings to me only after taking its share—and how none of those rules applied to people with enough money to buy exemptions or pay bribes. I had considered myself free there.

"So, what do we do?" I asked. "We can't make a deal with them."

"No, and there are too many, too well placed for me to fight our way through," said Alice. "We have to find another way into Hierophantia."

We turned our bikes around and remounted.

Laughter echoed down the canyon after us, erased only by our growling engines.

9

We rode back out of sight of the canyon.

At a place beyond reach of the scattered campfires, we left the pavement for rough terrain. We covered a mile or so before the ice and snow forced us off our bikes, then we walked from there, wheeling the bikes with us. The lights of Hierophantia beckoned. We followed an arc toward the city's northern quarters. After a few hours of tracking, we reached a canyon that gave passage through the rock wall that divided the city from the rest of the world.

There we camped in a shallow crevice to rest. Cold bit at us, held at bay by a small fire Alice tended and our thermal blankets. We slept in shifts, a few hours each. When we rolled out later, almost no light revealed the ground ahead. We didn't dare use our headlamps this close to the city. So, we followed Alice and trusted her guidance.

None of us saw the rockfall. We only heard it.

Alice kept us hugged tight against the north face of the ridge, which in some places rose higher than we could see in the dark, and along one of those stretches, a cascade of stone and ice pushed us near panic. We only heard it rumble at first—then pebbles rained on us, clacking off our helmets, striking the unprotected sisters, who yelped in surprise and pain. Alice ordered us to rush forward. The rockfall accelerated, building into a massive, sloughing wave of boulders and ice. Alice's quick orders spared us the worst of it, but enough debris spewed up to batter us and the bikes. We hunkered down behind them. I covered Greta as best I could. Alice did the same for Talia. When the rush of broken mountain finished, we came up bruised and frightened but still alive if only by inches.

Inspecting the bikes revealed no serious damage, and we continued our journey.

Hierophantia seemed farther away than ever, although I knew only another eight or ten miles lay between us and the city. We covered the distance in five hours, and then we dug down behind a low hill and camped again. Alice refused to go any farther until we rested. She wanted time for observation too and before dozing off she spied our way into Hierophantia. Later, with the city quiet and settled, we approached, cutting still farther north, and coming along a trail that led northwest into the darkness. From the debris and rubbish scattered along the way, I took it for the road to the garbage dump, a guess proven right when we entered a truckyard full of pickups and hauling vehicles, ripe with remnants of the trash they'd carried. Alice led us creeping across the yard to an alley that connected to the main roads of the city.

A few blocks later, we mounted up and rode our bikes. No one gave us a second look.

We either blended in well enough or they just didn't care. Gray buildings and lightless windows rolled by, shopfronts caked with dust and grime, narrow alleys loaded with menacing shadows. It resembled places in photographs in old history books, locked down by governments that controlled all aspects of life. The kind of places people tried to escape—and yet here the four of us had sneaked in and planned to stay for a while.

At an intersection, Alice spotted an inn with its lights lit.

We took rooms there. The innkeeper hesitated because we had no papers to show our legal entry, but Alice stacked cash on the registration desk until he agreed to house us and hide our bikes in his garage.

Alice and I took one room, the sisters the one next door.

Within minutes of entering, Alice had stripped down to her bottom clothing layer and lay snoring on the bed, while I sat wide awake, stunned at the journey behind us and how much my life had changed in so short a time. A soft knock at the door roused me from bed. Greta stood in the hallway outside.

"Talia's asleep, but I'm too wired and awake," she said.

"Me, too," I said. "You owe me a story."

"I do at that," said Greta.

We crept downstairs and found seats in the back corner of the inn's bar. Two people sat at the bar itself, a few at the scattered tables. At one table, two women played senet while a man followed the game. Greta's gaze danced across the dice sticks and the pieces arrayed on the grid. I ordered us a Riesling wine then watched her watch the game until the server brought the bottle and glasses. Greta didn't notice as I poured then raised my glass to her.

"Greta?"

Her attention returned to me with an abrupt change.

"Yes?"

I gestured at the full glass in front of her. "Your wine."

"Oh, thank you." She blushed as she raised her glass and clinked it against mine. "Sorry, I got distracted."

"I've seen an entire gaming hall enrapt by a senet game. But you promised me the story of why you and your sisters came here," I said.

"Right. Talia saw a vision of us in this city, so we came."

"To do what?"

"We don't know yet. In her vision we weren't alone. I'm not sure it's you and Alice she saw with us. Donia was here, though, so maybe she got that wrong. Her visions aren't always literal. There's a dreamy unreality to them sometimes." Greta sipped her wine then set down the glass. "Poor Donia. We left her all on her own—and how will she get in past the checkpoint to meet us?"

"Your sister seemed tough and smart. She'll find a way."

"I suppose," Greta said. "What Talia saw seemed important in the sense that what we're meant to do here is important. Helping someone. Maybe stopping someone from doing a thing dangerous not only to them but a lot of people. Like someone playing with a loaded gun. You understand?"

"Did Talia see anything specific?"

"Yes and no. She saw us, this place, and she saw motorcycles, so you and Alice are part of it. We were supposed to run into you on the road, I believe. She saw some people we haven't met yet, so maybe we haven't hit Talia's vision point. She felt tension here in Hierophantia and violence in the air. She saw another thing that made her desperate to get here, hoping we could change part of the vision."

"What was that?"

Greta took a long drink of her wine then let out a slow breath.

"She saw a lot of blood and fire."

10

In the middle of the night, Talia screamed.

Her cries woke me and Alice in the next room, woke the entire inn. We rushed from bed, from our room. In the hall, the innkeeper, eyes wide with anger, urged us to shut her up before she drew attention from outside the inn. Greta opened the door of their room for us, and then, as if at the snap of fingers, Talia fell silent. She stood at the window and stared out. Alice said her name. Talia turned in response then fainted onto her bed. The innkeeper watched as Alice and Greta positioned Talia and pulled the covers over her.

"Is she done screaming bloody murder?" he asked.

"She had a nightmare, that's all. She's a vivid dreamer." I pressed some bills into the innkeeper's hand. "Won't happen again."

"Listen, I took a chance boarding you four without documents. Don't make me regret it."

I gestured to Alice. "Do you see my sister there?"

The innkeeper nodded.

"Her last name is Atropos." The innkeeper's eyes widened again. His face paled. "We took a chance on overpaying you to let us stay here. Don't make *us* regret it."

Giving out a snort of frightened indignation, the innkeeper scurried back to his quarters.

"They come on her this way sometimes," Greta said. "She wasn't awake for it. She'll sleep soundly now and remember it in the morning. The vision, at least, not the screaming or you and Alice coming in here. She's going to have something to tell us when she wakes up. It's best if we all go back to sleep."

So, we did. Except I couldn't after that. Alice resumed snoring within moments of her head hitting the pillow. Not another bump or whisper came from the sisters' room. I laid awake and replayed our journey over and again in search of an answer to a question I hadn't yet asked. I had expected in Hierophantia to find a step toward our journey's resolution, like drawing sixteen at the blackjack table and knowing your next draw decides your hand, win or lose. Instead, new possibilities arrayed themselves across my mind. I turned each one over and over and considered them for so long that when I heard the noise of the staff prepping for work downstairs, I found myself no closer to rest or an understanding.

Soon, Alice awoke.

As she dressed, she explained her plan to scout the northernmost quarters of Hierophantia for passage to the Psychopomp Road. While the sisters still slept, we rode out and navigated a maze of approaches to the final checkpoint. It lacked defensible installations beyond a pair of watch booths stationed at the entrance to the bridge that connected it to city, and only a few guards staffed it. I suppose fear of what lay beyond provided ample security.

"Leaving here will be easier than arriving," I said.

"This is all for show. There's no benefit to stopping people from exiting this way when none of them come back."

Along our return ride, a caravan of pickup trucks passed us, bound for the city center. Each truck carried new arrivals, people willing to pay any price to enter Hierophantia and those who could no longer tolerate the deprivation of the campgrounds. Alice and I stopped to watch them roll past us. A familiar face looked out from one of the trucks.

"Donia," I said.

We lifted our visors, made eye contact, but none of us showed any sign of recognition.

Only the faintest curl of a smile suggested Donia found our presence reassuring. If Alice and I had reached Hierophantia, her sisters most likely had too.

Before going back to the inn, we purchased gear and supplies for riding the Psychopomp Road. Winter coats and sleeping kit. Jerky and other dry foods. Thermal blankets. Lighters. Flint and fire wool. Canteens. LED lanterns. A set of binoculars. Three handguns, two of which Alice added to her belt beside her first gun and her knife, and the third which I strapped on under my coat. Our lack of documents required us to pay triple for our purchases in bribes yet neither Alice nor I felt confident the sellers would keep their word if placed under duress. When we returned to the inn, the keeper eyed us with fear and relief that we appeared ready to leave soon.

Greta and Talia occupied a table in the corner of the barroom, so we joined them.

"Did you see Donia?" Greta said.

Alice and I shared a surprised glance.

"How did you know?" Alice said.

"I saw her here in my vision last night," Talia said.

Her eyes glistened with the flicker of the electric candle at the center of the table. She looked drained and pale except for the constant flush in her cheeks, a remnant of her fever or the sign of her tumultuous night.

"We saw her," Alice said. "In a truck with others who struck deals at the city gates."

"I wish you hadn't," Talia said.

"Why?" I said. "Now we know she's here, we can get you three reunited."

Greta shook her head. "Remember what I told you of Talia's vision that brought us here, how it ended in blood and fire?"

Alice raised an eyebrow at me, startled I hadn't told her, but between Talia's vision in the night and our scouting mission, there hadn't been time to bring it up.

"My vision last night added some missing pieces," Talia said.

"What did you see?" asked Alice.

"That before my first vision can happen, we'll be reunited with Donia—and the blood is yours, Alice Atropos, and the fire will burn us all," Talia said.

11

Despite Talia's warning, Alice insisted we rescue Donia.

"I don't care what Talia saw. I won't leave Donia a prisoner here and you two sisters likely to follow in her footsteps," Alice said.

The irony of "follow in her footsteps" struck me and Alice at the same time. We laughed. Greta and Talia stared at us, confused, and when we calmed, I winked at them, and said, "Family joke."

"We got you here," Alice said. "If you mean to stay, you'll need documents, identities, all that. First, we need information."

Alice parceled out instructions and a share of her remaining cash to each of us, and we split up. When we all met back at the inn, I'd struck a deal with a forger who worked out of a nearby gambling den. Greta and Talia had located Donia, at a holding house off the city plaza, where her auction would occur. Alice returned with more weapons and gear, and then we cleared out our rooms and loaded our bikes. Whether we succeeded or failed, we couldn't return to this inn.

We waited until the hour of worship when the faithful gathered in Hierophantia's myriad temples and halls to offer spiritual sacrifice to the gods of their choice. The streets emptied then, and Alice knew guards not released for worship often took this hour to nap, hit the lavatory, or even duck out for a rendezvous with a blasphemous lover. Nothing much happened outside the holy places during worship hour. Even faithless criminals laid low because punishment for any crime, large or small, during the hour meant immediate death at the hands of the few police still on duty. No trial or plea. If they caught you in the act, on any reasonable suspicion, they shot to kill, and so they would treat us if our plan foundered. That frightened Greta and Talia, but not enough to deter them.

At the holding house, Alice kicked down the front door. Only one of three guards who should've met us stood at his post. She killed him with her knife before he finished rising from his chair. A second guard arrived from the back, unawares, with a sandwich in his hand. Alice downed him too. Guard number three never showed, out for a quickie with his sweetheart or napping somewhere. We searched for Donia among rows of cells filled with cowering men and women. Fear etched itself in their dirt-streaked faces, and their eyes widened with apprehension at the sight of us. When we found Donia, she wept to see her sisters, and the three grabbed each other's hands through the bars.

With a hammer and chisel Alice had bought, we smashed open the lock on her cell. Donia rushed out and embraced Greta and Talia.

Her three cellmates pressed as far from us as they could into the corners of their cell.

"You're free to go if you choose. You can free the others with these." Alice offered them the tools. "Use them to smash the locks and run. No one will see you during the hour of worship. You can disappear into the city."

The oldest of the women shook her head. "And if someone happens to see us running, it's death. No thanks. We won't be a distraction for you."

"We don't need a distraction." Alice dropped the tools. They clanged on the cell floor. "Suit yourself. In the end, we're all prisoners of fate, anyway."

We fled the holding house. Donia rode pressed tight against Talia, who squeezed herself between Alice and her sister. She came close to flying off every time Alice hit a hard bump or took a sharp curve. Soon, though, we reached an isolated alley where my forger contact had promised to meet us. He brought five armed men with him.

"We had a deal," I said.

"The bounty on fugitives is much higher than anything you can pay me," he said. "I'm a businessman, first and last, nothing else. You do the math."

Alice lunged off her motorcycle. Talia and Donia scattered as it toppled, knocking them down. Alice hit the apogee of her leap and descended into the forger's group. She drew her knife and cut the threads of three out of the five before her feet touched the ground. The other two died in the moments after she found her footing. The forger tried to run, but Alice dragged him by the throat deeper into the alley.

"What were you going to do with us?" she said. She smacked him when he didn't answer, loosened her grip a bit, and repeated the question. When he still didn't reply, she twisted his head to face the corpses of his men, bleeding on the ground. "I had no use for them. If you won't talk, I have no use for you. Do you understand?"

The gasped out a "yes," and then Alice eased her grip so he could talk. "I was going to take you to the police," he said.

"Trying to herd the five of us, armed, and skilled enough to survive in Hierophantia without documents? You're smarter than that. How long do we have?"

"What do you mean?" he said.

Alice's grip tightened. His throat crunched, and his face brightened ruby red as he struggled to breathe. After a few seconds, Alice's fingers loosened.

"What time did you tell the cops to meet you here?"

The forger tried to shake his head, but Alice knocked it against the wall and squeezed his throat again. He sputtered, and his eyes bulged. When Alice next relented, he looked frightened and defeated.

"What time is it now?" he asked.

I glanced at my watch and told him.

"You have ten minutes. We only needed to hold you till they came to collect the bounty."

Alice punched the forger in the face, cracking the back of his head against the wall again, and then dropped him in an unconscious heap. At her order, we jumped on the bikes and sped out of the alley. Police sirens filled the empty streets. Red and blue lights flashed to the south, and so we rode north. We didn't know Hierophantia, though, and took some bad turns and had to double back twice. The police gained. The sirens wailed louder. The lights flashed brighter. Our engines roared. The city flashed by us. People emerged from houses of worship, stunned at the sight of us and the fleet of police vehicles dogging our trail.

Doubling back from another dead end, I shouted at Alice to leave Talia and Donia with me, to go on her own. She could ride faster without us holding her back. Whatever punishment the city dealt us seemed a fair price to pay for Alice's freedom. She refused, as I'd known she would. Alice could never accept defeat. She had set her mission to rescue Donia and protect the sisters, and she could accept no compromise other than death.

"If we reach the Psychopomp Road, they can't touch us. It's forbidden to interfere with anyone making the Journey to Erebus after they cross the bridge," Alice said. "And they can't set foot on the road to come after us, unless they plan to make the Journey to Erebus themselves."

"The sisters can't come with us," I said. "They never meant to make the Journey."

"They don't have a choice now. Their fates have spoken."

"She's right," said Donia. "We're with you all the way now."

Alice accelerated back into the flow of the streets. I sped after her, Greta clinging to me. The police drew closer. Their lights painted the street ahead of us, limned the shops and homes with lurid colors. Far ahead, much too distant for comfort, spotlights flared at the Psychopomp Road Checkpoint.

12

Reinforcements awaited us.

Police blocked the checkpoint entrance, and police closed the distance behind us. We skidded to a stop in the last open patch of road and weighed our options. None looked promising.

"You should've gone without us, gotten here before the backup arrived," I said.

Alice sneered. "They sent backup here before we left that alley."

"Then why did we come this way?"

"It's our only out, and they don't know who they're dealing with yet."

Alice climbed off her bike. The cops aimed guns at us, front and back. Using a megaphone, one ordered us to surrender, to get down on the ground, but we ignored the command.

"What are you going to do?" I asked Alice.

"Can any of you girls drive a motorcycle?" she asked the sisters.

Donia stepped forward. "I can."

"Good. You and Talia take my bike. Follow Brennan. He'll know when the time is right to ride through the checkpoint and cross the bridge."

"How? What are you going to do?" she asked Alice.

"What I was trained to."

Alice put up her hands and took several steps forward. Showing them her left sleeve, still speckled with bright threads.

"Do you see who I am?" she called out.

Through the megaphone, a voice replied," You *were* a Thread-Cutter. So, what? Here you're nothing but a trespasser, and we outnumber you."

"Numbers matter less than fate," Alice said. "I'm only here to complete the Journey to Erebus. Let us pass, and we're gone. We don't want a fight."

Fear flashed across the faces of the cops, but they held their ground. Thread-Cutter or not, a woman alone taking down any of them, forget about all of them, must have seemed laughable, but they didn't understand Alice had no need to take them all down, only the right ones.

"If you don't want a fight, surrender." The cop's amplified voice echoed.

"I will complete my journey whether you like it or not," said Alice.

"Then it's your funeral."

A dozen cops cocked their weapons and aimed at Alice.

She dropped to a crouch, made a swift gesture, and sent a dark sphere about the size of a tennis ball shooting away from her, over our heads, and into the first line of police cars behind us. The grenade exploded, swathing half a dozen cars in flames. A second struck the cars along the checkpoint and created a parallel cloud of fire. Alice became a shadowy blur in constant motion, her body frigid for fractions of a second as the muzzle flashes from her guns lit her. Shouts and screams rose from the police. Bullets flew. I pressed Greta to the ground behind my bike. Donia did the same with Talia. Shots ricocheted off the pavement around us, pinged off Alice's armored bike. Low walls of fire boxed us. I strained my eyes to keep track of Alice, to watch for her signal. She moved so fast and with such surety that she terrified me—but then at the height of the chaos, her signal came. Two more police cars exploded. Cops scattered, seeking cover, dodging debris, trying to kill Alice, and that's when she nodded to me.

She paused long enough I could see her clearly and gestured at me with her right pinky finger extended, a signal only I'd understand, one we'd used since childhood to wish each other good luck.

I dragged Greta with me onto my bike. Donia and Talia followed my lead. All four of us mounted up, started our engines.

Before we could ride, before Alice could hurl herself back into the melee, two shots hit her. I shouted her name as she folded to her knees, but she waved me back, and then so fast my eye could barely acknowledge it, she shifted back into motion. Torn between rushing to help her and taking the opening she'd provided, I gunned my bike toward the checkpoint. Donia rode after me. We sped through the wall of flames. The searing heat licked at us as we climbed the ramp onto the bridge. Guards emerged from the watch posts ahead. I drew my gun and fired at them, shot after shot going wide but close enough to drive them inside for cover.

We sped past the booths, each of us on fire. Our tires touched the bridge surface A half a mile to Psychopomp Road lay ahead of us.

With a wordless shout of anger, frustration, and worry for Alice, I led us across, and the wind from our race extinguished the flames.

13

From the start of the Psychopomp Road, we watched the checkpoint burn.

I picked out Alice's dark, flashing figure in the fighting, like an insect dancing around a flame. Gunshots turned sporadic, then stopped.

"Should we go before they come after us?" Greta asked.

"They won't," I said.

"What if they're so angry they don't follow the rules?" said Talia.

"They have to. There's more at stake for them than catching us. If they commit sacrilege to pursue us," I said, "if they break that rule, they blaspheme. If they set foot on this road, they must complete the Journey to Erebus before they return, or they blaspheme."

"They could just shoot us from the bridge," said Talia.

"They won't," I said.

"He's right," said Donia. "Their authority only lasts as long as people believe they honor the gods. If they transgress the divine order, they place all of Hierophantia at risk, and they'll be seen as unfit to govern. There will be a revolution. Always has it been that way in Hierophantia. These rulers aren't the first to rise and fall here. They won't be the last."

That quieted the debate, and we waited.

When the fighting seemed to stop and Alice didn't appear, worry consumed me.

Wounded cops moved around the scene of the battle, limping, holding onto each other for support, crawling across the ground among motionless bodies. Had Alice killed only those she needed for victory or had she gone further? Or, a sickening notion, had she gone only so far as to allow us to escape but not herself?

"Where is she?" Talia said.

"Hush and be patient," said Donia.

Wind carried ash and heat across the bridge and the wail of more sirens as Hierophantia's first responders rushed toward the scene.

The city seemed to quiet in reverence or fear except for that rising and falling wail.

It echoed off buildings and along avenues.

It filled the air, resounded in my mind.

I thought of how screechers had hounded me awake and driven me toward a type of madness. I feared the uncertainty of waiting for Alice might do the same.

Greta wrapped her arm across my chest and hugged me.

When the checkpoint booths exploded, we flinched and nearly fell from my bike. Heat jumped around us, and the shockwave took our breath away.

The fire and explosion spread. A piece of the bridge splintered into rocky chunks and fell away into the crevasse below. Fresh flames masked the city from our view. Smoke flooded the air and set our eyes watering. I welcomed it because it hid my tears for Alice. Tears I cried in sadness—and then relief when my sister's unmistakable figure emerged on our side of the fire, our side of the bridge, dropping through smoke and flames on a stolen police motorcycle like a true angel of death. Her bike slammed down on the bridge, and as she approached, she gestured for us to mount up, and then blew past us at full speed, dying tongues of flame still licking from her jacket. We raced to catch up, the five of us hurtling along the Psychopomp Road, leaving death and fire behind us, smoke wafting off Alice, heat shimmering from her body in the cold.

We rode until Hierophantia shrank to a burning dot on the horizon.

When we stopped, Alice staggered off her bike and made to fetch the first aid kit from her cargo box, but she didn't reach it. Her knees buckled. Donia and I caught her before she hit the ground then laid her out gently on the frigid dirt. Blood soaked her clothes, some of it crusty as it coagulated and froze. We searched her for wounds and found one in her left shoulder above her heart, another on her right hip, both clean. Each one had eaten away at flesh, no more. Donia and I cleaned them, bandaged them, then wrapped Alice in her thermal blanket, while Greta and Talia brought out nutrient bars. We explored the extra gear Alice had purchased and found food enough for days, more shining silver blankets, water purifying filters to drink from snowmelt, a dozen flashlights and lighters, and a stock of fuel pellets for campfires.

We made camp there so Alice could rest. She slept for hours. The sisters slept in shifts. I stayed awake, unable to close my eyes or quiet my thoughts, my ears alert for the engine noise I worried would follow us, signaling pursuit by the Hierophantia police or worse. None ever came, though. As the checkpoint fire dimmed and full darkness bled back into the horizon, I wondered if anyone in the city watched our tiny light burn.

When Alice awoke, she shrugged off our attempts at conversation and ordered us back on the move. No one knew the distance from here to our journey's end. After six hours, Alice's bike ran out of fuel. Our supply would last longer split between two engines, so she ditched it at the roadside. She resumed riding her old bike with Donia and Talia squeezed on behind her. We traveled with no sense of time except that provided by the clock and the slow, steady decline of our fuel gauges. Darkness embraced us, filled every void and seam in the world except for the meager reach of our headlamps and our instrument lights. It telegraphed emptiness more horrifying to me than that on the road to Hierophantia. Dangerous as it had been, things still lived in that darkness. Here, nothing did. The darkness equaled nothing which equaled absence which equaled nonexistence, and at times I wondered if we were real anymore or had exited the world into some space of unreality. Inside our tiny bubble of life, we rolled along a dead road, like crossing a wild, black, lifeless river, its waters washing from us all the artifacts of our lives, cleansing us down to souls, adrift in a universe that held no love or acknowledgement of us, and provided us no other place to live than the one we carved out of it with our own hands, by our own will. We lived now on Old Jack Chance's senet board, pieces moved by an unknown and unknowable player, by the fate in which Alice believed, or the random luck of the dice sticks across the final squares, ahead of our equally ineffable opponent's pieces.

I lost track of how many hours and miles passed by the time we filled the bikes with the last of our fuel.

Hours or days later, I couldn't say for sure, we exhausted even that.

We pulled off the road as our engines sputtered then died.

With no way to ride onward, we gathered in the yellowing glow of our headlamps, and tried not to think about the immensity of the void around us, and how it might swallow us whole when our batteries died, and those lights winked out.

14

Now we walked the Psychopomp Road.

Carrying provisions split equally among us and with flashlights to show the way, we trudged along the double-yellow line. No one said much. We wore our thermal blankets tied around our shoulders like cloaks against the falling temperature. Without a clock or an odometer, time and distance lost their meaning. I couldn't read my watch.

My brain refused to acknowledge the concept it represented. When we grew so tired our feet dragged, we camped and slept around small fires Alice made. We ate nutrient bars and drank snowmelt through our filters. We burned through the flashlights, dropping them when their batteries died, and choosing another from the supply. We camped three times and by our fourth we each held one working light.

On our next session walking the road, Talia's died first, then Donia's a while later, then Alice's. Greta and I led with ours, until Greta's flickered and blackened, and I carried our only working light. The others followed me, even Alice, a weird sensation, my much more capable big sister now trusting me to lead her to her goal. At my light's first flicker, though, she insisted we camp for the night and start a fire before it died. That night, Greta, who usually slept close to me, as if riding pressed together for so long had bred a physical link neither of us dared to break, huddled in with her sisters under their thermals. I sat beside Alice, who tended the fire. We took turns, one sleeping while the other kept the flames going, feeding them fresh burn pellets as they waned. We had enough pellets for one more fire, one more camp.

I asked Alice how long she thought remained ahead of us, how long we might last with no light. She smiled then shrugged, fire shadows dancing on her face. Her indifference revealed what she left unspoken: Whether we reached the Houses of the Gods or not, the end of our journey neared.

Not long after we resumed walking, my yellowing flashlight died.

Our eyes adjusted to the darkness after a time, enough so at least to perceive the shadow edges of hills and mountains along either side of the road and distant, squarish clumps suggestive of old cities and skyscrapers. I avoided thinking about what might live or might once have lived there. They helped us navigate. The double yellow line caught whatever meager, ambient light escaped the sky and magnified it to visibility, glowing faintly.

Hours or minutes later, impossible to say, but worn down and ragged, we camped. Alice built a fire with our last pellets. We spoke little, each of us haggard, downtrodden, weary, victim of a physical malaise that emanated from our psychological one as the darkness took hold inside us and extinguished our last spark of hope. We faced the possibility that all we'd suffered so far meant nothing. The gods remained unattainable. The road too long. Our lives' desires amounted to zero. Our lives themselves, meaningless. The things that drove and shaped us only fabrications of our minds, providing an excuse to live, an instinctive fantasy that shielded us from our own insignificance.

I expected the next time we camped we might not return to the road.

This time we did, and uncounted hours later, a dim glow appeared far ahead of us. All of us saw it; none of us believed it. We walked closer until we couldn't deny it.

A golden light burned farther down the road.

We stared at it, both grateful and terrified.

Our pace picked up, and the light grew as we approached it. A few more hours brought us to the crest of a steep rise in the road, and from the height we saw a magnificent sight.

The end of the road and the Houses of the Gods.

Their golden buildings sprawled across the black landscape and glowed with an intensity I'd never experienced. A hot, yellow glare, the heat of which reached us even so far away. I thought of children's books and myths about bright, open skies where a thing called the sun burned and sent light and warmth down to the people, and I wondered if it felt like this. I tried to imagine such brilliance hanging in the sky, raining itself down over the earth. Absurdity.

Alice laughed for joy. She started down the other side of the hill.

Donia stepped into her path and stopped her.

"Your bravery and integrity have earned you this much, Alice Atropos, that you may see the Houses of the Gods, but you may not go any closer," she said. "Your journey ends here. You have reached Erebus, the night, and you must stay with Erebus. Look upon the brilliance. Savor the fact that you are one of very, very few who've ever laid eyes upon it, who've ever traveled this far, who've ever survived the darkness and deprivation along the Psychopomp Road—and be grateful."

She lunged at Alice, wielding a long knife drawn from a hiding place in her clothes, and slashed at my sister's neck. Alice's reflexes saved her life. She recoiled. Donia's blade missed her throat. In the same moment, Talia and Greta seized my arms and held me from interfering. In the brilliance radiating from the Houses of the Gods, the sisters' appearances changed and grew both more beautiful than before and at the same time utterly horrible. The light changed them. It catalyzed a revelation of their nature.

"Don't fight us," Greta whispered in my ear. Her voice resonated with an ancient, strident tone, every lover's sweetest promises, every murderer's last threats. "We are the fate of all those who Journey to Erebus. We are the true Moirai, the Morrigan, the Orisha, the Anunnaki, and the Norn. Fate is ours to decide. The Psychopomp Road runs so long as we say, and we've granted you this gift. But no one may enter the Brilliant Place. No one may touch its heat and light. They don't belong to the world anymore. We have enjoyed your company and your righteousness, so we granted your sister this much to know that such a place exists and that she plays a part, however infinitesimal, in something grander than herself. But here fate claims you both."

I struggled to free myself. Greta's and Talia's hands held me like cold steel.

Donia thrust her blade again at Alice, but now Alice drew her own knife.

The two danced then in the palm of death's hand, but neither landed a blow.

Their bodies moved like fluid, like wind, like voices in the night, or rainwater spilling on the leaves of a tree.

I pled with Greta to free me, to stop Donia, but she refused.

"I saw a vision of blood and fire," Talia said. "We have witnessed the fire. Now the blood must flow."

The longer Alice evaded, the more terrifying Donia's aspect grew. I couldn't explain what emerged from the sisters now, how Greta and Talia's fingers burned cold against me, how their voices clawed at my ears, how their scents hinted at death, and how their suddenly revealed beauty terrified me. My mind reeled at their transformation. I struggled and yanked myself free, only to slam facedown to the road when Greta leapt on my back. She sat on me, pinned me. Talia yanked my head up by my hair so I could watch Alice and Donia fight.

"This was not your journey to make, not your fate" she said.

"We've craved your sister since she was born," Greta said. "The gem of her soul will add to our treasure."

"We have no need, or use, or desire for you," said Talia. "You must know, before you die, how little you mean. You're nothing in the shadow of Alice. In the eyes of the gods, in the turnings of the universe, you may as well have never existed."

"Or, better yet, had died as a child," Greta said.

"Or, better still, never been born," said Talia. "Nonexistence is a blessing."

I cried out for them to let me go. Talia pressed her hand over my mouth to silence me. Alice fought hard, but I saw signs of fatigue. Donia looked as if she might never tire.

The first blood came when Donia sliced Alice's upper arm. The second, Alice's thigh.

Sensing victory, Donia leered. It made her face truly monstrous. Somewhere in there her human features remained, but they floated on the surface of an alien and primal beast, a force of nature constrained by semi-human form. A mask over an elemental hunger.

I sensed the same in Greta and Talia.

Liars. Deceivers. Tricksters. Fates. Spinning, spinning, weaving, cutting.

They were all these things. And, in some part of my mind, still three stranded sisters in need of aid, which we gave freely and sincerely, only to find ourselves betrayed and repaid with horror. The fates. The indifferent, mercurial, and heartless fates.

They would have it all as they wished it, no thought given to the condemned.

My will to fight waned. This, too, played a part in their game, meant to wear me down to acceptance, to acknowledge their control of me, of Alice, of all people.

A scream pierced my ears, then. An unrestrained cry of agony and fury.

Alice stood by Donia, who doubled over and clutched at her chest where Alice's knife had bitten into her up to its grip. Donia wailed again as Alice withdrew the blade with a splatter of blood on the pavement. In the strange light from the end of the road, Donia's blood steamed like molten copper. Alice struck again, too swift for my eyes to understand. She stabbed Donia several more times in fast, powerful jabs. Each one spilled more blood and created a luminous mist that clung to Alice's legs. Donia folded to her knees. Alice swiveled her body behind her and landed her knife deep into the base of Donia's neck. She fell facedown to the road. Her appearance reverted to the Donia we had known as if all her life and power fled.

Greta screamed. Talia released me and leaped at Alice. Alice proved faster. She left her knife in Donia's neck, drew her guns, and shot Talia five times before she could get close, launching coppery clouds of blood. Instead of landing in a savage attack as intended, Talia hit Alice as dead weight then dropped to the pavement.

Greta sobbed. I pushed myself up, throwing her off my back, rolled over, and landed on top of her. I held her down and reached for my gun. She clawed at my eyes. I thrust my head out of reach, but it put me off balance. Greta seized the opportunity to shove free. She clambered to her feet and ran toward the Houses of the Gods, toward Alice. She evaded Alice's gunfire long enough to land emerging claws into Alice's torso and drag her to the ground. Teeth like knives popped from between her lips, aimed at Alice's neck.

I drew the gun Alice had given me and fired.

I pulled the trigger until it clicked empty. Greta lay in a pool of her own blood.

By the warm light from the Houses of the Gods, the three sisters looked ordinary, though I knew they weren't. Such is the nature of fate, a thing in which I had refused to believe until this moment. It looked like anything else, like life, like love, like opportunity or need, like mercy, or just another day in the city, another hour at work, another second's breath until it claimed you.

Alice helped me to my feet.

We gathered what supplies we could from the sisters.

Their blood gave off an intoxicating aroma. It lingered in our nostrils when we left them.

No matter what the sisters thought of my insignificance, I owned this journey too, shared it with my sister as we took the first step on its ultimate length.

15

We basked in the radiance of the Houses of the Gods.

At a certain distance, the heat and light from the buildings reached equilibrium, and the darkness inside me melted, and hope returned. I saw in Alice's eyes that it did the same for her.

The buildings sprawled toward the far horizon and seemed to stretch on even beyond it where darkness returned to the land. Maybe darkness never returned, and the Houses of the Gods stretched on forever. Or the Houses continued into a bright pocket carved from the darkness. Or all of it came down to a trick of the eye, of forced perspective, a matter of perception. I gave up trying to figure it out and accepted whatever my eyes showed me.

The Psychopomp Road ended at double doors, thirty feet high, twenty feet wide, set into a golden wall. Heat swirled in the wall as if liquid metal and fire flowed under its surface. Cool, black spots appeared in places then sank back into the glare. Flame tongues licked out, leaving wisps of smoke in the air, but we didn't feel their burn. The doors swung open as we approached. Impatient and buoyed by expectation, we entered the Houses of the Gods.

Soul-deep feelings of well-being, of purpose, of belonging, of tranquility, of safety, and so many other welcome and all-too-rare sensations flooded me. For several moments, Alice and I couldn't take another step. The wonder and vitality of this place rushed through us and erased all other feelings, all other actions. I don't know how long we stood there. The intensity of the light equaled the intensity of the deepest darkness we'd encountered on the road. All-encompassing, it became our world and shut out every other thing, even time. It cleansed us, purified us, held us by the entry until it prepared us to go farther into the house, and after an indeterminate time we walked forward.

Alice and I explored the Houses of the Gods.

We entered and crossed room after room, walked corridors that looked longer than the road itself, and gazed out windows onto worlds other than our own, worlds full of light and sun. In dining rooms, steaming, fresh food lay piled on tables, goblets dripped with wine, all of it untouched, unsullied. A fine, golden dust coated chairs and tables. Unwrinkled pillows lay on daybeds and lounges. Bathing pools held water so clear and still our reflections stared back at us like a movie. We found rooms full of treasure, rooms full of weapons, rooms piled with books and recordings, or stacked high with screens and consoles that showed images from every part of the dark world, of the cities, of our city. We found workshops for blacksmiths, carpenters, weavers, painters, and engineers, each one overloaded with materials and projects abandoned in half-finished states. One high-ceilinged room stood empty but for the projection onto its walls of a countdown numbered out to hundreds of digits. We wandered vast spaces and shouted so that our voices echoed all around. We found not a single living thing. No gods. No fates. Not even divine vermin.

No one and nothing. Absence. A darkness within the light.

No one dwelled in the Houses of the Gods.

When it came time to rest, we ate from the set dining tables and reclined on soft pillows.

We remained very still and silent. We listened. We waited. We hoped.

Nothing came. No one appeared. No voices or footsteps sounded anywhere.

Not even wind whistled along the corridors.

"How can there be no one here?" I said.

Alice said, "Don't the gods live in the Houses of the Gods?"

"Alice," I said and saw hope in my sister's eyes for an answer I couldn't give. "Is this real?" She scowled at me, disappointed. "I mean, I never doubted the gods and the stories of them stealing our light were all kid's stories and myths, but here we are, in a place that shouldn't exist, that seems like it can't exist, a place where light is simply part of everything, and I'm no more certain now than I was when we left the city because…"

"Because there are no gods here, only their Houses that go on forever."

"Yes."

"Empty."

"Yes. Have the gods abandoned us? Are they hiding?"

"Why would they hide?"

"I don't know, Alice. Why would gods do anything they do? If no one's here, why did Donia and her sisters try to kill us?"

"So that we wouldn't learn these Houses stand empty."

"How long have they been empty, do you think?"

"How should I know?"

"All of people's prayers. All of those who took the Journey to Erebus. All directed here at this forsaken wonder."

A vision of the burning church filled my thoughts. Its cross collapsing into the charred and smoking ruin. The one-time worshippers sitting on the hill, surrounded by torches, to watch it all go up in flames. I felt an urge to set fire to the Houses. Instead, I grabbed a silver pitcher off the table, screamed, and hurled it at the wall. A flash of light came on impact. Wine spewed out all over. The pitcher clattered to the floor.

"They're not worth your anger and frustration," Alice said. "They're not even here to see it or hear it. We're on our own."

"This place, though. Some mechanism keeps it, replaces the food, runs its power. What if they're coming back someday?"

"What if they are? Will they be any less deaf or indifferent to our needs then? They took our light for themselves. They hold it hostage here for this unused place even after they've left. They robbed our world of everything bright and discarded it like garbage."

"How could they?"

"They're gods. They can do anything."

Alice lifted a crystal glass from the table and dropped it to the marble floor.

It shattered.

"Except I killed a god, two of them, in fact, and you killed one. Or at least we killed their servants. Doesn't that make us their equal? We killed our fates. You were right. Choice rules fate because you chose this of your own will when I let fate make my choice for me, and I would've died within sight of this place without you to save me. Now *we* are fate, Bren. This belongs to us." Seeing my confusion, Alice held me by my shoulders. "Little brother, you asked me why I did this, why I wanted to come here. It was because I didn't know what I'd find and couldn't ask anyone to share that risk. Yet you did. Now we know. Light and heat are ours for the taking. This place belongs not only to you and me, but all of us who live in the dark. We only need to find our way out of the endless night to reach it. We can bring others here, bring light back to the world. The light will quiet the voices of all those I killed and wipe their faces from my memory."

"How will it do that, Alice?"

"By lifting the darkness from us all. Gods feel no guilt, no burden of conscience, and you and I—we're the gods now."

The idea sank into my mind, but it felt off, close, but still wrong in some integral way. I gazed at the opulence and beauty all around us, and it somehow felt like home to me, or more of a home than my city ever had, and a terrible thought formed.

"Alice, what if this was *always* ours?" I said.

She squinted and frowned, not seeing my meaning.

"What if we always *were* the gods, and we abandoned our light for the darkness? What if we've always had power to reclaim the light for ourselves?"

Alice thought it over. I ran my fingers along a wall, marveling at its coolness despite the furnace beneath its surface.

"Why would we do that, Bren? Why would we give up all this?"

A spark formed between the wall and my fingertips.

I pressed my hand harder until it gently broke an invisible membrane and sank into the wall, into the burning plasma. Frightened, I yanked it back, and light came with it in delicate, golden strings that dripped from the breach, from my fingers. I poured them into the palm of my hand then reached into the wall again and drew more. I tossed the radiant material into the air. It scattered into the shapes of tiny winged creatures I dimly remembered from long ago bedtime stories. They flutter-danced and then returned to the wall.

I smiled at Alice.

"We did it to know what it's like to be human."

Author's Notes

The Price of Faces

I first attempted to write this story around 1996 as part of a collection of ideas for a multimedia project an artist friend invited me to work on. I started with a classic "What If?" story concept, in this case: "What if an individual became trapped in a single physical body in a world where people changed bodies like clothes?" The artist liked this idea and several others. I started writing but soon stumbled with this piece because of the need to develop speech mannerisms for a society in which pronouns became inapplicable for actual persons and could only describe their current body outfit. The language of the story sounded awkward, and I needed to refine it. The project never progressed, though, so instead of solving the problem then, I set the story aside. Every so often, I revisited it and played with its language and structure, the ideas behind this world, and so on, never dedicating too much time to it because I felt it would be a difficult story to publish given the odd phrasings in some of the prose. It wasn't until the anthology call for *Qualia Nous*, edited by Michael Bailey, that I saw a potentially good home for it, one that made sense for a more experimental story. This time everything came together, and, fortunately, Michael liked and published it—nearly twenty years after its initial inception.

The Flying Rock

Danielle Ackley-McPhail asked me to submit a story to a new anthology she was co-editing, the first in a new fantasy series: *Bad-Ass Faeries*. The theme took faeries back to their roots as mercurial, sardonic, cruel, and vengeful. No happy, Tinkerbell-style faeries, but the kind people feared in the old days, the true Sidhe. I'd never written anything on the topic, so I researched the folklore and created a story, "Sally Smiles," set in an ongoing series of stories and comics, *The Midnight Hour*, which I co-create with artist Jason Whitley. That story made the grade for the first anthology, and I was asked back for the next three volumes produced by Danielle and her co-editors. My next two contributions featured Gorge, a fallen faerie musician exiled to the mortal world. He proved popular enough to spin off into a novella, *Three Chords of Chaos*. For the fourth volume, though, I wanted to do something more personal, more human, less fantastic, and more intimate. "The Flying Rock" is about many things. At its heart it's a meditation on the importance of remembering in adulthood what it means to be a child and why parents must open their children's eyes to the magnificent potential that exists inside them even when they might have lost or squandered their own—all wrapped up in the guise of a literal faerie tale. There's a vague sense of impending darkness in the world at large here, and, I hope, a balancing sense that children are the ones who will preserve the light.

Upon Waves, Wind, and Tide

I'm a beach person, love the sand, sun, and shore, love to swim. On childhood trips to the town pool, I probably spent more time underwater than above, so when editor John French asked if I'd like to write a mermaid story, I gladly agreed. I like water stories and enjoy writing them. But I didn't want to write a typical mermaid story, or at least my conception of a "typical" mermaid story. As a result, I wound up creating an entire new mythology and world unique to this story, though there's still a touch of classic mermaid tales in the land/sea romance aspect. One of the Amazon reviews for the anthology in which this first appeared, *Mermaids 13*, described each story in turn, and when it came to this one, the reviewer wrote: "A strange story that was almost too bizarre to enjoy, but at the same time was very imaginative." Thus, I feel I succeeded in my goal of writing an off-beat mermaid tale.

Meet the Tuskersons

It's not often an editor asks if you'd like to write a walrus story. What kind? Any kind—as long as it features walruses. So it went when Kevin Donihe asked me to submit something for *Walrus Tales*, perhaps the most unusually themed anthology in which I've been published. I remain grateful to Kevin for the opportunity because the odd challenge inspired one of my favorite pieces of writing. I started with fond memories of childhood TV shows and connected them to my cynical view of television in adulthood, seeking a happy medium where those feelings coexisted. I greatly enjoyed creating Ernie McCabe, an underdog who fell into a taste of all-too fleeting stardom. The anthology took a long path to publication. Sometimes I wondered what I might do with an oddball, magical realism walrus story if it never appeared. It did, of course, and the anthology received excellent reviews. I'm thrilled to see this story in print once again.

The Kind Old Fellow

Among the oldest of the stories collected here, this one first appeared in *Sick: An Anthology of Illness*, edited by John Edward Lawson, Raw Dog Screaming Press's first anthology, way back in the post Y2K hazy days of 2003. The theme of "sickness" was broad: anything from the individual level to an entire society or anywhere in between. I chose societal sickness for this one because it aligned with an idea I'd been knocking around. The idea? Well, the working title for this story was "Instant Karma." I enjoyed the opportunity to play with ideas of good and evil, justice and authority, role models, liberty, and oppression, all of which form part of the fabric here, and the experience in that context of a lifelong do-gooder, who finally succumbs to the temptation to lash out at the ills of the world. I also savored the chance to create a futuristic, dystopian vision of New York City. Unsurprisingly, perhaps, to anyone familiar with the often Kafkaesque nature of New York's bureaucracy, it wasn't too much of a stretch.

Brides of Fire

I've been fortunate over the years to have connected with a handful of editors who've offered me chances to try something new now and again. The most frequent culprit in this regard is Danielle Ackley-McPhail. This story came about when she invited me to submit to an anthology with a very loose theme of the Phoenix, Phoenix-like creatures, and other mythological fire gods. In particular, she was hoping for stories about more obscure beings and suggested I consider doing something with the cherufe, a fire god from the lore of the Mapuche people of Chile, a being who lived in magma pools inside volcanoes. For me that resonated with the trope of making sacrifices to the gods to quiet a volcano from erupting. *Joe Versus the Volcano* is one of my favorite movies, and there is a nod or two to the film hidden in the story. If people lived within proximity to active volcanos, I thought, such sacrifices would be routine, and, over time, lose their novelty, become just another part of domestic life. With that springboard, I dove into research on the Mapuche and the cherufe. The humorous tone felt right, like a story told by a mischievous uncle to his young nieces and nephews around the hearth.

Super-Villain Showcase #53: "Enter the Deep Loa"

A rare opportunity to tap into my vast, detailed, and mostly useless knowledge of comic books and comic book trivia, this story first appeared in *With Great Power*, an anthology edited by John French and Greg Schauer. John and I chat about comics whenever we see each other (which isn't often enough), and he knew I loved the super-hero genre. I chose to write this story as if it were an issue in an ongoing comic book series, something out of the Bronze Age (loosely the 1970s). It contains some moderate parodies and commentaries on classic characters and super-hero themes mixed with voodoo. With all the crazy mysticism flying around in super-hero comic books, the "meta" path of the story seemed natural, yet another commentary on how different creators click—or don't—with characters to make memorable or forgettable stories and how characters can "take over" a comic series when they become breakout popular. The voodoo aspects are also a call back to one of my earliest comic book series, "The Revenant" in *Shadow House*, in which a voodoo bocor, who fled from Haiti to Florida to escape the Tonton Macoute, was a major character.

Mother of Peace

A tip of the hat to Mike McPhail for this one. Editor of the Defending the Future series of military science fiction anthologies, Mike invited me to contribute to all but one volume (*No Man's Land*, which featured only female authors) of the series, and he let me do pretty much whatever I wanted. He also provided excellent editorial back-up to make sure I got the military aspects of the stories correct. Mike has a military background; I do not. I struggled with his genre at first because of that. By the time I wrote "Mother of Peace," though, I felt myself getting a handle on it. While most of my contributions to the DTF series, including this one perhaps, read less like serious mil-sci-fi and more like stories from back issues of DC's old *Weird War Tales* comic book series, I feel this one comes closest to capturing a little bit more, an echo of the horror and confusion of long-term war, of the emotional dynamic that drives people to survive or make the ultimate sacrifice. Or, my idea of those things, set in a world where cybernetics designed to end war swiftly only served to let it drag on year after year, for the traumatized and wounded to carry on long past the time they should've quit, a comment on the unrealistic expectations often placed upon and created by new technology.

Grilg Friendly

An alien contact story, this one mined my interest in connecting weird occurrences to everyday life and exploring the consequences. I wanted the aliens in this piece to be weird and monstrous not due to their nature but because of their non-human physique and mode of communication. I wanted them to capture that unsettling sense created by things such as spiders, which share our world but are utterly unlike us, unrelatable. I linked this to the theme of having your everyday life abruptly shattered by circumstance, of losing control of your existence in the space of a few hours, of losing one of the things most near and dear to you before you even understand how and why—or *that*—you're even losing it. The abrupt shattering of an otherwise serene and ordinary life.

I Am the Last

This story riffs on the theory floated in pop culture ever since *The Matrix* that we exist in a living hologram, that nothing is real, that at our most fundamental level we are brains inside jars that generate sensory experiences in response to nothing more than the coded stimuli that create the impression of a reality. If so, who created it? Are the creators of our hologram living in the same kind of manufactured reality? If so, what about those who created that reality? And so on up the chain—until, as the title suggests, a bug occurs in this system of infinite realities. Who then is the ghost in the machine and who the deus ex machina? As I write these notes in late 2020, a time of plague and tremendous sociopolitical upheaval, the idea of a "bug in the system" seems more frighteningly plausible than ever.

He Who Burns

I never thought I'd write a dragon story. I've loved dragons, ever since reading *The Hobbit* and discovering Smaug as a kid. They're the ultimate mythical creature, with variations in many cultures around the world. Dragons are wonderful and they capture the imagination—but they've been done so many times and so well by so many authors from Tolkien to McCaffrey to Martin and many others, I never seriously considered writing about them. At least, not until I was asked to do so for an anthology, *Dragon's Lure*. Even then, I wrote about a related mythical creature, a salamander. My favorite idea in this story, though, is the forensic alchemist, a position I assume would exist in the police department of any world where magic and mythology were real. This is the very first (and to date only) Maximillian Toth story, but I don't believe it will be the last.

The Star Gazers

I wrote this story for *If We Had Known*, an anthology whose title perfectly captures the theme. Re-visiting it for this collection, the influence of classic cosmic horror is clearer to me now than when I wrote it. The visuals of the titular statues, the strained father-daughter relationship, and the backdrop of a seemingly endless cosmic war all, I hope, bring a different flavor to it. I liked using the parent-child dynamic to drive the plot in this story, that sometimes insurmountable, irreconcilable gap in perspective between generations that can lead to terrible consequences.

A Cat's Cry in Pluto's Kitchen

This is the first Machinations Sundry story. This steampunk series usually stars Morris Garvey, inventor of the steam-powered chimney sweep and favorite son of New Alexandria. Morris often works with Inspector Daniel Matheson, as in this story, as well as other recurring characters, such as Anna Rigel, New Alexandria's Queen of Witches. For my first venture in steampunk territory I sought to create the feel of a living, breathing city from alternate history. I had tremendous fun writing these characters and this world and have written about half a dozen more stories in the series since, all published in various anthologies. Interestingly, while this was the first Machinations

Sundry story I wrote, the second one, "House of Automatons," was the first published, in the anthology *In an Iron Cage*. Such are the mysterious ways of the publishing world.

Long the Night, Low the Flame

The first draft of this novella, written many, many years ago, was a traditional fantasy story, with less mythology, more barkeeps, torches, and a quest on horseback. I promptly set it aside, completely unsatisfied with it. I loved the basic concept, the notion of this journey through darkness in search of a divinity with a tangible presence in the world, but I didn't like the dynamics of the setting or how the fantasy elements worked in the context. When considering how best to conclude this collection, though, the story leapt back to mind. A piece to provide an epic conclusion, a deceptively dark tale that, in its finale, reaches a surprisingly bright and hopeful note. In rewriting, I cast aside all the old fantasy trappings, finding a new path for the tale when a news article about the discovery of the oldest known senet set, an ancient Egyptian game of divination, headlined, "Ancient Egyptian 'Board Game of Death' Identified by Scientists," captured my interest and sparked a research jag into ancient games and divination. This led me to the ideas of fate in various lore systems, and the notion of a futuristic world where all mythologies remained relevant. Recasting the story as futuristic, urban sf/fantasy provided a fresh new take. I wrote it from scratch specifically for publication here, even taking inspiration for the title of this book from it. Along the way, I also took liberties with how senet is played and why the ancients played it. Historians report it remained popular at all levels of Egyptian society for roughly 2,500 years. Perhaps one day, it will make a comeback.

About the Author

James Chambers is an award-winning author of horror, crime, fantasy, and science fiction. He wrote the Bram Stoker Award®-winning graphic novel, *Kolchak the Night Stalker: The Forgotten Lore of Edgar Allan Poe and was nominated for a Bram Stoker Award for his* story, "A Song Left Behind in the Aztakea Hills." *Booklist* described his collection *On the Night Border* as *"...a haunting exploration of the space where the real world and nightmares collide." Publisher's Weekly* gave his collection of four Lovecraftian-inspired novellas, *The Engines of Sacrifice*, a starred review and described it as "... chillingly evocative...."

He is the author of the short story collection *Resurrection House and* several novellas, including *The Dead Bear Witness* and *Tears of Blood*, in the Corpse Fauna novella series, and the dark urban fantasy, *Three Chords of Chaos.*

His short stories have been published in numerous anthologies, including *After Punk: Steampowered Tales of the Afterlife, The Best of Bad-Ass Faeries, The Best of Defending the Future, Chiral Mad 2, Chiral Mad 4, Deep Cuts, Dragon's Lure, Fantastic Futures 13, Gaslight and Grimm, The Green Hornet Chronicles, Hardboiled Cthulhu, In An Iron Cage, Kolchak the Night Stalker: Passages of the Macabre, Qualia Nous, Shadows Over Main Street (1 and 2), The Spider: Extreme Prejudice, To Hell in a Fast Car, Truth or Dare, TV Gods, Walrus Tales, Weird Trails*; the chapbook *Mooncat Jack*; and the magazines *Bare Bone, Cthulhu Sex*, and *Allen K's Inhuman*. He co-edited the anthology, *A New York State of Fright: Horror Stories from the Empire State.*

He has also written and edited numerous comic books including *Leonard Nimoy's Primortals*, the critically acclaimed "The Revenant" in *Shadow House*, and *The Midnight Hour* with Jason Whitley.

He lives in New York.

Visit his website: www.jameschambersonline.com.

CPSIA information can be obtained
at www.ICGtesting.com
Printed in the USA
BVHW071421051021
618194BV00004B/120